Lizzy,

Great website, lady!

I'm so glad to have
a chance to be a part
of it. I hope you enjoy
Rafe's story as much as I
do.
                    ~ Cindy Gengler

FALLEN ANGELS
✝
RAFE'S HEART

BY
CINDY GENGLER

DEDICATION

For my family, whose love and understanding gives me the strength to stand strong and the courage to fly high.

Acknowledgments

I would like to thank Elizabeth Collins, President of Gardenia Press, for every e-mail and letter she took the time to answer and for not looking on persistence as one of the seven deadly sins. You took a chance, Elizabeth, and there is no greater gift you can give a writer than that.

All of my heartfelt love and thanks to my husband for not batting an eyelash at the mention of vampires and fairies. For understanding that I do my best work at two a.m. Without you to remind me that writing a book is the "easy" part, I might have given up on getting it published.

To my mother, who, after reading it for the first time, called with tears in her eyes to tell me how proud she was. My dad, who never once voiced a concern for what tiny part of my brain thought up such a world where vampires were the good guys. And Melissa, for reading every line a million times without complaint, for underlining the good scenes (I won't tell mom which ones!) and for laughing at all the right parts.

I couldn't have done any of this without the support of my family and friends. Thank you so much.

PROLOGUE

LONDON 1802

Katherine Darien stood back in the shadows, watching with amused black eyes while the party went on all around her. She didn't often venture out in public like this, but her mission tonight, and not much liking the company she was keeping, left her with little choice. Katherine wanted to meet the three who had built such a reputation for themselves in just a few years of residing in the city. She wanted to meet those the *Ton* had dubbed *The Fallen Angels.*

A tug on her bodice caught her attention, and she was barely able to repress a shudder as the man at her side groped her with rough, intrusive hands. Justin Lyons may have been a lord by birth, but his manners were that of the most base born peasant. To stay calm and accepting of his attentions was a hard fought battle because, as much as she wanted to accomplish her goal, self-sacrifice hadn't been her motto for many years

Katherine held no illusions as to what had drawn Lyons to her side. The Viscount's covetous nature had won her the rather dubious honor of being his mistress. Not that taking him as a lover made him special in any way. Any man would have served her purpose just as well. Her dark, exotic beauty gave her the power to attract a large number of admirers. Of all the men who had begged to offer their protection, Lyons had been the easiest to direct and manipulate.

Hidden in the recesses of the balcony, Katherine allowed Lyons to continue with his inelegant fondling, all the while bidding her time and biting back all the nasty words that pressed at the back of her throat. She couldn't believe that he was so blind to the disgust that filled her at his touch, at his very nearness. Nevertheless, he was, so she used that inattention as her jet gaze sought out her query.

The three men were incredible to look upon as they stood together, an impenetrable force that refused to bow down to the dictates of a society that alternately shunned and embraced them. They drew attention without seeking it, garnered accolades without effort. They were the center of speculation and malicious whispering everywhere they went.

Katherine stared at the three men and felt her curiosity stir. She looked at them for long moments, letting her eyes take inventory of the male flesh before her. The one who laughed was as fair and bright as the sun. The big man in the middle was as rugged and entrancing as the crashing sea. However, it was the silent one, the dark one that was as seducing as the beckoning shadows of night, who captivated her.

Any one of them alone would have served her purpose. Together they would be the answer to her every prayer. With the three to protect her, no longer would she have to fear those who hunted her without end.

"M'lord," she purred into her brutish lover's ear. "Introduce me."

"What?" Lyons couldn't comprehend the simple command for the lust firing his body to a feverish pitch as he attempted to stick his hand down the front of her dress.

"Introduce me to the three standing together over there."

Shifting his impatient gaze away from her, he sought out who had caught her jaded fancy. He snorted in disgust as he recognized the men in question. "Rotten bastards," he muttered in aggravation.

"Pardon, m'lord?"

The sultry voice sent a shiver down his spine. "They are nothing but savages, cads, rogues. I won't lower myself to speak of them." Lyons felt a surge of anger at her obvious interest in the three men he hated most in the world, if the truth be told.

His heated indignation brought a slight smile to Katherine's full lips. She didn't need him to tell her about them. There was nothing he could tell her that she hadn't already learned on her own. All she wanted from Lyons was a chance to get close.

"They are only men, Justin, just like you. Well, maybe not *just like you*. My, what plans I have for them." She gave a small laugh.

"You will do nothing until I'm done with you," Lyons snapped, his infamous temper quick to flare at her insult to his pride. "You're nothing but a street corner whore!"

"Oh, I'm worse than that, lover." Katherine turned her onyx-like gaze on him, malice gleaming in the darkness there. "You were just the means to an end. I thought I needed you to get here." She smirked at his seething disbelief, no longer trying to hide her contempt from him.

Years of training under a master manipulator allowed her to admit she'd made a mistake in thinking Lyons could help her in the quest. She could get rid of him now that he no longer had a purpose. "I don't need you anymore. I never did."

Katherine didn't even flinch when he grabbed her by the shoulders and shook her hard. Instead, she gave him the freedom to rant and rave about her vile character. Soon, enough was enough, and with cool disdain she pushed him to the ground.

Lyons sat on the cold, hard marble in stunned silence. No man had ever dared to treat him in such a way, let alone a mere woman. Pulling himself to his full height, he stared at her, the amusement she made no effort to hide further fired his rage.

"We are leaving," he grated through clenched teeth as he grabbed her wrist. Lyons wasn't afraid of witnesses out on the balcony; it was very dark with no moon in the sky to lend its all seeing light to the struggle taking place.

Katherine had that same assurance.

"You're nothing but a whore," he snarled when she pulled her wrist free of his hand. "How dare you treat me this way." Again, he reached for her, incensed at her continued defiance.

"I am Justin Lyons." He caught her arm in a grip that grated bone against bone. "I own you. You're nobody, just some stupid little bitch. It's time you were put in your place!" Control completely deserted him when her laughter echoed in his ears. Pulling back his arm, he slapped her full across the face.

His delicate little lover didn't stumble or cower from his strength as he expected from his women. Katherine just stared at him through eyes that had gone as dark and unforgiving as death. Lyons stared into those eyes and wished to God he had never come out onto this balcony on this night with this woman.

For the first time in his life, Lyons knew fear and he fervently wished that her laughter was back. Even that would have been preferable to the look of satisfaction that crossed her face as she wrapped talon-strong fingers around his arm and twisted.

CHAPTER 1

LONDON 1803

After a year of planning and plotting, Katherine was about to capture the prize she'd coveted for so long. Standing by her latest protector's side, she refused to be overwhelmed by the appearance of the three men she had so cunningly pursued in the last year. Hand-picking David Mallory as her lover had paid off just as she'd hoped it would.

The elegant, richly appointed study did little to tame the vividness of the three men who dwarfed her with their very presence. Even David's broad-shouldered frame did little to keep him from looking like a child when compared to the three. Their height alone would have set them apart in any crowd but there was something else about them that commanded attention. Something more than raw muscle and blatant masculinity that kept a person's eyes locked on them. They exuded power, intensity, and strength.

"I want you to meet Gabriel Arden, Michael Wyhndym, and Raphael Fahlan."

Katherine didn't need David's gentle prodding to know which of the three was the savage Scot. Arden's very nature shouted from his ruthless green eyes, just as Michael's seductive charm seethed behind that teasing smile he wore so well. Rafe Fahlan wasn't as easy to read. He was as dark as the devil himself. An icy challenge that beckoned a woman to foolish deeds.

"They call you *The Fallen Angels,* don't they? You do not appear very angelic to me," she teased. Michael and David laughed outright at her words, Gabriel's smile was slight but forced, and it seemed that Rafe, with his cold indifference, had never been amused in his life.

"We do have that honor, I even believe that David gave it to us," Michael explained, his slight French accent flowing through his words like music.

Katherine glanced at her lover and asked with contrived innocence. "You named them, David? You are so very clever. What drew that name to mind?" Her smile was so sweet, the silly man failed to notice the cunning in her eyes.

"It wasn't very hard to decree that name, my love, not if you had seen them as I did that first night four years ago," the older man explained, his hazel eyes bright with memories. "I'd been meeting with an old friend when ruffians tried to rob me, that's when these three walked out of the fog. They looked like warrior angels as they fought off my attackers. I just knew in my dazed state that they had to be arch angels sent to save me."

"Not that he couldn't have helped himself, Katherine. We just happened to be near and in need of entertainment." Michael tried to downplay the praise David loved to heap on them.

"There is no need to lie, Michael, she is aware of my faults, and that fisticuffs is not one of my strong suits," David said in his easy manner.

"We would protect you with our lives."

For the first time since Katherine had entered the room, Rafe graced them with words. Instantly, his voice drew her, so low and smoky, it slid across her skin like dark velvet. That voice. She wondered for a moment what it would be like to have her name whispered from those lips. Would it sound the same as it had when spoken so long ago by a man whose very face, very essence, never left her thoughts?

"We would be lost without you," Gabriel added with his quiet drawl. His words further softened by a husky highland brogue.

There were no secrets kept long among the *Ton* and it was common knowledge that the three would do anything for the man they had rescued four long years ago. After that night on the docks, David Mallory had taken them under his wing and made sure they were widely accepted in London.

For the most part, his championing of the outcasts had worked. None of the *Ton* wanted to cross the wealthy, influential lord. None wanted to be the one to give the *cut direct* to the three that the Duke of Stratford had claimed with such affection.

Katherine intended to put the affection between them to good use. With soft words and smiles, she excused herself.

"What do you think of her?"

"She's lovely," Michael answered David's question.

"What are you going to do with her?" Rafe asked.

"I would marry her, of course. Unfortunately, even I could never defy convention to that extreme." Sadness tugged at David's throat. "I fear her past will be our undoing."

"We were accepted thanks to you. I'm sure you could work that same miracle for her," Michael argued.

"Society is much more forgiving of a man than a woman, no matter what the sin." David's words rang true. "Promise, that if something were to happen to me, you would see Katherine taken care of. She is so fragile and not meant to be on her own," he requested.

"You have our word," Gabriel replied.

"We will keep her safe if need be, but most of all, we will keep you safe." Michael was vehement.

Ŧ   Ŧ   Ŧ

Later that night, Katherine asked the question that had plagued her for months. "Why is Rafe like that?"

"Like what?" Distracted by the warm body snuggled so intimately against his own, David only half-listened to her words.

Katherine had been his lover for five month and while she had never disclosed her age to him, she was so childlike that some times he felt like a lecher for touching her. He'd never taken a woman so much younger than himself to his bed, but she had sought him out with persistence, making light of his every attempt to deny his attraction for her. She had made him feel like a schoolboy, not a mature man of forty-two years, with her loving smiles and gentle touch. When she looked at him, he knew she saw behind the good looks that had granted him whatever he'd wanted.

In return for that beautiful gift, he tried to be everything she desired, everything she needed. He tried to give her every bit of his love in hope that she would give all of hers in return. "Why is he so cold?" Patience laced her words at his preoccupation. From lords to peasants, men were all the same, so easily led that sometimes it still amazed her.

"He has no heart, my love. From what I've gathered, nothing can touch him." What else could he say when she pressed for more? "His mother ran away and took all the children with her, but Rafe. She left *him* with a father who hated the very sight of him. Rafe had a hard life that was further complicated when his young wife and newborn son died of fever. To escape from his father and his grief, he came to London." David sighed his sadness. He could never hate a child. If only...

"Did Gabriel really kill his cousin over a woman?" Katherine asked, eyes bright with fervent interest while she ran fingers through David's silver-streaked brown hair.

"His cousin, my sweet, was very jealous of him. In order to get even with Gabriel, Alan misused a young serving maid at their grandfather's estate. When he learned of Alan's perfidy, Gabriel challenged him. When it was over, Alan was dead and he was cast out."

"What of Michael?" she whispered against David's mouth, her tongue snaking out to tease his upper lip.

"Michael got his mother's ward with child." David could hardly breath for the need that consumed him, but he forced himself to continue. "When the girl confronted him, he turned her away. She killed herself after that. Michael's parents wouldn't stand by their son when the scandal hit and forced him out." David moaned as her mouth settled softly on his.

He pulled her supple body under his, struggling to go slow, to please her when all the wild need she inspired in him demanded urgency. David reined in all that fire with difficulty. Katherine deserved better from him than a rough, hurried tumble. She was delicate, gentle. Everything about her touched something in him, made him long for the future. He couldn't give his name, but he could give her fidelity and love for the rest of his life.

Katherine lay awake long after her lover surrendered to the passions she had stirred within him, the information she had obtained buzzing in her head. So much to do. She smiled with dark delight, her obsidian gaze settling on David's sleeping face with cold calculation.

ᛏ   ᛏ   ᛏ

Their mentor was dead. David's battered body had been recovered from the docks two nights past. The three stood in the back of the crowded room and struggled to contain their grief. The *Ton* assumed that thugs had robbed and killed him, but Gabriel didn't believe that story. He made no secret of his disbelief. The others agreed.

"He never would have gone there alone!" Gabriel's rage resonated in his voice.

"This wasn't as random as it appears." Rafe's eyes locked with his.

"There was a plan," Gabriel stated it as fact his green eyes narrowing at the possibility.

"Is that possible?" Michael asked.

"We've learned the hard way, what is and isn't possible." Rafe was somber.

"What should we do? They're treating as negligently as when they found Justin Lyons with his neck broken. While Lyons was no great loss, the same can't be said for David." Michael observed.

"I think we should find out," Rafe drawled out slow as he looked over the crowd, searching without success for the woman their late mentor had insisted they protect.

"Where should we start?" Michael asked, determination in every word.

"Not *we*, Michael, *you* need to stay with Katherine. If this was planned, she could be in danger. Stay close to her tonight. Find out what David was doing there. If anyone knew of his movements, she did." Rafe's orders brooked no arguments.

"How did I get saddled with the grieving mistress?" Michael complained with a spark of his usual taunting humor.

"Stop whining and put some of that charm you're so proud of to good use for a change," Gabriel retorted before his mood turned dark with purpose.

"Meet us at the garden gate at midnight. We should have some information by then, a name at the very least, if not a head on a pike."

Gabriel's words left little room for doubt.

ϒ   ϒ   ϒ

When the last mourner had left the townhouse, Katherine allowed her composure to dissolve in a convincing show of tears and heartbreaking sobs. She could have smiled with glee when Michael sat on the sofa beside her and gathered her into his arms. To bend the pretty one to her will would be so easy. All she needed to do was gain his sympathy, his trust. Then when she needed him, she would slowly forge the bond between them.

Michael didn't speak as he stroked a soothing hand down the curve of her back. He had learned long ago that physical contact was all he could provide for a woman. Words, no matter how sincere, seldom made the hurt go away. All he could do was offer comfort in the only way he knew how.

"What am I going to do, Michael?" Her voice broke. "He was all I had. I loved him so much. We both loved him. I can't believe he's gone from us."

Katherine's tears ran unchecked as she stared into his eyes. She was prepared for trite promises, for well meant murmurs of shared grief, but not for the gentle hand that reached out to caress the tears from her cheeks. Physically moved in a way she hadn't ever been before, she buried her face in his chest.

"What will I do?" Even with her confusion mounting, she continued as planned. "I don't want to live without him." Katherine angled her head back until her face was only a heartbeat from his. She fought to keep her focus while sinking into the depths of his vivid blue eyes. When he slid his arm around her narrow waist, urging her onto his lap, she lost every thought. What in hell was going on? Her breath caught, her body betraying her grand plans.

"He loved you very much." Michael voice was husky. He edged closer, fitting her body to his until he could feel the frantic beat of her heart against his chest. "The last time we were with him, all he spoke of was his love for you, how he wanted to marry you. You are very special, *chérie*." Michael watched as her eyes misted with surprised desire. "Everything will be fine. I'll take care of you."

His breath fanning her throat gave Katherine a sharp thrill of pleasure. Tossing all plans aside, she willingly fell victim to a master of seduction.

A mere child when it came to passion, especially when faced with an expert of the craft, Katherine didn't hesitate. The need to explore the unfamiliar was paramount and she gave in to the hot sensations burning in the pit of her stomach.

Wrapping her arms around his neck, she edged closer to the hard heat of his body until she straddled the masculine spread of his thighs, her tender breasts crushed against the ridged muscles of his chest. Nothing in her past prepared her for the shock waves that crashed through her as he touched her.

"Please, I want you," Katherine moaned against his mouth, surprised that the words were true. Not since Christian had she wanted a man with any degree of true desire.

Even as she sank under the force of his seduction, a nagging awareness of the situation filled her. Michael's every move was calculated. Every caress, every kiss, was so honed that it bordered on perfection. But there was something missing, an emptiness that the pleasure and lust couldn't ease. Sensing that didn't stop the fire that flowed through her when he rotated her hips against his.

"Is this what you want?" Michael's question was a husky taunt as he cupped a soft breast with his hand. "Is this what you want from me, *chérie?*"

Katherine was deaf to the contempt that colored the silky edge of his soft words, blind to the derisive gleam in his jaded blue eyes. She saw nothing of the clinical way he searched her face for signs of her pleasure.

Nor would she. Michael was an expert at hiding the lust that drove him, good at pretending that the women he took mattered to him in those hours he gave them what they sought.

Some part of him rebelled at what he was doing. Some part knew that taking David's lover was wrong, but he didn't care. Michael had never denied himself when it came to women. Physical pleasure had always been his downfall. If this was what she wanted, what she sought, he wouldn't deny her. Long ago he had learned to take what he needed, whenever he needed it, without consequence. Only the dreams made him pause.

"Be sure this is what you want, because it's what you're asking for."

The harshness in his voice further aroused Katherine's heightened senses. Instead of replying with mere words, she reached up with hands that trembled and struggled to remove his coat and shirt.

"Oh, Michael," she barely managed, her breath seductive with each exhale. Black eyes feasted on the taut ridges and muscles she uncovered. He was so beautiful, so perfect in body that she had to force air into her lungs. Before she could stop herself, she ran her hands over the golden skin with the reverence of a child. "You feel so alive, let me be a part of you." Leaning forward, she raked a masculine nipple with her teeth, relishing the salty taste of firm flesh.

She was unprepared for the heat, the need, the hunger that bombarded her as he used hands, lips, and tongue to undress and drive her over the edge. Nothing could hold back the throaty moan of pleasure that escaped her when he finally invaded her arching body. The mindless whimpers continued as the power and size of him filled her so completely that in seconds, she was writhing and gasping with the intensity of her release. A release so consuming that it broke the thin threads holding back the darkness within her soul.

Michael didn't feel the sharp sting in his back as her fingernails tore skin and drew blood. Caught up in her body, her pleasure, nothing registered until her eyes began to glow within the beauty of her face. Then it was too late. With a low growl, she sank sharp, tearing teeth into his throat and began pulling the life from his body.

Katherine held him still, her arms binding him close as she continued to slide against him, bringing forth another burst of intense pleasure.

After a few moments, Michael felt his body weaken until all he could do was stare into her fiendish eyes. What he saw there made him rear away one last time in desperation, but it was too late. Pain mixed with the most enthralling ecstasy was the last sensation he felt before the abyss pulled him down into the warmth of its deceitful embrace.

Chapter 2

Katherine stared at Michael as he lay unconscious in her arms. The ugly wounds in his neck, the trail of blood seeping into his blond hair, stood in silent testimony to her lack of control. She, Katherine of Darien Glen, in four hundred years as a sorceress turned immortal, had never lost control of her bloodlust.

"Oh, this is just wonderful! What am I going to do now?" She spoke to thin air, the noise bringing her little comfort. Knowing he would die in a matter of minutes if he wasn't brought over did little to improve her displeasure. Even as she watched his life ebb away, Katherine knew she should just let him go. Knowing had little to do with her grand plans though.

Ignoring the human part of her that demanded she do the right thing was easy. What worried her was that after all these centuries, she could still hear that little voice in her head at all. Life as an immortal didn't leave room for a conscience, not if she wanted to stay one step ahead of the cruel vampire that had created her. Not if she wanted to avoid the wrath of the *Sidhe* princess who sought them both.

With her decision made, she lay him down and crossed to the mantle. There she opened the ornate, craved chest that had appeared at her silent command. Bringing out an ancient dagger fashioned in the shape of a dragon's claw, she stared at the razor sharp blade with fondness. This was the same blade she had used to end David Mallory's life.

Katherine crossed back to Michael's side, filled with confidence even as she knelt beside the sofa and turned his head toward her. No expression marred the beauty of her face as she drew the blade across her breast over the steady beat of her heart, there was only the half-formed hope hidden deep in her soul that he wouldn't grow to hate her for what she was about to do.

But if he did hate her and nothing could persuade him otherwise, she would just get rid of him as she had David and so many others. Katherine smiled at that little bit of cold-bloodedness. A long time had passed since she'd been accused of being sentimental.

т   т   т

Rafe leaned against the gate, his expression guarded as they waited for Michael. Something evil was lurking, waiting. He knew that as clearly as he knew anything. The voices on the night air called to him, and he felt a dark promise beckoning within those whispered words. If Michael had been less of a friend or he less of a man, he might have left the darkness to close in on itself. But fear was a luxury the cold-eyed man didn't allow himself.

"What should we do? It is not like him to keep us waiting."

Gabriel's words echoed Rafe's own concern for their friend. "We have only one choice." He searched Gabriel's face for any reluctance.

Forcing open the window was the easy part, fitting a giant like Gabriel through such a small opening proved much more difficult, but very amusing for Rafe. "You need to stop eating," he chided.

"This is all muscle, little boy, and as soon as we find Michael, I'll beat the hell out you to prove it."

The challenge was an old one, issued so many times in the four years since he had wandered onto Gabriel's ancestral estate that Rafe no longer took heed. With a mocking smile he stood back and watched as the big man landed on the floor with a thud.

"Your concern is touching," Gabriel muttered with a fierce

scowl as Rafe left him sitting on the carpet while he went to the study door.

"There's light from down the hall," Rafe warned, their banter forgotten.

Side by side, they crept down the hall to the salon. Opening the door, they glanced inside. What they saw transcended their caution, and as one, they rushed to where Michael lay.

Gabriel turned from the blood that covered Michael's throat and chest. From the stillness that blanketed the unconscious man like death. If anyone else had been lying there, he wouldn't have felt the need to look away. However, it wasn't someone else, it was Michael. A friend. A brother.

Clutching the dagger in his fist kept Rafe focused. The steady beat of Michael's heart under his palm quelled the fierce rage that threatened to break past the solid wall of his icy control. Forcing himself to see beyond the brutality to the fact that Michael still lived took an effort. Rafe let the dagger drop to the bloodstained floor, his cold eyes sweeping the room for answers.

ᛏ   ᛏ   ᛏ

Katherine heard the crash that echoed through the quiet house. In a moment, she had a mental picture of Gabriel and Rafe, kneeling over Michael's slumbering body. This was working out so much better than she'd planned.

Standing in front of the mirror in the bedroom, she was pleased with what she saw reflected in the glass. Her hair, still tousled from Michael's skilled attentions and the blood on her cheek and neck added a nice touch of authenticity. All her appearance lacked was the sign of a struggle. With a delicate hand, she ripped the bodice of her gown from neck to waist with a slight flick of the wrist.

Katherine allowed herself only a second to thank the impulse that had caused her to dress Michael's slumbering body before leaving the salon. Finding him unclothed would have left the field open for too many questions. With her spirits high, she glided from the bedroom, down the stairs, and into the morning room.

This was as good a place as any, she decided. In little time she turned the once spotless room into a scene of utter chaos and violence. Not a single chair or table escaped her noiseless destruction. When she was convinced it looked as it should, she settled herself into the far corner. Dragging the edges of her tattered gown around her, she began to weep, low at first, then with more volume as she waited for the answering sound of footfall in the hallway.

Gabriel rose from his kneeling position next to Michael. Slowly he turned his head in the direction of a sound more felt than heard.

"What is it?" Rafe asked, not taking his eyes from Michael's pale features.

"Just a noise," Gabriel replied with a thoughtful frown. "I'll go."

"I'll go with you." Rafe was already moving to the door.

Gabriel stopped him with a firm hand on his shoulder. "I don't need you. He does."

Rafe took a moment to look at Gabriel's face. The fires of hell he saw reflected in his friend's eyes forced him to retrace his steps and resume his vigil. His silence was statement enough.

As Gabriel entered the hall, the faint sound took a familiar shape. When he recognized the sound of a woman weeping, he sprinted the rest of the way. With a quick glance, he took in all the destruction, all the chaos. Following the sobs, he walked across the room to where Katherine huddled in the far corner.

The way she cringed back from the candle he had brought, reminded him of an abused animal, seeking refuge in the dark. The shock and disbelief on her face reminded him of the expression that Emily had worn when she had made her accusations against his cousin those years ago. He hoped to God it wasn't as bad as that, but his heart told him, that once again, God wasn't listening to his prayers.

"Katherine," he whispered as he went down on his haunches in front of her. "I'm here, lass. Give me your hand and I'll help you. I'll get you away from here. Away from the dark. Rafe is waiting for us. Come with me, that's it, come to me," Gabriel spoke soft and low, not wanting to frighten her further.

Much to Katherine's delight, his distress caused him to lapse into a lilting highland brogue that time had lessened but not erased. She had always had a weakness for soft, honey-sweet words. Keeping in character with Gabriel proved easier than she had thought possible. His presence was very comforting and for a moment, she almost forgot that she could crush every bone in his body. To feel fragile and protected was a nice change, even if the circumstances were false.

"Please, take me upstairs." Her voice was ragged.

"Let me tell Rafe I found you," he murmured against her ear as he swung her up in his arms.

Katherine shivered at the feeling of *déjà vu* that flooded her as she leaned her cheek against his broad chest. For a moment, she hesitated in her planning; these three men brought back too many memories better left buried with the one who had inspired them so long ago. They were muddying her mind with the mixed emotions they'd stirred within her, and in her position, it wasn't intelligent to become so distracted. Inattention could mean the end of her unnatural life.

With her two-centuries-older-blood-sister, Sasha, just a step behind, she had learned the hard way to stay ever vigilant. If Sasha ever learned of her little plan for the three, the *Sidhe* fairy was certain to be upset with her. But with a nonchalance born of four centuries of supremacy, Katherine shrugged off her concern. Even if Sasha was still angry with her over the antics of their vicious sire, Katherine knew in her heart that Sasha could never harm her. The little wood sprite didn't have it in her to hurt another.

T   T   T

Rafe glanced up when Gabriel walked into the room with

Katherine in his arms. Concern for Michael remained utmost in his mind, and he came to his feet in a rush, naked aggression replacing cool civility. "What the hell happened here, Katherine?" His smoky voice was as sharp as broken glass in the silent room and he watched in disgust as she shrank back into Gabriel's embrace. "Who did this?" A clenched fist pointed at Michael's still form. "Who?" He remained unmoved by the damp eyes she turned his way. Unlike the others, a woman's tears had lost any effect on him long ago.

"There was nothing I could do," her voice broke on a sob. "Michael tried to stop him but the man had a knife. They fought and I ran, but it was too late. He hurt me, Gabriel." She turned her attention back to the one cradling her close to his heart.

"He was so strong and I was afraid. Please, forgive me." She let her head fall back against Gabriel's shoulder, as if the weight had become too much for her to endure. "How is Michael?" she asked after a moment.

"I don't have a clue. Why don't you tell me what really happened?" Rafe responded before Gabriel could utter a word.

Katherine found it hard not to break the self-righteous bastard in half. The fool was getting on her bad side. She was putting on her best act here. She'd even managed to squeeze out a few galling tears and a pitiful apology, but he still had the nerve to doubt her sincerity. Ignoring Rafe altogether, she locked wide, misty eyes on Gabriel. "Please, take me upstairs, Gabriel."

"Whatever you want me to do," he promised her, attuned to the tension that flowed between her and his best friend.

"Watch your back," Rafe warned him, unconvinced of her innocence.

T   T   T

"Stay with me. Please. I can't stand to be alone," Katherine tried her best to sound needy as he lay her down on the bed, her grand plans already spinning through her devious mind.

For all his size and confidence, Gabriel was at a complete disadvantage and longed for a hasty retreat. Trying to hide his reluctance, he sat beside her, doing his best to soothe her fears. "He didn't hurt you, did he?" He hesitated in asking, already dreading the answer.

"No." What good would it do to push her luck at this stage?

"Good," he said, breathing deep in relief. "You've been through too much, to add that."

"What did I do to make Rafe so angry with me?" Her eyes widened with feigned hurt.

"This isn't about you, lass. He's just angry with this whole mess." Gabriel tried to reassure her, although he didn't believe his own answer. "Rafe likes to be in control of every situation, and this one is beyond all of us. This is going to drive him insane until we find out who's responsible."

"You're looking for who killed David?" Katherine couldn't mask her surprise. She hadn't counted on their interference in *that* matter. Even with as well as she'd covered her tracks, one could never be too careful.

"We failed David. In any way we can, that has to be set right. I would have died for him, Katherine. Still might, but I won't be the only one." The fire in his green eyes would have ignited the bedcovers had it taken form.

Katherine pitied his dead cousin for a moment. No way an ordinary man could have competed with a creature like this. He was magnificent, the very barbarian he was accused of being. With a champion like him, she would never have to fear Sasha or her vile sire again.

"Please, hold me. I need to forget this horrible thing, if only for a moment." She gazed up at him, the darkness of her eyes luminous with unshed tears.

Gabriel looked around in desperation, searching for a quick escape. Not seeing any, he scooted closer to her on the bed and pulled her into his arms.

"Kiss me," she beseeched, pushing a little further than she'd planned.

He jerked away from her clinging arms, his shock and disbelief clear on his face.

"Make me forget that man, forget how he ripped my clothes, how he hit me. Please, touch me, Gabriel. Give me something to fill my mind with." She improvised, trying to regain her advantage. When he walked away from the bed, she knew that she had overplayed her hand, but that didn't slow her down. Things didn't always have to be easy and she was more than up to the challenge.

"What game are you playing?" Gabriel demanded, incredulous at her audacity. He whirled around to face her, loathing etched in every line of his rugged face. "Whatever it is you're selling, I'm not interested. David was my friend. If you won't remember that, then I will." Disgusted dripped from his tongue.

"Not interested?" she seethed, bounding from the bed. Her temper flared as his rejection hit home and her plans crumbled before her. "How dare you refuse me? I was good enough for your precious David. Men lust after me. They'd do anything for me. What makes you so bloody high and mighty?" she demanded, her heaving body inches from his.

"Leave David out of this. You're not fit to mention his name. He was a true gentleman, and if he availed himself of your dubious charms it was no more than a brief escape from good taste," Gabriel berated, looking down at her through eyes brimming with contempt.

"How dare you? I'm beautiful..."

His humorless laughter cut through Katherine's words. "Outer beauty is little compensation when all that is inside of you is corrupt and rotten. Even animals show more discretion, Katherine," he sneered.

The significance of the insult went much deeper than even he could have imagined. His cold words stripped away the last traces of humanity that had clung to her. With a howl of outrage, she flung herself at him, striking out, fingernails raking a burning path down the curve of his cheek.

His large hand slapping her across the face left Katherine sitting on the floor where she'd landed in stunned silence. This man, a puny mortal, had the ability to hurt her.

Gabriel watched as she rubbed at the hand print that stood out bright red against the exotic hue of her skin. He'd never hit a woman before and having done so now shamed him. The need to make peace, to beg forgiveness, overrode even his disgust at her sluttish behavior, had him stepping toward her.

Brushing at a tickle on his cheek, he was unprepared for the blood that came away on his questing fingertips.

Katherine couldn't believe the expression of absolute fury that crossed his abused face. Fear consumed her as he closed the distance between them. This man, a barbaric throwback to his highland ancestors, was intent on murdering her, of this she had no doubt. Even with her great strength, she didn't know if she could stop him.

Crawling backward on hands and knees, she made for the far side of the bed. There, with the distance separating them, she took a second to conjure a weapon worthy of vanquishing a barbarian. Rocking back on her heels, she grasped the hilt of the broadsword her magic had wrought. She waited in tense silence as Gabriel stalked her.

"That wasn't very smart, Katherine. You should never back yourself into a corner."

He sounded so calm, as if they were talking about the weather. That bothered her the most. A man out of control was one thing, a man so enraged that the fire turned to ice was a different story. As much as she wanted to keep him as her champion, she had no choice but to kill him. There was no other way to handle him, not if she wanted to survive.

Katherine had never felt so much like the animal he accused her of being until now. Feeling like a helpless mortal woman didn't set well with her, and she vowed he would regret this night's actions before she ended his miserable life.

When he was close enough that she could see the fury etched into every line of his face, she brought up the sword and drove the blade into his chest. His shock gave her a moment of satisfaction. His last words took it away.

"I wouldn't have hurt you, lass," he rasped.

His sincerity was reflected in those highland green eyes and Katherine knew then that he spoke the truth. He wouldn't have harmed her. His honor wouldn't have allowed him to. Only her stupidity let her believe otherwise.

Consumed with anger over her foolishness, she took it out on the only person she could. Grasping the sword in both hands, she dragged the blade down his body with a vicious yank, leaving a trail of ripped skin, torn muscle and a river of glistening red blood from mid-chest to thigh.

Gabriel was in too much pain to do more than watch as she pulled out the sword, dropping it to the floor at their feet. With the last of his strength, he reached out a bloody hand and touched her bruised cheek.

᛭   ᛭   ᛭

Rafe stood at the window, looking out into the night. His thoughts were as dark as the endless blackness that stared back at him. He didn't believe Katherine. Not that he thought she was physically capable of attacking Michael, but if she had an accomplice, someone who would have a reason to come back to this house at midnight, anything was possible. At this point, all he wanted to know was what in hell was going on, and what she had to do with it. With those questions churning in his mind, he didn't at first notice that Michael had spoken.

"Rafe?" he whispered again, his words nothing more than a raspy murmur. Rafe heard him then, and in seconds the other man was at his side.

"Are you well?" At this point, all of Rafe's concerns were for his friend. The rest could wait. Katherine wasn't going anywhere. The highlander would see to that.

"Where is Gabriel?" Michael's words were slurred with fatigue and shock.

The fear he couldn't hide was something Rafe had never seen in him before and all his reflexes went on alert. "He's upstairs with Katherine. What happened?"

"Get him away from her, he's not safe." Michael was desperate as he fought to rise. Rafe pushed him down with a firm hand before sprinting for the door. Michael felt peace then, knowing that together, Gabriel and Rafe were unstoppable. No matter what kind of fiend she was, she didn't stand a chance.

As Rafe raced up the stairs to the master bedroom, all he could think about was breaking her damn neck. If she had as much to do with this as Michael's words implied, there wouldn't be anywhere the bitch could hide. As he turned a corner, he collided with Katherine full-force. The motion sent her careening into the wall as he fell backward to the floor.

Rafe gained his feet in a rush and pushed past her, self-preservation the last thing on his mind as he took in the blood that splattered the front of her torn gown.

The sight of Gabriel distracted him from the fist Katherine aimed at his temple. Pleasure filled every crevice of her fractured soul as she watched him crash to the ground at her feet. "Now we're going to do things my way." She said no more, instead, she planned her next move with malicious glee.

Chapter 3

Sasha stood over the fallen warrior for long minutes. There was no guesswork needed to figure out what had happened to the dying man at her feet. This little drama had Katherine written all over it.

Luck had been on Sasha's side that she'd been able to find Katherine at all this time. The sorceress had grown careless in the last weeks, her need for adventure leaving her exposed to those who searched for her. Sasha couldn't quell the irritation that waiting had caused her. She wasn't afraid of the little immortal her sire had made. Their black-hearted sire himself was the one who moved her to caution. Wherever Katherine was, Jamison was never far behind.

The only things left to wonder over now were how close their sire was and if she had time to mend the wrongs done before he arrived. Dropping to her knees at the dying man's side, Sasha saw his face for the first time and felt a sharp stab of recognition. Endless time had passed since her first dreams of him. At last, those haunting visions were flesh and he was so much more than she'd expected.

Gabriel moaned in protest as awareness pierced the blessed numbness filling his body. Burning agony flared then faded as something pressed against the wound in his chest. "Am I past hope, Rafe?" Even as he forced the words out, he knew the truth. The coldness slithering over his skin like a snake hissed the answer to him over and over. No hope. No hope. Death was coming for him but he wouldn't hide behind closed eyes in meek acceptance.

An angel knelt beside him, not Rafe, her delicate hands slick with his blood as she stroked the wreckage of his chest.

Gabriel stared in disbelief at the ethereal creature. Battling the weakness sapping his strength, he reached for a spiraling curl the color of autumn. All russet and golden, the silken strands slid through his fingers like sunshine through the trees. And those amber eyes, filled with so much love and compassion he wanted to cry out against it.

Didn't she know what he'd done? Couldn't she feel the darkness in the heart pounding under her hand?

Bedtime stories learned as a small child had him searching for gossamer wings even as the strong body he'd grown into quickened under her touch.

"Are you an angel?"

The awe in his whispered words caused her to smile despite her sadness. "Not an angel, just someone who exists to help you. Will you let me help you?" Sasha asked.

"It's too late, angel. Will your God forgive what I've done? Will you come with me if he doesn't?" Her heaven or his hell. What did it matter so long as she was with him?

"I'm not an angel, sweeting, but I'll go with you." The end was close and she couldn't lose him now. Swallowing her fear, she tried again. "Let me help you." She prayed for the strength not to do what had to be done without his permission.

"Help me." Bright bubbles of blood stained his lips with every ragged breath that escaped him.

Framing his face with gentle hands, she pressed her lips to his. The innocent pleasure of the kiss was lost to her with the first coppery taste of his blood. Darker needs exploded inside of her, needs that her dreams had kept hidden.

Sasha pulled away from him and the new, unwanted sensations tormenting her. She couldn't do this. For all her searching, her waiting, she would lose him.

With a last, desperate surge of strength, Gabriel wound his fingers into the wealth of her autumn-hued hair and pulled her face close to his. "Don't leave me now that you've found me, my angel. Don't let me go."

He brushed his lips over hers and in that kiss, mingled with his blood, Sasha could taste the helplessness of her tears. There was no longer a choice for her in this. Damned or vindicated. Angel or demon. Lost or found. He was hers now and she would give everything to keep him. Even her soul.

She stroked a bloodstained hand over his face, letting her fingers memorize every rugged curve and hollow. With each touch the ugly marks of Katherine's bruised pride healed until nothing remained but the mortal death that dimmed the magnificence of his deep green eyes. There was nothing she could do for that except take his life.

"I have to take so much away from you to give you my gift. Please, forgive me," Sasha whispered against his ear. When his eyes fluttered closed, she brushed her lips against his throat, fighting urges she'd never experienced before. With one last breath, she bit deep, taking that first addictive swallow.

T   T   T

Rafe turned his throbbing head with caution, making out the boundaries of the wine cellar. It took his dazed mind a moment to realize that chains held him to a stone wall, with his arms secured high and tight above his body. His total defenselessness started a fierce anger smoldering deep in his soul.

"Katherine." Her name bounced off the walls as he gave into his fury. "There is no place you can hide. Even hell won't be a safe haven for your rotten soul." He pulled against his bonds, wanting only to strangle the life from her body.

"Why would I hide from you?"

Her laughter echoed around them. She seemed to take form from the shadows, drawing herself from the very walls that held him captive.

Entertained by his frustration, she made no secret of her amusement. She approached with nonchalance, stopping a hairsbreadth from his struggling body. "Are the accommodations not to your liking?" she cooed against his ear. He met her fascinated gaze with a look of such loathing that she wanted to slap his face.

"Well, well, just as high and mighty as your green-eyed friend. Look what happened to him. I would suggest you remember who is in charge here and act accordingly. You wouldn't want to make me angry, I might not let you live." Taunting him lit a fire in her blood. For once tonight, she had the upper hand with him.

"What do you think you've accomplished?" he asked, his emotions buried under ice.

"I have you at my mercy. What more could a woman want?" Reaching up, she drew her fingertips in slow, sensual exploration from his shoulder to hip.

Rafe arched into her until they were nose to nose. "You had better kill me now, because I will get free. And when I do, I'm going to rip your heart out and eat it, while I watch you die at my feet."

The cold menace in his voice provoked the devil in her. "You have a choice," she snapped, loosing all humor with her prey. "Either cooperate with me and I'll see you don't suffer much, or I'll cut you into little pieces and take my time doing it."

Katherine's smile was sweet while every part of her hated him with a passion. His cold, soulless eyes reminded her so much of her sire that it was all she could do not to break every bone in his mortal body. But she wouldn't do that, yet. She had the upper hand with the dark bastard now, and she relished the chance to do to him all the things she couldn't do to her sire.

"I could let you go, Rafe, if you're nice to me." Katherine's whisper was suggestive. Bluffing in truth. She didn't want him in her bed as she wanted Michael. There would be no lovemaking between them when the time came for them to join. Rafe didn't inspire that heated, mind-weakening ripple in the pit of her stomach. What Rafe brought out from her soul was a viciousness that her sire would have been proud of. This man, she could take, possess and savage. He made the demon inside of her howl with anticipation.

"I need your answer, slave," Katherine purred the words against his neck as she slid her body against his.

"I'll never be your slave, Katherine, not on this side of hell." His answer was as blistering as the center of the hottest desert at noon.

"If you're so eager for hell, Rafe, I can take you there, very slowly."

"I've been there before." He didn't try to hide his contempt. "I wasn't impressed." The memory made his words sound remote. "There is nothing you can do to me short of death that I can't survive and come back from."

"My plan was to keep you with me for awhile, but now I think I'll just slice you into little pieces." The wicked taunts she forced on him thrilled her more than lustful thoughts of Michael's lovemaking.

"You're out of your mind."

"Not at all," she countered. "There is little I can't do to you."

"Go to hell." His words rasped through gritted teeth.

"You and your fixation with hell. I'm going to take you there, Rafe."

He struggled as she drew the dragon-claw dagger from thin air. When he saw her delight at his resistance, he stopped and looked her straight in the face. His determination burned like molten silver in his eyes.

Katherine knew it in that moment. He would never beg.

She reached up, wearing a smirk and pulled the chains from the wall. When Rafe didn't move fast enough for her, she slashed at him with her blade, cutting the arm he raised in defense.

In the struggle that followed, Rafe wasn't at first aware that he didn't stand a chance. He never admitted defeat, not even when Katherine straddled him to the ground and held the tip of the blade to his heart.

"Beg me, Rafe," she challenged, panting, her body thrumming with the lust their fight had stirred within her. She wanted a taste of him so much that she couldn't breathe for the need that gripped her. "Beg me."

"Never." The one word was fierce and driven.

"So be it." She tossed the dagger aside and grabbed a fist full of silky black hair, her hold vicious as she jerked his head back. Her excitement rose to an unbearable pitch at the sight of his throat exposed for her pleasure. Moaning under her hunger, she met his gaze.

Rafe refused to pull away from the ugly gleam he saw in her eyes. With an arrogance and determination borne of years of torment and abuse, he did the only thing he could do; he held her gaze and never lowered his gray eyes from hers.

Katherine didn't hesitate another moment. Brutally she mauled his neck with her teeth. Over and over again, she opened his throat until the blood flowed hot and thick against her tongue. She fought off the waves of ecstasy that crashed over her as she drew his essence into her body, fighting the strange, dark needs that demanded something of her. Just what, she couldn't name.

Not realizing what she was doing, she reached for the dagger. Without conscience thought, she dragged the blade across her chest until her blood mingled with his. Leaning down, she pressed his mouth to the wound on her breast. That was what she had needed; to have him tasting her while she bled him dry.

Rafe felt as if he were floating above the scene, not taking part, but watching in appalled fascination. The vision in his mind was frightening. Katherine had her mouth buried in his throat, her body convulsing over his. All the while he drank from her until their blood mingled as one within his heart, his soul.

Reality hit him like a closed fist. He was getting just as much pleasure as Katherine seemed to be from this depraved union. But no more. With a fierceness borne of vengeance and self–preservation, he began ruthlessly drawing life from Katherine's trembling body into his own. Pushing aside all thought, he focused only on her destruction.

As a wave of dizziness rolled through her, Katherine heeded her instincts and tore away, only to fall back in exhaustion. She wasn't sure how much he had taken, but knew that she had never felt so weak and muddled before. Closing her eyes, she courted sleep without fear of Rafe intruding on her peace. There was only the knowledge that he hadn't taken enough from her to begin the change, and that his death was imminent.

ϯ   ϯ   ϯ

"What's wrong, Katherine, too much treachery for one day?"

The question came from the one person Katherine hadn't expected to hear from again. The voice, so low and smoky, sent shivers down her spine. She looked up in shock and found herself staring into Rafe's frigid eyes as he leaned over her.

"You seem surprised to see me. Did you forget about me already? It's not a mistake you'll ever make again."

The brutal finality of his words slammed into Katherine like a sledgehammer. "You shouldn't be alive. How can you be alive?" She could feel the panic welling up inside. "I don't understand. You couldn't have taken enough blood." Her words stopped as Rafe wrapped his hands around her throat, about to make good on a vow of vengeance, no doubt.

"I can't let you do that." The words were soft, the voice like warm honey.

As Rafe turned to locate the new presence in the room, a woman stepped into the light. He froze at the sight of the angel who appeared so glorious before his eyes. "Am I dead?" he asked, aggravated at the possibility.

Sasha took pity on him amused by his chagrined expression. "No, you're not dead. However, it is time you took a rest. It's going to be a long day tomorrow, and I need you wide awake so I can answer your questions." She dropped to her knees beside him, unconcerned with the dirt that marred the purity of her white gown. With a touch to his forehead and a soft-spoken word, she completed her spell and sent Katherine's latest creation into a deep slumber.

"You were always so good at putting men to sleep." Katherine tossed out the insult as she struggled to pull herself together.

"What a silly child you are, Katherine. Don't you know better than to bait me? You are weak from your greed, and I would like nothing better than to drain you dry for this bit of stupidity." Sasha flowed to her feet, the motion like poetry.

Katherine rose as well, not the least fooled by Sasha's pleasant smile. For centuries, she had eluded the *Sidhe* immortal. She wasn't likely to fall for that soothing voice and fairy magic now.

"You don't scare me." The second the words slipped from her lips, Katherine wanted to call them back. To be called a silly child was one thing, to act like one, another.

"He should scare you." Sasha warned as she nodded to the man sleeping at their feet. "I'd stay away from him if I were you. He's more dangerous than you think. This one is likely to finish the job our sire started with you."

"As if you care." Katherine snorted in disbelief. "You wouldn't help me when I needed it. All you could do was stand there with your high morals and preach to me about right and wrong. I didn't need you though, did I? Jamie did what you wouldn't. He gave me immortality."

"At what cost, sweeting?"

Katherine had to look away from the sympathy she saw in those strange amber eyes. Sasha knew first hand what their sire was capable of. There were no secrets between them when it came to Jamie's creative streak.

"I have protection from him now." Katherine spoke with a confidence she didn't feel. There would be no help for her against Jamison. Rafe and Gabriel had eluded her plans, and now she only had Michael to stand between her and the thousand-year-old vampire who insisted she belonged to him.

"The fair one won't help you," Sasha replied. "He will know what you did to the others and he will hand you over with a song in his heart. The warrior I saved will also hunt you. As will the dark one." There was a deep sorrow in her over the panic that filled Katherine's pretty face. The little one had delved in too deep this time and had left herself with no escape.

"I will find others." Katherine struggled to remain calm in the face of such hard truth.

"Can you take that chance? Can you risk any more enemies?" Sasha didn't need an answer. "Let me help you."

"Never."

There in that one word was all of Katherine's hatred for the golden one. For the *Sidhe* princess that had denied her the gift she had needed to save her very soul. They stood there for a long time, neither speaking of the past that had changed them both, until a faint shiver in the very air forced Sasha to bridge the distance.

"He's close now."

Sasha didn't need to say his name, his very presence hung like a dark pall over them. Maybe a day kept them safe from his wrath, maybe less.

"He will destroy the three." There was no pleasure in Katherine's voice, only a quiet acceptance of what would come.

"I won't let him. It will be years before he knows of their existence." Sasha knew her magic could keep them cloaked, much as it kept her. Only Katherine remained vulnerable to him. "I can help you, keep you safe from Jamie."

"But not from them."

Sasha knew Katherine spoke of the three, just as she knew the other immortal was right. Not even her ancient magic could stand between the newest immortals and the one they would hold responsible.

"You asked me the cost for going to Jamie?" Katherine's slight smile was bitter. "You of all should know the torment, the agony, the terrible suffering he can inflict with such joy. I would rather lie with my Christian, under the dirt for all eternity without the chance of ever gaining peace, then endure at Jamie's hands again."

"Don't." Sasha couldn't stand the pain that filled Katherine's ebony gaze. She reached for her, wanting only to give comfort.

Katherine jumped away from hands that would have touched her. She didn't need the pity she saw on Sasha's face. There was nothing the golden one could give her. Not now. "Jamie is the known evil in this lovely little farce. Unfortunately, I know what he can do and I know how far to push. He will seek me until the end. The choice doesn't belong to me in this."

She shook off the desolation that plagued her and continued with a mocking smile. "So off I'll go, pretending this was nothing more than a big game of hide and seek. Jamie will demand obedience, and for awhile, he'll have it of me."

"No, sweeting, you don't need to go to him. I'll do my best to hide you." Sasha forced herself not to grab for Katherine. Forced herself not to use magic to make the little one see reason.

"Too late, Jamie knows I'm near. He won't stop until he has blood and it might not matter whose now. Unless you feel up to the sacrifice, that leaves me." Katherine took Sasha's silence as a no. She stepped back a little more until half the cellar separated them. "Guard the three well,

Sasha. They may be the only ones able to bring Jamie down when the time comes." Katherine glanced at Rafe then, where he slept so peacefully on the floor, her black eyes blazing with hatred for a brief second before she gained control. "Keep that one away from me, fairy. There is nothing breathing that can keep him safe if I decide to finish what *I* started."

Chapter 4

"My name is Sasha." Her voice flowed around the three, sweeping away the last wisps of sleep. She waited, patient while they stumbled over questions and demands. "I will do my best to explain but I need your cooperation."

The three men drifted into silence as they stared with varying degrees of awe and confusion at the angelic creature holding court in the night-darkened salon.

Sasha turned her attention to the one whose cold gray eyes searched the room with such ruthless determination. "I can assure you that she no longer resides in this house." She watched Rafe tense at the mention of Katherine. "It will do no good to search for her. You will not find her." There was no reason to add that she wouldn't allow them to hunt her. They didn't need to know her plans to protect the sorceress. No one did. Not even Katherine.

Only when Sasha felt some of the tension leave Rafe, did she focus on another. "You are well?" she asked of Gabriel, hesitant to look at him for fear he would see the hunger she couldn't hide.

"Better now, angel, for seeing you." He drawled out the words, soft and low.

The sensual promise in his voice caused heat to clamor though Sasha's body. She dropped her gaze to where her hands clenched in her lap, trying to hide the blush that crawled into the ivory perfection of her cheeks. No one had ever spoken to her as Gabriel just had. Like a mortal woman. Like a lover.

"Say you're real, angel. Tell me you aren't a dream," he demanded as he dropped to his knees in front of her chair. Gabriel didn't allow her to escape as he caught her chin with gentle fingers and brought her amber gaze to his.

The fire burning in his green eyes made her catch her breath and pray for strength. "I am as real as you," she whispered, unaware of much else but him.

Rafe and Michael watched the by-play in fascination. They had never seen Gabriel so taken with a woman. Any woman. The man lived like a monk, his social life limited to the time he spent with them.

"Do you think he's going to take her on the floor?" Michael murmured under his breath in utter fascination of the heat the oblivious couple was producing.

"At this stage anything could happen." Rafe's answer was just as quiet as he leaned forward in his chair, equally captivated by the emotions Gabriel made no effort to hide.

Those emotions changed in the span of a heartbeat as aggression edged out passion and Gabriel lunged across the room, his hands fisting in Michael's shirt. He lifted the other man off the ground until startled blue eyes were even with glowing green.

"Don't even look at her." The words emerged through clenched teeth as Gabriel tightened his hold.

Rafe didn't hesitate to place himself between the growling highlander and Michael. Nor did he think to question the sudden surge of strength that enabled him to shove Gabriel against the wall with enough force to crack plaster.

The silence that followed the violent outburst was broken only by the harsh rasping of in-drawn breaths as the three struggled to regain control.

"So much for doing this the easy way." Sasha swallowed the bitter regret that pooled in her throat. This was not how she had planned on breaking the news to the three, but Gabriel's jealousy had left her little choice. "Katherine is a vampire." She waited for it to sink in, but they remained guardedly silent. "That in turn makes all of you vampires." She had never been good at this part. "Vampires, night walkers, blood drinkers."

That got a reaction.

Rafe was the first, his eyes blazing as he pushed past an equally stunned Michael to confront her. "There is no such thing!" He was vehement in his rejection.

"Vampires, demons, that's all make-believe," Michael added his less explosive opinion.

Sasha looked to Gabriel, waiting for his denial. Nothing prepared her for what she saw. Pain, raw and crippling, reflected from his eyes and edged the bitter curve of his mouth. Struggling to focus on anything other than the terrible emotions she could feel inside the highlander, she tried again.

"Think back to the moment you realized Katherine was different. Try to remember what happened when she took you." She motioned Michael to her. When he was close enough, she drew attention to several details. "See the marks on his neck? Look at his eyes, Rafe, the paleness of the blue. Were they like that before?"

"What about you?" She asked the dark man. "Isn't everything clearer? Sharper? Can you feel the strength? The power that pulses through your body? What about where she cut your arm? Pull back your sleeve and tell me what you see. Just a scar, correct? What of Gabriel? See the blood on his clothes? By all rights, he shouldn't ever draw breath again. That blade cut through flesh and muscle. Show them."

Her words held such conviction Gabriel could do no less and with undeniable grace, he shrugged out of his shredded and bloodstained shirt. There was complete silence as they looked at the angry red scar that marred the length of his chest.

"Do you remember the pain?" she asked. Her voice nothing more than a breathless murmur from the unexpected effect his body had on her system.

"What I remember, *angel,* is that she left me after she did this." He pointed to the mark, then with fierce, unforgiving eyes, he pinned Sasha to her chair. "Then you came, with your sweet words and soft kisses."

"I gave you a choice, Gabriel," she whispered in desperation, unable to bear the thought that she had taken what he hadn't willingly given. "I couldn't let you die. I would have given anything to make your decision easier, but there wasn't time. Katherine hadn't left me any time. Please, understand. Please."

Michael and Rafe looked away, unwilling to watch her beg or Gabriel's determination to make her.

"You're just like her," Gabriel accused, all the gentle passion from minutes before replaced with unforgiving condemnation.

Sasha tensed at the bitter coldness of his expression. The suppressed hatred in his eyes. "If you mean that I'm immortal, then yes, I am like her." Drawing a steadying breath, she waited, some part of her already knowing what was to come.

"It goes deeper than that." Gabriel's laugher grated the back of his throat. "You're the same conniving bitch that Katherine is, only you're worse. You sit there looking like an angel when there are nothing but fiendish intentions in your black heart."

"I had no choice," she whispered, tears shimmering within the golden mystery of her eyes.

"I'd have rather died then be like you."

Nothing had ever hurt her as much as those bitter words and she could only watch in bone-crushing agony as he turned away from her.

"Where shall I begin?" She asked when the pain lessened enough to allow breath.

"Tell us about you and Katherine," Michael requested, desperate to break the tension that filled the room.

Gabriel continued his silent perusal of the deserted street, not trusting himself to gaze upon the woman who had changed his life, his duty.

"I was immortal long before the vampire came to me. I lived in an area that the Saxons and Normans had battled over from a time beyond memory. I came from a very special people. War, famine, and sickness never bothered us. We were revered. Then everything changed and it was no longer safe to live."

"You speak as if your race no longer exists," Rafe interrupted.

"My people hid deep in the forest to avoid persecution and became as one with nature. They were absorbed into the very hills and valleys they sought refuge in until nothing remained of the people I had loved." Sasha explained.

"What were they called?" Michael's question was little more than a whisper.

"We were the *Sidhe*."

The foreign sound of the word, S*hee*, was nothing more that a revered escape of breath from her lips, but the reaction it brought was anything but gentle.

"Fairies!" Gabriel's explosive response revealed his disbelief.

"Do I have wings and pointy ears?" Sasha shot back, her anger over his defection rising. "Fairies are make believe, Gabriel, a bedtime story spun by the *Tuatha Dé Danaan* that came before us. The *Sidhe* were the golden people, the Harbingers of Light. We were magic."

"Magic?" Rafe scoffed at the idea. "I don't believe in magic."

"You don't believe in vampires either. Look what that got you." She chided with a gentle smile, again controlling the turmoil within her. "That magic did nothing to save us when a stranger came to our land. He was vile, barbaric, cruel, and invincible. He destroyed anyone that opposed him, decimated anything that stood in his path. Armies quaked in fear at his very name. Kings gave him anything he demanded in order to protect their people."

"What did your king give him, Sasha, to keep the clan safe?"

She took a deep breath before she answered Rafe's question. "Jamison wanted magic. Our magic is in the blood, not something gifted on a whim. The very essence of it resides in our heart, our soul. He was enraged." She shuddered at the memory. "He went on a rampage, destroying and raping and maiming. In desperation, they offered him anything he wanted."

The terror that lingered in her eyes gave Rafe added insight into her story. "Jamison wanted you," he said.

"What happened?" Michael prompted.

Sasha didn't answer, only turned her face from their curious eyes, but Gabriel refused to let the matter rest. Crossing the room to her chair, he dropped to his knees beside her. Catching her fragile hands in his large fists, he ignored her gasp of surprise. When she would have pulled away, he tightened his hold and focused on the memories that danced through her mind.

"They came for you on what should have been your wedding day. As they dragged you to the meeting place, you begged and pleaded for mercy but nothing stopped them. Jamison had chosen and the others were more than happy to sacrifice you for their own well-being. Magic was used to bind you and you were left alone to await the devil." Gabriel paused at her pained whimper.

"Don't do this," she pleaded, trying to escape, but he only tightened his hold and stared more deeply into her anguished eyes. "Please, I'll go away, just don't…" Her words died when he began to speak again.

"He came, shrouded in the night, so big he blotted out the moon. You knew he brought eternal torment and prepared for the worst. But he didn't touch you; instead, he let you go. Overjoyed to be free, you dropped to your knees at his feet, kissing his hand, the tears of gratitude bathing his cold skin.

"That was your mistake, wasn't it, angel? Showing tender emotions to a monster with no heart." A ragged breath escaped him as the next nightmare slammed through her mind. "You ran from him but it wasn't enough. The violence of his rape left you broken and bloody."

Gabriel felt her every torment of that night, but still he continued. "Into the darkness he carried you, laughing his pleasure as you begged for him to end your agony. For death. Before the sun rose, he raped you again, this time taking your blood and giving back his own. When it was over, you lie there on the ground, calling out for help. For your family. But their arrival brought no comfort. Knowing what he had done to you changed their love to fear, their compassion to scorn. They gave no help that day or any other as they deserted one of their own." Gabriel finished then. "You had just seen your sixteenth year that summer." He let her pull free, staying on his knees as Sasha gained her freedom and fled.

Rafe and Michael walked past him as they left the room, each in turn placing a hand upon his shoulder. As they entered the night air, they went their separate ways, each feeling a deep remorse for the beautiful enchantress and the highland warrior who silently suffered for her pain.

Ⴕ   Ⴕ   Ⴕ

Morning brought no comfort to Rafe and Michael as they returned to the townhouse, their thoughts in turmoil, their emotions stretched to the breaking point. Everything was so different now, every sound, every sight brought forth such unparalleled sensations that it was a struggle to focus on the very things that demanded their attention.

They found Gabriel in much the same place they had left him the night before. He had taken over the chair their fairy savior had vacated in her haste to escape the highlander's cruel insight into her past. He sprawled in that chair, his eyes locked on the piece of parchment crumpled in a large fist.

No one spoke for long minutes as they waited for Gabriel to return from the place that had put such grim suffering in his deep green eyes.

"She's gone." The words were hollow, his expression bleak.

"Did you really think she would stay after what you said to her?" Rafe asked. "Did you think she would see beyond the cruel words? To what you hid underneath? Some things don't change, Gabriel, no matter how hard we wish."

Michael was clueless as to the meaning behind those stark words. Rafe and Gabriel had secrets between them that he wasn't privy to, but he buried the hurt that the exclusion brought him. He had secrets of his own to hide, his night with Katherine just one of the many things he would never be able to share.

"So what does that mean for us? Are we supposed to wander around like freaks? Afraid of our own shadows? Biting virgins after dark?" Michael drawled out. The parts of himself he kept hidden behind a flashing smile and smooth charm evident in the tiny flash of rage that flared to life in those pale blue eyes.

"She left a note," Gabriel responded in a tired murmur. Unfolding the rumpled parchment, he handed it to Rafe.

My Fallen Angels,

I am unable to stay with the contempt I know I will see in your eyes. I could not prevent what happened to me, but I tried to give Gabriel a choice. May he forgive me.

I will try to answer the questions I know you have. When my blood mingled with Jamison's, it changed us both. That change made him stronger, different.

Jamison is not like the others of his kind. Night no longer confines him.

The sun is not his enemy. Thoughts and dreams are his to read at will. Magic is his weapon.

He is in this moment and all others, a demon set free on the world without limitations. With a lust for blood that brings him pleasure.

I in turn am no longer a creature of light and magic and innocence. He bestowed upon me hatred and rage. He would have all believe that his way is the answer to peace, that the taking of human life eases the darkness, but he lies. His blood he gave me, his darkness, but unlike Jamison, who lost his soul when the demon entered, I did not.

The same is true for any immortal made from the same blood that Jamison and I share. Katherine is one such immortal, but she chooses to follow his path, to glory in the darkness.

The three of you now have a choice of your own to make.

Do you follow them and forsake the soul that lives within your body, or do you fight the dark need and exist as I do? I can only hope you make the right choice.

There are so many things you should know to survive in the new existence that was thrust upon you. So many things that I would spare you.

Our emotions are so strong. Love, rage, jealousy, hatred, passion, grief, all are intensified by the magic that flows through our veins. Control is a necessity for us, a way to keep others safe.

So many gifts are now open to you if you choose to explore them. So many things you will learn as time passes. Magic is a part of you now and all the gifts that that magic entails.

There is no amount of forgiveness I can ask for, nothing I can say to ease the pain you will experience. All I can do is be at your service when you need guidance and offer what answers I can when you have need. Please be well and know that I would change all if I could.

Sasha

Chapter 5

New Orleans, Now

Gabriel Arden strolled through the crowd that spilled out of the discreetly lit, high-priced French Quarter nightclub as it closed its doors for the night. The number of patrons Heaven's Gate brought in never ceased to amaze him. Not even the small hours of morning lessened their enthusiasm for music, play, and booze.

Michael and Rafe had made a good investment when they'd bought and renovated this place on Royal Street several years ago, but he didn't dwell on that as he entered the elegant four-story building. The hellish night he'd just lived through had him on edge and all he wanted now was the seclusion of his personal domain.

Functioning on autopilot, Gabriel shed the hardware that accompanied his job. Unloading his police issue automatic, he stored it and his gold shield in the desk, all the while replaying the events of the day.

The job he'd taken with the N.O.P.D. wasn't always so upsetting but tonight had been different. He had a new partner, an aging pretty boy that felt his advanced years gave him an advantage. A new partner who'd made no secret of his contempt for Gabriel's youth.

A resounding knock on the door pulled Gabriel from the unpleasant path his thoughts had taken. He didn't even have to guess who it was as he opened the door.

Rafe stood there, two chilled beer bottles in his hand. "I thought you might need this." He offered a beer with a rueful smile.

"You could say that," Gabriel replied, tension radiating from his big body in waves.

"Did he really call you a punk?" Rafe didn't bother to keep the dry amusement out of his voice and was pleased when the tension in the other man lessened.

"That and more," Gabriel admitted, a slight smile on his generous mouth.

"I find it hard to believe that any man would call *you* names." Rafe was incredulous at this unknown man's audacity. Very few people tried to poke at the big man.

"He's been in homicide for eighteen years. He makes his opinion known that I'm a thirty-year-old-child that has no place in his department. My being there for the last three years doesn't matter. He's seen everything, knows everything, and if I have an idea or thought, I had better keep my damn mouth shut because he doesn't want to hear it. His words, not mine." Gabriel ended his tirade with a deep sigh, wincing at Rafe's laughter.

"You've been on this earth for more than two hundred years, have worked different homicide departments for fifty. Your record for the last three is flawless and you let this jackass talk to you like that?" Rafe asked, when the laughter was under control. "I can't believe that the mighty highland barbarian has mellowed that much. God, if Sasha could see you now."

Rafe had stepped over the line with that one and Gabriel rose to his feet and walked to the window, not trusting his reaction.

"Go see her, Gabriel. Put the past to rest." Rafe left the words hanging in the air. Any mention of Sasha ventured into forbidden territory. The subject was just about the only thing that stood between them and perfect accord.

"I see her sometimes."

Rafe kept his surprise to himself over those whispered words. Any mention of their immortal savior in the past had been met with open hostility. Never before had Gabriel spoken of seeking out the ethereal Sasha.

"She's never mentioned it to me." He picked at an imaginary speck on his white linen shirt while he pretended not to see the bitter pain that flashed across Gabriel's face at the casual mention of his own meetings with Sasha.

"I stay with her for hours and just look at her while she sleeps." Gabriel explained, the bleakness in his voice a mere echo of the desolation in his soul. "She never mentions it, because she doesn't know. I leave before she awakens. Sometimes I lay beside her, almost close enough to touch."

"Why?" Rafe didn't question the need to touch, only why he didn't.

"If I touched her I could never let her go, and then I'd be forsaking not only my honor but my heart, my soul, all to a woman who made me into a wandering freak." Gabriel's words were so brittle a rapid heartbeat would have shattered them. "Where is Michael by the way?" he added, desperate to change the subject.

"We had a problem on the floor tonight." Rafe was glad for the distraction. He had never seen Gabriel like this and it worried him. "He's going over it with your buddies from the 8th. The fights are getting worse and we aren't always around to mellow the irritation before it breaks into a brawl."

"That's the third fight this month. Have you looked into security? I have a name if you're interested." Gabriel broke off when the door swung open without warning. He winced as the heavy wood bounced off the wall with a resounding thud.

"Thanks for leaving me to clean up the mess." Michael accused as he caught the door and slammed it shut behind him, centering his aggravation on Rafe. "What the hell gives with the disappearing act? Do you think I haven't noticed the pattern lately?"

Gabriel and Rafe exchanged amused glances. The fierce glower and puffed-up aggression were out of place on their Armani-clothed friend. However, Michael in a foul mood was too good a source of entertainment to pass up.

"Nice suit." Rafe took a second to admire the shiny silver silk. The flashy stuff actually looked good on the younger man but he wouldn't be the one to tell him.

"Bite me." Michael all but snarled as he started his complaint again. "I'm tired of this crap, Rafe. Laugh all you want, but do you think the cops were any help tonight?"

"Does Brad Pitt know you're borrowing his clothes again?"

Michael ignored that from Gabriel. The guy considered khakis and a T-shirt a wise fashion choice. "All they did was take their little notes and tell me what they thought I wanted to hear," he continued even though most of his frustration had evaporated. "All the while they were mentally undressing the hot blonde that sings backup in the band. Cops are nothing but worthless, mindless jackals." The grin he flashed was devilish as he feigned innocence and focused laughing blue eyes on the *worthless cop* advancing on him. "Hey, buddy, I didn't see you there," he lied, taking Gabriel's black glower in stride as he dodged the less than gentle fist aimed in his direction.

"We have a state of the art monitoring system we don't use and a pair of bouncers that wouldn't say boo to a Girl Scout." Michael began his favorite rant. "I'm tired of playing the heavy. Have a heart, Rafe and let me hire someone."

"If you stop whining, I'll make some calls in the morning." Rafe offered that olive branch in payment for dumping the cops on him and running.

"You don't need to call." Gabriel interrupted before Michael could take exception. "We have an expert coming in from Texas to give a seminar next week. From what I understand, he was a part of St. John Securities. Before he branched out on his own two years ago, he worked for them as both a protection team leader and a security specialist. If we get in an early bid, we might be able to contract him."

"Is he any good?" Rafe asked, knowing Gabriel's gift for separating the truth from what people assumed was the truth.

"I would trust him with my life."

"So, does our new muscle have a name?" The absolute

conviction in Gabriel's praise was enough for Michael.

"Montgomery Sinclair."

ᛏ   ᛏ   ᛏ

"When does he start?" Michael questioned Rafe as they approached a quiet section of the long black glass and chrome bar that dominated a large portion of one wall of Heaven's Gate.

"He should be here tonight," Rafe replied.

"What did we offer him?" As personnel manager, Michael needed to know and he was still rather pissed that Rafe hadn't kept him updated on the negotiations he'd made via e-mail and fax with their new security specialist.

"The empty apartment on the fourth floor, use of the weight room, the sauna, etc." He mentioned a salary that brought a low whistle from Michael.

Rafe shrugged it off with a reckless grin. "Don't worry, Michael, I won't cut into your clothing budget. Besides, this guy's the best and I had a lot of competition. He'll be worth it. Gabriel checked his records and he's amazing. Some of the stuff he's done is unbelievable. A lot of Sinclair's casework was so restricted even Gabriel couldn't break the security codes. We should thank…" He stopped at Michael's low murmur of appreciation.

"Look at what just walked in."

"Damn, Michael, get your brain north of your belt for a second or two." Rafe would have been a fool not to realize what had caught Michael's attention. "Women are still only good for one thing you know," he reminded.

When that didn't draw him back to reality, Rafe scanned the room himself. Not a single female his gray eyes wandered over was so phenomenal that she could possibly have such a hold over Michael and his jaded inclinations. "What the hell are you looking at?"

The words froze in his throat as the crowd parted. For the

first time in memory, Rafe couldn't stop himself from staring. The woman was as sleek and muscled as a panther, her movements as graceful as any jungle beast he had ever seen. He felt a hunger rise within him he had never experienced before. As she moved closer, he could see the red highlights that brought her mink-brown hair to flaming life.

The dress she wore was no more than a sheath of liquid copper silk that hugged every curve and hollow of her supple body. Held by thin straps, it draped full breasts, nipped in at an impossibly tiny waist and flowed over feminine, narrow hips. As she walked toward them with a sensuous grace that left Rafe breathless, his eyes focused on the high slit in the gown that showed an impossibly long length of leg.

"She has to be six feet tall. I don't normally like the athletic type, but for her I'll make an exception. What do you think, bro? Hey, Rafe." Michael couldn't help but grin at the other man's unguarded expression. A sharp elbow to his ribs had those silver eyes focusing on him again. "Knock it off before you scare her to death. You look like you're going to throw her down on the floor and go at it right here. The idea is to entice a woman, not send her running for cover. Watch real close and I'll show you how it's done." He moved away from the bar, but a strong hand gripping his shoulder pulled him back.

"Don't."

"What are friends for, bro?"

"Friend or not, if you turn this into a game, I'll make you regret it." Rafe kept his tone gentle but that did nothing to soften the impact of his words.

Michael wasn't quelled by the threat. If anything, the mere thought of competing against Rafe sent a dark rush of pleasure pulsing through his veins.

Rafe had always treated him like a little brother. A nuisance. His every effort to gain equality over the countless decades had met with little success. Just once, he wanted to go toe to toe with his *big brother* and come out on top. Was this woman who'd managed to get a reaction from Rafe, while all others had failed, his chance? "Where's your sense of fair play?" he chided, ignoring the fingers digging into his shoulder.

"There's nothing fair about this."

"Then don't expect me to play the game by your rules." Michael saw the brief flash of rage that flickered to life in those cold eyes and didn't bother to hold back the smirk demanding freedom.

ᛏ   ᛏ   ᛏ

"Hello gentlemen, I've been lookin' for you two." The voice was soft and sexy, with a slow Texas drawl that gave it an erotic edge.

Rafe and Michael reacted to that voice and found themselves looking into gold-flecked hazel eyes set in a face that could have graced a thousand magazine covers.

"How can I help you, *cher*?" Michael didn't feel a second of shame over the colloquial endearment he'd just tossed out. A lot of time had gone into perfecting the loose, flowing Cajun dialect that seemed to draw women without exception.

"I'm looking for Raphael Fahlan. The bouncer said you could help me."

"I'm Rafe Fahlan." A sharp flash of lust stabbed through him as she turned her attention his way and those beautiful eyes widened with something equal to the unfamiliar sensations burning inside of him.

"Pleased to finally meet you. I'm Montgomery Sinclair."

The two men she'd come hundreds of miles to meet were so busy checking out her cleavage that it took several seconds for her actual words to sink in. When they did, it was all she could do not to laugh at the mixture of shock and surprise on their too handsome faces.

"We assumed you'd be a man." Michael recovered first.

"That's funny, sugar, I've never heard that one before." Montgomery didn't bother to hide her sarcasm. "Is there going to be a problem?" Rafe's recovery was a little slower, but when it came she was wasn't prepared.

"I don't think there'll be a problem as long as you don't plan on sleeping your way through the male staff." Rafe wasn't sure if it was irritation with Michael or disgust at his own momentary weakness that had him tossing out insults cold enough to turn Lake Pontchartrain into a skating pond.

"Don't you fret, Mr. Fahlan, that's not a situation you'll ever find yourself in." Montgomery returned the insult without blinking an eye.

There was no way she could have known the impact his smile would have on her, or how it would turn her well hidden anger into something completely different. The man was dangerous without half-trying and she felt her stomach tighten with long repressed needs. As if he sensed her dilemma, his smile changed, taking on a sexual edge that no man should be able to accomplish.

Michael glanced from one to the other and knew he had lost this battle, but he didn't let that bother him much. Losing was one thing, letting Rafe have her without a single shot being fired was another. There was still some fun to be had here, a few ways he could stir up mischief just to see if Rafe would drop his guard again.

"Let me show you around, *cher*." Interrupting the fierce tension mounting between the two, Michael drew their new security advisor across the crowded dance floor.

Rafe watched her walk away, saw the speculative glance she tossed back over her shoulder at him and had to fight down the low growl that edged up the back of his throat. This one thinks she can play the game, but there was no way he'd let Montgomery Sinclair play with him. No way he'd let a woman take his control. He was in charge here and she would be ever so easy to bend to his will.

With his immortal gift, he could already feel the heat burning in her body for his touch. He would enjoy her in his bed, and Michael's little power play could be damned. Rafe hadn't missed the silent challenge the other immortal had sent with those bright, taunting eyes. Michael wouldn't get the reaction he sought.

There was no jealousy in him to stir, no emotions to prod to life. Even with Michael running interference, taking her wouldn't be a problem. What did it matter if the fire flaming in his gut was new?

†   †   †

Montgomery Sinclair was very impressed with her new surroundings. The club was stylish, the employees well-trained, and the patrons in a class of their own. Her apartment was superb and the workout facilities guaranteed her the regiment she preferred. Michael was another surprise. A long time had passed since she'd felt so desirable and it benefited her greatly to see the male adoration shining in his baby blues.

For all of her busy thoughts and planning, her mind wouldn't stop wandering back to another pair of eyes. Not laughing blue, but brooding silver. As she lay in her queen-size bed, her body reminded her again of how she had ignited deep inside when Rafe Fahlan had smiled that illegal smile of his.

The man looked like the lover that had always dominated her darkest midnight fantasies. Deeply bronzed skin shouted his Italian heritage. His black hair was styled so the close-cropped sides drew attention to sculpted cheekbones that any high-priced male model would have killed to possess. However, it was the rest of his hair that hinted at a sensual side; the top boasted a hint of curl and he left it just long enough that a woman could twist her fingers into those silky raven locks.

He could have been the basis for every movie or book that had a dark, brooding lover as the hero, but it was his eyes that had touched her. Eyes that could turn from ice-cold steel to molten silver in a heartbeat.

Montgomery slid against the cream silk of the sheets and groaned aloud at the lust that bombarded her to the point of almost physical pain. She would have preferred pain to the uncontrolled sensations plaguing her. The desire to touch him was so strong she shook with it. For all of her limited experience, nothing had prepared her for the sensations that had hit her when he'd let those eyes glide over her body.

Giving up on sleep, she threw back the blankets and flung herself from the bed. Unable to fight the tension filling her, she pulled on the minimal of black spandex her abused nerves would allow. Grabbing a few of her favorite compact discs, she headed for the gym.

After turning on the lights, she set about programming the music into the sound system. In no time, she was stretching out to the upbeat rhythms. When her muscles had relaxed enough to avoid injury, she began to move in a twisting, turning dance that utilized almost every muscle in her lithe body.

Caught up in the pulsing warmth of the music, she was unaware of the man that watched every twist, turn, and thrust of her body with clenched teeth and fisted hands.

Rafe had never seen a woman move with such abandon. Mink-brown hair flowing around her shoulders in erotic disarray, all that barely covered sun-kissed skin glistening with sweat. He drew in a harsh breath. There was nothing about that body that didn't inflame the hunger clawing deep in his belly.

Escaping to the gym had been his solution for working out the frustration filling every pore of his body. He hadn't counted on her beating him to the punch. So, he switched gears instead. Maybe he would put all her slick, damp energy to better use.

The brief second of hesitation was enough to destroy his intentions. He could only delay as he sensed Gabriel's presence. Rafe struggled to subdue the anger that flashed through him as his friend leaned against the door frame, appreciative eyes exploring a lush female body he had no business looking at. Just when Rafe felt his jealousy slip past his control, Gabriel stepped forward.

"Good morning." Gabriel smiled as her startled gaze flew to his.

"Good morning," she returned. The tone of his voice was friendly enough, but she refused to lower her guard. Even dressed in nothing but a pair of cutoff sweatpants and running shoes, the man was huge. When he lowered his massive arms and took a step forward, she noticed the scar. She couldn't help but wonder what had inflicted that scar and how he had survived. As he stepped closer still, she forced her taunt body to relax. Then she moved into position so she could strike if it proved necessary.

"That won't be necessary," he drawled out nice and slow, his faint brogue softening the words into poetry.

Montgomery's attention flew back to his face as he bridged the distance. Her breath caught as she found herself staring into the gentlest green eyes she had ever seen. "You're a handsome one, aren't you?" she asked. His chuckle vibrated around the room and she found herself smiling with him, her caution forgotten in the warmth of those eyes.

"I'm glad you think so," he replied, his voice deep and husky.

"I'm Montgomery Sinclair." She extended her hand in greeting, trusting her instincts.

"I've heard about you, Montgomery. I'm Gabriel Arden," he added, clasping her hand in his.

"Great record you have with the homicide department, Sergeant Arden." Her eyes widened as she recognized the name. The man was a legend on the New Orleans police force with his habit of solving murder cases deemed lost causes. He could ferret out impossible leads, find reluctant witnesses, and hunt down murder suspects with a skill that was almost scary.

"I try my best. Call me Gabriel."

There was that smile again. "I'm sure you do, Gabriel." Her answering smile was just as warm.

"This is all very touching, but shouldn't you be protecting our fair city from ax murderers?" Rafe stepped out of the shadows, no longer able to stand back in silence.

Gabriel felt the tension that exploded in Montgomery as Rafe drew closer. Out of habit, while he still grasped her hand, he took a second to delve into her thoughts. What he saw in her mind surprised him. Images of tumbled sheets and sweat-slicked limbs entangled in sensual combat flooded him. The faces were hard to decipher at first, but then the image became clear and he saw her and Rafe locked in an embrace as old as time.

Montgomery slowly pulled her hand away, her eyes never leaving Rafe's bronzed chest while dark fantasies swirled in her head. Unwilling to stay and take a chance on blurting out an indecent proposition to her new boss, she tossed out a weak goodnight and cut a strategic retreat.

"In her mind, you're already lovers." Gabriel waited while Rafe digested that little piece of information. "What do you intend to do?"

The question was direct and Rafe was surprised at Gabriel's interference. "I won't turn down what she'll offer." Rafe ignored the rush of hunger that slammed through him at the thought of joining his body to hers.

"She's not like the others, brother. This one will reach your heart if you're not careful," Gabriel warned. "I see a difference in you already. You stood in the shadows watching me watch her and you wanted to break my neck. Jealousy doesn't suite you, my friend, not with your temper and our blood. It's a dangerous combination."

"Are you warning me off?" Rafe's tone could have formed icicles on the sun.

Gabriel didn't answer right away, but continued to stare at Rafe. "Wouldn't dream of it," he vowed, watching as Rafe followed Montgomery's lead and escaped. "Hell, you don't stand a chance," he murmured, rolling his eyes as the music ended.

ᛏ   ᛏ   ᛏ

"Come on, *cher*, what's wrong with me?" Michael continued to tease Montgomery as he moved her body against his in time to the music. "You and Rafe been hittin' sparks off each other for weeks now. He isn't gonna give in and neither are you. Let me take care of you, *cher*."

His words purred whisper soft against her ear as he swung her around the dance floor. Montgomery had to admit that at another time she could have been tempted. If Rafe hadn't caught her attention from the start, she might have taken Michael up on his bold invitation.

"Now, sugar, we've been through this before." She teased back, at ease with him in a way she could never be with Rafe. "I need a friend, not a lover. With his Highness and I disagreeing all the time, I need all the friends I can get."

"Do you feel that dagger digging into your back yet?" he inquired with casual interest.

"Huh?" Her repartee lacked its normal flare.

"He's been watching us for the last half-hour," Michael replied, nodding in Rafe's direction. At her doubting look, he spun one more time, giving her a clear view of Rafe's glaring features.

"Just what I need, another lecture on not getting tangled up with a hound like you," she drawled out, fluttering her lashes for effect.

"Rafe doesn't mean it, *cher*, he loves me like a brother." Michael tried to coax her into another dance. Anything to give Rafe a bad moment.

"That's what Abel thought of Cain." She tossed that last dig over her shoulder as she walked away.

The finger Rafe crooked in her direction put her on edge but she obeyed the silent command knowing she would repay the little insult later. As she crossed the distance, she tried not to think about how badly her relationship with this gorgeous man had gone in the last six weeks.

That Rafe was everything she wanted in a lover but loathed in a man kept her in a constant state of confusion. He was arrogant and condescending to the point of rudeness, but she couldn't look at him without wanting to drag him to the floor. She wanted to possess him, heart, body, and soul until he couldn't think straight. Maybe then he wouldn't be able to criticize her job performance.

"Did you want something, sugar?" Montgomery couldn't hold in the smirk. Calling this specimen of blatant masculine hormones *sugar* was ridicules in the extreme. Nevertheless, old habits died hard and the term was a great equalizer; one she had used repeatedly in the male dominated circles she'd traveled in. And right now, with her urges stuck in overdrive, she needed all the advantages she could get.

"Do you have to cling like that?" Rafe demanded, ignoring her endearment. That grating little word she threw at him so often was nothing compared to the things he'd learned to disregard in order to keep his sanity. The way she walked, smelled, the flash of gold in her hazel eyes when she tilted her head. The sound of his name on her lips. The caress of burgundy velvet over ripe curves. Those were the things destroying his determination to let her come to him.

Montgomery didn't have to guess what had him in a snit this time. "I thought the idea was for me to stay on the floor as much as possible. Dancing with Michael keeps me on the floor, Mr. Fahlan." There was no reason to veil the sarcasm.

"People think you're lovers, Ms. Sinclair,"

His cold tone put her back up. With a careless shrug, she brushed off his concern. "I can't help what people think about my relationship with Michael."

"Relationship?" Rafe had to force the word out.

"Now, sugar, don't get upset, Michael and I are just ... friends." Her deliberate pause brought a fire to his gray eyes that sent a thrill shooting through her. She just loved upsetting the Ice Prince.

With a visible effort, Rafe brought his temper under control. After a quick glance at his watch, he gave the signal to close up. "I want you in my office in an hour." It wasn't a request and with one last hard look, he spun on his heels and left her staring after him.

"But you don't always get what you want, do you?" She smiled at her own words. Out of anyone, she knew best the truth of that sentiment.

"What did you do now, Gomery?" Gabriel asked, using a shortened version of her name as he joined her at the deserted bar.

"I tweaked the boss' nose again." Her warm eyes were alight with mischief.

"Why fight it? You know what you want. Go get it," Gabriel urged, wanting peace to reign once more. Heaven's Gate had turned into a war zone in the last weeks and the constant bickering was about to drive him nuts.

"Just forget the fact that the man has absolutely no respect for me? Just get over my aversion to arrogant, cold-hearted bastards and let him seduce me?" Montgomery asked, shooting her questions with dead-on accuracy.

"If that's what it takes."

His answer surprised her. Gabriel had never by word or deed hinted that he cared about her lust/hate relationship with Rafe. "It's not always that easy, Gabriel." She had learned her lesson the hard way, and some things a person never forgot.

Needing to unwind, she stood and extended the nightly invitation for their ongoing rendezvous. "Same time, same place, sugar."

Gabriel watched the sway of her hips as she departed and almost felt sorry for Rafe. Almost.

Chapter 6

Montgomery hesitated outside of Rafe's office. More than forty minutes late for her appointment, she stood there, hot and sticky, in the workout clothes she hadn't bothered to change. Squaring her shoulders, she opened the door. Immediately she sought out Rafe and found him standing at the third floor windows, his back to her.

"You wanted to see me, master?" She saw him tense at her taunt, and wished she had kept silent. Usually she tried to avoid baiting rabid dogs.

"I wanted to see you an hour ago." Rafe turned from the view and froze when the full impact of her attire hit him. "Been working out with Michael?" He missed nothing of her flushed and disheveled appearance.

"Gabriel," Montgomery corrected him, her mind not on the conversation so much as the best way to escape the derisive rake of his eyes.

"How the hell do you keep their names straight in the dark?" He snapped then, unable to remain silent.

She gaped over his crude accusation. They had taunted and insulted each other in the past weeks but he had never crossed *that* line since the first day. She held out for a whole second before she gave in to the devil inside her and answered him, playing her part to the hilt.

"Why that's easy, I just call them both sugar. That cuts down on embarrassing mistakes in the heat of passion." At the sight of his clenched fists, she should have stopped but she had never been one to back down, and she continued without caution, "But don't you worry, Rafe, I'll strive to keep *your* name straight."

All of his discipline was required to remain on his side of the desk. Every ounce of restraint he possessed went into leashing the ugly frustration that howled within him. God, he was a fool! While she'd been screwing the others, he'd stood back, his stomach in knots, praying for enough strength to let her make her own choice.

But not now. No longer would he rein in the lust, the need. All it would take to rouse the beast within him was a little push. Then all bets would be off and the victory would be his. He'd be damned though, if he would let her think, even for a minute, that she had an advantage.

"Sorry, Gomery, I've learned to appreciate the road less traveled." He denied his desire for her with a derisive smile as he eased himself into the leather chair behind his desk, his disregard as insulting as possible.

"They're just friends, Rafe. That's all, just friends," she defended herself, trying to ease the situation. His disbelieving snort triggered her temper and sent her around the desk.

"I had more respect for you when you were honest. I could never tolerate lying whores." He delivered that little gem even while his eyes devoured her.

The sound of Rafe's muffled grunt when she tipped his chair and dumped him on his butt at her feet took a lot of the sting out of the wound his nasty words had inflicted. Nothing could take the satisfied smile off her face as she ignored his sputtering and picked her way over the toppled chair to make good her escape.

Nothing except finding her path blocked by Rafe's massive chest.

The fire in his gray eyes sent her backing into his mahogany desk. Before she could form a defense, he had an arm around her waist and with the other was clearing the desktop in a single violent sweep. Then he had her sprawled on the smooth surface, his firmly muscled body following her down to pin her there as his mouth ravished and his hands roamed over vulnerable flesh.

Montgomery's heart raced at the intensity of his reaction. Her outrage melting in the heat of her desire. From the very first, she had known what would happen between them. But it couldn't be like this. Never like this. No man would ever take from her what she was willing to give.

"You want to play rough, sweet thing? I'll play rough with you." He promised against her ear.

She shivered at the sensations his words aroused, torn between lust and self-preservation. "Rafe." His name slid off her lips before she could decide. Only when he eased back in response to that whispered word did she realize that she'd already made the decision.

"You want me to stop?" His voice was uneven with desire and something more. Something just outside of his understanding.

"Don't hurt me." That was as close to a plea as she'd ever come.

Rafe felt that unfamiliar something inside of him shift and growl. Bringing his mouth down on hers, he delved into the heat. In the back of his mind, in that little part still sane, was the knowledge that in the morning she would bear the marks of his possession. That control, no matter how hard he wished it otherwise, had no place between them.

Montgomery's ragged moans of pleasure rang in his ears as he peeled the taut spandex from her lush breasts and replaced it with his mouth. Her low, throaty whimpers brought his hunger to the flash point.

For one moment sanity reigned again and Rafe was aware of a burning in his chest that radiated outward, taking control of that hunger and making it unbearable. He heard a vague echo of Sasha's long ago warnings about uncontrollable emotions and blood lust, but he had never lost control before and he wouldn't let himself now. Pushing everything else aside, he sought the pulsing heat of the woman flowing like molten copper in his arms.

Montgomery rocked against the hand that sought access

to her deepest, most intimate places. When those questing fingers slid beneath the final obstacle and glided into the moist heat that awaited, she arched into the pleasure, raking her nails down the broad back she'd uncovered in her urgency.

She didn't care when her clothes hit the floor in shredded tangles. All that matter was his strong, rough hands on her skin, his mouth tasting her, taking her higher. That and the near desperate need to have him deep inside of her where the terrible ache demanded release.

The tidal wave of lust that crashed though Montgomery made her greedy, aggressive. Tugging and pulling, she striped Rafe until nothing but his hard, heated skin rested on hers. "You feel so good." She moaned against his chest as her tongue foraged through the crisp black hair to lave a flat nipple.

The feel of her wet mouth on his body was the last push Rafe could take. He lost the battle he'd been fighting then and there. With a low groan, he pressed his mouth to the sweat-slicked skin of her throat. He settled his lips around the pulse that throbbed under the honey-gold skin with ease borne more of instinct than practice. Body taunt, eyes blazing silver, he raked his teeth across her neck, drawing small beads of crimson to the surface. Spurred on by her husky purr, he slid his tongue along the welts.

The coppery taste of her blood in his mouth was pure ecstasy and he had to force himself not to sink his teeth in and drink until his mind exploded from the pleasure. Rafe fought through the darkness that threatened him, denying himself the exquisite feast.

Montgomery gasped in surprised when Rafe rolled over, taking her with him until she lay atop his muscular body. Riding on a surge of raw desire, she pulled her long legs up until she straddled him.

They moaned in unison at the slick, slippery play of aroused flesh on flesh. Passion-glazed eyes locked as he arched and she rocked. Need stalked closer, demanding release. Montgomery fell first, mindless to anything but the fingers caressing her. Rafe brought her to the edge of insanity but still denied her that final push.

Giving in to the forces driving her, Montgomery rose to her knees, determined to take him herself and end the desperate power play. Firm hands on her hips stopped her downward slide.

Defiant hazel eyes questioned him until he answered. "Not yet, sweet thing, I want to taste all of you, touch all of you." His breathing was ragged and matched hers in the quiet room. He lifted her from the tempting hold she had on his body with easy, fluid strength and settled her on his powerful chest.

"Next time we'll take it slow," she promised, trying to wriggle away from his restraining hands. That he was able to hold her captive with such ease thrilled her in a dark, wicked way she'd never experienced before. His easy domination taunted her, challenged her.

She answered the challenge.

Rafe almost lost it when her tongue snaked out to wet her parted lips. He fought against the tide of animal aggression that rolled through him at that simple action. The woman was dangerous. Almost more than he was. He watched as she threaded burgundy-tipped fingers through the waves of rich, mink-brown hair surrounding her slender shoulders. The fingers continued their deliberate journey over those moist lips, down the tempting curve of her throat, stopping to cup hard-tipped breasts.

Montgomery didn't take her eyes from his face as she ran her hands over her sensitive skin. She liked the way he matched her pant for pant, moan for moan when she wrapped fingers wet from her own need around the demanding hardness of his.

"Do you want me to beg?" she drawled out the question, soft and low. "Or should I make you?"

"Do what you will," Rafe rasped through clenched teeth, releasing his hold on her.

Montgomery took his mouth in a deep, wet kiss that left them both reeling. Having him beg wasn't a priority this time. The need for his body and seeing his eyes as she took him inside inch by inch was. Grasping his shoulders, she shifted her body to his.

The glint of gold on that hard-muscled chest caught her attention. "What's this, sugar?" she asked, distracted as she slid the gold band along the chain.

ᛏ   ᛏ   ᛏ

The sound of that word on her lips caused Rafe's heart to stop. That one little word killed the pleasure, leaving in its place a burning rage that came close to striping away his mortal guise. Clenching his fists at his sides, he drew a deep breath and prayed he wouldn't give in to the urge to drain her lack of fidelity along with her life's blood out of that beautiful body.

"It's my wedding ring." He answered her with what he hoped was a steady voice.

The band slid through her nerveless fingers to land on his chest with a hollow thud. Her shocked eyes dropped to the ring gleaming dully on his dark skin. "Wedding ring?" she mumbled, unable to raise her eyes past that circle of gold.

"Don't tell me that bothers you, *sugar*," he taunted, wanting to strike back, if not with force, then with words. "I wouldn't think that would stop a woman like you. After all, I'm much more discriminating and if I'm willing to share with others, why can't you?"

Sliding off him with unsteady legs, she stumbled away from the desk. Grabbing his blue shirt from the floor, she slid into it, hugging the expensive silk against her aching body. She looked at him then and found him watching her through hooded eyes as he zipped his trousers. Any sign of the impassioned lover that had touched her seconds before was replaced by the hard, contemptuous man watching her every move with insulting disregard.

"Change your mind?" he asked, soft as velvet, at her hesitation.

His scornful laughter followed Montgomery as she fled

from the room. She didn't stop her anguished flight until reaching the relative safety of her suite. Once there, she shed the shirt and staggered into the bathroom, needing to remove the scent and feel of him from her body.

When Montgomery crawled into bed twenty minutes later, her body was in agony from Rafe's lovemaking, her face streaked with tears.

Ͳ   Ͳ   Ͳ

Rafe slammed out of his office, her blood tingling on his tongue, his body still tight with unsatisfied need. Upon reaching his apartment, he wasn't surprised to see Gabriel waiting for him. Ignoring the other immortal, Rafe crossed to the window, staring out into the darkness. His thoughts were as tumultuous as the sultry New Orleans night that greeted him.

"How was your meeting with Gomery?" Gabriel inquired, feigning casual interest as he rose from the black leather sofa.

"Why do you ask?" Rafe countered, his voice tight, edgy, as he turned frigid eyes from the view.

"Because you're missing your shirt and I can see the nail marks down your back," Gabriel chided.

"Are you asking as my friend or her lover?" Rafe ground out through clenched teeth, his hands fisted for battle as he advanced on the highlander.

"I'm not Gomery's lover, but I'll be more than happy to kick your ass." Gabriel rolled his massive shoulders to loosen up.

"Okay, little boy, let's see what you've got," Rafe taunted, circling his impromptu opponent. He doubled over with the first blow to his midsection. Welcoming the pain, he quickly returned with an uppercut to his adversary's jaw that didn't even turn the immortal's head.

"Is that the best you can do?"

The taunt sent Rafe's temper up in flames. Overcome with rage, he threw a flurry of blows that would have killed a mortal man. Gabriel took the punishment without returning a punch, allowing his friend to work off some anger before he drew back his large fist and caught Rafe square in the face, sending him reeling into the far wall. Rafe slid to the floor, wiping blood from his nose as he went.

"Well, I feel much better now." Gabriel's smile softened the terse words.

Rafe smiled back, deeply satisfied with the blood that trickled from the cut under the highlander's right cheekbone and the swelling that guaranteed his friend's left eye would be black and blue for a few hours at least.

"Did I miss all the fun?" Michael called from the doorway.

"Come to take your share?" Gabriel invited, dabbing at the blood on his cheek with the hem of his beige T-shirt.

"Sorry, I have a better way of expending energy. *I'm* heading over to Fritzel's. The music there's been giving us a run lately. I thought I'd have you come along, but hell no. You'd scare all the ladies away with that face." He laughed at the silent threat Gabriel glared in his direction before he turned his attention to where Rafe rose from the floor.

He stepped farther into the room, closing the door behind him when he saw the fresh scratches down Rafe's back. "Unless Gabriel has changed his fighting style, I'd say you already took care of your problem. What I want to know is, if you just took a tumble with our resident goddess, why are you brawling with the brute?" He nodded in Gabriel's direction. "You know he kicks your ass every time." His words held a verbal slap that stiffened Rafe's spine.

"What's the problem, Rafe?" Gabriel joined in.

"Why are you going whoring, when you've been sleeping with Gomery?" Rafe shot the question at Michael. "Go to her room if you need to fuck.. I have her so primed, all you'd have to do is crook your little finger and she'd beg."

Rafe's words were brutal and unlike him, but that didn't stop Michael from starting toward him, his intentions clear as he rolled up his sleeves.

Gabriel grabbed him by the back of his white shirt, stopping him inches from his target. "That's enough." The hard tone discouraged argument. "Tell us what happened."

Rafe bristled under the invasion but answered just the same. "She came to my office straight from her workout with you. Do you at least have enough restraint not to screw her on the weight bench?"

"I'm not her lover," Gabriel denied with a feral smile, refusing to be baited.

"We exchanged words. I commented on her ability to keep her lovers' names straight in the dark. She told me it was easy, she just called them all *sugar*. Then she assured me she'd keep my name straight." Rafe speared Michael with a heated glare. "I told you to stay away from her," he accused, unreasonable in his anger.

"I never touched her," Michael countered, looking straight into Rafe's smoldering gray eyes.

"Funny, that's what she said, right before I called her a lying whore."

There was so much rancor in those words, all Michael could do was shake his head in disgust. "Do you really think I'd make her my lover and then her share with you? If she was mine and I thought you'd laid a single finger on her, I'd take your head off, not stop to ask the where's and how's." Michael's displeasure echoed through the room.

"What did she do then?" Gabriel pulled the conversation back.

"She flipped my chair and dumped me on my ass." Rafe turned from those all-knowing green eyes. "I met her at the door, picked her up and carried her to the desk. Then I cleared the top and tossed her down."

"Well, well, well, The Ice Prince finally went over the edge. I didn't think rape was your style." Michael didn't bother to hide his animosity.

"There was no question of consent." Rafe was so sure of his answer that he convinced them without saying more.

"What went wrong?" Gabriel was incredulous.

"She saw my ring and asked about it."

"So what?" Michael wasn't impressed.

"Her exact words were, 'What's that, sugar'. She called me sugar, the same thing she calls all of her lovers. 'That way there's no mistakes in the heat of passion.' She tied me up in knots, then she called me that. It was like a system overload. I was afraid I'd hurt her so I froze up and told her it was my wedding ring. I just failed to mention my wife's dead." He looked across the room at the others, his eyes bleak. "I need you to back me on this."

"Why should we?" Gabriel asked.

"I need the barrier. After just one taste of her, I'm lost. I don't know if I'll be able to stop myself from taking her next time," he explained, bitter with self-disgust.

After a slight hesitation, they did what they'd done for centuries. They banded together, swearing to protect each other as friends. As brothers.

CHAPTER 7

Gabriel was in a fine temper as he dealt with the chaos that always abounded at a murder scene. God, he hated this. The girl was maybe eighteen, and she lay in a pool of her own blood, her sightless blue eyes forever staring up at the stars. His chest tightened at the waste.

"What happened?" He focused on the officer who had responded to the disturbance call.

"Usual story, Arden. Victim got in a fight with her boyfriend and he beat her up. After he finished with her, something must have set him off again because he took a baseball bat and smashed her head in." The veteran walked away when another officer called his name.

"What've we got, Arden?"

"Nothing I can't handle." Gabriel took a deep breath to calm the fury that exploded within him as Seth Jordan reached out and snatched the notepad from his hand.

"Why don't you just tell me what happened then, since you have it all figured out." Jordan made no effort to hide the deep dislike he harbored for his latest partner.

The forty-four year old veteran was on a rampage, and Gabriel knew he wouldn't slow down until he had picked the situation to death. So he recounted the facts without inflection, trying his best to control a temper he had leashed years ago.

Jordan wasted little time in cutting him to ribbons, so much so that Gabriel retaliated. Focusing his attention on the new tires gracing Jordan's vintage Mustang, he released a small stream of energy, then watched in satisfaction as two of the four tires deflated.

By the time they asked all the questions and cleared the scene,

Gabriel was ready to call it a night. The sound of his name stopped him before he could reach the sanctuary of his black SUV.

"I need a ride, Arden. I've got a couple flats."

His partner sulked like a spoiled child and Gabriel cursed his own short-sided act of revenge.

The ride was thankfully short though, with no conversation to distract him from the injustice of his night. Only Jordan's stilted invitation to come in kept him from escaping with a squeal of tires.

"Sarah, where are you, girl? I want you to meet my partner." Jordan announced his homecoming with a shout from the front door.

Gabriel was kept waiting only seconds before a slim female joined them in the hall. "Hello, Sarah." He greeted her with a soft murmur, extending his hand. The beat of his heart stuttered when she raised her head.

Sarah Jordan felt much the same way when she lifted her eyes to his to acknowledge his words, but she wasn't as good at hiding her response. As her breath caught in her throat, all she could do was stare. Seth's rough nudge brought her back to reality.

"Hello, Sergeant Arden," she mumbled with a guilty glance in Seth's direction. "Would you like something to drink, sir?" Her eyes were on the floor now where it was safe to look and not on the incredible man standing in front of her.

"No, thank you, Sarah, I need to get home." Gabriel took pity on the girl. There was no reason to give her father more ammunition to badger her with later. Seth walked him out and in an effort to make conversation, he said the first thing that came to mind. "Your daughter is beautiful."

"Sarah is my wife." Jordan pushed the words out, not bothering to hide his animosity.

Gabriel paused on the steps and faced the other man. "She's too damn young for you, Jordan." His usual tact deserted him. "Does she still have Girl Scout meetings?"

The age difference between the two wasn't what upset

Gabriel. He had lived in times where years meant nothing in a marriage if there was something to gain from the union. No, what bothered him was the thought of that young girl stuck with a bitter, self-centered bastard.

"Sarah is twenty-four. We've been married eight years." Jordan stepped in closer, clenching his fists as he sized up the chances of knocking his partner to the ground.

Gabriel let it drop. The man was already a pain in the ass. What good would it do to further alienate the person he spent the largest part of his day with? Keeping an eye out for Sarah on the sly would serve his purposes just as well.

What would it hurt to make sure that Jordan wasn't taking advantage? What did it matter that Seth Jordan's wife looked exactly like the golden angel whose bed he had stood over the night before until the hunger had driven him away?

ϯ   ϯ   ϯ

Jordan mounted the steps, not at all surprised to see the curtains twitch back into place. He headed back into the two-story house with a smile. His night had just gotten better. "Did you like looking at him, Sarah? Did he turn you on?"

The words were cold, furious, and Sarah knew there would be no escape. On trembling legs, she faced her husband. Wiping her sweaty hands on her jeans, she tried not to cringe as he towered over her. "I'm sorry, Seth. I didn't mean to look at him. It won't happen again, I swear." She hated herself for begging, for appealing to tender mercies that didn't exist.

"Damned right it won't." He grabbed a handful of copper hair, tugging on the ponytail until her head snapped back. "You need to learn another lesson, Sarah, for your own good."

ϯ   ϯ   ϯ

Montgomery glanced at the clock over the bar and wondered if she should even bother with the pretense of going to bed. Once there, on the cool silk sheets, she never slept. Not since that night three weeks ago. All she did was stare at the ceiling, berating herself for still wanting that man. She hated him fiercely. Hated him for being nothing but a rotten, cheating bastard. But, it was a tossup who she hated more; right now, she was winning.

Life would have been so much easier if she was really the whore he'd accused her of being. Then she could use him until the wanting went away. The agony of it burned deep and ugly, knocking down the walls she had spent years constructing. Fear of those walls crumbling completely forced her to avoid Rafe like the plague. She avoided the others as well, sulking in her room instead. The time lost with Michael and Gabriel only added to her resentment of the situation.

A soft footstep and the subtle scent of cologne alerted her to Gabriel's presence long before a non-professional would have noticed him.

"Don't be shy," she extended the invitation without turning. "You don't have to tip-toe around me. Come have a seat."

He winced at the dig, but joined her just the same. After meeting Sarah Jordan, he needed a drink. "How'd you know it was me?" He filled a glass with scotch.

"Survival of the fittest," she replied. "I was taught that it's best to know who's sneaking up behind before you determine fight or flight."

"Fight often?" Gabriel was curious. Sitting beside her, he waited.

"Every chance I get. Even when I don't have a prayer," she reflected with a rueful smile. "When you're the only child of a man who made no secret of his hatred; you learn at a young age to sacrifice life and limb to make a good impression."

"Did you ever make a good impression?" He probed deeper.

"There was never a chance of that." She didn't bother to disguise the bitterness in her voice. "So I made as many mistakes as I could. I ran wild hoping he would notice. Nothing worked, not who I dated, who I slept with."

Montgomery wasn't blind to his expression. "Surprised, Gabriel? I slept with his commanding officer's son to gain his attention. All I got was a warning not to get pregnant. Is that the kind of thing you'd tell your fifteen-year-old daughter?"

"Did he ever notice you?" Gabriel asked the question before he could stop himself.

"I took a job protecting a top government advisor. A hitter opened fire on us. I was in a French hospital fighting just to breathe when my father showed up. He laid it all out for me. I was nothing more than a disappointment to him, not fit to live while another died due to my carelessness. He never came back and when he died a few weeks later, I was glad. That way I didn't have to live with his disappointment. Only my own." She blinked once to clear the memories, giving Gabriel a tired smile.

"What can we talk about now, sugar?" She flinched at the word. "Did Rafe tell you about that night?"

"Not really," Gabriel lied. "Do you want to talk about it?"

"What's his wife like?" Montgomery hated herself for asking.

"She's hard to describe." He was at a loss as to how to handle this twist. The promise made long ago between the three kept him from saying more.

"Forget I asked." She rose from the stool, refusing to look at him.

"Can you keep track of someone for me, Gomery?" He spoke to her departing back, half-hoping she hadn't heard him, but then she turned back. "A woman." He refused to acknowledge the color that invaded his face at her knowing look.

🕇   🕇   🕇

"How long will Gabriel be gone?" Rafe asked Michael several nights later as they sat at the bar dealing with the loads of paperwork that went with the club.

"Depends on how long narcotics needs him. Probably a

month or so. Why?" Michael threw back his own question, not taking his attention from the paperwork he loathed doing.

"I'm thinking of having Sasha come for a visit." Rafe kept his tone light as if he hadn't just dropped a major bombshell into the conversation.

Michael's head snapped up and he forced his frozen mouth to form his next thought. "Are you crazy?" His words bounced off the walls with the force of a ricocheting bullet.

"I need a wife." Rafe met his startled gaze head-on. He didn't even flinch as ugly awareness dawned in Michael's eyes, or when the other man rose to his feet.

"Coward." The word seethed with Michael's contempt. "You've hurt her enough. There isn't any need to involve Sasha, not unless you're trying to force Gomery out. Is that the plan? To make her leave because you can't stand to have her so close?" He was nose to nose with Rafe now, more than ready for a fight.

"Problem, boys?"

Rafe turned as that drawl caught his attention, taking a second to bring himself under control. A control that shattered when his restless eyes focused on her.

What she wore had both men stopping to draw calming breaths. No more than a mid-thigh length sheath of clinging red silk, it hugged every curve and hollow, showing more golden skin then it covered.

"We thought you were upstairs." Michael plowed tense fingers through his pale hair in frustration, not at all pleased with the interruption. He wasn't finished with Rafe yet.

"Not hardly, sugar, it's my night off." She cocked her head to the side, a smile flirting across her lips.

Rafe watched in fascination as a chestnut-hued spiral escaped the loose knot atop her head and slithered over neck and shoulder to rest temptingly against her breast. What he wouldn't have given to twist that curl around his fist and pull until she was so close to him she could never get away. He ignored the hard elbow Michael jabbed into his side as warning. He ignored everything but the hunger that clawed deep furrows in his belly at the very sight and smell of her.

Montgomery sauntered closer, swaying on stiletto heels. An intoxicated giggle bubbled from her lips as she slid her arms around Michael's waist. "How's my favorite boy doin'?" she murmured, her Texas twang more pronounced than ever. "Come back out with me. I want to have fun."

"I think you've had enough fun," Rafe contradicted.

She arched an eyebrow at the sharpness of his tone, then blew him off altogether as she focused her attention on convincing Michael. "Come on, *cher*, who needs the cheating bastard anyway. O'Brien's is hopping tonight. Just you and me, what do you say?"

"You're done for the night, Montgomery," Rafe cut in, refusing to react. "You've had enough to drink already." He anchored her to his side with a strong hand. "You need to call it a night before you completely disgrace yourself."

The coldness of his voice pierced the pleasant haze she'd fallen in. She jerked away from him, her resentment boiling over. "You're the disgrace, not me. I'm not a cheat, or a liar, or a whore."

Rafe reached for her again, anger dancing across his hard face. Only Michael getting to her first stopped him. "Let go," Rafe muttered, clenching his fists in silent warning.

Michael's smile wasn't pleasant. "I'll see her up." He purred the offer, drawing her closer within the curve of his arm.

"Over my dead body." The dark immortal growled low in his throat.

"Nothing so drastic as that. I just thought you'd need the time to discuss travel arrangements with your wife." Michael smirked at the mayhem he saw reflected in that silver gaze. There was a moment of regret when Montgomery stiffened in his embrace, but he continued for her own good. "Playing it this way was your idea, Rafe. You can't drag Sasha into this and expect to have everything go your way."

As much as Rafe would have liked to drag her away from

Michael, he wasn't blind to the loathing on her face. He swallowed down all the harsh threats demanding freedom and conceded the battle. "Go then." Stepping back, he physically removed himself from temptation.

Only as the fair immortal led her away, supporting the gentle sway of her body, did it hit Rafe. "Michael," he called out, the open challenge in his tone stopping him on the stairs. "Don't begin to think it's you she really wants tonight."

ϯ   ϯ   ϯ

Montgomery didn't give a thought as to how he opened her door without the key, or how he managed to read her intentions so effortlessly. Nothing much pierced the fog the clouded her awareness, and for what she had in mind, that suited her just fine.

The evening hadn't started out with a plan to seduce Michael. That thought had evolved as the night progressed, as the loneliness closed in. She was tired of being empty inside, tired of the need that invaded every space within her. Michael was the one person she could trust to get her through it. He could keep her from begging Rafe for what she wanted so badly.

Tossing a smile over her shoulder, she left him to follow.

Michael paused in the doorway of her bedroom. For the first time in two hundred years, he wasn't sure. Gomery wasn't like the others. This wasn't a woman he could take and walk away from as if it didn't matter. She was a friend. Someone he could even love if his heart was capable.

A part of him, the ugly part he kept hidden, couldn't help but wonder how far she would go. There was no secret what she wanted from him. Words hadn't been necessary for the invitation offered with the subtle press of her body against his, for the hot promise issued by those gold-dusted hazel eyes. There was everything for him to lose in this little game. If he was still here when the sun came up, Rafe would have his head on a platter. If he was still in that bed beside her, Gomery could very well have claim to his heart. Either way he was damned.

Michael had never seen anything so breathtaking as Montgomery standing in a pool of moonlight. The chestnut silk of her hair gleamed, her hazel eyes seduced from a face just as stunning as her body. Stepping through the threshold, he closed the door.

"Do you want me?" Montgomery asked before she lost her nerve. That the man in her bedroom was every woman's fantasy with a fallen angel's face helped her focus. What did it matter that he wasn't the one who destroyed her reason with nothing more than a glance? Michael might not be the one her body cried out for, but if taking him kept her sane, then he would do.

"What's not to want, *cher*?" Michael was unable to tear his eyes away as she unhooked the halter and let the red silk slide down the length of her body. Before he was conscious of the action, he had her cradled in his arms, carrying her to the bed.

"This is what you want?" he asked, giving her a last chance to turn him away. Stillness claimed him as she took the initiative. The kiss she pressed to his lips left little doubt in his mind as to what she expected. The desperation in her touch pulled at him. Reminded him. He'd felt that same need in himself for too many centuries not to understand the agony it created.

"Touch me, Michael." Montgomery's fingers were clumsy as she struggled to edge the white cotton of his T-shirt over ridged muscles. "Help me!"

"Anything you want, *cher*." Pulling the shirt off, he tossed it in a crumpled heap on the floor. This was familiar ground now. Only the original offer had thrown him off guard. Women always wanted something from him. Montgomery wasn't so different from the others after all. Pushing away the small twinge of hurt that stabbed at him, Michael took over.

Nothing of her escaped him as he drove her to the edge of reality. Strong arms clung to him, that supple body arched to the stroke of his hands, damp skin heated under his lips but still it wasn't enough. When he finished with her, she would remember him always. That small comfort, that small piece of her memory, was all he could allow himself.

"Please!" Montgomery wasn't above begging. The torture he was inflicting had to end.

Michael's jeans joined the red silk on the floor. Engulfed in the hunger that tormented him with merciless claws, he reached for her. Darker passions ruled him now. The need to be inside of her eclipsed thoughts, emotions, vows. Nothing existed but the momentary escape release brought him.

"Rafe."

The breathless whimper broke through his lust-filled haze even as her long legs urged his taut body closer. That single word kept him from taking, from possessing. Women had offered themselves to him for many reasons but never as a stand-in. That was one he couldn't settle for. Wouldn't settle for.

"Michael?"

The hesitant question his name represented was just too much. Mocking laughter flowed from him as he untangled arms and legs. "I don't do masquerades, *cher*. Not even for you." Disgusted that he couldn't even be pissed at her, Michael took a second to breathe in the warm musk of her skin before he slid from the bed.

The depths she had sunk to, and how much lower she would have fallen if Michael hadn't walked away, stunned Montgomery. That she had attempted to take a lover to get over Rafe was bad enough, to make love with him pretending that Rafe held her was inhuman. She couldn't even form words to express regret, all she could do was bury her face in her arms, crying out her misery.

Michael didn't desert her in those moments it took to cool the fire in his blood. Instead, he tossed his shirt back to the floor, approaching the bed as a completely different desire drove him. Murmuring soothing words, he lay down beside her, pulling her trembling body against his. He held her until the flood stopped and when he would have finally left her, she stopped him.

"Please, stay with me. I don't want to be alone anymore."

He conceded to her desperate whisper, staying beside her while every part of his damaged soul demanded he walk away.

ϯ   ϯ   ϯ

Someone banging on the door woke him a few hours later. With more tenderness than he thought himself capable of, Michael eased Montgomery out of his arms. The face that greeted him when he opened the door would have made a saint pray for death. He wasn't a saint. "You're a little late, Rafe. I expected you hours ago."

"I trusted you." Rafe tensed every muscle in his body, forcing himself not to strike out.

"No you didn't. Last night was a setup. What game do we play this morning, brother? Are you the outraged lover? Or do you thank me?" Michael watched the unfamiliar emotions that danced across the other man's face. Jealousy. Rage. Guilt. They were all there and he felt each one like a fist.

"This isn't a game," Rafe denied even as he looked away.

"Yes it is. I started the game, but somewhere along the way, you changed the rules on me. What should I say now? What's the right response, Rafe? Did I take her? Or did I walk away?"

"Bastard."

Michael ignored that. The name didn't bother him; men had called him worse with better reason. That it was Rafe playing the betrayed cut at him, though. *He* was the one setup in this little farce.

"Let's try the truth then. The game played out right 'til the end, Rafe. Just like you planned. She offered and I accepted." Michael deflected the blow aimed at his face. "Funny thing is? She didn't really want me and even I won't stand-in while a woman plays make-believe."

Gray eyes surveyed the unbuttoned jeans, flicked over the telltale marks Montgomery had left on his skin. He *had* set Michael up last night. He had sent her off with him half-hoping the other man would take her, removing the temptation she presented. That plan had changed at some point and now he needed to know. "Prove it," Rafe demanded harshly. All it would take was a touch. A second to share the memory and it would be over.

Michael stepped away from the hand Rafe reached out to him. He hid darker things within his soul than last night. Those things would stay there. "Trust," he countered. There had to be that between them. For two hundred years he had hung on every word the dark man had ever said to him, tried his hardest to impress. To be his brother.

He didn't share with Rafe the easy friendship that Gabriel claimed. Still excluded from that little click in so many ways, he tried not to let it matter. They had welcomed him to the group long ago and if he still struggled to feel worthy, it was only because Rafe was his hero. The coolness, the control, Rafe was everything he wanted to be.

"Do you trust me?" He waited while minutes ticked away in his head, but no answer emerged from the man he idolized. Michael gave a little laugh, nothing of humor coloring the sound, as he walked away.

Rafe stood in the hall for a moment, torn between the desire to go after him, and the need to see her. His need won out and he entered the suite, locking the door behind him.

The soft light from the rising sun cast the room in a golden glow. He missed nothing of the T-shirt and red silk crumpled on the floor; missed nothing of the sleeping woman sprawled in the tangled silk sheets. With a gentle hand, he moved the tumble of curls from her face. At his touch, she stirred, seeking the comfort of his caress.

"Don't leave," Montgomery mumbled without opening her eyes. "Stay with me." She rubbed the spot next to her.

Rafe slid out of his clothes and into the empty space beside her. Her purr of contentment as she curled her warm body against his and drifted back to sleep eased some of the tension inside of him. Using the morning light, he took his time exploring all the things he hadn't seen that night in his office.

There was a birthmark on her left hip. The small freckles that dusted the curves of her shoulders. A trio of scars that marred the hollow of her stomach. Looking closely at the lone mark that puckered the skin below her left breast, he would have sworn that they were healed bullet wounds.

"Michael."

Burying the fury that reared its head at that whispered name, Rafe touched her, focusing on the information *his brother* had denied him. Only when the events of the night had played out did he allow himself the peace of sleep.

ϯ   ϯ   ϯ

Ignoring the pounding in her head, Montgomery took stock of her situation. Disgust at her actions from the night before swamped her. The warm male body pressed against her back didn't help matters.

Luring Michael to her bed wasn't even the worst part of last night's transgressions; pretending he'd been Rafe won that dubious honor. *That* would no doubt give her nightmares for the rest of her life. Nevertheless, she was an adult and would deal with it. How she planned to explain it all was still a mystery, but they would work it out. All she had to do was open her eyes and face the bold Cajun.

When a possessive hand settled on her hip, she cringed. God, she'd never touch rum hurricanes again! Getting drunk and having a one-night stand all in the same night wasn't something to brag about. Or relive.

Startled eyes shot opened in disbelief when she heard the voice purring against her ear. The tousled black hair that entered her line of vision drained the color from her face. The gray eyes that met hers sent the color crashing back. Unable to speak, she could only stare.

Rafe didn't bother to hide his amusement as he drew her unresisting body on top of his. "Good morning, sweet thing."

He drawled out the greeting.

"What are you doing here?" she demanded, when her power of speech returned.

"I would think that's obvious."

Unable to meet the undeniable taunt in his eyes, she dropped her forehead to his chest. Where the heck had he come from? *That* part of the night was definitely a big blank. Was that bare skin under her hands? Oh, God, please don't let this be as bad as it looks! "Did we…" She couldn't bring herself to finish.

"I'm insulted, sweet thing. Why don't I refresh your memory?" He didn't wait for a response. With cool deliberation, he grasped her chin, plundering her mouth in search of surrender. The low moan that escaped her brought a surge of satisfaction. She wanted *him*, not Michael. The fire that burned inside of her was for him.

As difficult as it was to admit it, the obsession he felt for her wasn't going away. Wanting her was taking over, obliterating every thought, every seed of caution. There was nothing left of him that could breathe without the smell of her, the taste.

No longer did it matter whom she had taken to bed with her in the past. She was his now for as long as he wanted her. If he caught her slipping out on him, he'd just drain her and her little lover dry. No matter who that lover was. The cold-blooded scenario stopped him for a heartbeat. Where the hell had that come from?

Ignoring the warning bells in her head, Montgomery allowed her body to melt, her lips to trail across his shoulder, her tongue lapping at the salty skin. Determined to gain his undivided attention, she found the strong beat of his pulse with her mouth and bit down.

Rafe almost lost control at that aggressive nip. The urges her action unleashed prodded his hunger higher. Clenching his fists was the only thing that keep him from giving in to the beast, from taking everything she had to offer in a rush of ugly, feral need. That control slipped further at the low purring sounds that slid from her lips against his skin. Only the sound of another in the room stopped him from finishing what she had started.

"Am I interruptin' anything, *cher*?"

Montgomery groaned when she recognized Michael's Cajun twang.

"What are you doing here?" Rafe demanded. Rolling out from under her sprawled body, he raised up on an elbow.

She was just as quick to react and with an undignified squeak, buried her head under the nearest pillow. Shielding people from flying bullets had never prepared her for this situation. Her reprieve was short lived when Michael sat down beside her, swiping the barrier from her grasping fingers.

"You can't be shy with me, *cher*, not after last night." The plea in her eyes stopped him from saying more. The hurt she had inflicted last night was minimal compared to what he could do, but he didn't have the heart to strike back. Instead, he turned to Rafe. "Nothing happened last night." He wanted the simple statement to be enough.

"I know exactly what happened." Rafe watched as the method he'd used to obtain that information sank in.

"Michael?" Montgomery reached out to him, the pain on his face concerning her. "Are you okay?"

"All I wanted was your trust." He addressed the quiet words to Rafe.

"I can't give it in this."

"Play the game as you see fit." Michael rose from the bed, his steps unsteady for a second as he struggled against the wound Rafe had dealt him. "But it's not just me on the field anymore. Sasha's here."

"Who is Sasha?" Montgomery asked, her confusion over the whole conversation mounting. What had passed between the two men to put that shuttered look on Michael's face? Why was Rafe tensing as if for a fight? Then, in a second, she knew. Wrapping the sheet around her with as much dignity she could muster, Montgomery rose from the bed.

"Don't keep her waiting on my account, sugar." She tossed a mocking smile over her shoulder. "We've established I'm not picky about where my lovers have been, but she might be. Wives are like that." Closing the bathroom door behind her, she stood in front of the mirror and prayed for the strength to walk away.

CHAPTER 8

"Maybe you'd care to explain why I'm here?" Sasha asked Rafe later that night as they dined on spicy chicken gumbo in his apartment. "It's not like you to tempt Gabriel's anger for a simple visit."

"We like having you around, no matter what he says." However, just to be on the safe side, Rafe would make sure she was gone before the highlander finished his assignment.

"She's very pretty." Sasha hid her disappointed when he gave no response to that comment. The sparks that had flown between Montgomery Sinclair and the dark one on the floor earlier had been a revelation. Part of her hoped for more of the same.

Long moments of silence reigned as Rafe formulated a polite way to tell her to mind her own business. "Butt out, Sasha." His smile softened the rebuke.

"No can do, Fahlan. You've been in my business for years, now it's my turn."

"I wouldn't dream of telling you how to live your life!" He couldn't meet her eyes after speaking that lie.

"Right. Why am I here?"

The dryness of her tone caught him off guard. "I need a wife," he answered before he thought better of it.

"A wife?" Sasha sputtered, choking on her red wine. "You're not my type, sweeting, no matter how much I love you."

"God, not a *real* wife. I'd never do that again." Rafe shuddered at the very thought. "I just need you to pretend for a few weeks. Besides, Gabriel would kill me if I ever tried to touch you."

"Do you think so?" Sasha smiled wistfully as she dabbed

the red splotches from the lap of her pale yellow slip dress. "Why do you need a wife?"

"To keep me from taking Montgomery. This thing between us is dangerous and I'm afraid of going too far." He left nothing out then as he recounted the last months. "Do you understand?"

Sasha nodded, long copper tresses dancing around her shoulders with the motion. "Tell me about your marriage," she asked of him with quiet determination. That was a story he had danced around as long as she had known him. Not any more.

"My marriage." His words were a furious hiss.

Ignoring the risks, she pressed on. "What did your wife do to you?" There was no way she'd back down now. "What did she do to you, Rafe?"

Rafe exploded from the table, overturning the heavy oak chair in a rush of fury. "You want to know about my wife?"

Sasha stood slowly, amazed to see his cool demeanor blown apart for the first time. Then he was stalking her, backing her against the wall as he closed the distance. "What happened to her, Rafe? To you?"

"I would stop while you're ahead," he warned, his growl that of a dangerous animal.

She breathed a sigh of relief when he backed away. "Tell me what happened. You can't keep running from the past. I won't let you," she persisted. The coldness in his eyes was completely at odds with the rage that emanated from him in waves, and she couldn't help but wonder how he contained such conflicting emotions within himself.

"My father brought home a bride for me when I was twenty." Rafe started his tale, the words a mere echo of the past. "Elizabeth was so beautiful. To my young eyes, she was the perfect English lady. Her gentleness was such a change from my father's hatred that within mere hours she had me completely under her spell." The laughter that escaped him was harsh, bitter.

"We were married a week later. Our wedding night was a revelation; my sweet, innocent bride was as experienced as a whore, but I believed her pitiful story of foolish seduction. I was so desperate for her love that I welcomed her into my bed, into my life with open arms.

"She came to me later and spoke of a child. I was in heaven with that news. What did it matter that she had shunned me from her bed? What did it matter that I couldn't touch my wife, couldn't hold her? When things fell apart I did my best, but nothing satisfied her. Only my father was capable of holding her affections."

"How could she turn from you? What woman would prefer another?" Sasha was incredulous. The man was stunning. Everything about him called to a woman. Beckoned.

"I am very like my father." Rafe explained. "If not for our coloring you would have thought us brothers." His derisive chuckle vibrated through the room. "Not that he ever noticed that fact. When he looked at me, all he saw was an unwanted, dark-skinned child who dared to taint his pure English line. If not for our identical gray eyes, I think he would have accused my mother of foisting her bastard on him. Funny how fathers only see what they want to in their children." He shook his head to clear his thoughts.

"The baby came early and my beautiful wife recovered. Night after night, I'd go to her and plead for some crumb of affection. Night after night, she turned me away. When I'd finally had enough, I went to her room, determined to make love to my wife. She wasn't alone."

"Your father was with her." Sasha turned away from the savagery she saw in his face.

"Clever of you," Rafe taunted. "Elizabeth was quick to confess that they'd been lovers for years. Only on the verge of discovery did he marry her to me."

"He had his mistress sleep with you?" Sasha couldn't believe the lord would go to such extremes to keep a woman only to let his son have her.

"There was never any intention on his part for her to bed me. That was all her idea." He ran agitated fingers through jet-black hair. "There was a fight when I tried to take her from him and in the confusion, she fell against the headboard. Elizabeth was dead before she hit the ground. In the end, it was truly pitiful. There was my father, bleeding on the floor, holding his dead lover, damning me all the while for killing her."

Rafe felt drained but he continued. "Before I could leave, my son was struck with a fever. He died in my arms a week later. Only then was my father free to tell his little secret. The child wasn't mine. Elizabeth had been pregnant when she married me. When I recall all the nights, I held that baby in my arms, all those nights, I blinded myself to the fairness of his features, the blond silk of his hair. All that innocent sweetness and he wasn't even mine. I buried my heart with that little boy, Sasha."

She came toward him and with a gentle hand cupped his chin. "Why do you still have the ring?" She questioned, drawing the chain from inside his shirt, her shaking fingers twirling the band.

"It's another reminder of how there is no love in this world for me."

The slight smile that curved his lips sent a chill down her spine, preparing her for the worst. "Another reminder?"

"My mother took my brothers and ran away one night when I was five. Despite all her promises, she never came back for me. Every day after that my father forced me to my knees to beg forgiveness for the shame she had brought on his proud name. When I was old enough to refuse, he moved on to other tactics." At her perplexed expression, he turned away. With the grace befitting a sleek jungle beast, he pulled his linen shirt over his head.

Sasha's stomach clenched as her amber eyes traced the white scars that marred the tawny flesh from shoulder to waist. Not even immortality had erased the marks that crisscrossed his broad back. "How?" The single word escaped the tight knot in her throat.

"I was eight when he started with the lashes. Some days it would last until I begged him to stop. Most of the time begging wasn't enough. The whippings ended when I could finally hit back. He never touched me after that first swing. In the end, marrying me to a whore so his pure English heir could inherit was the worst he could do."

ϯ   ϯ   ϯ

What should she do now? Montgomery wondered as she watched Rafe and his wife circle the dance floor. The other woman had been in residence for three weeks and the situation hadn't gotten any better. She'd hoped a wife by his side would kill the fierce longings he inspired in her. However, the woman's presence seemed little barrier against the fierce lust that plagued her.

Rafe and his scorching silver eyes were to blame for that failure.

A woman like Sasha Fahlan in a man's bed should have been enough to satisfy even the most jaded of lovers, but not him. With every glance, every look, Rafe shouted his intentions to take her to bed in his wife's place. Part of Montgomery pitied Sasha for her blindness to the obvious, while another part damned herself for being tempted to accept.

The ending of the dance pulled her back to the present. Montgomery watched as Sasha approached the stage with movements so graceful, she seemed to float across the floor in a velvet gown that echoed the amber of her eyes. A quick glance down confirmed that her black dress still looked dowdy in comparison.

The polite conversation that had started when Michael joined Montgomery at the bar ended abruptly as the moaning of the saxophone pulsed through the room. The voice that mated with the music was a throaty purr that seemed to coat the room with its honeyed sweetness. This was the first time that Sasha had performed in the club and not a soul could take their eyes from the exquisite creature in the spotlight.

The man frozen in the arched doorway was no exception as he stood there for a moment, his longing painful to see.

"You're back early!" Montgomery focused on Gabriel as he edged closer. She was as happy to see him as she was for the excuse it gave her to ignore Rafe when he joined the group.

"What's she doing here?" Gabriel spoke first, his voice a rough rasp of sound.

Michael didn't doubt whom the highlander's grim question referred to. "Rafe needed a wife and Sasha had the time." He was pleased to see the mayhem that glowed in those green eyes.

"It's not what you think, friend," Rafe broke in.

"Then how is it, *friend*?"

The dark immortal flinched slightly at his harsh tone. "Trust me." Rafe couldn't say more.

"Go ahead, Gabriel, trust him. Just don't expect it in return." Michael tossed out the taunt with a tight smile.

"I don't have a problem trusting *him*, Michael." Rafe drawled out nice and slow, as if talking to a child.

Montgomery watched Gabriel leave without another word as loud applause signaled the end of the song. All of her questions over Sarah Jordan were answered in that moment. A blind man would have seen the pain in those green eyes when he'd looked at Sasha Fahlan. Gabriel was in love with his best friend's wife. And he didn't want to be.

After a few moments, Montgomery followed Gabriel. He was in the gym, sitting on the bench, his elbows on spread knees, his head buried in large hands. She hesitated, unsure of her welcome. Hesitation turned to puzzlement when a softly spoken question came from another of the room's entrances.

"Why did you run from me, my warrior?" Sasha asked, her voice catching on the words.

Gabriel's head flew up at the sound of her voice. He hadn't expected her. "Doesn't Rafe need you to play at happy-ever-after?"

"He needed my help, Gabriel. Something you'll never admit to."

"What happens now that I'm back, angel? Do you run and hide? Or, are you going to stick around and finish the charade? Heaven forbid you leave poor Rafe to deal with her on his own." He lashed out, the fact that Sasha cared for the other man cutting at him still.

"What do you want me to do, my warrior?"

"I want you to go away." His order was harsh, but she didn't obey. Instead, she tested his resolve by drawing close enough to stroke a gentle hand across his jaw. "Don't touch me."

"Still not forgiven me?" Sasha asked as she sank down between his denim-clad legs.

"Never."

Sasha closed her eyes in defeat, flinching from the impact of that single word. "So be it."

The world stopped for Gabriel when she opened her eyes and met his. "Why do you do this to me, angel?"

"I ask only for one last token before I leave you to your unbending righteousness."

"What more do you want from me?" he demanded, grasping her shoulders in a ruthless grip.

"You've taken my honor, my heart, my blood, even my life. What do I have left?" A strangled groan escaped him.

"Just a kiss," she whispered as she threaded her fingers through his thick brown hair. "Just the warmth of your lips on mine. One last time, like before. When I was your angel and you would have followed me through hell." As a single tear slid down her cheek, she brushed her lips against his. "Please. I have waited for you forever. If you won't forgive me, then please, give me this."

The plea brought him to his knees in front of her. The smell of her forced his arms around her waist. The heat of her body pulled him closer. "You ask too much of me, angel."

"I ask for no more than I need."

"Just one kiss," he vowed, unable to deny himself a moment

of heaven he could carry with him through eternity.

ϯ   ϯ   ϯ

Rafe closed the club down that night with Michael, the silence surrounding them a week's old development stemming from their trust issues. As easy as it would have been for him to end the standoff, Rafe couldn't do it.

He couldn't discount the nagging thought that the fair one was a bigger threat to his hold over Gomery than he claimed. Instead, he let Michael leave for his date without a word. Settling down on a barstool, he reached for a bottle. Maybe a drink would help ease the knot in his gut.

A couple hours and an empty bottle later, he felt able to cope with what he'd been going through the last months. Enough at least to know it couldn't go on any longer, not if he wanted to keep his sanity. Gomery had two options, she could get the hell out of his club or she could put him out of his misery. At this point, he didn't give a damn which she picked, only that it happened soon.

Walking through the dark, he sought his bed, kicking off shoes and unbuttoning his shirt along the way. A note on his bed stopped him in mid-motion, with clumsy fingers he reached for it, only grasping it on his third attempt.

Montgomery wanted to see him.

A fifth of vodka overrode centuries of caution and allowed him to enter without knocking. Only feet from the bedroom door, he found himself flat on his back. The forearm on his windpipe and the knee nestled against his groin forced him to admit that maybe he'd had a little too much to drink. The lurking shadow hadn't even caused a ripple in his awareness. Not until it was too late.

"Don't move or I'll break your neck."

"Move your knee a little to the left, sweet thing, I might as well enjoy this." He chuckled when Montgomery jumped as if a fire had suddenly flared to life under her. "Does that mean no?"

She snapped on a lamp, refusing to answer his little taunts. That he remained sprawled on the floor did nothing to alleviate her righteous anger. "You lied," she accused. "You lied to me!" The more she said it, the madder she became.

For once, Rafe was at a disadvantage. "What in the hell are you talking about, woman?" He demanded, standing up on unsteady legs.

"This." Reaching past the unbuttoned shirt, she pulled the ring from his neck, breaking the chain. When no response was forthcoming, she took a second to look at him. To *see* him. God, he was drunk. Falling down, half-dressed, tousle-haired drunk.

Had she been thinking clearly, she would have let him go. She wasn't. "Rotten lying bastard!"

Rafe caught the ring she'd aimed at his face. Turning the gold band in the light, he stared at it. "You know." Nothing of his liquid good humor remained.

When he raised his head, the fire in his eyes took her by surprise.

"By the time Gabriel and your *wife* realized I was there, it was too late. I know the truth now, Rafe. I know about your real wife's death."

"Sasha being here was the last thing keeping you safe, " he drawled, slipping the gold band on his finger. Moving with a swiftness that mocked his current condition, he caught a fistful of her nightshirt, pulling her body hard against his. "I lied about her being my wife for your own good." The confessed came without remorse. Slowly then, as the silence lengthened, he lowered his head, giving her a hundred opportunities to pull away.

Her lips met his halfway and the contact jolted Rafe to his toes. Hunger overwhelmed him, threatening his resolve. Stepping away from her required all of his control.

There was nothing standing between them this time. She was his now and nothing could stop him. Except Montgomery. Even as he prayed she would turn him away, he knew there would be no escape. Not tonight.

"Tell me to leave, sweet thing." Rafe ordered even as he reached out a hand to her. "If you don't turn me away, there's nothing that will keep me from taking you until nobody can ever separate us."

He didn't bother with soft words once she put her hand in his. Need demanded more than pretty murmurs and empty whispers. Fierce hunger screamed for release, begged him to taste her again. The press of her body against his, the stroke of her fingers on his skin gave the darkness strength. Every moan, every desperate caress that send clothes falling to the floor taunted his discipline, weakened his hold on the demon that howled for freedom.

Unable to quiet the beast, he grasped her hips with bruising fingers and took her to the floor. Nothing of the man remained as darkness took over. Wrapping long, feminine legs around his waist, he drove deep.

All of his frustrations went into his possession. With every withdrawal of his body, he arched her up with him; with every thrust, he slammed her back to the floor. Savage hands caught at her hair, holding her captive as he pressed his lips to her shoulder, her throat. He tasted the salt of her skin; savored the faint twang of coppery blood as skin broke under the demand of grazing teeth

Then nothing but pleasure existed as rough hands demanded, as nails raked and bodied arched, shuddered, and writhed before exploding with mind numbing intensity.

CHAPTER 9

He lay in the huge four-poster bed, his harsh face bathed in the gentle morning light. The dark, vibrant beauty of the woman lying beside him was a perfect contrast to the pale roughness of his own features. As she stirred, his black eyes met her sleepy gaze.

Katherine Darien came awake in an instant. The satisfaction reflected in the deadness of her sire's ebony eyes spoke to her as clearly as shouted words. "He gave in to her." Her excitement at the revelation stole the breath from her body.

"Yes, my pet. The hunger reared its head and the beast took the sacrificial lamb." Pleasure over the long awaited occurrence slithered through his every soft-spoken word.

"We strike now." She leaned against his muscular chest, her raven hair sliding over his wide shoulders.

He brushed away the long strands with a battle-scarred hand. A patience he seldom felt lingered in the smile that twisted his thin lips. His little pet was always in such a hurry. All the lessons he'd given her in savoring her victims forgotten in her lust for revenge. "We wait, my pet."

"Why should I wait?" Katherine didn't even try to hide her resentment as she left the bed. What right did he have to dictate to her? Who'd died and left him a god? Actually, she couldn't fathom the number of people who had died in her sire's pursuit of divinity. Little had he understood back in the days of his mortality that a demon had nothing in common with the gods. The differences between the two, was an endless, ugly torment that her cruel sire deserved.

"Right now, there is only hunger for him," Jamison explained, watching in idle fascination as she paced the floor with furious strides, her glorious body still nude from his earlier enjoyment. "If you deny him the woman now, my pet, there will only be a brief moment of irritation before he finds another. There has to be more than hunger. To hurt him, he has to love her. A man, or woman, denied the very sustenance of his heart would suffer a thousand agonies for the want of it."

"Will he take her into his heart?" Her sulking came to an end as the idea gained appeal.

"He will not be able to help himself. Love is the greatest weapon ever forged, my pet. People sell their souls for just a taste of it. They would give their own life to preserve it," Jamison assured her.

"We'll let him keep her for a while longer then. When she becomes the essences of his soul, the very air he breathes, then we'll rip his heart away until nothing but the pain remains."

The laughter that accompanied Katherine's vow was chilling even to Jamison and as arousing as her tiny flash of defiance had been. Rising from the tousled blankets, he stepped closer, using the mere threat of his big, brutally honed body to crowd her back against the bed.

"Very good, my pet. You have learned well." He praised even as he anchored her to him with merciless intent.

Katherine knew the futility of refusing. Instead, she planned. A dozen scenarios filled her mind as Jamison turned her from him until her back was locked to the hard prison of his chest. The bulging arm hooked around her waist held her defenseless against whichever form his desire would take this time. "When will we know?" She forced out the question before whatever he'd decided upon could begin.

"We cut a little bit at a time until he bleeds," Jamison replied as he trailed his lips over the curve of her shoulder.

"Until he bleeds to death," she corrected, relief leaving her dizzy as his teeth raked furrows along her collarbone. This particular desire of his was easy to appease. Wounds healed and were soon forgotten but what he could inflict on this bed when the urge struck was a different story. Those wounds never healed.

"Yes, my pet, until he bleeds to death." Jamison bit deep, the hunger for her blood a visceral need that increased with every hot, crimson bright swallow.

†   †   †

Michael's steps dragged as he entered Heaven's Gate with the first bright rays of morning. He'd allowed what could have been an enjoyable night to fizzle into nothingness, and there was no one to blame but himself. His mind had been elsewhere and his stunning companion had not taken kindly to playing second fiddle to his errant thoughts.

"I need to get a life," he muttered as he dropped onto a barstool.

"I've been telling you that for years. But look on the bright side, we only have eternity to go." Gabriel's mockery was a double-edged sword.

"We're getting too old for this." Michael sighed as he dragged his fingers through silver-blond hair. "Maybe I need to find a woman and settle down for a while." He put his thoughts into words for the first time.

"Sasha's gone." Gabriel ignored the sharp look Michael shot at him.

"Serves the bastard right."

Something had happened in the days he'd been gone. Things had changed between the two men he considered brothers and Gabriel needed to know why. "Gomery knows he lied to her."

"What did she say?" Michael asked when his curiosity could no longer be contained.

"She was furious." What an understatement that was. The woman had taken him apart after Sasha had left. She'd fired questions with deadly accuracy, leaving no aspect of Rafe's perfidy in doubt.

"How furious?" Michael persisted, crystal eyes bright at the prospect.

"Had Rafe deserved it, I would have warned him ahead of time, but he didn't. So, I didn't." Gabriel's smirk spoke volumes.

"Maybe I should offer Gomery a shoulder to cry on." He rose from the stool, but Gabriel's next words stopped him from leaving.

"You underestimate him. Sasha was the last excuse keeping him from her bed. When Gomery confronted him with it, it was taken away. In your place, would you have let her go? No matter how angry she was?" Gabriel asked. "She's just one woman, Michael, don't let this come between us." The highlander was unprepared for the deep rage his words provoked.

"Rafe let her come between us, not me," Michael denied. "He let it come to this. All I needed was for him to believe I didn't take her. But he wouldn't trust me. Instead he went to her and took from her memory what I wouldn't give." He watched awareness dawn in Gabriel's eyes.

"Didn't he fill you in, brother? Are you out in the dark with me now?"

"Why don't you fill me in?" Gabriel's request was more of a demand.

"Will you trust me?" Michael couldn't stop from asking. "Do you know me enough to believe that I took her to bed without taking? That I stopped myself from taking her when I heard his damned name on her lips? I held her against my heart while she cried out for him, Gabriel, and still he accused."

"Rafe can't control what he feels for her, brother."

"He doesn't deserve her! He'll use her until there's nothing left." Michael snarled, his fist striking the bar with enough force to crack the smoke-colored glass. "He won't give her what she needs. He'll leave her broken and hurting. He won't love her like she loves him." He stopped at the shocked sound that escaped Gabriel.

"What, didn't you know? Didn't you wonder what could make a woman like that fall for his heartless line of crap? Or are you surprised that *I* care?" He could see the confusion on the highlander's face and before he said too much, he stormed toward the stairs. "Regardless of what you think, you're not the only one around here capable of selfless emotions."

Gabriel reached out a strong hand to stop his retreat. Never having seen Michael in such a state, he was unprepared for the fist that flew back and caught him under the chin.

𐤟   𐤟   𐤟

Black sheets. Black sheets? But hers were cream. Montgomery stared at the ebony pillowcase for a second before reality slammed everything back into perspective. Stretching to ease the ache in her severely abused muscles, she bit back a low moan. All he'd had to do was crook his little finger last night and she'd given in without so much as a whimper of protest.

Like a mindless bimbo, she had screwed him on the floor; caution and restraint tossed aside for the glorious sensations every stroke of his body had inspired. There hadn't even been a pretense of lovemaking in those small hours of morning. Lust had driven them to mate like animals, biting and scratching, each struggling to control the other.

That cold little piece of reality did nothing to stop the slow smile of satisfaction that curved her lips. Montgomery hadn't thought the ice prince had that much raw need in him. Reaching out a tentative hand, she wound a lock of raven hair around her finger. Even that simple touch had her body edging closer, wanting more of him. How long could she hold him before the fierce heat burned itself out?

The first thing Rafe saw when he awoke, were big, gold-flecked hazel eyes filled with sadness and need. He felt his body harden with the need and his chest tighten at the sadness. Heaven help them all if she turned him away now. Having her one time wasn't going to be enough to feed the hunger that plagued his body.

"Gomery." That was as close to a plea as he would ever come. He caught the fingers in his hair and pulled her closer until sleep warmed skin pressed against his own.

"What are we doing here?" she asked.

"I wanted to wake up with you in my bed." The whispered words were a husky reminder of what he'd denied her last night. Guilty eyes took in reddened scrapes and vivid bruises. He searched for a sign that he'd taken more, that the beast had bared its teeth. He had taken her with rough hands and brutal strength, but he hadn't wanted to take everything from her.

Montgomery leaned into him, her heart pounding against his chest as he seduced her with nothing more than the fire in his eyes. "Not as much as I wanted to wake up beside you." She breathed out, her lips brushing his. "Do you think we can try it again? Just to see if it feels the same on a bed instead of the floor?"

Rafe didn't need words as he firmly reined in the darkness and proceeded to show her that on the floor, on a bed, nothing mattered but feeding the hunger.

ᛏ   ᛏ   ᛏ

Gabriel stood on the sidewalk as he had repeatedly in the last six week and watched Sarah Jordan leave her home. The pleasure that lit her face when she looked his way made his breath catch, until that look was replaced by the usual one of guilt-laced caution.

"Hello, Gabriel." Sarah glanced at him only briefly as she joined him. She still wasn't used to the attention he showered on her, to the wonderful way he made her feel with nothing more that a few words.

"Ready for lunch?" He softened the faded brogue of his homeland, trying to soothe the tension she couldn't hide from him. Her tentative smile was answer enough and he took her hand in his, pleased when she didn't flinch away this time.

Their conversation at lunch began much the same way it had for weeks with each dodging the other's questions while they lobbed back some of their own.

"Any family?" she asked as she nibbled on a fry. Her sherry-brown gaze sought his at the prolonged silence. For the first time, she felt able to discuss personal subjects and wasn't up for a rebuke.

Gabriel tried to answer with as much honesty as he could. "My family's been gone a long time." Centuries in fact. "It's okay though." He didn't need sympathy. "I have some great friends and we take good care of each other."

"Have you known them long?" She was glad to hear that Gabriel wasn't as alone in the world as she was.

"Forever. What about you? Anybody other than your husband?"

Sarah glanced away, unable to look at him. "My mother died when I was six and my father died when I was fourteen. Melissa, my sister, is four years younger than I am." Her voice had taken on a hard edge.

"How did your father die?" Gabriel couldn't hide his curiosity.

"He was a police officer, shot and killed in the line of duty."

"Who took care of you and Melissa?" he asked as he stirred his Coke with straw

"My father's partner at the time had a sister living with him and he took us in."

Gabriel only needed a second to draw his own conclusions. "Seth was his partner."

The harsh statement brought her head up. Nobody ever spoke that way about Seth. Everyone loved his perfect, golden image. "How did you know?" she asked, expressive eyes wide in surprise.

"It's a talent of mine." His grin bordered on wolfish with its ferociousness. "How long did his sister live there?"

"Not very long. Just until the county was satisfied that we were settled." The beauty of his deep green eyes distracted her enough that she spoke the truth instead of what hard experience had trained her to say.

"Where is your sister now?" Gabriel fought the desire to

read her memories.

"I sent her away to school as soon as I could get enough money saved to enroll her." She remember her role then and snapped her lips close.

Gabriel knew he wouldn't find out anything else with her on guard so he asked a final question. "Did you send her away before or after you married Seth?"

Sarah stared right back, daring him to question her answer. "After we married."

Gabriel let the subject slide on the way back to her house. Short of invading her mind, there was nothing he could do. Seth might be a son of a bitch, but nothing more. In all the time he'd spent with Sarah, she'd never by word or deed implied otherwise. Now his time was up. The slight of hand he'd used to obtain the six-week transfer had run its course.

He'd miss the time spent away from the club with Sarah. He was fond of the little one, maybe too fond. Now things would go back to they way they'd been. She'd have her husband and he'd stand back and do his best to keep Michael from killing Rafe over the increasingly frigid way he treated Montgomery.

Gabriel was sure it was only a matter of time before that little triangle exploded into something nasty and when that happened only heaven could help them. Deep in his soul he felt a tempest brewing, he just wasn't sure from where it would hit first.

"I had a great time, Gabriel. Thank you."

Sarah pulled his thoughts back, her soothing voice sounding sweet to his ears. "No problem, Sarah."

"When do you start working with Seth again?" She was hesitant to bring up her husband's name.

"Another few days if all goes as planned." He wasn't looking forward to it. Seth's presence would mean no more visits with Sarah. No more walks in the park or sherry-colored eyes across the table at lunch. The time had definitely come to break away. While this was still innocent and he still could.

"Will you stop by tomorrow?" she asked, trying to sound

indifferent. This was the part of the day, when he left her at the front door, that was getting harder and harder to handle.

"I don't think that would be a good idea, Sarah. It's best if I don't come around anymore." He marveled that he could say the words without flinching from the pain in her eyes. "I wouldn't want to cause any problems between you two. Seth might have a problem with me dating his wife." Gabriel made the comment with a humor he was far from feeling.

"That's fine. I understand." She smiled brightly; her eyes opened wide against the sting of tears.

He reached out and caught her chin with gentle fingers. Lowering his head, he slowly brushed his lips against hers. This was their first and only kiss. There could be nothing more. "If you ever need me, Sarah." Touching her cheek one last time he turned and walked away, all the while wondering how such a tiny mortal could have the power to touch his heart.

ᛐ   ᛐ   ᛐ

"Morrigan, it's great to hear your voice. Yes, I've missed you too. No. Now is not a good time. We'll talk about that later. Yes, I want you to come visit me if you can spare the time. I know we missed Christmas and New Years together. Not a lot was going on to celebrate here."

Montgomery's voice echoed down the hall into Michael's office. Tilting his head to the side, he listened to the one-sided conversation.

"Can you come down this weekend? Saturday night? That'll give us a week. Great! You can stay with me. No. Nope. No one will mind. What can anybody really say about who I let stay with me? It's a queen size, right. Plenty of room. No flying elbows. Not like the last time I shared a bed with you." Her laughter echoed. "Are you going to drive down? We have a lot to discuss when you get here. I'm thinking of taking you up on that proposal. Yes I agree. I think we could do very well together. Okay, sugar, I'll see you then. Mmm. Yes, bye."

Michael rose to his feet when he heard the telephone click. He had a few things to say to Montgomery that wouldn't wait any longer.

She was sitting behind the desk, her eyes glued to the papers in front of her, a contented smile curving her full lips. He clenched his fists at that smile.

"Hello, sugar." Montgomery didn't bother to look up as she tossed out that little greeting. "Still not talking to me?" she asked at his continued silence.

"What makes you say that, *cher*?"

She looked at him, speculation bright in her eyes. He'd ignored her completely since she and Rafe had become lovers. At first, she'd put it down to anger or jealousy, but now she wasn't so sure. There was something more than those petty emotions egging him on. It was almost as if he didn't trust himself to speak to her for what he might say.

"Just a hunch," she returned with false sweetness. "I have a friend coming to stay for a few days. Do you think you can behave yourself?" She smiled at the irritation that flared his nostrils. "Come on, sugar, it's an easy question." She dug in deeper as she walked around the desk to stand nose to nose with him. There was no way she'd back down now, not when there was finally an emotion reflecting from those pale blue eyes. "Scream at me, Michael. Get it out of your system. There's no one here to stop you. Go ahead." She tilted her head and waited.

"Go to hell," he gritted out through clenched teeth.

"That's a start." She refused to take the defensive. "Anything else?"

"You bet there is, *cher*." He snarled as he grabbed a fistful of chestnut curls. Using it as a rein, he pulled her head to his.

He crushed her lips under his with a ruthlessness that was completely at odds with the playful seduction she had experienced at his hands that night. The taste of her blood on his tongue brought him back to his senses and had him letting her go.

That was when he took a moment to look at her, to really see what had changed about her in the last weeks. She was as breathtaking as always, but there was an uncertainty in her eyes that made a mockery of the self-confidence he had come to expect from her. A blind man could see the torment Rafe was putting her through. His brother was hurting this woman in ways his cold heart couldn't understand. When this ended, Rafe would lose much in order to retain his control.

Blue eyes fell to a mouth bruised from his anger and with shaking fingers, he wiped the tiny bead of blood from the cut on her lip. "Damn! That's not what this is about. I'm sorry, Gomery." His voice was a hoarse whisper as he denied that lust was what had fired his emotions. He was sorry for the pain he had just caused her and for the pain he wouldn't be able to protect her from. He hadn't ever wanted to defend a woman before her and it scared some part of him to realize how deeply he wanted to now.

She reached up and wound a lock of silvery blond hair around her fingers, with a gentle tug she pulled his head closer. "No, I'm sorry, Michael. I had no right to use our friendship the way I did. I only hope you can forgive me."

Her sincerity humbled him. Lacking his usual grace, he clumsily pulled her into his embrace, cradling her to his chest. "There is nothing to forgive, *cher*. It's not your fault that you chose him over me. From the beginning, I knew you would. I just don't want to see him hurt you. You deserve to be cherished, *cher*. Loved. He can't do that. I'll be here for you when you need me though, for whatever reason. That's what friends are for and no matter what happens, I am your friend." He cleared his throat on the last.

Michael stroked her hair as she rested her head against his shoulder, ignoring the furious gray eyes that watched them from the doorway.

Chapter 10

Sarah sat down on the stairs and watched Gabriel walk away for the last time. She'd never known a man like him before. While it hurt to see him go, she wouldn't have missed it for the world. He had shown her a whole other side of herself. A side that she was surprised still existed after all of her years with Seth.

Pressing a hand to her mouth, she swallowed the sob lodged in the back of her throat. She hadn't thought she would ever fall in love. Hadn't even believed it possible. Not for her. Love was for people like Melissa. Her young sister was in love. The last letter she'd sent had gone on about her lover and their plans for the future. That letter had hurt as much as Seth's ever-eager fists. She didn't begrudge her sister happiness, she just wished there might have been just one day to experience the love that so many took for granted.

Just one day with a man who loved her above all else, but that small piece of happiness could never be hers. Seth had seen to that. Even if she could break away from him, no one would ever love her. She wasn't even sure if she could love herself.

Heaving a shaky sigh, Sarah pulled herself together and entered the house. Stopping in the hall to hang up her jacket, she was surprised to see the living room light on. "I don't remember leaving that on." She broke the silence; the sound of a voice, even her own, bringing her comfort.

"You didn't," Seth answered from the depths of the armchair.

Sarah hid her fear and plastered on a pleasant smile. "Seth, you're home early." Her eyes darted to the front window. She breathed a silent prayer of thanks at finding the curtains closed.

Even with them slightly parted, he couldn't have a clear view of the stairs. She didn't move as he got up from the chair and walked toward her, his expression completely blank. Her smile faltered, but she held onto it.

"Where have you been, Sarah?" No emotion colored his simple question.

Guilty brown eyes flickered to the window again. "Out. Out for a walk. With a friend." She stumbled over her answer.

"You're lying."

"With a friend, Seth. Just a friend." She tried again.

"You're *lying*." His eyes never left her face.

"Just a friend." She clasped her hands together to stop their trembling.

"You're lying, Sarah."

"Please, Seth," she pleaded, giving up.

"I saw you." His eyes came to rest on her mouth.

"It's not what you think," she denied in a rush, resisting the urge to touch a finger to her lips.

Reaching out with a large hand, he stilled her words with a gentle rap on her nose. "You were out with Gabriel Arden today. And yesterday. And the day before. For weeks in fact." He spoke calmly as if he were reading a criminal their rights.

"Please." She tried to look away, but strong fingers under her chin locked her head in place.

"You like him, don't you, Sarah? You close your eyes at night, in my bed, and think about him. About what a pretty boy he is, how perfect he is, how young he is." He spoke soft and low, as if soothing a frightened animal. He bent down close and whispered in her ear. "You screwed him, didn't you, Sarah?"

He asked the question so gently that it took a moment to register. "No!" she denied, rattled to her soul.

"You're lying!" Seth snapped then, his hazel eyes wild.

The rage twisting his face almost brought her to her knees. The open-handed slap to her face did. He grabbed her arm, dragging her to her feet, fingers digging into bone as he pulled her nose to nose with him.

"Unfaithful bitch, you took that bastard and you fucked him."

"No!" Sarah denied it again, so terrified in that moment that she raised her voice for the first time in eight years, desperate for him to understand. "No, Seth, I didn't touch him." Her throat hurt from the force of her words. Another slap silenced her for a second. "Please, believe me!"

She was too frightened for the tears that stung the back of her eyes to fall. A closed fist knocked her to the floor. A brutal kick rolled her to her side. Seeking refuge, she scrambled on hands and knees, her pleas a strident echo in the hall. Seth stalked her, well placed kicks stopping her retreat at every turn.

"I'll teach you, you little whore. I'll teach you to spread your legs for that son of a bitch." He ignored her cries. A booted heel coming down on fragile fingers stopped her desperate crawl across the floor. "It's not that easy, Sarah."

His return to calmness was disturbing in its suddenness. Casually he went down on one knee beside her, grinding his heel a little harder. The sound of breaking bones brought a smile of satisfaction to his face. "We need to have a lesson, Sarah."

A smartly delivered smack brought forth a trickle of blood from her right nostril. "What's mine, *is* mine." Another slap and blood from a split lip dripped onto the floor. "You *are* mine, Sarah. You're brought and paid for." A closed-fisted blow and her head hit the wall with a thud. "Do we want to keep Melissa happy?" he asked pleasantly.

A handful of hair stopped her as she tried to pull crushed fingers out from under his boot.

"Do you want sweet little Melissa to know what you had to do for her? All in the name of sisterly love? That her big sister's sacrifice was the only thing that kept me from bending her over the kitchen table? How do you think she would look at you? If she knew all the things you let me do to you? Do you really think she would thank you for lying on your back while I screwed your brains out?" He laughed at his own questions.

"Seth, please," she whimpered, trying again to pull her

throbbing hand free.

"Quiet! The lesson isn't over." Grasping her head in both hands, he slammed it against the wall.

She heard his demand from far away as she tried to focus on the black spots dancing before her eyes.

"Let's see, shall we tell her about the baby we had to rid you of? I couldn't let you give birth, now could I? It would have ruined everything."

Her weak moan brought another whack to the face, this one splitting the delicate skin under her eye.

"Maybe it's time I let you have a baby. That should tame your whoring little butt down, don't you think?" he asked with a satisfied smile. "Let's go upstairs, Sarah. I think we need to start this little project now. The sooner we get you knocked up the better." Seth held out a hand for her to take.

Cradling her crushed fingers to her chest, Sarah shook her head. Refusing to lower her pain- filled gaze, she fought against the waves of nausea that threatened to overwhelm her.

"Now!"

The rage in his voice showed on his countenance, turning his handsome features into an ugly mask in the fading light of dusk.

"Never," she gritted out through clenched teeth.

The smile that crossed his face was hideous in its intent. "That's fine then," he sneered as he kneeled down beside her. "You want to be Arden's whore? I'll teach you how to be a whore. I've been gentle with you in the past. Not anymore. I'll show you what choice a whore gets." With brutal and grasping hands, he tore at her clothes. "I say where and when, Sarah, not you. I say how, not you. If you think anything I've done to you before unpleasant, just wait," he promised.

Sarah struggled against his hurting hands, praying even as he drew blood for the strength not to beg.

ϯ   ϯ   ϯ

"Is it time yet?" Dark red lips pouted in an olive hued face, her gaze following the movements of her sire as he dressed for the evening.

"Patience, Katherine." Jamison's black eyes met hers in the mirror. "Time can only aid your cause now."

"I don't want to wait any longer. This is my revenge and I want to end it now. As for patience, I've waited two hundred years to have that dark bastard at my mercy again." She didn't need anyone's permission to finish this, least of all the ruthless vampire that continued to look at her with such amused indulgence. Jamison was here for his own purposes and it was time she reminded him of that.

"If I don't finish this and bring Fahlan to his knees, there is no need for your fairy princess to come out of hiding to rescue him. You can't get to her until *I* finish with him." Katherine couldn't resist adding that in an effort to goad his temper.

"I'm not trying to *get* Sasha. I just wish to see my golden angel again." Jamison's eyes were dreamy with memories only he could see.

"Your sweet angel wants to rip out your heart," she reminded him, disappointed in his lack of response.

"There is that, but I'll get the upper hand this time and make her see reason." He turned from the mirror, focusing his full attention on Katherine. "How do you know she seeks me? Have you seen her?"

He sounded like a child eager for news about Santa Claus. That a woman could control this cold, merciless immortal amazed Katherine. She reveled in her superiority to him; never again would love or affection color her judgment. Only once, in her long existence had she made that mistake and Jamie had taught her well the price one paid for love.

"I haven't seen her since that night in London. But if I remember correctly, *she* had been looking for you." Katherine played upon his weakness, waiting for the moment she could use it against him. "Why do you seek her out when she has shown you no affection? Did she not betray you when she left your side after your time together? You're lucky you escaped with your head still attached. Peasants are so easy to rile when they are given news about a nightwalker in their domain."

"She was so beautiful that night when she led the mob to our castle. I couldn't help but admire her spirit," he reminisced.

Katherine rolled her eyes in disgust. Men were so stupid that it continued to astound her. "What has she ever done for you, Jamie, to inspire such devotion? Sasha has troubled you for centuries, plotting and planning your downfall. Why let her continue?"

"There is nothing that will lessen the gift she gave me. Sasha brought light into my life after centuries of shadows. You don't know what it was like, my pet, to exist only in the night. To feel the craving for blood burning in your stomach until you thought you would die, until you prayed you *could* die. Mixing her blood with mine gave me freedom to hunt, to take, to feed at will. After a thousand years of darkness, she gave me the sun." He turned back to the mirror, his hunger clear in his stark face.

"The taste of her was like nothing I had ever imagined. That pure *Sidhe* blood rushing through my veins was like liquid fire. It burned until nothing of the cold remained. That was as close to heaven as I had ever come. I would give anything to have her again, for her to take of me, but my princess will not partake of such dark pleasures."

"What do you mean?" Katherine asked when she had digested all he had revealed.

"She will not drink of nature's sweetest nectar." He shrugged his broad shoulders to show he didn't understand. "She swore there was nothing on earth worth giving up her soul for and if she drank, she would be forsaking all."

"If she did this, if she gave her blood to a mortal, what would that prove?" Katherine paced herself as she set up her sire.

"Such an act would take a great sacrifice, a great amount of love. I know her, she wouldn't give up so much of herself," Jamison explained after some thought.

"That's interesting." Katherine's smile was nothing more than a slight curve of lips. "Is it time?"

When she asked the question this time, the promise of Sasha's appearance was incentive enough for Jamison. "We'll go to the club tonight and stir up the waters." He relented, craving the mayhem he so loved to breed.

"Jamie." Katherine called his attention back to her as she moved in for the kill. "That night in London? When Sasha and I were there with the three? I didn't change the highlander. I had stabbed him with a sword and left him to die. Your precious fairy did that on her own. Your golden princess drank from him, taking his blood without hesitation as she gave him back her own, along with her soul. Wasn't that sweet?" She turned away with a smirk of satisfaction, leaving him to burn with a cold fury. Maybe she wouldn't have to deal with Jamie *or* Gabriel. If her luck held, they would kill each other.

ፐ   ፐ   ፐ

Rafe tugged on the gold hoop in his ear, thankful for the pain and the reminder it served. In a moment of weakness, his thoughts turned to Montgomery and the desperate power struggle that waged between them. For the last month and a half, he had played a dangerous game and he knew it was close to the end. The few innocent, little tastes he'd taken of her had left a deadly craving inside of him. No longer could he ignore the hunger that filled him whenever he had her body hot and clinging under his.

All those weeks ago, the urgency to have her hadn't seemed so desperate. Even his momentary loss of control when he'd almost taken her on the desk hadn't been as consuming as the hunger that taunted him now. Using all of his unnatural restraint in the last weeks had kept her safe, but to exercise that restraint cost him much and the coldness he wrapped himself in refused to thaw, in or out of the bedroom.

Montgomery was learning to hate him and herself for not being able to turn him away. They were strangers in the light of day; the politeness only melting when the heat in their bodies took over and they came together in an explosion of desire.

Even the urge to take her to his bed was something he hadn't given into again. Only in the night did he go to *her*, when the darkness hid the hunger that glowed silver in his eyes, and the shadows could mask the scars on his back. The scars on his soul. Only when she couldn't see the monster inside the man did he take her body with his, suffusing her with pleasure until she trembled in his arms. All the while he denied his hunger and left her heart and soul empty.

Rafe tugged the earring again. He'd had it made from his wedding band the day he had woken up staring into Montgomery's sad, gold-flecked eyes. The jeweler had been shocked by his wish to have the antique band transformed into a plain gold hoop, had even done his best to talk him out of it, but no other would do. Only this one could satisfy him, this ring, given to him by the faithless whore that he had called wife. Always would he wear it. The style didn't matter, only the reminder it served of the treachery that had shaped his life.

Determination had driven him as he'd pushed the post of the hoop through his earlobe. Cold rage had filled him as he'd gritted his teeth and wiped away the blood. Never would he forget what Elizabeth had done to him, or what his mother and father had put him through. If the scars on his back weren't enough, then the cold feel of the gold would do. With one last tug on the earring, he allowed himself a moment of regret.

Tonight, he would end the game.

ϒ   ϒ   ϒ

Montgomery stood back and watched the crowd, trying to gage the mood in the packed surroundings. Valentine's day was always a real treat and this one was no exception. Filled to capacity, surges of aggression and temper pulsed through the place in invisible waves. Experience had taught her that nothing would subdue the wild emotions, but a long sweeping glance assured her that all was calm for the moment. Only then, did she allow herself to focus on the man working the crowd.

Rafe returned her stare from across the wide expanse of dance floor and just that brief flash of silver awareness in his eyes was enough to steal the strength from her knees. Montgomery turned away from that too knowing gaze, ashamed of the need that unfurled in her belly. How easily her body betrayed her to this man was disgusting. All it took was a moment of his attention and she was hot enough to ignite.

Little of her need for Rafe had changed in the last weeks. No matter how many times she took him into her arms, her heart, they were still strangers. He ignored every effort she made to get close to him, to reach out. Questions asked went unanswered. Promises demanding freedom went unuttered. He denied her even gentle affection when he came in the dark and claimed every part of her being.

What did he care that he shattered her heart every time he touched her? In the end, it was her problem, her responsibility. She had let it come to this and had only herself to blame. Let Rafe keep his secrets, let him look through her in the light of day as if she didn't exist. Rafe Fahlan was nothing more than a marauding pirate with his gold earring and cold eyes. A marauding pirate all ready to ravish her body and steal her soul. What hurt the most was that he already had it and didn't care.

When this had started, she had thought that his body coming together with hers in the obscurity of the night would be enough. She'd been wrong and tonight this *thing* between them would have to end.

Montgomery stood there and waited, some part of her hoping he would break the pattern and come to her here, now, that he would acknowledge her. Love her. Giving in to the weakness, she sought him out again. Her breath caught in her throat at the impact of those silver eyes clashing with hers.

As he continued to hold her captive with nothing more than the sheer power of his gaze, she prayed for something, anything, but it wasn't to be. He left her there, her every emotion on her face as he walked away. He wouldn't seek her out until the darkness was at its peak and his lust had reached its zenith. Only then would Rafe need her.

The thought of escaping his rejection filled her as she made her way through the crowd. Intent on reaching the private elevator that would give enough privacy to pull herself together, she failed to notice the shadow that followed.

"Excuse me?"

The lilting little voice caught Montgomery's attention. Drawing a deep breath, she slapped a pleasant smile on her face and found herself staring down into intense black eyes.

"I'm looking for a friend of mine. I was wondering if you knew where he could be?"

The girl's dark beauty intensified with the gamin smile that brightened her features. Hell, the girl barely looked old enough to be in the club. Montgomery felt ancient by comparison. "Who would you be looking for?" she asked instead of carding her.

"Michael Wyhndym."

"You're looking for Michael," Montgomery repeated. Now why wasn't she surprised? "I'm sorry. I don't expect him in until after midnight. Can I give him a message?"

"No. I'll be back another night. I plan to stay in the area for awhile. You work with Michael?"

"Yes I do. I'm Montgomery Sinclair."

"Katherine Darien." She extended her hand in greeting, dark eyes searching the other woman's face when their hands touched.

Montgomery disregarded the faint shock of electricity that zinged through her at the contact. There was something about this girl's involvement with Michael that concerned her. The poor little thing wouldn't stand a chance against a playboy of his caliber.

"You're not what I expected of Rafe," Katherine murmured, tilting her head to the side as she looked up at the woman she planned on sacrificing in her quest to destroy the dark one.

Montgomery hid her surprise at the comment. The girl

must be closer to Michael than she'd assumed if she knew
Rafe as well. "You're not what I pictured as Michael's type
either," she couldn't help teasing. There was something
about this girl…

"Does Michael really have a type?" Katherine challenged
with a slight smile, liking the warm laughter that greeted the
blunt honesty of her words.

"Not that I've noticed. Are you sure you don't want to
leave a note or a number?"

"That's not necessary. Please, don't mention you saw me.
I'd rather sneak up on him later."

Her smile held a secret that Montgomery didn't think she
wanted to unravel. Instead, she watched, a little envious, as the
dark beauty walked away to disappear within the crush on the
dance floor. The girl had a lot of confidence for one so young.
Giving up on her need to escape, she followed Katherine's lead
and pushed into the throng of people.

"Busy night," Rafe commented as he fell into step beside
her. He'd been avoiding her all night, but he hadn't been able
to stay away a minute longer. He had in fact, broken his own
rule by seeking her out for nothing more than the pleasure of
touching her, breathing her.

"Yes it is," Montgomery replied, keeping her eyes off him.

Rafe was glad she didn't notice the hand he reached out to
her. Didn't see the fist that clenched as he let his arm drop back
to his side. "I'll see you tonight." With that grim warning, he
walked away.

Montgomery wondered as he left if those words were a
threat or a promise.

CHAPTER 11

Gabriel had to see her again even if only to check on her while she lay sleeping. Just to make sure she was well. To make sure that the wild threats Seth had made to him just an hour ago were nothing more than the empty words he wished them to be.

With a little magic, he opened the front door of the house.

Sarah lay on her side, curled into a ball on the bed, her hair a coppery tumble around her face. Easing down beside her, Gabriel combed the strands aside. In that moment, he forgot how to breathe. Nothing in Seth's ugly accusations had prepared him for this. A harsh sigh escaped him as he slid away the sheet. Biting back the low growl that clawed the back of his throat, he searched out every purple bruise and raw abrasion that covered the majority of her fair akin.

"Sarah?" he whispered, his breathing ragged in the silence. Reaching out a trembling hand, he traced the shallow cut on her cheek. The need to know what that bastard had done to her was fierce and immediate. Cupping his palm to the curve of her bruised jaw, he closed his eyes.

After an agonizing hesitation, her memories flooded his mind. Leading the way, he drew her back to that afternoon where he'd left her on the steps. Fury grew inside of him as he *saw* Seth's accusations through Sarah's eyes. He felt her fear, her pain, endured her shame when Seth threatened to reveal her dark secrets to Melissa.

It was a struggle to hold it together as the last of Seth's deeds assaulted his mind. Wolves showed their prey more compassion than that monster had shown Sarah. Gabriel would have walked through hell on Sunday to erase from her mind what happened after that son of a bitch came down on his knees beside her.

Only when Seth had sufficiently amused himself had he left her there, lying on the floor, ragged, beaten, and bleeding. For a long time, she'd stayed that way, too stunned to speak, too paralyzed to move until fear of Seth's return had forced her to her feet. Using the last of her endurance, she had fallen onto the bed, only closing her dazed eyes when she had pulled the flower sprigged sheet over the tremors that racked her.

"Gabriel."

The soft sigh of his name pulled him from his murderous thoughts. "I'm here, baby." He crooned the words, hiding his hatred for her husband behind the gentleness of the hand he smoothed over her tumbled hair.

"How did you get here?" she whispered, her voice raspy from her pleas. Only when those words scraped her swollen throat did the rest come flooding back. Fear and shame slammed into her like a fist, outweighing even the sharp, biting pain that followed her every movement as she turned away, hiding her humiliation in the shadows.

Evading him was useless and he eased her into his arms with little effort. "Let me go! Let me go!" Her cry was nothing more than a broken sob as she pushed against the solid wall of his chest.

Gabriel gentled her the best he could, but in the end, her strangled cries were too much and he let her go. "I'm not going to hurt you, Sarah."

"Get out." She refused to look at him as helpless tears streaked down her battered face. "I don't want you here."

He recoiled as her words struck him. "Sarah?"

"I can't let you see me like this."

Her voice cracked on that and he glimpsed the desperation that drove her. Ignoring her struggles, he again gathered her close. Making use of a gift he had received directly from Sasha's blood, he focused his mind and began to drain as much of her pain into his body as he could. When he had finished, he found that she had cried herself to sleep in his arms.

Gabriel took a moment to assimilate each throb and ache of the agony he had released from her that now rattled around in his chest. He knew he could disperse the suffering he had absorbed, but he chose to keep the pain so he could share it with Seth Jordan when the time came.

Holding her within the warmth of his embrace, he left his mind to healing the internal injuries that she couldn't question. The glowing eyes of the immortal missed nothing as he mended cracked ribs, broken fingers, and a fractured wrist. He allowed the cuts and tears received from her husband's brutal lesson to close and heal. In the end, he regretted the need to leave the ugly bruising as testimony to her torment at the hands of her spouse.

There was no hesitation in him when he decided what to do next. Wrapping her in the sheet, he closed his eyes and pictured his apartment. A tingle raced through his body and when he opened his eyes again, he found them in his bedroom. He laid her gently on the antique canopy bed, covering her with the bronze silk comforter. Sure that she was safe, he left her to recover in the healing arms of sleep. Walking into the kitchen, he wasn't surprised to find Michael lounging in one of the turn-of-the-century oak chairs.

"What's up?" Michael asked, his face a picture of mild interest.

Gabriel released a deep sigh of regret. He'd hoped to regain some control before he faced the others. "Have you ever wanted to shred somebody until there was nothing left of them?"

"Do you need my help?" Michael offered without reserve. He'd kill anyone that dared put such deep suffering in those green eyes.

"I can take care of him on my own." The smile Gabriel flashed was savage in its design.

"Can I watch?" Rafe asked as he broke another of his own rules and *popped* in. Traveling by magical means wasn't something he did without protest. He hated even that brief moment of dependence on Katherine's dark influence. However, given the agony he'd felt coming from his brother, he'd decided stealth might be to his advantage.

"I would be honored. Maybe you can give me a few suggestions; some of the things you learned at your father's knee for instance." Gabriel drawled the backhanded invitation. Goading Rafe wasn't something he did often but he needed the distraction a fight would bring. He needed to ease some of the rage inside of him before the beast broke free.

"If need be. You would be amazed at the inventive streak my father possessed. Who do you have in mind?" Rafe refused to rise to the bait. "Where are you hurt?" he asked when Gabriel didn't answer. His gaze not wavering as he stared at the highland warrior.

"I'm not hurt," Gabriel denied even as he wondered how Rafe knew.

"I can feel your pain, brother," the dark immortal chided him for lying.

"It's not mine." He turned away from probing eyes, fearing they would see too much.

"Sarah?" Michael asked the question in a low murmur.

"Yes." He wasn't surprised that the others knew about her.

"She's asleep in your bed," Rafe stated it as fact.

"What is she doing there?" Michael asked that, looking at him with open curiosity.

"Jordan was at the station tonight. He accused me of sleeping with his wife and warned me to stay away from her. He said he'd put her in her place, that she wouldn't be spreading her legs for me again." Gabriel closed his eyes to keep the others from seeing the wild emotions that tumbled around inside of him. "He hurt her, Rafe. Seth hurt her and it's my fault. If I had stayed away, she wouldn't have had to go through what he did to her."

"It's not your fault," Rafe contradicted as he placed a comforting hand on Gabriel's shoulder. "Men like Seth Jordan don't need a reason to mistreat others. If not you, then maybe how she fixed dinner or how she cut her hair." He watched those green eyes fly open but didn't flinch from the molten fury that bubbled there.

"What Jordan did went beyond *mistreat*, this was defilement, violation, desecration, rape!" Gabriel's voice rose with each word he spat, until his shouts rattled the windows.

"I'll kill him for you," Rafe promised.

"He's mine." Gabriel forced himself to focus. "I'll crush him until he's nothing but a pile of blood and guts at my feet."

"What about Sarah?" Michael threw that into the silence.

Gabriel contemplated the question. He hadn't given the future much thought. His only concern had been in getting her away from that son of a bitch. "She can start over away from here. Her sister lives in Chicago. Sarah will want to see her again."

"Do you love her?" Michael asked.

"Love?" Gabriel couldn't stop the harsh bark of laughter that escaped him. "There is no one I will ever let myself love."

"What if she loves you?" Rafe wanted to know.

"That's something I can't allow."

ᛏ   ᛏ   ᛏ

"'I'll see you later.' Arrogant bastard," Montgomery mumbled under her breath in the small hours of the morning as she prepared to crawl into her lonesome bed. "He can go straight to hell!" She swore a little louder this time.

"I have no doubt I will, sweet thing."

Montgomery refused to be seduced this time by that smoky drawl. What did it matter that it filled her mind? Her dreams? "I have a headache. Go away," she snapped out, turning her back on him as she flipped off the lights, hoping he would take the hint.

"What's wrong, sweet thing?" he purred out soft and low in her ear.

She jumped at that whisper of air, the warmth of his breath

on her skin sending a shiver down her spine. Resisting the urge
to lean against him was near to impossible, but she stiffened her
resolve. The game had to end now.

"I'll not be your whore tonight, Rafe. I'm done with you."
She spoke the words and for a second almost believed that she
could walk away with her heart unscathed.

"Don't I please you?"

His lips brushed the nape of her neck, and Gomery had to
grind her teeth together in an effort to hold back a moan. She
had to be strong this time. No one could treat her like a con-
venience and get away with it. Michael's little friend wouldn't
let any man get by with this. Katherine Darien would have
brought him to his knees by now, begging her forgiveness.

Rafe smiled in the darkness, he could feel the excitement that
rushed the blood through her veins. Could feel the heat and the
lust that flooded every inch of her body even as she shrugged
off his touch. He felt his own need soar to meet hers and knew
that he needed one last night with her. One more time to possess her and then he could walk away a free man. One more time
just to prove he could. That everything was under control.

"You're wonderful between the sheets, sugar, but outside
these walls you fall short." She mocked him, angered by his
indifference. Feeling his desire growing against her hip, she
tried to turn his attention before she gave in to the fire burning her insides. "I find myself bored with your company. I need
a change." She lied as bold as sunshine, desperate for a reaction
from him. Any reaction that kept him from touching her again.

Rafe slid his fingers under her hair, pulling the thick mass
aside. Resisting a temper that would have shattered his control, he leaned forward and slid his tongue along the side of her
throat. He didn't need to hear the words as she surrendered to
him, knees buckling at the contact. With sure movements, he
lowered her to the bed, keeping his muscled chest pressed
against her back. When she melted at the hard press of his body
on hers, he continued the erotic exploration of her neck and
shoulders, stopping on occasion to suckle a bit of skin between

his teeth.

Montgomery moaned deep in her throat when he bit down, leaving damp bruises in his wake. "You want me to stay, *sugar?*" he jeered as his teeth closed down on her earlobe.

"No!" She wouldn't beg, couldn't let him know how much she needed him.

Rafe's anger kicked up a notch at that blatant lie. Some of his control slipped as he pulled her gown up her thighs, ignoring the sound of tearing silk. Knowing hands sought out the wet heat that pooled at the center of her body. "You want me to stay?" he growled against her cheek as he slid a finger into the waiting heat. At her hesitation, he slid in another. She cried out sharply as he found a spot hidden deep inside of her and thrust his fingers against it.

"Oh, God!" Montgomery sobbed as pleasure flooded her body. Another thrust and she couldn't control the trembling. Burying her face in her arms, she clenched her fists in the blanket as she struggled not to cry out.

"Do you want me to stay?" he whispered against her ear, his breathing ragged in the silence of the night.

"Rafe." She broke down. "Just for tonight. One last night..." her words choked off as he pulled away and stripped the silk over her head. Just as quick, he removed his own clothes.

"For as many nights as I want you," he grated out with ruthless determination. He felt the tremors that racked her as he pulled her hips against him. Felt the need that shuddered through her as he spread her thighs and took her.

Rafe lunged again and again, careless in his intensity. Ignoring his anger and everything but the feel of the woman under him, he closed his eyes and focused his senses on the pleasure. To the feel of her body rocking back against his thrusts. For the first time in his life he put his own desires above the protection his control granted him.

This time there was no alcohol to dull his hunger, or icy disdain to coat his cravings, and as their passions exploded with the brightness of a nova, he couldn't hide from it any longer.

With his head pounding and his body shaking, he grabbed a fistful of chestnut hair and pulled her neck taunt. Arching her slender back against his chest, he closed his mouth around the vein that
throbbed beneath the golden skin.

Growling a low rumble of warning, he bit down hard, releasing a heated flood of sweetness into his mouth. Running his tongue
across the wounds, he collected his bounty, uncaring of the con-
sequences as the coppery fire that was her life burned down his
throat. Pulling her even closer to him, he slid his lips along her
neck. Unable to stop himself, he sank his teeth in again, harder
this time.

"Rafe." She moaned his name, awash in the sea of sensations
wrought by their lovemaking and the startling eroticism brought
forth by his unholy possession. "Rafe," she moaned again. Pleasure
she had never dreamed of covered the discomfort caused by his bite
as he sank his teeth in yet again. Her body convulsed as wave after
wave of ecstasy crashed over her. "Rafe, please."

Her faint whisper broke through the rush of his hunger and
with a suddenness that left her sliding to the bed, he threw himself away from her. Stumbling to a safe distance, he resisted the
urge to spring back to her side and sink his teeth into her exposed
throat yet again. Locked within a silent battle of willpower, it took
him a long moment to notice the shallowness of her breathing. Fear
banished his hunger as he slowly approached the bed. His stomach lurched at what he saw there. He had done this. He had…

"Rafe," she whispered as her lashes fluttered open. "I love
you."

Her eyes closed and for a moment, he feared the worst.
"Arden!" he shouted at the top of his lungs. In his distress, he
didn't even think to use his mind to call for the highlander.

Gabriel appeared moments later and the sight his green eyes
took in was something he had hoped never to see again.

"Help me," Rafe begged him. The control he prided himself
on was lost in the terror that darkened his silver eyes. He held
Montgomery in his arms, her face turned into his shoulder.

When the dark one released his lover into the highlander's

arms, it only took Gabriel a second to realize that she bled from several wounds on her throat.

"Who did this?" he asked as he examined the ragged wounds.

"Help her." Rafe closed his eyes against the sight and left without another word.

Gabriel laid his burden on the bed and with gentle fingers, he touched her. Within seconds the injuries closed and healed. Within minutes, they had almost completely disappeared. When he was sure that she slept, he washed away the evidence and covered her nakedness with the quilt. She would be tired in the morning, but that was better than dead.

He went in search of his friend then. This whole mess was going to require a hell of a lot of answers and he meant to get them.

Rafe wasn't hard to find.

"What in the hell happened?" Gabriel demanded when he cornered the other man in his office, digging through his desk.

"How is she?" Rafe countered, looking up from the drawer.

"She's fine." The panic in Rafe's eyes was so foreign to his character that Gabriel stared for a moment before he asked again. "Who did that?"

"Will she be all right?" he asked again, ignoring Gabriel's question.

"She'll survive." The highlander narrowed his eyes. Something was definitely wrong. The dark one was dressed for the road. Why wouldn't he stay? "Where are you going?"

"Out." Rafe refused to explain himself. A hand on his shoulder stopped his leaving.

"Who did that?" Gabriel wasn't letting go until he had his answers.

"I did," Rafe replied as he shrugged off his restraint. Gabriel didn't try to stop him this time as he walked out the door.

ᛏ   ᛏ   ᛏ

"Let me go!" Sarah shrank back from the rough hands that

grabbed her. She fought against the cruel fingers that pulled her hair. "Let me go," she screamed again. The hands shook her and she struck out with trembling fists. "Leave me alone." Her fist connected with something solid and she gasped against the pain that speared through her fingers.

"Sarah," Gabriel soothed her, trying to break through the terror that held her in its suffocating web. "Wake up, Sarah, you're having a bad dream. It's going to be okay."

Strong arms held her close and as the dream faded, she burrowed into the warmth the embrace offered. She opened dazed eyes and the sight that greeted her was more beautiful than words. Gabriel sat on the bed, sleep rumpled and concerned. He held her cradled on his lap; her head nestled against a bare shoulder. Unable to resist, she rubbed a bruised cheek against his chest, sighing as the dark hair tickled her nose.

"Good morning," he murmured by her ear. Startled brown eyes flew to emerald green and he could read the sudden understanding that filled those rich sherry pools.

"Where am I?"

Her voice was horse, and he could tell from her slight wince that it hurt to talk. He knew it was from her screams the night before. From all the agonized pleas that her husband had ignored. He buried his rage before it could raise its feral head.

"Home. With me."

His uncertainty made Sarah want to cry. He looked at her as if he feared she would run away from him.

At her slight nod, he cupped her face with gentle hands. With strong fingers, he drew her closer until their foreheads touched. "You're safe now, Sarah. He'll never touch you again."

She nodded again, knowing he meant every word. If anyone could keep her safe, this guardian angel would. As she moved closer to him, the blanket slipped and she looked down to see the bruises that covered most of her arms and chest. Feeling more ashamed than she had ever felt before, she slid out of his arms and crawled to the far side of the large bed. Seth's actions left her feeling humiliated, dirty. If Gabriel touched her, the obscenity of it would rub off and he was too special to have his hands sullied with her shame.

"Sarah?"

His hand brushed her shoulder and she scrambled away from the bed as fast as her sore body would let her. "You shouldn't touch me," she rasped, refusing to look at him. "I'm not clean." Her words faltered when he walked up behind her and pulled her to his warmth.

"You are perfect." That soft-spoken tribute was all it took to shatter the last hold she had on her tears. Turning her in his embrace, Gabriel rocked her in his arms. "Would you like to shower?" he asked when the storm passed.

"Yes, please," she whispered in a small voice.

Gabriel swept her up into his strong arms and carried her into the bathroom. Holding her to him, he turned on the water. Only when steam filled the room did he set her down. "If you need me, I'll be outside the door." With a brush of his fingers through her hair, he closed the door behind him.

On trembling legs, she stepped under the hot spray. The water was harsh on her tender skin, but she held back the tears that burned her throat and grabbed the soap and began to wash. As her eyes took in all the marks that flawed her skin, she began to shake.

Every memory of the past twenty-four hours that her brain had tried to block came flooding back. Unable to stop the nausea that churned her stomach or the tremors that shook her small frame, she fought against the shower door, wanting only to get away. Unaware of everything but her misery, she forgot about Gabriel until her wild flight sent her crashing into his solid frame.

His arms closed around her as he pulled her wet, shivering body flush with his. "Back in the shower, lass." Through the damp fall of copper hair, anguished brown eyes peeked up at him but he refused to back down. "I'll help you." With sure movements, he swept her naked body into his arms and carried her back to the shower door. Stepping under the water with her, he didn't let her go until the warm wetness had eased her shivers.

"You're in the shower with me!" She stammered the obvious

when reality dawned, staring at him in open-mouthed amazement.

"I kept my clothes on," he offered with a crooked grin. Her bubble of laughter surprised them both and Gabriel had to fight the urge to hug her. "Will you be able to finish?"

His slight smile brought a blush to her bruised cheeks. "Yes," she stammered, remembering her nudity.

Gabriel stepped out of the shower, grabbing a towel as he went.

Sarah watched him move through the steam, the water rolling and sliding from his short hair and navy shorts. She took a deep breath. In all her life, she had never thought a man could look like that. Not even the cover models that graced the novels on the romance shelf at the bookstore looked like that. Even as he stood in front of the mirror and shook the water from his brown hair, she continued to stare. Her eyes never wavered as they took in the bronze skin and hard muscles that flexed and bunched as he ran the towel over the broad expanse of his chest.

Afraid he would turn around; she slid the glass door almost closed. Leaving it open an inch, she watched as he slid the wet shorts down his long muscular legs. She felt her skin tingle as she looked at his bare body.

Her gaze never wavered when he wrapped the damp towel around lean hips and ran his fingers through his hair. When he turned from the mirror, she caught sight of the scar that marred the perfection of his chest. The pain he had to endure to survive a mark like that brought back her tears. Try as she might, she couldn't hold back the sob that followed, or the gasp that rose when he pulled the door open.

"Are you okay, Sarah?" he asked, full of concern.

"I'll be just fine," she replied with a watery smile.

"I'm here when you need me."

ϒ   ϒ   ϒ

Montgomery woke up with her head spinning and her body aching. She felt sick. Really sick. She groaned as she sat up.

With an unsteady hand, she pushed back a face full of hair as she braced herself on an elbow and waited for the room to stop spinning. Maybe she had the flu. She slid back amongst her pillows, wondering if you really had to call in sick if you were sleeping with the boss.

Closing her eyes, she counted to ten hoping she could control the rolling motion her belly had decided to follow. On another bad note, she didn't remember all that much of last night, at least not the part that came after the flood of pleasure she'd drowned in after Rafe had come to her room. That was becoming a very disgusting habit of hers, this not remembering.

"Morning," the boss said as he walked out of her bathroom. His shirt clung to his damp skin as he used a towel to dry the silk of his ebony hair. Walking across the room, he made his way to the side of the bed.

He had never stayed the night before and Gomery couldn't help but wonder if this wasn't a fever-induced hallucination. "I feel like hell," she mumbled just in case, looking away from the intensity of his silver eyes.

Rafe was glad she didn't notice the agitation that tightened his fists as he searched her neck for any sign of their encounter. Blanching when he saw the faint marks at the base of her throat, he knew he had to get away before it was too late. Next time the demon that lurked in his soul just might end her life.

"I'm in total agreement with what you said last night. We're going to end the game between us now." He threw out the cold statement with no lead in or gentle let down attempted on his part. He had only come back this morning for one reason. To finish this. He felt that in the harsh light of day he stood a chance. When he could see the evidence of his betrayal. When he could see the damage his hunger had wrought.

"I don't understand." Montgomery blinked in confusion. Hadn't she told him last night that she loved him? Hadn't he stayed with her all night? Didn't she matter to him at all?

Rafe turned away from the bed and finished dressing. He

didn't want to see that look in her eyes. Didn't want to see the marks he had left on her body. Caught up in thought, he didn't sense her until a hand touch his shoulder.

"What's wrong?" she whispered as she pressed her weakened body to his. Her fear grew at his continued silence and in desperation; she blurted out something she'd never planned to tell another person again. That she vaguely remembered saying it last night only added to her desperation. "Rafe, I love you."

Her husky plea splintered into the vast hollowness that was his heart. Fighting down the hunger that her mere touch evoked and reinforcing his resolve, he shook her hands away. "Love?" he sneered, refusing to look at her. "You only love the ride I give you. But look on the bright side, you give almost as good as you get. You'll find some other playmate soon enough. Your kind always does. Unfortunately, I'm no longer interested in what you have to offer. The challenge is won, *sugar*. The game is over." Without looking at her, he gathered up the rest of his things and left her standing in the middle of her room.

Her quiet sobs and shattering heart were the only sounds he heard.

CHAPTER 12

"I quit," Montgomery informed Michael several hours later.

"What'd I do now, *cher*?" he demanded, almost falling off his chair in his haste to stand up. Motioning her into the office, he watched as she walked in and closed the door behind her.

Only then did he really look at her.

Never had he seen her looking anything but perfect in the past; today was the exception. He didn't think that she had even bothered to run a brush through her hair, let alone perform all the normal rituals most women participated in every morning. "You look like hell," he blurted with none of his usual charm.

"Thank you." She smiled without humor. Sinking into the chair, she drew her knees to her chest.

Sitting down on the arm, he ran his fingers through the tumbled mass of chestnut curls. "Talk to me, *cher*," he encouraged.

"Rafe loved his wife very much, didn't he?" she asked, looking up at Michael with wide, pleading eyes.

Taken by surprise, he didn't answer right away, but came down on his knees at her side, caressing her face with gentle fingers. The pain in those gold-flecked pools astounded him. "What's wrong, Gomery?" His thumb stopped the tear that rolled down her cheek.

"That's the reason he can't love me, isn't it, Michael? Because he loved her so much? No one else can take her place?"

He closed his eyes at her words. There was no joy in his every prediction coming true. "Rafe doesn't talk about her. He keeps that part of his life to himself." Michael opened his eyes just in time to catch another tear. "You're not the problem in this, *cher*. It's him." He couldn't hide his bitterness.

"I don't know about that. Nobody has ever loved me but Morrigan and I don't think that counts." She gave him a weak smile.

"What's not to love, sweetheart?" His blue eyes showed his surprise. "You're beautiful, and smart, and…"

"All my life, people have walked away from me." Montgomery interrupted him. "They've made no secret that they hated me. My own parents didn't even want me to be born. I was maybe five when I realized that things were different at my house than at others. When I got home, I asked my mother what was so wrong with me that she couldn't love me. All she said was that I couldn't help being born, but she wasn't going to sacrifice her life for a child she never wanted. That if she ever came to love me, she would always be tied to me.

"She left in the middle of the night when I was eight. My father was out of the country and I was alone. Two days passed before the school sent a counselor to find out what was wrong. When Dad came home, he blamed me. He never believed me when I told him it wasn't my fault." Montgomery covered the hand cupping her face, needing the comfort.

Michael fought hard as he blocked her thoughts from his mind. He didn't think her private misery was something he should delve into. Watching her for a long moment, he made his decision. Knowing that this wasn't the time did little to stop him, and he bared his soul with an honesty that hurt.

"Come away with me, *cher*. We should be together. I'll take care of you, give you what you want. I'll hold you in my arms and give you what you deserve. Will you come with me?" He swallowed hard at the shock that flooded her face.

"Oh, Michael," she murmured with a sigh.

"Don't answer now." He rushed to stall the refusal that brimmed in her eyes. "Give yourself time to think about it."

Moving closer to him, she placed a silencing finger against his lips. "You are an absolute wonder and I love you with all my heart, but I'm not in love with you. A part of me would like nothing better than to be held in your arms forever, but that wouldn't be fair to you." She stopped his protest. "It wouldn't be fair, Michael. You deserve a woman who can love you. Someone with a whole heart, not just the broken pieces."

"Let me decide what's fair, *cher.*"

"You say that now, but you would grow to hate me. There isn't a man alive who could live with the thought that their lover isn't their own. I would never be untrue, but the heart is much harder to tame. My love for Rafe would slowly destroy all three of us. When we saw him, you would never be sure of how I felt. *I* wouldn't even know until it was too late and I couldn't live with the thought of hurting you." She ran a hand over his shoulder.

"You're hurting me now," he whispered.

"The truth can only hurt you once," she countered. Her eyes soft with understanding.

"We make a sorry pair, don't we?" he asked with a sad smile. "If you change your mind, *cher*, you know where I'll be. Don't be afraid to come to me." As he spoke those words, his pale eyes took in the beauty of her face. those same eyes missed nothing as they came to rest on the very faint marks on her throat. "Are you sure?" he questioned as they stood.

"I think so." Montgomery gave him a sweet, simple kiss on the lips. Stopping at the door, she turned back. "I still quit."

Michael watched her go, a hard expression on his angel face. He'd have to deal with Rafe. Soon.

T   T   T

I love you. Those three words whispered with such reverence and he had slammed his rejection home with the force of a jackhammer. He lay on his bed, focusing all his strength on not crawling back to her on his knees to beg her forgiveness. What he'd done had been for her own good. Montgomery didn't know how close she'd come to the monster that lurked under his skin. How close he'd come to sacrificing her to his unholy appetites. She would never know if he had his way. If he had to run to keep her safe, then so be it.

"It's not always that easy," Gabriel spoke then, his rugged features as hard as stone.

"Don't you ever knock?" Rafe demanded, not even glancing to where the highlander leaned against the dresser. "What the hell do you want anyway?" He came to his feet in a rush.

"What happened last night?" Gabriel was determined to get to the bottom of it this time.

"I ended the game."

"Explain it to me."

"She decided it was over between us. Then she told me she no longer needed me and I lost my temper and showed her how wrong she was. I thought I had mastered this hunger. I was wrong."

"Did you..." Gabriel couldn't bring himself to finish.

"Did I what? Did I take her like an animal? Did I grab her hair and bare her throat to my hunger? Did I rip into that beautiful skin with my teeth? Did I glory in the rush of her blood as she trembled in my arms? Is that what you want to know? Yes I did! I did all of that and more." His laughter was harsh as he slammed his fist against the wall. "She told me she loved me, Gabriel." Rafe turned his head away, hiding from the scrutiny of those ageless green eyes.

"Do you love her?" Gabriel repeated the question put to him the night before.

"He doesn't know what love is," Michael taunted from the doorway.

The fire that burned in the fair one's eyes slowed Rafe for only a second. "I think you should go," Rafe responded with cold menace.

"I don't think I will." Michael took a step in, closing the door behind him.

"What do you want, Michael?" Gabriel asked.

"Montgomery just gave notice on her contract. She'll be

leaving at the end of the month."

"It's for the best." Rafe spoke to no one in particular. "I'll survive this much better if she's not here to tempt fate. Maybe in time she'll find someone else, someone who can love her as she deserves." The mere thought of her in another man's arms had him clenching his fists.

"I wouldn't concern yourself on that count. She's already received an offer of an understanding shoulder to cry on." Michael's smile was a thing of cruel beauty.

"You didn't?" Rafe rasped out in disbelief.

"Didn't what?" Michael's smugness was tangible.

"You son of a bitch." Rafe growled even as Gabriel grabbed for his arm. "I saw you with her in her office the other day. I saw you touch her." The anger over that kiss was something he could no longer hold in.

"Let him go, Arden. Let the bastard reap what he's sowed."

Michael issued the challenge with a cold fury that raised the highlander's hackles. "It's not that easy, Michael," Gabriel countered, trying to calm the men he considered brothers.

"Sure it is." Rafe pulled free from Gabriel's hold. "I told you to keep your hands off of her." He advanced on the fair immortal.

"You set this up yourself, Rafe. You gave her to me, then walked away hoping I'd screw her so you could hate me more than you wanted her. Didn't work out though, did it? I didn't screw her but you still want to hate me so it'll all be simple for you. Why shouldn't I help you out?" Michael ducked under the first swing. The second, a swift uppercut to the jaw, staggered him back a step. "If you can't trust me, why shouldn't I take her away from you?" He launched his body high in the air, catching Rafe around the waist as he tackled him to the ground.

Sometime later, Gabriel could only shake his head in amazement as he watched the two, sitting on the floor, too tired to move and in too much pain to do more than lean their backs against the wall. "Are you finished?" he asked, disgusted with the both of them.

"Not yet." Michael's statement coincided with a straight-armed right that rattled Rafe's teeth. "Now I'm finished," he conceded as he watched Rafe flex his bruised chin.

"I'm letting you live out of the goodness of my heart," Rafe gritted out through clenched teeth.

"What do you know of hearts or goodness or trust?" Michael demanded as he tried to gain his feet.

"Want to go again?" Rafe challenged as he lurched up on unsteady legs.

"Sit down!" Gabriel roared the words, growing tired with their juvenile antics. "I've had enough!"

They sank back against the wall, each refusing to look at the other.

"What are you going to do until she leaves?" Gabriel demanded into the strained silence.

"I'm leaving. When she's gone, I'll make my way back here. In a year or two maybe," Rafe answered, resting his head against the wall, his eyes closed against the future.

"You're afraid of what you'll do to her? From the marks on her throat this morning, I'll assume that fear didn't stop you last night! Why stop now? Hell, why not take everything she has. Isn't that what you're dying to do?" Michael demanded.

"What the hell do you care, Michael? You don't love her. You'll never love a woman. You're too busy screwing anything in a skirt to let yourself care about a woman's heart." Rafe accused him as his eyes met the chilling anger in those pale blue orbs.

"No, I don't love her. I'll never love her, but I can't walk away from her either. I need to protect her, I need to know that she's safe, that's she's happy. I don't know why." He didn't understand himself the need forcing him into the foreign role of protector.

"Have a nesting instinct, do you, lover boy?" Rafe taunted.

"Maybe it's time I made amends for the past."

"Stay away from her, Michael. Don't make me do something I won't be able to live with."

The silver eyes that opened to meet his were filled with such torment that Michael didn't say another word.

ϯ   ϯ   ϯ

Katherine paced back and forth, black hair writhing, ebony eyes flashing. The air seethed with the force of her rage.

Jamison lounged on the bed; his big body relaxed despite the venomous daggers Katherine shot his way. His soulless eyes never left her as she stalked the room.

His open amusement only served to loosen the leash she kept on her explosive temper when she was in the company of her inhuman sire. "Do you think this is funny?" She spoke with less care than normal. "All my planning ruined!" Katherine's voice rose, the exotic purr disappearing under the harshness as she continued. "He's leaving! Fahlan feels nothing for the woman. Nothing!"

Jamison's smile faded as she ranted on.

She ignored the silencing hand he held up. "This is all your fault! I should have never believed you! What are you compared to sorceress such as I..."

The words choked off as he wrapped a brutal hand around her slender throat. With a small smile, he lifted her with one arm until her feet dangled high above the ground. "Don't test me, Katherine," he commanded in a soft whisper. "I drained you once, don't tempt me to do it again."

The complete lack of emotion in his dead eyes frightened her to the depths of her fractured soul. He tightened his big fingers further until she couldn't breathe.

"Do you understand me, my pet?" He shook her like a cat toying with a mouse. "Do you?" he asked again.

"Yes." She gasped, struggling to draw air past the death grip he held her in.

"Good," he replied as he released his hold.

She crashed to the floor at his feet, choking as she held her throat with trembling hands.

"Your dark angel will come back to his lady love. He won't be able to stop himself," Jamison explained as he returned to the bed. Stretching out again, he continued. "When he returns, we will be waiting for him. Soon he will give his heart into her mortal keeping and when he does, we'll cut it out. Bit by bloody bit." He closed his eyes, through with her for now.

Katherine lay there, fingers rubbing the vivid smudges that stained her throat as her dark gaze rested upon her sire with murderous intent.

᛭   ᛭   ᛭

Morrigan St. John appeared as if by magic that Saturday morning. No one else knew about the imminent arrival of Montgomery's long time friend but Michael. She had told him that she was expecting company. Being warned didn't necessarily lead to being prepared.

Nothing could have prepared him for the sight of the dark blue Prowler that purred up to the curb. Or the strange, bright eyes that were such an odd shade they appeared purple at first glance. Those eyes that gazed at him with curiosity from behind Lennonish sunglasses. He sure as hell wasn't ready for the platinum-haired fem who slid from behind the wheel.

He only had to stare at her for a second before he decided he hated tiny blondes with big pansy eyes. Only a second longer before he decided he should run the other way. Fast.

"What's his problem?" Morrigan asked her best friend in her soft whispery voice as they watched him stalk back into the club, his mumbled goodbye only half understood as the door slammed behind him.

"With Michael, you can never tell," Gomery replied, a puzzled frown on her face. She looked back at her friend, her throaty laughter filling the air. "I don't know how you do it."

"Do what?" Morrigan tilted her head so she could stare up the ten inches that separated their heights, her long hair cascading past her waist.

"How you always look like you just walked off a California beach. How you always manage to have that sleepy-just-rolled-out-of-bed-but-still look-like-a-playboy-bunny thing going. It's not fair. If I didn't love you so much, I'd strangle you." Gomery hugged her instead. "I missed you."

"I'll stay as long as I'm able," Morrigan promised, her silky little voice cracking.

Montgomery looked past her to the police officer approaching the illegally parked car. "Now you're in for it," she taunted Morrigan as he flipped open the ticket book in his hand.

The blonde slanted her a tiny smile. "Watch," she mouthed the word. Her eyes traveled to where he stood, writing up what would no doubt be a very expensive parking ticket. "I'm sorry, officer. Shouldn't I park my car here?"

Her breathy Dixieland drawl caught his attention. He looked up from his pad, startled eyes crawling up the curvy pleasure ride that was her petite body, stopping when he got to those wide, innocent, deep purple eyes.

He dropped the pad.

"Let me get that for you, honey." Morrigan bent from the waist, her low-cut blouse giving him the perfect view of her tanned cleavage. "There ya go." Morrigan handed him the pad with a syrupy smile.

He closed the book absently as she leaned against the hood of her car. He missed nothing of the tanned legs set off to perfection by her faded denim cutoffs. His dazed eyes wandered down to the Celtic braid that circled her ankle. He missed nothing of the black tattoo or the flirty sandals that allowed hot pink toenails to peep out. "We don't normally allow cars in a tow away zone, miss."

"Morrigan," she corrected with that cutesy smile again. "I'll only be another minute. But if you think I deserve that ticket, you go ahead and finish while I find a place to park this beast." She stuck her hand into a front pocket fishing for the keys. The movement pulled at the loose waistband of her cutoffs.

He gaped at the smooth expanse of flat stomach and tanned navel exposed by the combination of a short shirt and low-riding shorts.

Montgomery had to bite her lip to keep from laughing. Finally giving up, she turned and walked back inside. Sitting in a chair, she laughed until her sides hurt. God, she had missed her!

"You just set the women's movement back fifty years," she charged as Morrigan followed her in a few minutes later.

"I know," she answered, all breezy confidence. "But, since I didn't get the ticket, I can't bring myself to care." She sank down onto a stool, twisting her toned legs into a relaxed knot.

"You moved that blue monstrosity fast enough." Montgomery smiled, softening the tired lines around her hazel eyes.

"I didn't move it. George is gonna keep an eye on it for me. He's gonna make sure no one tries to tow it away." Her purple eyes were wicked.

"George?" Gomery couldn't stop the laughter that spilled out.

ү   ү   ү

Sarah pulled the sheet closer to her and with a guilty glance around the bedroom, tiptoed to Gabriel's closet. She felt more than a little sinful for having slept the clock round after her shower, but she wouldn't think about that now. What she did need, was something to wear. At this point anything that covered her bare backside would do. Digging through the hangers, she grabbed the first thing that looked like it would work.

Dropping the chocolate brown linen, she slid the navy button down on. The tails hung to her knees and the sleeves required several rolls before she could find her fingers, but she had never relished the feel of something against her skin as she did this. Pulling the collar up to her nose, she breathed deep. The smell of him lingered on the cotton. It wasn't cologne or after shave that marked the shirt as his, but the subtle masculine scent of soap and shampoo. The same things she herself had used in his shower.

Using his hairbrush, she worked the tangles from her hair. Checking the buttons one last time, she smoothed down the shirt. Hoping the tails wouldn't flip when she walked, Sarah went in search of her protector. She did all of this without ever once looking in the mirror. Experience had taught her that a few hairs out of place weren't worth the agony of her reflection.

Keeping her sore hand close to her chest, she crept down the stairs to the lounge, her eyes shifting left and right as she searched for Gabriel. Walking through the doorway, she was surprised to see two people already seated at a table. The woman with the dark hair looked up first.

ᛁ   ᛁ   ᛁ

"I'll kill the son of a bitch," Montgomery murmured low as her eyes took in Sarah's marred appearance.

Morrigan was puzzled until her own gaze landed on the battered woman. "Can I help?" she whispered back, knowing the abused girl wouldn't hear.

Montgomery rose to her feet and extended a hand. "Good morning, Sarah. I'm Montgomery Sinclair. Gabriel asked me to look after you this morning until he gets back." Her greeting was warm, but her hazel eyes missed nothing.

"You don't have to," Sarah protested, her cheeks flaming with embarrassment.

"I seldom do things I don't want to," Montgomery assured her. "This is a friend of mine, Morrigan St. John. She'll be staying with me for a week or so."

Sarah tentatively held out her good hand to the smaller woman. She had heard about Montgomery from Gabriel, but this blonde woman was unknown. And unknown scared her a little.

Morrigan took her hand, but she didn't shake it. She just

held it for a minute. Sarah's surprised eyes flew to that steady amethyst gaze. "How?" Morrigan wasn't known for her tact and the one word was question enough.

Sarah didn't bother to lie; she'd had enough of that. "My husband likes to hit."

"Do you want us to take you to a doctor?" Montgomery asked, concerned.

"No, thank you. I'll be okay. I just need some time and a little rest." Sarah was embarrassed having this conversation, but she couldn't seem to turn away from those steady purple eyes.

"This has happened before." Morrigan stated it as fact. Her gaze never wavering under the force of Sarah's discomfort.

"Yes it has, but it's been worse." Sarah's voice cracked and she wrapped trembling arms around her stomach.

"Why?" Morrigan didn't relent. Even Montgomery's sharp elbow failed to deter her.

"He has a bad temper."

Morrigan interrupted her with a shake of her head. "Not why does he hit you; why do you let him?"

"That's enough of that." Montgomery pulled the other woman to the table. "Sit," she ordered as she walked to the counter and poured Sarah a cup of coffee.

Sarah was thankful for the rescue, but after long moments, the awkward silence was more than she could tolerate. She looked from one to the other, then she settled her next question on Montgomery. That one didn't make her as nervous. "Where is Gabriel?"

"He had to go to the station. There was a problem with some paperwork, I think. He said he might be gone awhile. We're going out to lunch in a little bit. Would you come out with us?" Montgomery smiled at her, nodding her encouragement.

Sarah looked at the blonde, her expression unsure.

"Don't worry about me," Morrigan chided her. "I don't bite." Her smile was just as adorable now as it had been an hour ago when she had turned it on the poor unsuspecting George.

Sarah laughed then, more than a little sure that she could come to like this tiny five foot, two inch platinum blonde with the unnerving purple eyes. "I would love to." She was anxious to get on with the day. The first was always the hardest when the bruises were the darkest and the aches still strong. She rose from the table, needing to change clothes, when another thought hit her.

Montgomery saw the emotions that crossed her face and asked after them.

"I don't have any clothes with me." Sarah's face burned with embarrassment. "I need to go home. All my things are there." She wasn't sure how she had come to be here with nothing to wear but she really hadn't cared at the time. Now she wasn't so sure.

"That won't do." Montgomery shook her head. "You can use my things." She shot Morrigan an evil glance as the other woman laughed out. "What's so funny?"

"My mistake," Morrigan replied with barely restrained amusement as she looked her friend over with an arched brow. "You're not built like most of the women in the world."

While Morrigan and Sarah both had petite figures, they didn't possess the brunette's long legs and enviable curves. "You can use mine," she offered with a sincere smile. "You're a little taller than me but that shouldn't matter. I have a couple T-shirts you can choose from. The amber should be a good color," she said, her gaze taking in the sherry eyes and sunburst hair.

They went to Montgomery's rooms together, the three of them laughing as they dug through Morrigan's luggage. The size five cutoffs fit Sarah with little problem but the tailored shirt presented a difficulty that brought another round of laughter, this time at the small blonde's expense.

"What was that you said about not being built the same?" Montgomery challenged as Sarah held the loose bodice of the amber blouse away from her smaller endowed chest.

Morrigan didn't even blush as she pulled out a more neutral sweatshirt in a vivid blue and tossed it to her. "Then we go shopping." She couldn't help but see the panic that crossed Sarah's expressive face.

"I don't have any money," she mumbled, again reminded of her precarious position.

"But I do."

T   T   T

When Gabriel came back and found Sarah gone, he went in search of the only person in the club. He found Michael in his office, sitting in his chair, staring at nothing.

"Where's Sarah?" His concern for her foremost in his thoughts.

"Out with Gomery." Michael looked at the highlander, a sneer twisting his lips. "And her *friend*." He spat the word. "Morrigan St. John." He supplied the name before Gabriel could ask.

"*The* Morrigan St. John? From St. John Securities?"

"The only one I know." Michael's reply was sullen at best.

"If you thought Gomery's credentials were great, you should see the file on this guy. Even if only half of it is true St. John is unreal." Gabriel let out a soft whistle.

"You can say that again," Michael mumbled under his breath.

"Is he staying here?" Gabriel was eager to speak with him.

"It's a she, and yes *she* is."

"A she? You're sure?"

"Kind of hard to miss," the fair one snapped out, catching Gabriel's puzzled frown. "Just wait until you see her."

"What is it about Morrigan St. John that has you all in a tizzy?" Gabriel asked.

The change in subject caught Michael off guard. "Her body. Her face. Her hair," he blurted out with none of his usual finesse.

The highlander laughed at him.

"God hates me. That is the only answer for this." Leaning forward, Michael rested his head in his hands. "You won't think this is so funny when you see her. Just you wait."

"What does Gomery think of your little problem?" Gabriel asked. He smiled when he heard Michael's muffled groan.

"I don't think walking up to Gomery and telling her that I want to throw her best friend on the ground and jump her bones would go over very well. I'm just going to avoid her. I won't go near her, mark my words."

Michael's voice was strong and Gabriel was proud of his determination. Walking out the door, he chose to ignore the mumbled words his friend spoke as he buried his head back in his arms.

"Please don't let me get near her. Please."

CHAPTER 13

Sasha hadn't been surprised to see Raphael lounging on her couch when she'd come home last night. But she *was* surprised at the torment etched into his bronzed features. She hadn't asked him any questions then, had in fact just showed him to a guest room and left him to sort out his mind.

Breakfast the next morning had brought no conversation above simple small talk and by evening she was frustrated by his preoccupation. Over dinner and a bottle of wine, she verbally dove into him with claws sharpened and bared.

"Why are you here?"

She startled him with her bluntness but he recovered well. "I ran away from home." There was no humor in the twist of his lips that resembled a smile. "I have a problem with…" He wasn't able to find the words.

"With your hunger," she finished for him.

He nodded, guilt flashing across his face. "I lost control." Sasha was in awe of the raw pain that filled his cold gray eyes. "I hurt her."

"Is she okay now?" she asked, her hand gentle on his.

"Gabriel healed her." He rose from the table and paced the room.

"There is that weakness in each of us. Even I had that urge once," she confided, walking up behind him.

"What did you do?" He was curious to know how she dealt with her hunger.

"I brought Gabriel over," she replied, the dimple in her cheek flashing.

He didn't like her answer at all. "I'll just stay away until she leaves."

Sasha was surprised at that bit of news. She hadn't pictured

Montgomery as one to run and she said as much.

"I was very unkind when I saw her after. I said things that ensured she wouldn't ever come near me again." His confession was hollow.

"How bad could..." She protested until she saw the coldness in his eyes. For a moment, she'd forgotten how savage his tongue could be. "Now that you have tasted her and quenched your thirst, you should be able to go on with her if you want. It was that way for me with Gabriel." The lie caught in her throat but she wanted so much for Rafe to be at peace.

"I don't think that it's the same in my situation." Rafe was thoughtful. "You had never seen Gabriel before that night. He was dying at your feet and you did what you felt you had to do. I've held her in my arms for weeks and fought this urge with everything I had. I controlled it until there was nothing left. This wasn't the saving of a soul, Sasha, but the taking of life. It wasn't a single moment of insanity. I took her again and again until her blood rushed down my throat. Until the taste of her filled my every thought. If she hadn't called out my name, I'd be burying her now. If that ever happened, you would have to bury me."

Sasha closed her eyes against the vivid picture his words produced in her mind. As much as she loved Gabriel, Rafe had always been her favorite. For all of his cold and cynical humor he had always been there when she had needed him. Had always provided a shoulder when she had *felt* too much.

"Everyone has a weak moment, Rafe. You can't let that shape your life. This is the first time it's happened to you so the feeling is new and scary but you stopped yourself. The remorse you're feeling is a good thing. This way you can make sure it never happens again."

Seeing the disbelief on his face, she chose to share something with him she had planned to keep to herself. "I think your mistake was in running. She is a part of you. Your soul picked her, as much as mine picked Gabriel. You've seen what good it's done me to avoid him. He fills my every thought. My every dream. He's my heart. To each of us, there comes a person who is our other half. It took six hundred years to find mine. Two centuries of his scorn hasn't changed that feeling. Some people are lucky in that they can love at will, some of us can't. I hate to say it, sweeting, but welcome to my world."

"No," Rafe denied, but no urgency marked his words, just a cold certainty.

"If it's true, there is no fighting it. This obsession will fill you. As long as she walks this earth, it will haunt you. You won't be able to hide. I know, I've tried."

He wiped away the single tear that rolled down her smooth cheek.

"That your actions upset you is a good sign."

His expression showed his confusion.

"Taking her blood filled you with revulsion. That's good. Most likely it won't happen again." She watched in surprise as those silver eyes froze and his face hardened. She blinked at the darkly wicked smile that curved those sensuous lips.

"You have it all wrong, Sasha. Her blood didn't repulse me. That thought didn't even cross my mind. What did cross my mind was the fact that I liked it so much, I want to do it again."

ⲧ   ⲧ   ⲧ

Sarah sat in the middle of the bed, her eyes taking in all the new clothes Morrigan and Gomery had helped her pick out. Those two cracked her up. A more unlikely pair of friends she didn't think existed. The tall brunette was the more serious of the two but she had a quick wit that kept her from being daunting. While the blonde was such a free spirit it was hard to keep a straight face in her company. She owed them a lot, they had helped her today by keeping her spirits up and she would always be grateful for their companionship.

As she sat there reflecting on the day, she pulled the tags from her clothes with restless fingers. When she finished, she stacked them in neat piles. She's never had this many new things at one time before. Never bought so many beautiful things in her whole life. If it killed her, she would save the money and somehow pay Morrigan back. She had told her she would, but the blonde had shrugged her off with some cryptic response about her having a million reasons why that wouldn't be necessary. Regardless, she would give her back every cent. Even if mental tally of the sales tickets managed to rob some of the color from her face.

Rising from the bed, she folded her new garments into the carryall Montgomery had picked out for her. She was hesitant to put the bag in Gabriel's closet, not wanting to take too much upon herself. After all, she was just a visitor. An unwanted one at that. Opening the door, she slid her bag into the far corner, wanting to hide it from his sight.

The bag didn't slide very far across the carpet before it bumped and knocked over something with a muffled thump.

Sarah wallowed in guilt as she reached past the bag to the wooden frame lying on the closet floor. What right did she have to paw through Gabriel's things? What if it was broken due to her clumsiness? Would he be angry? Would he hurt her?

"Of course not." Sarah shook off her fear. Gabriel was her hero. He would never hurt her.

The frame wasn't all that heavy and it only took a tiny effort to ease it out into the light. The glossy wooden frame held a painting. An oil painting of a woman in a long white gown; her long sun-kissed hair curling down past her hips as she knelt beside a fallen warrior. The lady held his face turned toward her as she caressed his hair with loving hands.

Oh, God! This woman looked like her. Not identical, but close enough.

Sarah reached back into the closet and pulled out another frame. This one was an actual photograph. She reached in again and pulled out another and another and another, until the floor around her was covered with pictures and paintings of this woman whom she resembled. She picked up another, this one worn around the edges from repeated handling.

Sad brown eyes wandered over the picture and Sarah felt a stab of envy at the long vivid curls, the princess perfect face captured forever young in peaceful repose. A lover had taken this picture. Only a lover would have memorialized on film every inch, every curve of his woman covered with nothing but the rosy blush of slumber.

This was why he'd never hurt her. This was the reason Gabriel had rescued her from Seth. He must have loved this woman very much.

Despair over the truth crushed her as she slid the assorted paintings and pictures back into the darkness with all the others, where no one else could see them. Never would she hold his heart, share his love. She was nothing more than a weak imitation, a pale shadow of the woman in those paintings.

She needed to go. There was no place for her here. The decision was easy to reach as she walked back to the bed, taking her packed bag with her. No longer could she delude herself with thoughts of a future with the man she loved. When Gabriel looked at her, her saw instead the mystery woman who owned his heart.

If she went to her sister, things would be better, at least until Seth found her. And he would find her. He had before and it hadn't been a pleasant experience. Memories of his retaliation over her defection still made her quake. She hadn't lied to Morrigan when she'd said he'd done worse to her in the past.

Some of his past beatings could make this last one like a cakewalk. So had been the case a few years ago when he'd found out about her pregnancy. What had followed that little bit of news had been a beating so excessive that she'd almost hemorrhaged to death on the kitchen floor. A beating brought on by no greater reason than the fact that he hadn't given her permission to conceive. The mistake was one she'd never made again.

She had learned the hard way and repeatedly not to expect anything from life. But this time she wanted something. More than anything, she wanted free of Seth and Gabriel could give her that.

ᛏ   ᛏ   ᛏ

Morrigan and Montgomery walked the night, both unable to sleep. Even at this hour the French Quarter was bursting with activity. Passing building after building, they spoke in low murmurs.

"Who's Raphael Fahlan?" Morrigan lobbed her first question. "I heard pretty boy talking about him with Gabriel. I also heard him mention you. Anything you want to share?" She watched the emotions that played across her friend's face but she couldn't bring herself to believe them.

"Rafe is Michael's partner. They own the club among other things. He left right before you showed up." Montgomery wouldn't meet her eyes. The continued silence unnerved her, but she was afraid to look up. She didn't want Morrigan to see her pain. If anyone could read her emotions, it was the tiny woman at her side.

Morrigan just waited. She didn't need to say anything else. Instead, she would do what she did best and give Gomery just enough rope to hang herself. The tall Texan could never keep anything from her. Not from the first time they had met in the school dorm, when a group of the in-crowd had decided that the new girl would make a great target for their barbs. Not when Morrigan, the most popular student at the all girl academy had deflected those barbs with a few taunts of her own. Taunts sharp enough that several of the little prima donnas had run to their rooms in tears.

Montgomery could keep nothing from her. They'd gotten kicked out of school together. Twice. They'd gotten their ears pierced and their tattoos together. Had climbed out windows, *borrowed* beer and cigarettes to party behind the head mistress' quarters with a group of boys from the military academy. She'd held Montgomery and wiped her tears after that army brat took her virginity and told everybody who would listen. She was the one that put the tampons in his gas tank. There was nothing Montgomery could keep from her.

"You would like him. He has your sharp wit." Montgomery spoke to fill the silence. She hated when Morrigan did this to her. "He doesn't look anything like Michael. He's all brooding dark intensity. He's just as stunning as Michael, but he doesn't have that careless charm. Rafe has more of a commanding air about him." She closed her mouth then. Morrigan always got her to spill her guts like this by doing nothing more than throwing out a loaded question and leaving it to fall where it may.

"Was he good?" Morrigan dropped another and was amused by the flush that spread across Gomery's high cheek bones.

"He was incredible," Montgomery confided, rolling her hazel eyes in exasperation as she gave up. "All he had to do was touch me and I'd go up in flames. When we made love, he would look at me with those silvery eyes and I'd want to die. He's so beautiful, Morrigan, just like a dark angel from a fantasy. There's a lot a woman would give up for that man. There's a lot I would have given up for him." Gomery raised her head then and let Morrigan see her pain.

Morrigan wasn't pleased. "Where did he go?" she asked. She had gone past petty vandalism long ago. With experience had come bigger and better forms of revenge.

"He's cold, Morrigan, unlike anyone we have ever met. I thought I could change that. I thought the heat we shared could melt him. The ice in his eyes when we weren't in my bed made me feel like a whore. I felt like my mother."

"Sweetie, your mama was a whore." Morrigan didn't mince words. "She slept with your daddy so she would get pregnant and he'd marry her. Your daddy was a sorry piece of trash, too. How he couldn't realize that you were worth a thousand of your mother is beyond me. I think you need to tell me what happened with your Rafe, and not just the pretty parts," Morrigan ordered as her purple eyes searched for something in the night.

The telling of the story took awhile and with the end in sight, Morrigan couldn't contain her surprise. Gomery had never told a man she loved him, and for Raphael Fahlan to throw that away was a mistake Morrigan wouldn't let him live down. Big, dark, fallen angels didn't scare her.

"How is Adam?" Montgomery asked after Morrigan's older brother in an attempt to change the subject. The ploy didn't fool Morrigan but she allowed her friend to distract her.

"He married Jillian last spring. He still goes out in the field from time to time but he's trying to stay out of it now that he has her to worry about. Accidents seem to be the order if you own too many St. John shares." Her smile was cryptic.

"What is your dear uncle up to these days?" Montgomery drawled out, her eyes alight with malice.

"Running for cover. When you and Adam sold me your shares, that put me over the top. I keep him on his toes." Morrigan spoke of the stock her brother had sold her before his wedding. He hadn't been pleased with the idea but a long skid on a short road had convinced him it was no longer safe to hold even the ten-percent he had received from their father when he came of age.

"Malcolm has lost twenty-three security contracts in the last nine months. People have little tolerance when the unbreakable is broken. He's nervous and that's making him desperate, careless. It's really a shame, St. John's did so much better before my father died and we left. It seems to be doomed to fail now. He's pulling assets and if Adam didn't own the commercial sec, I think Malcolm would have sold it out from under him long ago," Morrigan explained.

"Did they find anything out about that night in Boston?" Montgomery was very quiet when she asked about the death of Morrigan's father.

"No more than in Paris. Anyone who had a thought about Boston quickly developed amnesia. You and I are the only ones who still live with the doubts. Not even Adam knows. To him it was all a tragic accident. Paris was a little clearer cut. You survived." Morrigan looked away before the guilt she felt showed in her eyes.

The pain she hadn't been able to save Montgomery from that night still haunted her dreams but she'd learned a powerful lesson from the whole bloody mess. Never trust, never forget. The simple motto served her well. "Uncle Malcolm's time is coming. Soon his stolen company will lie in ruin at his feet. Sooner than even he knows."

"Could he still come out of this unscathed?" Montgomery clenched her teeth against the thought of Malcolm St. John gaining anything from his perfidy.

"He's liquidated everything and sunk his own assets into this latest system. It's still in final testing but he's jumped the gun and installed several already. If the system works, he'll float another two months before going belly-up. That would allow him to pull enough out of the company to live comfortably for the rest of his miserable life. Failure now means he drowns in a sea of his own deception. No life raft to save him. No rescue from on high." Morrigan smiled her pleasure at the thought.

"How many more do you need?" Montgomery slowed her pace as they came upon a house set back from the others. It was a large house, the security gates tall, strong and impenetrable.

"Just three more and this will all be over."

T   T   T

Michael kicked his feet up on the desk in his office. He'd been hiding in here for the better part of the day and the cowardice of the act didn't bother him nearly as much as the rottenness of his luck of late.

There is no way he deserved to have his resolve tested with a woman like that. Sure, his past sins didn't garner him a lot of mercy from the powers that be, but this went beyond cruel and unusual punishment. Not to mention it just wasn't fair.

Stunning.

That was the only word he could think of to describe Morrigan St. John.

A stunning pain in the ass. A pain he didn't need. He wasn't in the market for a platinum blonde with endless legs and big pansy eyes.

What he needed was an undemanding woman who could soothe the scars of his past. Someone with a good heart and a trusting soul. Someone he could tell his secrets to. All of them. Even the scary ones. He doubted if such a woman even existed, but it sure as hell wasn't this one.

Morrigan St. John wore her defiance like a badge of courage. Her recklessness like a shield. She was all long hair, fierce eyes and silken limbs, not what he needed in his life. He needed peace, contentment, and acceptance.

"Have you seen Montgomery?"

Her whispery little voice beckoned him against his will. Looking up, his eyes adhered to the petite blonde who leaned in the doorframe. Michael missed nothing of the faded bib overall shorts that molded the curves of her body or the lavender tank top that clung to every hill and valley. He had managed to avoid her for most of the day, but now it seemed his luck had run out.

Morrigan watched him look her over, from the top of her wild, curly ponytail to the brown shoelaces that knotted her hiking boots. As his eyes wandered back up, she waited. When his gaze finally met hers, she smiled. Not the insincere one she had graced the cop with, but one guaranteed to melt solid steel if she wanted it to. In that moment, she made up her mind. She wanted it to.

Michael saw that smile and took a much-needed breath of air. In that moment, he knew to the depths of his scarred soul, that he was doomed. For the first time in centuries, he actually wanted a woman, not just the release he knew he would find in her arms, her body. But the woman herself.

"Interviewing another bouncer," he answered her question just to prove he was still capable of speech. "She'll be done soon if you want to wait in the lounge." His words lacked all subtlety, but she refused to take the hint. Instead, she settled on the edge of his desk. *Inhale* he reminded himself as she crossed one long leg over the other.

He gazed at those legs, watching the lean muscles ripple under that honey-hued skin. They weren't soft and curvy in a classic feminine way, but they weren't hard and bulging either. There was nothing masculine or butchy about those finely honed legs. Michael shifted in the chair as his mind took a whole other track. They were perfect for wrapping around a man's waist and holding him where she needed him until she'd taken all she wanted. They were prefect for holding wide as he … *Exhale.*

"Was there something you wanted?" he demanded as she just sat there and stared at him.

"No," she answered and smiled again. Her head tilted to the side as she continued to watch him.

In turn, he watched those white curls as they brushed against her thigh. Over and over and over they swayed, the difference between fair hair and golden skin an erotic contrast. *Inhale* he reminded himself again.

"Don't you have some place you should be?" His mood darkened as she continued to stare at him.

"No," was her one word reply. Her purple gaze never stopped its perusal of his features; it missed nothing of the high cheekbones, straight nose, strong jaw and chin. Only a blind fool would have missed the beauty of his pale eyes. He rivaled Mel Gibson with the blue of that clear gaze. She wasn't a fool and he *was* beautiful. Men weren't referred to in such terms, but handsome didn't do justice to the fairness of his features. Morrigan smiled again, this wouldn't be such a difficult job after all. She might even enjoy it. All she needed to do was push him. Just a little.

"What are you staring at?" he snapped, his patience at an end.

"You."

"Do I have a smudge?" His control returned with a sarcastic lift of his brow.

"You would never let that happen," she assured him with a certain little smile.

That smile erased his cool again. "You think you have me all figured out, don't you? In the few minutes you've spent in my company, you think you know everything about me." He bristled at her condescending smirk. Boy, did he have a *few* things she would never guess about his nature! A few things that would send her running back to the security of her safe little world.

Michael smiled a little smile of his own. She might have figured out a few things but he would always have the last laugh because she would never guess what he kept hidden behind his polished façade. "How did you gather all this useless information?" His tone of voice reflected his boredom with the whole conversation.

Morrigan didn't answer his question. "You aren't at all what I imagined." She waited to see what his reaction would be.

"What makes you think I'm not?" He was curious to hear her opinion. He settled back in his chair, certain it would be entertaining if nothing else.

"I watched you last night as you worked the crowd. I saw the clothes and the practiced smile, heard that cute little drawl I'm willing to bet you can turn on and off at will. There were the women watching you as you moved on the dance floor but you didn't notice that, did you? I think the clothes, the hair and the show, are all for you to hide behind. You want them to think you'll have an attitude so they'll keep their distance."

Michael didn't respond, but waited for her to continue.

"A woman would chance her luck just to see if you're as good as you look. Just to see if you can move your body as well in bed as you do on the floor. To see what all the fuss is about. You may ignore the rumors that fly the minute you step out into the crowd, but they are fascinating. Some even go so far as to wonder why you don't have the required society dress up doll clinging to your arm. Why don't you?" she asked to appease her own curiosity. Morrigan didn't understand why he chose to remain apart from the crowd. He might walk among the patrons of his club, but he wasn't *there*.

"Are you applying for the job?" he asked, letting his eyes slide over her body with a heat that left no doubt to which *job* he meant.

"I've never been able to do the adoring trophy thing. It's not my style."

She smiled at him, a wicked little smile that had him asking despite himself "What style would that be, *cher?*" he drawled out the words, his pale blue eyes alight with mischief.

"Maybe I'll show you sometime." She leaned forward, her lips mere inches from his.

All at once he got a hold of himself and drew back, his body temperature dropping several degrees as he realized what he had almost done. This was not a good thing. "Sorry, Morrigan. You're not my type." His smile was anything but sincere.

The look in her eyes should have warned him. The little curve of her lips should have had him diving for cover. The way she tilted her head as she gave him a long considering look should have been a dead give away. Had he known anything about her, he would have realized that look didn't bode well. He didn't know her, so he wasn't prepared for the next words she drawled out in that little southern whisper that was hers alone.

"That's all right, Michael, you're not mine either. I don't think you're any woman's type." Her eyes speculative, she gazed across the desk at him. "You're so busy being what everyone expects you to be, that you don't have the time or the courage to be yourself. What do you hide under that pretty face, Michael? What's inside of you that's so terrible that you choose to hide it behind all those fake smiles, all that empty charm? What do you hide behind those empty blue eyes?"

Michael sat there long after she had left, his mind in absolute turmoil as he turned over every word that had spilled from those pink lips. Never had a woman seen through his act so clearly. She didn't fall for the jaded camouflage he put on for the world. She looked deeper, and that scared him. He could never let anyone see what lurked inside, of the things he had done for his own pleasure. No one could ever know. He wouldn't let them.

ᴛ   ᴛ   ᴛ

Sasha let her restless fingers move over the keys of the century old piano as her mind focused on the thoughts plaguing her mind. She'd *dreamed* last night of things that would come to pass. Two visions had haunted her sleep. Both saddened her. The first for what it would mean to her friend, the man who had taught her to pour her heart out through the piano. A man whom she had come to love in many ways. She didn't know how Rafe would take her vision or if there was any way he could change the outcome.

The second was something she would have to deal with on her own. That vision was what had her sitting here, wanting nothing more than too never feel again. It was what finally made her give up hope that she had a chance of redeeming herself in Gabriel's eyes. Now she knew, he may want her but he would never forgive her.

"Bleak thoughts?" Rafe asked as he sat beside her on the bench.

"Bad dreams," she replied, her fingers stopping on the keys.

Rafe waited for her to continue. He knew the power of her dreams and what they meant.

"How do you fair so far from Heaven's Gate?" she asked, her fingers again moving on the keys.

He recognized the melody in a second and with a skill taught by the masters, he joined her, their beautiful music flowing into the room. "When she's gone, I'll go back," he answered when the music ended.

"It's not that easy," Sasha countered, looking at him with

something that might have been regret. "She is your heart, your soul. She will be with you no matter where she is and fill your mind until there is nothing left. Until she no longer walks this earth, she will be your obsession. There is nothing you can do. Nowhere you can hide. If she leaves now, you will search for her until you find her again."

"That won't happen. I won't allow it to," he denied as he turned from her.

Sasha followed him as he stalked through the house. Time had given her much strength and she stopped him at the front door. "You will stand by her bedside and you will watch her sleep. If you have enough control, maybe you won't wake her. If not, you'll take her, if she wants you or not. You won't be able to stop yourself. You'll fill her with your body, until briefly, you slack the need, the wanting. Then, just when you think you have it under control, it will flood back fiercer than it was only seconds before."

He pulled away from her, his fury a living thing. "No!" Rafe denied, his hands clenching as he fought both his anger and his fear.

"Yes," she contradicted. "And may God help her if she isn't alone when you find her. Just the thought of her with another lover will haunt you, but to find her with one would mean the end of her and him. But more than that, it would be the end of you. I don't think you would be able to live with what you would do."

"She's leaving the club. She'll forget about me and find a man to love, to marry. They will have a long life together, with children and grandchildren. What do I have for her? I offer nothing, but the possibility that one day I'll go too far. That one day I'll end her life in a fit of lust and rage." He rested his head on her shoulder, his quiet suffering a physical thing.

Knowing that nothing else would console him, Sasha decided to reveal the other vision that had haunted her dreams the last few nights. "Gomery won't forget you, Raphael. She won't fall in love, or marry, or have children. You are all she'll have out of this life. If you don't go to her now, she'll die with nothing. She'll die alone."

He pulled away from her comforting embrace and gave her a grave smile. "In the end everyone dies alone. She's strong, Sasha. She'll survive without love, without me. Just as I'll survive without her."

His cynical response was what she had expected from this barren-hearted man. She had known that he didn't love Montgomery on an emotional level, that it was his soul that reached out to the dark-haired woman. The cold that surrounded him would never allow him to admit that he felt love for anyone. His past had taught him well.

"Her time is coming sooner than you think. My dreams are haunted by her death. The end is coming soon." She flinched back from the rage that flared within that silvery gaze.

"You're wrong. The dreams are wrong. She's not going to die until she has lived a full life. She deserves a long and full life." His voice was harsh in the gathering silence.

"She won't have it. Montgomery will die very soon and from what I've seen of my dreams, it will be an ugly death. It'll be full of pain and blood and misery." Sasha's eyes brimmed with remorse.

"I won't let it happen." He was sure he could change the outcome.

"It can't be changed. What I dream will come to pass no matter what anyone does to stop it. Your lover will die, Rafe. Her life's blood will pour from her body until all that you know of her will be gone. Until all that remains of her will vanish into nothingness. It's up to you if her last days on earth are haunted by the memories of you walking away. Or if you'll get over your fears in time to hold her in your arms before the light fades from her eyes and the life spills from her body."

Chapter 14

Michael walked into The House of Blues hours later than he had planned. Scanning the tables with restless eyes, he searched for Gabriel's distinctive presence. He still wondered how the highlander had suckered him into joining him and the three women when everything inside warned him to avoid contact at all costs. Suckered or not, he was there and as he walked farther in, he noticed Gomery and Sarah seated at a table close to the dance floor. Their eyes were locked on something going on in a cleared space in the middle of the Sunday night crush. Closing the distance, he pulled up one of the two empty chairs that circled the small table.

Sarah was the first to notice him. "Hi, Michael," she piped up. The last few days had given her the courage to speak to the gorgeous man without fear of repercussions.

Michael could tell from the slight catch in her voice that she'd already had a few drinks. Narrowing his eyes to combat the haze of cigarette smoke that clouded the building, he took a good look at her and almost had a stroke. With the bruises faded to mere memories, she looked so much like Sasha that he had to take a second glance to assure himself he wasn't seeing things.

"Where's Gabriel, *cher*?" He strove for casual panic as he focused his attention on Montgomery. When she met his question with amusement shining in her eyes, he couldn't help but wonder what was so funny about the impending disaster Sarah's appearance represented.

"He wasn't back by the time we left and he was still at the station when he paged us an hour ago. I don't think he's going to come out when he finishes. There was some buzz about a robbery or something. The whole place is in an uproar."

She shifted her eyes back to the dance floor before he could ask what was so funny and he couldn't help but wonder what held both her and Sarah's attention. "What's the attraction?" he asked as the band segued into a Joe Cocker classic.

"Why don't you go find out?" Sarah giggled a little as she picked up her glass to take a healthy swallow.

"I think I will." It took a long minute and some strategic maneuvering, but he was finally able to work his way through the crush of onlookers. He was surprised that none of the couples were dancing, only standing in a circle. Staring. At her. Michael had to remind himself to breathe while he himself stared at what held the whole club so enthralled.

The woman was too dangerous to run free. She was a lethal weapon with a waist length tangle of wild, white-blonde curls.

Just to look at all the golden-brown skin left uncovered by the deep purple tank top that ended a few inches under her breasts hurt. That the matching skirt rode so low on her hips that he could see the small gold hoop that adorned her navel didn't help. Nor did it ease the ache in his chest to know that the clingy skirt only went down so far as to cover a few scant inches of firm thigh.

But it wasn't the package that held them; it was the movements of her body as she danced to the sultry tune. The way those lavender eyes flashed as she turned and dipped and swayed. There wasn't anything vulgar in the way she danced. Nothing he could hold against her. He had seen professional dancers who couldn't have moved with such grace and sensuality.

He tried to melt back into the crush before the need in his gut became too great but he had waited too long. Morrigan had already seen him and if her wicked smile was any indication, he was in for a rough ride. With a dramatic toss of her head and a saucy curve of her index finger, she beckoned him. Michael shook his head in denial; he didn't want to get anywhere near her.

Some people in the crowd recognized him from Heaven's

Gate and he heard more than one person cheer him on in the hope that he could match the moves of the woman within the circle. Everyone waited to see if he would accept her blatant invitation.

He took a step forward before he could stop himself. That single motion was all the prompting the band needed. In the next second, a heavy, erotic instrumental piece throbbed through the room. He had danced to the music before and some music just couldn't be danced from a safe distance. She smiled at him in triumph as he closed the distance and pulled her against the length of his body.

The next few minutes would be the talk of the club for weeks to come.

Alone, Morrigan had been the fantasy of every man there. Together they danced with such passion and brilliance, that they fairly exuded sex.

Their movements were smooth and sleek as if years had gone into the dance instead of seconds. Backs arched, arms clung, blond hair cloaked and flared as they pivoted and swayed. Bodies pressed, legs intertwined and hearts pounded as the two combatants seduced each other on the floor.

Michael struggled to keep a tight leash on the need that demanded he wrap those long legs around his waist and take her with a fierceness that erased any thought of another lover from her mind. Then, finally, it was over and he couldn't stop the small sigh of relief that escaped him as the last notes throbbed to a close and the crowd cheered them on.

Without giving the band a chance to play or her a chance to protest, he pulled her from the dance floor. She went with him, dragging the thick mass of her hair from her sweat dampened skin once they reached the relative safety of their table.

"Having fun?" Montgomery asked with an expressive arch of her eyebrow. She watched Michael as he struggled not to look at her friend, but even Montgomery had to admit that Morrigan was dressed to kill tonight. However, when she looked closer, she couldn't understand the emotion reflected in the bright purple of those eyes.

"I try." Morrigan turned to Michael and looked him square in the face. "Come dance with me?" she asked as the music changed to a slow, mellow number. Before he could even speak, she had her answer. "Never mind." She cut him off before he could reject her. "I'll find someone more my speed." She didn't look back when she sauntered off in the direction of the bar.

Michael caught Montgomery's eye, the question in his pale blue gaze one she didn't have an answer for. She shrugged her shoulders, her own confusion written on her face.

"Is she always so outgoing?" he asked as Morrigan and her new dance partner slipped onto the floor.

"Outgoing? Always. But I don't think I would use the word *outgoing* to describe *that*." She watched Morrigan wrap herself around the dark-haired stranger that she had propositioned away from his drink. This was way more reckless than she had ever seen her act before. Not counting work. Morrigan was so different now from the girl she had met and grown up with. Different from the woman she had seen two years ago. Different even than she had been just seven months ago when she had seen her last. Something was wrong and Montgomery was going to find out. "Let's get out of here."

"What about Morrigan?" Sarah waved a vague hand in the direction of the dance floor where the blonde still danced with her groping partner.

"I'll get her."

There was a speculative gleam in Montgomery's eyes as she watched Michael snake through the crowd until he was in grabbing distance of his prey.

"Time to go," Michael muttered as his hand came down on Morrigan's shoulder. She gave him only the slightest of looks before she went back to swaying in her partner's arms.

Michael absorbed that for a brief moment before he changed his tactics. Looking into the guy's clouded eyes, he stated a simple fact, "I suggest you let her go and walk away, before I hurt you." His cold smile promised pain and the guy couldn't get away from them fast enough. Even if his running was best, Michael had to hide his disappointment. He would have relished kicking his ass.

"That wasn't very nice." Morrigan pouted. "You're ruining all my fun." That Michael didn't care was obvious as he dragged her to the door.

The ride back to the club was accomplished in silence as Sarah dozed in the back seat next to a very relaxed Morrigan. That Michael wasn't relaxed was easy to tell from Montgomery's position next to him in the front seat, her eyes glued to the fisted hands griping the steering wheel. To the jaw that threatened to grind his pearly white teeth to dust with every shift of the gears. He was pissed about something and Gomery couldn't help but wonder what her friend had done to inspire such a response from a man who hid his every emotion behind a careless smile.

᛭   ᛭   ᛭

Jamison gazed out the window as he stretched his powerful, naked body. Watching the few people who walked up and down the quiet streets reminded him of one thing, he was hungry. He wanted something young. A female. Their blood was the sweetest. However, that would have to wait. He had to deal with Katherine's whims first. While she was out roaming and whoring, he would have to set the trap for Fahlan and his little bird.

When he finished that, he would deal with Sasha and her highlander. How dare she create one such as he, when she had denied *him* time and again. How dare she give of herself to another? He'd forgiven her much in the centuries they had evaded and hunted each other. But this time he would find her and he would remind her of what it had felt like when he had taken her body and soul. What it had felt like when he had shared his blood with her.

The knowledge that Sasha was the only woman to deny his will still fired his rage. She was the only one who didn't cower at his feet when faced with his displeasure. Even Katherine with all her dark magic still bowed down and begged at his feet when he had the urge to make her. But not Sasha. She might have shown fear at the very beginning when he had come for her. She might have pleaded for her life when he left her broken and bleeding. But that had changed after he had given her his gift.

When she had marched through the forest and found him after her people had cast her out, there had been no fear, no hesitation, only a deep-seated rage that had done him proud. That magnificent rage in addition to her *Sidhe* spirit had made her a worthy advisory. How he had loved that fire! He had adored every part of her, except that nasty habit she had of denying him everything he wanted from her.

In the brief time they coexisted together, she'd tried to behead him, burn him at the stake, and had set the local villagers on him as the devil incarnate. Each time, in each country, in each village she had almost succeeded. Her radiant, angelic appearance had aided her well. None had ever guessed what demons lurked under *her* smooth, glowing skin.

What he felt for Sasha transcended mere mortal affection or lust. She was quite simply his life. She had created what he was today. If not for her, he'd still be burning with an unappeasable hunger. He'd still be hiding under the cover of night, afraid of the great glowing sun in the bright blue sky. But not for many centuries now had he felt that fear.

Sasha had given him a bit of magic. The powers he'd had before were nothing compared to what he had received from her. Traveling to a place with nothing but a single thought aided him well, reading dreams and memories were priceless gifts he could never repay. That was why he had chosen the *Sidhe* as his prey all that time ago. He hadn't counted on getting a pure girl, but it had worked to his favor and he had relished the flow of her blood through his veins. Had relished the feel of her spirit. He wanted to feel it again. Needed to feel that rush.

A mistake had been made in thinking that if he took Katherine the effect would be the same. He'd been wrong in assuming the magic was what caused the deep, glorious pleasure. The black-haired witch had brought him none of that joy. Nevertheless, Katherine had her uses. She amused him and there were secrets she didn't know about that would bring him great satisfaction very soon.

Rafe Fahlan wasn't part of the secret and he couldn't help but wonder what it was about the dark immortal that had his little Katherine all in an uproar. What it was that set this immortal apart from the others in her eyes. He wasn't the only immortal she had ever made, but he was the one that called to her.

Jamison had never been in sight of Fahlan, but one didn't need to get close to feel the darkness that came off that one. That was why he had offered to help Katherine bring him down. Fahlan was a challenge he would relish. He longed to see if he could break down the icy contempt that kept all that danger locked away.

First, he needed to give the dark one a little incentive. A little test just to see if he was ready for the next step. Just to see that if he squeezed enough, could he make the beast bleed. From experience he knew the best way to bring down a man was to use a woman. He was curious to see if Fahlan would fall into that old trap. Curious to see if jealousy was still as powerful an emotion as it used to be. That new bouncer would aid his cause just fine.

ϯ   ϯ   ϯ

Gabriel drove home in the darkness, more tired than he had been in a long time. The latest robbery that had the whole station in an uproar wasn't what was bothering him. His problem was Sarah and the affect she was having on him. Leaving her on her own was worrying him more than he wanted to admit. What happened if Seth found her before he got to him?

The hours that made up the rest of Seth's life were numbered. When he got his hands on Sarah's husband, it would all be over. But, with the end of Seth's life so ended his illusion of humanity. Could he let the beast he'd fought for centuries take over now?

All the pain and fear he had taken from Sarah was still inside of him, rattling around in his chest, waiting for the day when he could let it all out. At times like this, when he doubted his right to revenge, was when the pain crept out and allow him to experience just a touch of what Sarah had suffered. The pain was harsh and sharp and he welcomed it. That suffering strengthened his resolve and focused his rage. Seth would pay for every indignity he had ever forced on an innocent who couldn't protect herself. He would see to it.

Parking his SUV, he walked thought the empty club with dragging feet. Letting his guard down, he opened his bedroom door. Sarah was waiting for him on the bed, cloaked in candlelight and bronze silk. She had never seemed more like Sasha than she did at that very moment. Gabriel closed his eyes and prayed for strength. He was barely able to hold back the shudder that streaked through his body at the gentle hand that came to rest on his forearm. He opened his eyes slowly. Had he been less of a man he would have fallen to his knees at what he saw reflected in those light brown eyes.

"Have fun?" In his confusion, the words came out harsher than he had intended.

Sarah flinched but held her ground. "It was fine, but I missed you." She slid her hand down his arm, her fingers coming to rest in his strong grasp. "Now that you're here, you can remedy that."

The look in her eyes made him think he was dreaming. Or maybe this was just some horrible hallucination his tired mind had conjured up. "Our flight's in the morning. We need to leave early." He warned her, his mind not on what he was saying so much as on the way the fingers on her free hand toyed with the buttons on his shirt. "We need to go to bed." The smile that lit up her face was so beautiful he couldn't stop the hand that came up to touch her cheek.

"That was what I had in mind," she murmured as her fingers released the first button on his shirt.

Gabriel couldn't have been more surprised had she reached up and slapped him. He stared at her for a long moment, looking into her eyes, searching for a reason for this turnabout in his charge. Then he caught the scent of a sweet and familiar alcohol.

"You've been drinking." He stated as two more black buttons slipped their moorings. "The rum has your thoughts clouded, Sarah. This can't go any farther. I won't let you embarrass yourself." Too late, he grabbed the nimble little fingers just as they finished liberating his chest from the confines of all those plastic fasteners.

"The only thing I'll regret is if I let you stop this. Unless the thought of touching me is repulsive?" Sarah hadn't thought of that. Since she looked so much like his lost lover, she'd assumed that would be inducement enough for him to make love to her. Wasn't she worthy of even that? Didn't she deserve a moment of pleasure? The sad part was, she didn't even care if there *was* pleasure. Just to have him would be enough; to make love with the man she loved even if only this once. Even if it meant nothing to him, it would be a sweet memory she could carry to her grave.

Didn't she deserve, after all she had been through, to have a few happy memories? "Please, Gabriel, make love to me. Just this once. Show me what it could be like." While he stood there looking as if someone had punched him in the stomach, she took advantage. Pulling her hands free, she placed them flat on his chest. Tentative at first, then with more curiosity when he didn't stop her, she burrowed her fingers through the soft hair that covered his tawny skin.

"I don't want to hurt you," he murmured, catching those gentle hands under his. "We can't do this. Some day you'll find a man to love and when you do, you'll regret ever having suggested this. Don't let gratitude be a reason to give yourself, Sarah. You're worth so much more than that."

"This isn't about gratitude, Gabriel. This is about wanting you to be the one I give myself to."

"I'm not the man you think I am, Sarah. I'm not a saint. I took you away from Seth, but in some ways I'm no better than he is." A finger against his lips stilled his words.

"Don't ever say that," she admonished. "You're nothing like him. Nothing!" She was shaking with her emotions. How could this man, her protector, ever think that he was even in the same category with that monster she had married? Then he was kissing her forehead and setting her away from him like a child. When he walked away from her, Sarah was stunned. He was going to leave her, just like that.

"Gabriel!"

The stridden plea in his name stopped him at the door. "I'm just a man, Sarah. Don't do this to me." He might have still had the will to leave if he hadn't caught the faint, whispered words that escaped her.

"Pretend I'm her if you need to, but please, don't leave me like this."

He didn't ask how she knew about Sasha, he didn't ask anything as he turned and watched her through green eyes that reflected not a bit of the turmoil that churned inside of him. How could he walk away from so much need? What part of honor had ever prepared him for this? Closing the distance between them, he cupped her head in his hands.

"Pretend, Gabriel." She couldn't stop the tears that slid down her face. He was so close she could feel the heat of his body but still there was too much distance. "Please."

"There'll be no one in this bed tonight, Sarah, but us. You. Me. No one else. Not tonight." Gabriel spoke the vow even as he lifted her slender body against his. Even as he took her mouth, he prayed to God that he had spoken the truth.

ᛏ   ᛏ   ᛏ

Unclenching her hands and stretching out her fingers,

Morrigan focused all of her attention on the purple of her nail polish. She focused on anything that would take her thoughts off the pounding in her head. Montgomery was already asleep in her room; she'd crashed almost the very moment Michael had left them at their door.

Morrigan hadn't been so lucky. After changing her clothes, she'd settled down at the kitchen counter, her eyes periodically searching out the small brown bottle next to her that contained the means to alleviate the pain screaming through her skull.

The bottle remained unopened though; pills were a quick fix and she had never been one to run from anything. This headache stuff was nothing new. She'd been through it so many times before. What did it matter if the pain was a little sharper this time, a little harder?

When the discomfort escalated, she left the stool, pressing the palm of her hand against her temple as hard as she could. For a second it helped. Then the ice-pick sharp pains returned.

Fresh air would help. That was what she needed. Fresh air. Morrigan ignored the convulsive shiver that ran through her body.

Letting herself out of the apartment, she edged her way down the stairs as quiet as her training allowed. There was no need to wake the others with her late night creeping. Punching in the security code, she walked out into the cool night air. Taking a deep breath, she picked a direction and started to walk, a little unsteady at first as the pain shook her, then with more confidence as she focused on her feet and held the pain at bay.

The route she took was no more than an aimless wander, her eyes locking on anything that blocked the agony. Lost to everything but the vicious misery that made her want to curl in a corner and heave her guts out, she failed to notice the tall shadow that followed at a discreet distance. The same shadow, that with a single look, managed to keep several unpleasant things that lurked under the cover of night at a distance.

Michael kept pace with her and couldn't help but wonder

what was so wrong that she had lost that natural grace of movement he had admired from the first. When she stumbled, he almost reached for her, but he hung back, wanting to see where she was going. He watched with a puzzled frown as she caught herself in time and leaned against the side of a building. Maybe she didn't have a head for alcohol. Funny though, he didn't think she'd had much to drink.

When she pushed away from the wall and began to walk again, he didn't miss the small hands she pushed against her temples. That he could blame on a migraine or at the very least a killer headache. Everything inside of him wanted to go to her and lead her back home, but he knew she wouldn't relish his interference. Hell, she'd be furious to know that he had followed her from the second she had crept from Montgomery's apartment. He hung back instead. If she needed him, he would help her. If she let him.

The longer she walked, the more time he had to think about what had happened on that dance floor tonight. Why had he let the little witch get under his skin like that? He didn't want to feel anything for this particular female, let alone the fist her very presence seemed to launch into his gut. Giving in would be a big mistake, not the biggest he'd ever made, but close. Another bad decision coming back to haunt him was something he could live without.

At first, his senses failed to notice the sinister looking man that slunk out of his dark alley to block Morrigan's path. When he saw the hand the man reached out to grab her shoulder with, he had to fight down the black rage that threatened to explode inside of him. Failing in that endeavor, he prepared to launch himself at her assailant.

Michael never got the chance to find out if the beast in him planned on ripping out the throat of his would be victim or not. Just as he closed in for the kill, Morrigan brought her knee up, catching the man in the groin. When he hunched over holding his injury, she caught him square in the face with a tightly-clenched fist, the force of which knocked him to his back on the ground.

Plans of rescue flew from his mind when she went on her way, stepping on the man's stomach instead of walking around.

After he got over his initial surprise, Michael wasn't as charitable. Once Morrigan was out of sight, he stalked over to the man writhing on the ground. With barely contained savagery, he pulled the now whimpering man up by his collar.

Face to face with the beast Michael made no effort to hide, the beaten man could do nothing but weep and beg. Even through frightened eyes, the thug knew he was looking at death. His own.

"You will never do this again." Michael growled low in his throat, teeth flashing in the streetlight.

The man nodded his head, willing to agree to anything just to have his limp feet back on solid ground. That and to be about a million miles away from the avenging angel that held him with one hand a foot off the ground.

"If you do this again, I will come back for you." Michael promised with a cold, malicious smile. With a flick of his wrist, he tossed the man away from him as if he was no more than a bag of garbage. Not looking back, he went in search of Morrigan.

Chapter 15

Sasha stood at the foot of the bed and watched them sleep. Even while he slept, Gabriel kept his new lover held close in his arms. Clenching her fists against the sight of them helped her cope. Seeing them in her dream had been like a knife to her heart, but this, this was like having her heart cut out. As silly as it seemed, she felt like a betrayed wife. A wife who heard the giggles from outside the bedroom door but wouldn't let it go until she opened that door and found her spouse in the arms of another. How she wished she'd kept that door closed.

A tear rolled down her cheek when Gabriel pressed his lips against Sarah's hair while he slept. He pulled the girl closer still, until nothing separated their bodies, but Sasha's wish that she could make it all go away.

Anger ate away her tears. Why didn't she just wipe this girl off the face of the earth? Why didn't she remove her from his memory? Doing it would be so easy. Raising her arms high, she let the magic build until it burned and flamed, hurting her with its need for release.

Why didn't she let it go? Then she could have him all to herself. She could do it. Wasn't she what Jamison had made her? Wasn't she the monster that Gabriel accused her of being?

Her arms dropped. Walking closer, she sat on the bed. With a gentle hand, she touched the girl's brow. Opening her mind, she let all that was Sarah flow into her. The anger was crushed under the weight of this little one's life. How could she hurt one who had already suffered so much? Tears fell in earnest as she remembered her own pain and suffering at Jamison's hands. She remembered how it was to be helpless, to suffer.

But nothing Jamison had done to her matched the pain of

losing Gabriel. Kneeling beside the bed, she reached out, needing to touch him one last time. Green eyes flew open at the feel of her hand over his heart.

"Angel," he whispered, his hand covering hers.

Sasha looked up from their joined hands and wanted to die. Through her tears she could see nothing in his eyes except fear for the young one at his side. "You think I'm going to hurt her, don't you?" Her laughter was a fragile sound in the quiet room.

Gabriel eased away from his lover and sat up, his hand still holding Sasha's to his chest.

She watched him through wounded amber eyes, the rapid beat of his heart under her palm answer enough. "I don't think you realize how truly pathetic I am." The struggle to keep her voice low was draining, but she didn't want to wake the innocent to the ridiculousness of this whole scene.

He reached for her other hand. To someone else it would have appeared that he sought to comfort her. Sasha knew better. He thought if he had her hands, she couldn't injure his lover. Or him. "You think I'm going to hurt her?" she asked again. He still didn't answer but she saw the wariness reflected in those deep green eyes. "You're killing me." She slid her hands out from under his before he had a chance to blink.

"No matter how much this is hurting me, I would never touch a hair on her head. Sarah has done nothing wrong. She and I suffer from the same dreaded weakness. She'll survive hers. I doubt if I will." She rose from the floor, and still he said not a word. Turning her back on him, she moved away. Disappearing from his sight would have been her best option but now, even the act of breathing hurt.

Sasha knew he was behind her before she felt his hands on her shoulders. She wanted so much to lean back into the heat of his body but she could smell *her* scent on him. Mere mortals wouldn't have noticed the faintness of it but to her it was as strong as cheap perfume.

"I won't touch her again," he whispered against her hair.

There was no doubt about what he was saying or why he said it. The promise had nothing to do with her lacerated emotions. He only promised so she would leave the poor girl in peace. He protected his lover with those words. "It doesn't matter anymore." She wanted to scream but she kept her voice down for Sarah's sake. "If you take her a million times, it doesn't matter." It was over. Gabriel had made his decision. If he had slashed his rejection into her soul with a razor blade, he couldn't have made it any clearer. "You love her."

Gabriel almost didn't hear those last words, she spoke them so low. Maybe she hadn't said it at all. Maybe she had thought it. Only her distraction gave him the courage to turn her around. His breath caught at the shattered look in her eyes. Never had he seen her like this, not even that night in London when he had laid bare her suffering at Jamison's hands.

He had to make it better. Never could he forgive enough to let his love for her become a reality, but he didn't want to see her like this either. "I don't love her, angel. She needed me. I was there for her. In the morning, I'll take her to her family and she'll get on with her new life. It's that simple."

Sasha almost buckled under the force of her pain. He thought that little speech would make it all better? "Anyone but me will do, right?" Her voice was horse with the need not to shout. "You will have anyone but me." She looked up, letting him see the agony that burned in her clear amber eyes. "Anyone but me, Gabriel," she repeated again. Pushing with all her strength, she staggered away from him.

"It's not that simple, Sasha." He reached for her, but she eluded him.

"Yes, it is. All of this doesn't matter now." She made a wide gesture with her arms. "You think I turned you into a monster that night. You say I took away your honor. Did you ever stop to think that when I gave you back your life, what that did to me?" She let him see the depth of her misery. "I made *myself* into a monster that night. For the first time in six-hundred years, I became the vile creature that Jamison had made me. I betrayed *myself* for you." Her voice broke and she turned away from him. "I gathered you into my arms and I took your blood into my body." She shrugged off the hand he placed on her shoulder. "*I gave you back my soul.*"

"Why?" he asked, for the first time in two centuries.

"How can you ask me that now? How can you ask me like you care when I can *smell* her on you?" Why had she done this? Did she have so little pride left that she could give him every part of herself? "Why doesn't matter anymore. It's over now." She only wanted to get away before she lost everything.

"Why?"

She could no more deny him her answer than she could have denied him her blood. "Because I love you."

ᛏ   ᛏ   ᛏ

A faint sound pulled Montgomery from her restless sleep. Turning her head to the side, she heard it again. The music was so out of place that her instincts went on full alert. Before her feet touched the floor, her gaze landed on where Morrigan huddled against the far edge of the bed.

Walking at a swift but silent pace, she headed out of her apartment and down the long flights of stairs, watching her back as she went. With her adrenaline pumping, she was oblivious to the cool air that brushed her legs under the short cotton nightshirt she wore. All her attention focused on finding out who was in the club.

Pausing outside of the doors to the main floor, she slid her back against the wall, listening to the now louder sounds of music. Concern for her own safety never crossed her mind as she ran a mental list of who had access to the security codes that opened the front door. With Morrigan asleep and Gabriel out of town, that narrowed the possibilities.

Michael was one but he was on a date, and even with it being a Tuesday night, she didn't expect him in until well after noon tomorrow. Edging around the door, she spotted a dark head bent over the ivory keys. She knew without seeing his face that it was Rafe.

"Come on in, sweet thing. Don't be shy," he called without looking up.

Resisting the urge to run for cover, Montgomery entered instead. "What are you doing here?" She decided she would play it cool as she joined him. He would never know how badly he had hurt her with his last words the other morning.

"A change of plans." His reply was as mysterious as his smile. After leaving Sasha's, he'd taken some time to think. Just a couple of days to decide his fate. Montgomery's fate.

"Oh?" Chestnut eyebrows rose above curious hazel eyes, but she refused to say more. Being strong in front of him was her goal, not finding out about his vacation activities.

"Let's just say I've given up fighting what I've been assured is inevitable."

Rafe lifted smoldering gray eyes and she fought the urge to back away from the fire that scorched her in that heated gaze.

"Did you miss me?" he taunted her.

"I've been busy. How long were you gone?" Her question was just as flippant as his had been. A few more minutes. She could talk to him for a few minutes, and then she would walk away. There was no way she'd let this man break her down again. No matter what she felt for him, she still had her pride. Never would he know about the misery she'd suffered in the four days he'd been gone.

"Touché, sweet thing." Skimming his fingers along the keys, he grabbed her wrist.

Before she could even think to pull it away, he had positioned her between his wide-spread legs with a gentle tug. Trapped between his hard body and the piano, she could only look into his brooding features.

"Where's your friend?"

Montgomery was surprised he knew about Morrigan. "In bed." She didn't understand the tension in his fingers where they gripped the keyboard on either side of her hips. She started to edge away, but his next question stopped her.

"Tired yourselves out, did you?"

The sarcasm that colored those words was hard to misinterpret, but she was clueless as to what his problem was with her having company. "We had a lot to catch up on." Her eyes probed his, trying to find a reason for the fire reflected within those silver depths.

"Who's bed is your *friend* sleeping in?"

Montgomery found it hard to concentrate as strong fingers began to caress her thigh through the worn material of her shirt. She slapped his hand away but he replaced it with the other. Her pulse raced out of control as he drew lazy circles on her bare skin. Holding her breath as those fingers slid higher, she braced herself. "Stop it!" She couldn't let him do this to her again.

"Do you really want me to stop?" His hand stilled under hers.

Montgomery couldn't lie to him anymore than she could lie to herself. In a few days, she was leaving with Morrigan and would never see him again. In the meantime, why should she deny herself the pleasure of his body? She knew the score now, had learned it the hard way when he'd trampled her heart. She could survive his coolness for a few days if it meant this intense pleasure. If it meant she could pretend he loved her, if only a little.

"No, I don't want you to stop." She let go of his hand, moaning as he caressed her through the thin lace of her panties.

Rafe stood in a rush at her ragged gasp and lifted her onto the piano with a discordant screech of abused keys, forcing her to hold onto his wide shoulders for balance. He was moving so fast, with none of his cool finesse, that she felt a rush of excitement. She had hoped to make it to a bed but this would do. With a single fluid movement, he stepped between her spread knees, forcing her legs wider as he kicked the bench across the stage.

"Rafe?" His frenzied actions left her breathless. She never

heard if he answered. By then, his hands had reached her hips and he pulled her flush with his aroused body. The feel of him pressed against the heart of her desire robbed her of all reason, and with a moan of wanting, she arched back against the piano lid.

Rafe followed her down, trailing a path of rough nips and burning kisses as he traveled up the length of her body. "Is Morrigan sleeping in your bed, Gomery?" he whispered against her ear.

"Yes." She moaned low in her throat, paying no attention to the harshness that entered his features at her answer.

"Why?" he rasped the word, his tongue darting out to lave the inside of her ear.

"Why are you doing this to me?" Montgomery forced herself to concentrate on his question. Why was he asking dumb questions when all she wanted was him inside of her? Then all thoughts flew as he rocked against her. Oblivious to the hard wood under her back, she wrapped long legs around his narrow hips. A shiver rippled through when he shredded the lace that kept her body from his.

This wasn't the lover she knew.

"Tell me you want me, sweet thing," he demanded, his voice husky, his breathing hard and heavy as his need reached an unbearable level.

"I love you, Rafe," she whispered instead, cringing even as she said the words. God, she hadn't meant to say that. She should leave him now, before she had no pride left at all. But, she didn't move. To deny her own pride was an easier feat than walking away from this man. With trembling hands, she pushed at his jeans until nothing separated them.

Rafe growled deep in his throat as he fitted his body to hers, but he didn't take. Not yet. He needed more. Dragging the T-shirt over her head, he tossed it away without a glance. Arching her up, he pulled a blush-colored nipple deep into his mouth, sucking hard until she writhed against him. Leaving the wet peak, he moved to the other using his teeth to shape the sensitive skin to the contours of his mouth.

"Rafe." She moaned when he pushed against her, hot and hard but still denying that final possession.

"Say you're mine, Gomery," Rafe commanded as he slid his body into hers a small fraction before he pulled back. "Say it, Gomery." He slid a little farther this time before he left her again. "Say it!"

"I'm yours."

He couldn't hold back his growl of triumph as he slammed into her. "You're mine now, Gomery. Only mine." He drove into her again. "Mine. Mine. Mine," he panted the word with each thrust until nothing existed for him but the pleasure.

"Rafe!" Montgomery screamed his name, oblivious to the teeth that sank into her shoulder as the world exploded all around her.

ᛏ   ᛏ   ᛏ

Rafe watched her while she slept in his arms, his eyes cold with self-disgust. It had taken an extreme effort on his part to keep from drinking of her, to stop and heal the small wound he'd left in his frenzy. He couldn't allow himself to take her like that again. There could be no emotion, no anger. Even the lover Montgomery had upstairs was a moot point.

The man would cease to exist in his mind, not because he wanted to, but because he needed to. If he didn't get over it, the Fallen Angels would have to bury one of their own beside her after he finished what he'd started tonight. He shelved the dark thought plaguing him when he felt her hand flutter on his chest, waiting as those hazel eyes focused on his face.

"I love you," she whispered as she smoothed an unruly lock of his black hair. When she felt his body tense, she knew it had been the wrong thing to say, but she could no more stop the words as her own heartbeat.

"I know you do, sweet thing. I know you do." Closing his eyes, he rested his forehead against hers.

"This must be Rafe," a whispery voice drawled from the doorway.

He raised his head, eyes widening in surprise at the tiny blonde girl standing only ten feet away, her avid purple eyes locked on them. Blushing under that vivid scrutiny, he lowered silver eyes to his lover.

"I think we've been caught," Montgomery whispered with a devilish grin.

Rafe paused in his strategic retreat as he considered her lack of embarrassment. Then with searching eyes, he turned back to the girl. This time his cool gaze missed nothing. Not the lush curves hidden under the old T-shirt, or the long legs that stretched from the frayed hem, or the amusement that danced in those unchildlike eyes. Least of all, he didn't miss the Smith and Wesson .357 that seemed so out of place in that fragile hand. He turned his gaze back to Montgomery and raised an ebony brow in question.

"Rafe," she purred with a kittenish stretch of muscles, "I want you to meet a friend of mine."

His eyes darkened as she moved against him, his body reacting to the sweet torment. Only then did he reach out a searching hand for the discarded T-shirt, trying to cover her bare skin. The blonde laughed outright at his belated attempt to protect his lover's modesty, never mind that he was bare-ass naked on a piano in the middle of a dance club. Gomery stilled his hands.

"This is Morrigan St. John."

Rafe's head shot up with a snap and he again found himself looking into amused amethyst eyes. This time with a whole new perspective.

"Nice to meet you, Rafe." Morrigan nodded her head in his direction, her pale pink lips twitching.

"Nice to meet you." He nodded back, refusing to acknowledge the absurd situation.

"I'll leave you two to get ... comfortable." Morrigan managed a straight face as she looked them over one more time before she walked away. "Gomery?" She paused at the door not bothering to turn back around.

"Yeah?" Montgomery waited, knowing that her friend was up to no good.

"You were right. He does make that fallen angel fantasy work for him, even on top of a piano. Not many men could pull that off."

ͳ   ͳ   ͳ

Some time later, they made themselves comfortable in Rafe's large black-sheeted bed. Only then did he bring up the subject of Morrigan St. John.

"So that's Morrigan. She's not what I expected," he stated the obvious.

"What were you expecting?" Montgomery asked, running her fingers through his ebony hair.

"Oh, I don't know. Someone more like you maybe." He lied rather than admit to the misleading information someone had fed him about the *friend* staying in Gomery's bedroom.

"She's more like me than you'll ever know. I met Morrigan at school when I was fourteen." She smiled as she explained. "The first day there, some of the girls started making fun of me. Morrigan stopped them. That was the start of it. From then on, we were inseparable. Any trouble I managed to get into, she made sure we shared.

"When they kicked us out, I was scared to death that she would get it from her dad but he didn't even blink. Instead he enrolled us in a less structured school and took me under his wing. I stayed with them a lot after that." She smiled as another memory hit.

"This one summer, I think I was sixteen, we climbed down from the third story in the middle of the night, borrowed her brother's Jeep and found this little dive and sat through the most painful tattoos." She laughed at that.

"What did your dad say?" Rafe asked, though in his heart

he already knew the answer.

"My father? He never noticed. I wasn't around him much by then. Morrigan and I were pretty much fixtures at St. John Securities. We learned everything we could and by the time we were twenty, we had our own teams. It just about killed us when Morrigan's dad died." She stopped then, embarrassed at all she'd said without any input from him.

"Why did you quit?" Rafe asked at her continued silence.

"We had a problem develop in Paris. Morrigan's uncle sent me and my team there to guard an American business advisor. Darn thing should have been a cakewalk, but I had a traitor on my team. He was a new member and I had complicated matters by going to bed with him." She confessed without shame for her past transgressions.

"I should have never fallen for his line. Nik opened fire on both me and our client. I tried to save Barnett but it was too late, he was dead with the first shot. Then Nik took great delight in using me for target practice. A member of the team killed him before he could finish, but he did leave me these lovely mementos." Montgomery shrugged off the remembered pain, running a hand over the scars.

"Morrigan helped me out. To pay her back, I joined her security team. After a year I went out on my own." She leaned forward and kissed the corner of his mouth.

"How old are you?" He only just realized he didn't know.

"I'm twenty-eight," she answered with a throaty chuckle. "How old are you?"

"Thirty," he lied with ease. "Why is Morrigan here?"

"She needs me to go with her."

Rafe could see the hesitation in her eyes. "Do you want to?" His eyes held hers.

"She has helped me with so much without ever asking for a thing that I can't refuse my help now. What would you have me do?" Montgomery left her heart open to him, praying he didn't kick so hard this time.

"Where would you be staying?" he asked, not betraying a

thing.

"Chicago." She looked away, not wanting to see the indifference in his eyes when he realized the distance the move implied.

"Chicago." Rafe rolled the word off his tongue. Tugging her chin up, he met her eyes, refusing to let her hide.

"Do you think I'll like Chicago?"

It took a moment for his words to sink in but when they did the sun at its brightest couldn't compare to the glow of her smile.

"I'll do my best to make sure that you do."

T   T   T

"What's going on?" Gabriel asked Michael the next morning when he *popped* back from leaving Sarah at her sister's house to settle in.

"Rafe is back," Michael lobbed his answer out as if it was a comment about the weather. "He must have showed up while we were out last night."

"Has Gomery seen him?" Gabriel was curious about her reaction.

"She's with him," Michael returned with a slight smile. "The girl has nerve. You would have thought she'd have run for cover after the last time."

"Are you good with this?"

"He doesn't need to worry about me so much as the witch plotting his downfall."

Gabriel had no idea what Michael was talking about, but it didn't take Michael long to enlighten him. Tilting his head to the side, he nodded in the direction of the weight room. Standing outside the door, they watched as Morrigan worked her way through the high end of one hundred sit-ups.

"Gomery must have told her something. What Gomery is willing to forgive is more than what this one is going to do. Rafe should be down in a minute. She sent up a message about an hour ago." Michael motioned Gabriel to stand back. He did-n't want her to see them. "We'll watch the show," he explained when he saw Gabriel's puzzled expression.

They didn't have but a few seconds to wait before Rafe strolled in.

Morrigan finished her routine while he stood back and waited. Even basking in the glow of his physical contentment, he would have been blind not to appreciate the perfection of the damp-skinned woman.

"Good morning." He waited while she wiped the sweat from her face with a towel. She met his cool gaze with eyes as cold as frost. This was not the laughing woman he had blushed in front of last night. He wondered at the change. She didn't leave him to wonder long.

"Where is she?" Morrigan's tone was sharp as glass.

"Sleeping."

Dropping the towel, she crossed the distance to stand so close to him their bodies almost touched. Rafe was worried. He didn't need her to put a move on him. He didn't want to offend Gomery's friend, but he knew it would be necessary when he turned her down. Preparing himself, he waited to see if at least her line was unique.

"If you hurt her again, Rafe, I'll cut your heart out." She spoke the words with no expression on her face.

He was stunned. You couldn't get more unique than that.

"She might have forgiven you, but I won't forget, Fahlan."

Rafe felt the rage that emanated from her slender body. "You think you can hurt me?" He spread his arms wide with an amused smirk as he waited for her answer. The cold smile that settled on her face wiped away his humor.

"I could rip your lungs out and give them to you to wear as a hat before you even realize you can't draw a breath." She placed her hand on his chest.

He looked down into her bright eyes and saw the sincerity reflected there, felt her fingers as they settled over his heart and didn't doubt she would try.

"Don't make me hurt you," Morrigan drawled out with that Georgia peach lilt.

"Gomery wouldn't like it if you did." Rafe found himself saying as he placed his hand over hers. She didn't even flinch from the pressure he exerted to keep her hand in his.

"Montgomery would never know. You have no idea what I've done to keep her safe and happy. No concept of what I'll do."

He believed her. She would kill to keep Gomery safe, but then, so would he. She continued to stare at him with those expressionless lavender eyes.

"I won't hurt her," he promised, removing his hand from hers.

Morrigan nodded as she dropped her hand. "Did she tell you she was going with me to Chicago?" she asked as if the last few minutes hadn't happened.

"I'm going along." He waited for her reaction.

"Gomery will need the company when I'm not there." She grabbed her towel from the floor. "Thanks for talking with me this morning."

"No problem," he replied for lack of something better to say.

"Do they always listen to your private conversations?" A nod of her head indicated the empty doorway.

Rafe watched as she walked out of the gym, humming a little tune in her wake. "Do you always listen to my private conversations?" He echoed the question as Gabriel and Michael stepped out of hiding. He gave them a tolerant smile while they stared after the blonde.

"That was different," Gabriel offered.

Rafe couldn't help but agree. "Interesting little thing, isn't she?" He didn't expect an answer.

"Yes, she is." Michael walked out after her.

"What's up with him?" Rafe was curious what had kept Michael from taking a potshot at him.

"I think your little assassin has been working some voodoo

on him." Gabriel turned his full attention on the dark one. "I thought you were gone."

"I realized it would be useless to stay away. We're leaving for Chicago on Friday." Rafe waited to see if he would object.

"Gomery's good for you, brother."

CHAPTER 16

"It's time, my pet," Jamison fairly purred the words that
Katherine had waited so long to hear. "The beast is hungry
and the trap is baited. Now we need to send in the hunter with
his weapon. What do you have in mind for ammunition?" He
would leave it up to Katherine, she always liked this part best.

"I think tomorrow night will do just fine. From what I
hear, they've planned a little going away party. Our man should
be back tomorrow and if he's not, I'll nudge him in that direction. Then I think I'll go see him in the evening. He should be
dying to know where his wife has been. I'll just send him over
there." Katherine smiled in anticipation. "It should be interesting to see who walks away from the party."

"I want the girl."

Jamie's demand broke through her happy thoughts. "What
girl?" She had no idea what he was talking about. "Jordan's
wife isn't part of this."

"Fahlan's woman. I want her."

"You can't have her. She's mine." She denied his request,
adamant in her planning.

"You can have what's left."

"She's mine, Jamie." He stopped her protest with a single
look that made the color drain from her face.

"Nothing is yours until I give it to you."

The truth behind his words froze Katherine to the bone.
Nothing was hers until her sire deemed her worthy. Everything
was a test for him, an excuse to torture and wound until death
threatened to steal his prey. Once upon a time, what he'd had
to offer had mattered more than her own life, but that hadn't
been his price. Jamie had demanded her survival.

To accomplish that, she had relied on her magic for strength. Repeated spells had been necessary to heal the damage he'd inflicted with his dark imagination. The brutality he was capable of was something he proved over and over again. There were times when the pain he had inflicted without a touch of remorse haunted her thoughts still. He had a talent, one he had passed on to her, but she had never excelled to his level of expertise.

"What could you possibly want with her? She is nothing in this but a lure to draw Fahlan." Katherine didn't want to give the woman to her sire. Her plans didn't include Jamie amusing himself with Montgomery Sinclair. Granted the woman would be involved in the plan, but she didn't want to see her hurt. Jamie would hurt her. From what she had seen of the woman, she had liked her. There was something about her that struck a cord deep in her soul, but Jamie couldn't know that. If he thought she cared, he would make the woman suffer while he forced her to watch.

Jamison was good at that.

He liked to make her watch while he did things. Mean things, terrible, ugly things that had failed to move her centuries ago. For as long as she'd known him, he had searched for something. At first, she had assumed all he looked for was Sasha, but it didn't take her long to realize she was wrong. Instead, he searched for the one. The woman who could match the other half of his ruthless nature.

In his quest for her, he would hunt out a woman. What he would do then was enough to make Katherine's skin crawl. None ever survived intact. They would die begging for release from their mortal suffering. Some he would finish off quickly, while others he would leave for days. A few she had killed herself, their pitiful cries reaching out to her. In all that time he never found the one he searched for.

"I want to see what draws the beast out from under the dark one's control. I want to see what she is all about." He smiled at the flash of panic in her eyes. "If you don't hand her

over, you'll serve in her place while I alleviate my boredom.
You know what I can do, Katherine. Do you really want to take
the place of a woman that means nothing to you? Do you need
your memory refreshed? Have you forgotten?" He took a step
toward her and it was all she could do not to shrink away from
the menace in his black eyes.

"I'll bring her to you, but I want Fahlan." She bargained
even as she backed up.

"I have a special plan in mind for him. If you're very good,
I'll let you help."

He moved so fast that she didn't see his hand until he had
it wrapped around her neck.

"Next time, don't question me, Katherine. I think I've
grown lax with you. For some reason, you've forgotten what
I'm capable of. Let me refresh your memory."

ፐ   ፐ   ፐ

Montgomery knocked on Rafe's door. She had woken alone
this morning and had been on edge ever since. Even a visit
with Morrigan had done little to improve her mood. At a loss,
she had spent the rest of the afternoon packing her clothes and
belongings for the trip to Chicago.

Feeling foolish for knocking after the number of times
they'd trashed the bed last night, she turned the knob and let
herself in. Setting an overnight bag on the sofa, she walked
back through to the bedroom she had spent such an active
night in. She reached down to smooth the silk of one of the pil-
lowcases, smiling as events from last night flooded her mind.
The piano was definitely a memory she would never forget.
The thought of it alone sent a trail of fire through her stomach. The boy was something.

But it was what had come after, that warmed her heart
the most. As they had talked last night in his bed she had felt
connected, as if nothing could ever ruin the beauty of the
moment. Reality had a way of intruding into even the most

beautiful of dreams though, and she was more than aware of the fact that Rafe didn't love her. On his part, this was nothing more than an affair.

For the most part that was fine with her. The rules were clear this time; they would be friends. Granted, very good friends that burned up the sheets whenever they got the chance, but friends just the same. As long as the rules remained simple, she could hide the love that would send Rafe scurrying for cover.

Hearing the water shut off in the bathroom, she opened the door and stepped in. The sight of so much muscled flesh gleaming with water went straight to her system. With avid interest, she watched him run the white towel through the wet silk of his hair.

"Hello, lover," she murmured as she wrapped her arms around his damp shoulders. Pulling his lips to her, she kissed him until she felt the heat clear to her toes.

"Hello, sweet thing." Rafe shivered as she licked a bead of water from his chest.

"Miss me?" Stepping back from him, she pulled her shirt over her head. The fire in his eyes was response enough. In short order she shimmied out of the rest of her clothes until she stood before him, proud and eager to do something she hadn't done with him before. She wanted to have him now with the sunlight shining through the windows.

No longer would she have to wonder what he hid from her in the shadows of the night.

Rafe pulled her close, a strong arm locked around her waist. "You're so beautiful." He pulled her closer until her legs tangled with his and her hips cradled the heat of his arousal. Sliding his free hand into her hair, he wove his fingers tight and held her still as he took her mouth with his.

The kiss stole the breath from her body. Never had she felt something like this before. For weeks, she had enjoyed the mastery of Rafe's kisses, but this went beyond that. This was a melding of spirits, a joining of souls. What the hell had gotten into him? Why was he changing the rules on her now?

"Rafe?" Did she dare hope for more from him? "I love you." She offered the opening, then watched in fascination as the shutters came down on his expression. Oops, so that wasn't what had changed in him. "I want you so much." Montgomery tried again and knew she'd gotten it right when he swept her into his arms and carried her to his bed.

After they spent their passions, Rafe held her close, gazing down at her as their hearts slowed and their skin cooled. Loving her in the light had been worth the control it had taken to bury his needs. Difficult as it had been to ignore the memory of her taste, he had managed it and the loss of that dark pleasure was slight when compared to the other. Even the hollow feeling in his heart was lessening, each time he took her the ice melted a little more. This contentment couldn't be love but it was close. As close as he would ever let it.

Montgomery Sinclair was his woman now. She was his to protect and contrary to what Sasha had said, he wouldn't let her die. He had finally gotten the golden one to confess that in her dreams Gomery died here, in New Orleans. That was why he was taking her to Chicago, where it was safe. He hadn't told Gomery yet, but he had arranged to leave after the party tomorrow night. Leaving that much sooner improved the odds.

No matter what, he was not going to let anything happen to her.

Montgomery stirred from her comfortable position in his arms. Reaching up, she pulled his head down to hers and met the guarded expression on his face. The coldness in his eyes caused her to panic. God, she couldn't go through that again. Not now. With a trembling hand, she traced the outline of the frown on his face. "What's wrong?" She didn't believe him when he shook his head in the negative. "Keeping secrets?" she chided him around the fist lodged in her throat.

Rafe stilled at that question. If she only knew what secrets lurked under his skin, she'd run for cover in a heartbeat. It wasn't even his demons that would scare her so, but the lack of a human heart. His wife had ripped that heart out long ago. At least the parts that had survived his father. But he did have one secret he could share with her. One he would no longer be able to keep hidden in the dark of night. With just enough of the late afternoon's light coming through the windows, he stood up and turned his back to her, then he waited for a reaction.

"Oh, my God." Her eyes moved over the pale scars that crisscrossed the bronzed skin of his back. There were so many she couldn't even start to count them all. Reaching out, she traced one of the raised welts. They were old. He would have been just a child when he received them. She would kill who had done this. With her bare hands, she would rip them to shreds until there was nothing left.

"Who?" She could barely speak for the pain and rage that gripped her. Then he turned around, and she saw the fierceness in his eyes. He would accept no sympathy. To do so would remind him too much of pity and he would never allow that, not even from a lover.

"My father," he replied with a cold little smile. "He had quite a talent. It took him almost six years to make that collection. He was ever diligent. Nothing kept him from his task. Every day he would administer what he deemed a worthy punishment for my sins."

He spoke with so much sarcasm that Montgomery wanted to weep for him. "What reason?" she whispered through bloodless lips.

"It was easier to blame a five year old boy for his wife leaving than to admit that his wife had left because she hated him. He never did like taking the blame for anything."

Montgomery wanted to wipe the hurt away but experience had taught her that words couldn't undo the past. She needed to fill his mind with other things until there was no room left for those memories. "Let me love you, Rafe, let me take your pain away." He didn't say a word as he pulled her into his arms, but she hadn't expected him to.

ᛏ   ᛏ   ᛏ

The impromptu celebration on Thursday night for Montgomery's birthday also doubled as a going away party. That was the reason they gathered around one of the large tables in the empty club. Gomery looked around the table at the group of people that had become so important to her in the last months. There was Michael, as beautiful as always with his angelic features.

Gabriel reclined back in his chair trying to play it cool as those ageless green eyes wandered from time to time to Sasha's serene appearance. And Sasha, beautiful and talented Sasha, who tried so hard not to look in his direction. She managed to say a thousand words without ever opening her mouth.

Looking in Morrigan's direction, Montgomery bit back every question buzzing in her head. Morrigan wasn't happy. That was plain to see no matter how hard she tried to pretend otherwise and it had to do with more than St. John Securities but she could wait until they got to Chicago to find out. Then she would know it all, even if she had to tie Morrigan to a chair and beat her.

Her eyes at last drifted to Rafe, her perfect, scarred lover. Shifting around on his lap, she trailed a kiss across his parted lips, all of her hopes and dreams reflected on her face in an expression he pretended not to see. "I love you."

"I know you do, sweet thing."

She was beginning to hate that patented little phrase of his but she wouldn't push it now. There would be plenty of time to turn him around to her way of thinking once they got to Chicago. Sure of her plans, she turned from him with a tiny smile.

Leaning back against her reluctant lover, she watched with

avid interest as Morrigan played helpless kitten to Michael's pit bull attitude. Never had she seen her friend so willing to put up with such blatant male stupidity.

"You can't tell me how to dress."

That was Morrigan's response to some comment Michael had issued but that Montgomery had missed.

"If I want to go out dressed like this tonight, then I will."

This referred to the black lace dress that clung to her curves.

"I just thought someone should let you know." He shrugged his broad shoulders to show he didn't care

"What's wrong with it?" Morrigan stood up from the table and allowed everyone to take an inventory of her outfit.

An outfit that offered a view of an extreme amount of tanned skin through the sheer lace pattern. The only thing that kept her from indecent exposure were the few strategic pieces of material that lined the dress only where necessary. On anyone else, the dress would have looked ridiculous but Morrigan was one of those people that no matter what she wore, it looked perfect.

"Nothing except the fact that at first glance you look like a *hooker*," Michael offered with an amused smile. "A high priced hooker, but a hooker just the same." He pretended blindness to the fire gleaming in her bright purple eyes.

"That was a little blunt, don't you think?" Sasha asked from her end of the table, her laughter as fine as music.

"I don't believe in using five dollar words." He was at ease as he lounged back in the chair, watching Morrigan as she settled back into her seat. His gaze lingered on the long legs she crossed and the way she didn't bother to smooth down her skirt as it edged even farther up her bare thighs.

"Why is that, do you think? That you don't use five-dollar words? Is it that you can't afford them? Or is it simply that your dates can't spell them?" She taunted him in return.

"Are you always such a spoiled brat?" he shot back, the complacent smile wiped off his face.

"Are you always such a narcissistic, egomaniacal,

presumptuous jackass?" she returned, her face aglow with the fire of battle. "Some of us don't mind using five dollar words, pretty boy."

Everyone was so caught up in the heated exchange, they missed the insistent pounding on the front doors. Not wanting to interrupt the entertaining exchange of insults, Montgomery decided to answer the summons. She didn't think whoever was knocking was going to go away, not even with the closed sign on the door.

There must be an emergency, Montgomery decided, for someone to stand out in the rain and knock like that. Sliding from Rafe's lap, she started for the doors. He caught her hand before she made a step. Pulling her back to him, he threaded his fingers into her loose hair and tugged her mouth down to his.

Their kiss left her breathless. "I love you," she whispered, desire burning in her eyes.

Rafe hated to see her need for his love reflected in that beautiful gaze, but he couldn't bring himself to say those three little words. Not even for her. He had lost too much to ever fall into that trap again. "I know you do."

Montgomery nodded her understanding at what he refused to say, then she walked away from him. Rafe almost called her back when he felt the backlash of her pain and disappointment. He had felt much of her emotions ever since the other night on the piano, when their lovemaking had stolen a piece of him and exchanged it with a part of her. Sometimes he hated himself for the confusion he made her feel.

What would it really hurt to make her happy? They were just words and he would know the truth in his mind. That was what mattered. He could tell her he loved her as he held her close to his heart and eased their passions.

Tonight. He would tell her tonight.

ᛏ   ᛏ   ᛏ

Montgomery unlocked the door and motioned the tall blond man out of the driving rain. "The storm has picked up," she said as a flash of lightening filled the night sky.

"Where's Arden?" Seth Jordan demanded.

She swung around to face him and it only took her a second to realize who the man was. A second longer to decide she didn't like the emotions flashing in his hazel eyes. "Gabriel's not here," she lied. There was no need to look in the direction of the gathering. A wall blocked the table from sight so Jordan couldn't see the party he was trying so hard to crash.

"You're lying." He reached for her arm, jerking her against him. "I know that bastard's here and I know he has my wife. Now show me where he is," he demanded as he shoved his service revolver against her ribs.

"There is no need for this. Please try to be reasonable. Put the gun away." Her training kicked in and with a steady hand, she touched his arm. "Put the gun away. You don't want to hurt anyone." She tried to soothe him while she figured out the best way to bring him down.

"Shut up, slut!" He jabbed the barrel against her side. Shoving hard, he started the two of them across the room.

Rafe felt the adrenaline that pumped through her body seconds before they rounded the corner. The stillness of her expression and the fact that any man dared touch her sent him surging up from his chair. Michael and Gabriel joined him on their feet a mere second later.

Morrigan was just as quick to react and was on her feet in a heartbeat, drawing a 9mm Beretta from God only knew where.

Sasha stayed in the shadows knowing her likeness to Sarah would only complicate matters. Fists curled as she explored every vile thought and deed in Jordan's mind. When she finished, she made her decision; the animal deserved to die. Slow. Painful. She would see to it.

"Let her go, Jordan," Gabriel ordered, the quiet menace in his voice sending a shiver through the air.

"Give me my wife," Seth countered with a grim smile.

Rafe kept his eyes locked with Montgomery's, waiting for any sign of fear, any sign that would enable him to rip this man limb from bloody limb.

"Is this your woman?" Seth asked, his heated gaze meeting that of his partner's. There was no attempt made by the veteran cop to hide the malicious intent that blazed from his crazed eyes.

"She's mine."

Rafe's emotionless statement drew Seth's attention. The death he saw promised in those icy pools caused his feet to stutter back a step.

"Let her go," Morrigan demanded as she brought Seth's head into her sights. She didn't trust the boys to play fair and she wouldn't let Gomery suffer while testosterone levels rose at such an alarming rate. "Let her go or I'll shoot you."

"I won't go alone." Seth jabbed the gun harder.

Montgomery didn't feel any pain for the adrenaline that ran through her veins. God, she had missed this. At one time, not so long ago she had lived for the sole trill of danger.

A sudden clash of thunder caught her attention then, a sound so loud it rocked the very foundation. It distracted Seth as well and she felt his grip lessen, but still she waited to take him out. There was no fear in her for this man who held a lethal weapon pressed against her back. She had walked away from professionals with more deadly intent than a jealous husband had.

"Where's my wife!" Seth shouted his demand against the rain lashing the windows. "Answer me!"

Lightening flashed through the windows, bright and blinding, giving everyone a chance to move in on their target.

Michael grabbed for Gabriel, holding him back from committing a vicious act they would not be able to explain to the mortals with them. Morrigan adjusted her aim, not wanting to shoot anyone other than the stupid bastard that held her best friend as a shield. Rafe sprang forward like a cat, landing within striking distance of the now struggling pair. They all ignored the shot fired from the gleaming revolver as Montgomery brought her elbow flying back into Seth Jordan's startled face. Using the few seconds advantage that awarded her, she sent him crashing to the floor, his weapon skidding across the room, useless to his searching fingers. Rafe ignored the burning pain in his stomach as he pulled Jordan to his feet only to drive him back to the floor again with a fist to his face.

He didn't get back up.

A few phone calls, Gabriel's influence, and fifteen minutes saw the last of Seth Jordan for that night as the N.O.P.D. escorted him swearing and resisting from the club.

Rafe watched it all with glowing silver eyes. Once they were gone and only immortals remained on the main floor, did he turn to the golden one. "I need your help, Sasha." The soft demand escaped him as he dropped into a chair.

Gabriel's head swiveled in his direction. When he stepped closer, he spotted the blood that seeped from between the long bronzed fingers pressed against a flat stomach.

"I've never been shot before. It burns like hell," Rafe commented, a crooked smile curling his mouth.

"Did it go through?" Sasha asked as she came to his side. She pushed his hand away, wincing at the ugly wound that peeked out through the hole in his shirt.

"No. It's in here somewhere." His answer was faint as he pulled the ruined shirt over his head.

There was absolute silence in the few minutes it took Sasha to work her magic and draw the mangled bullet from Rafe's body. Only when the bullet was in her hand, did the questions start again.

"That's really smashed up. Did it hit bone?" Gabriel asked as he eyed the flattened piece of lead.

"It lodged in the muscle. Why?" Sasha asked.

"You were two feet away from him, from that distance it should have passed right through." Gabriel looked at Rafe closely. "Are you sure you're okay?"

"It hurts over here, but other than that I feel fine," he

replied with a shrug.

"Over where?" Sasha ran her hands over his stomach searching for another injury. Rafe cringed as she probed the skin beneath his ribs. "There's nothing there," she concluded, her gaze flying to Gabriel as an unpleasant thought occurred. "If that had hit someone else first, then hit Rafe, would it look like that?"

"What are you saying?" Rafe didn't give the highlander a chance to answer.

"Montgomery was standing between you and Jordan. What if the bullet struck her first, went through, and then hit you?" Sasha hoped she was wrong.

"Where is she?" Gabriel rose from the table, his green eyes searching the room. When the cops had first shown up, Montgomery had mumbled something to him about going with Michael to his office, but a quick mental question to the fair one proved disappointing. When he looked back to the table, Rafe was already gone. He and Sasha followed.

CHAPTER 17

"Damn this really hurts!" Montgomery groaned as she slid to the floor of her living room, leaving a trail of crimson down the wall behind her. Somehow in the last two years she'd forgotten how excruciating gunshot wounds could be. "What do I do now?" she moaned around a desperate burst of laughter that only served to increase the pain in her back and stomach. What part of her had actually believed she could handle this on her own? The little voice in her head that had convinced her the wound wasn't so bad was still a mystery. Now she wished the damn thing had kept its opinion to itself. If she screamed at the top of her lungs, would someone come to her rescue?

"Leave everything to me."

The amused advise came from the dark depths of her bedroom. Montgomery staggered upright, pulling together a weak defense even as her life's blood pooled in an ever-widening circle on the floor.

"Who the hell are you?" she demanded, her voice growing faint as she swayed. The voice took shape as a woman sauntered closer. "Katherine?" The name slipped out as recognition hit. "How did you get in here? Did Michael send you?" Loosing her balance, she fell against the wall. Sobbing with the pain, she left another stark trail down the wall as her strength gave way and she slid to the floor. "Will you help me?" She bit her lip against another wave of agony.

"Don't worry, *sweet thing,* I have big plans for you."

☨   ☨   ☨

Rafe's eyes locked on the dark streaks that marred the wall

in front of him. The wide circle at his feet held the attention of the other immortals who had appeared in the room only seconds after the dark one had *popped* in.

"Is she alive?" Gabriel asked, missing nothing of the vast size of the stain.

"I can feel her pain," Rafe murmured, his eyes loosing their focus.

"Where is she?" Sasha asked as she tried to find a trace of the woman.

"I don't know." Rafe couldn't pin her down and his feeling of helplessness stabbed deep.

"Does someone have her?" the highlander asked, concern sharpening his voice.

"Katherine has her," Michael answered when he joined them. "I would know that perfume anywhere." The sandalwood was faint, but the scent was one he knew well.

"We can find her." Rafe struggled to remain calm, his even tone at odds with the fierce rage that burned through him.

"Wherever Katherine is, Jamison is not far behind. They are like murder and mayhem; you don't have one without the other." Sasha placed a restraining hand on Rafe. There was no way she could trust him not to get himself killed over the missing woman.

"I thought everyone stayed away from him?"

"They do, if they're not of his making." She answered Michael, but her eyes remained locked on Rafe. Only when she felt him waver under the soothing magic she directed his way did she start a story she'd neglected to share so long ago in London. "Six hundred years ago, Katherine went to him of her own free will. She was a sorceress with great ability, revered by her people, but she wanted something more. Immortality. First she came to me, demanding I change her, but I refused. At the time, I couldn't bring myself to condemn anyone to that bleak existence. I underestimated her determination. She went on from me and found Jamison."

No longer could Sasha protect Katherine from the three.

Taking Montgomery nullified the vow made so long ago. If Katherine courted death so eagerly, there was nothing she could do to save her now.

Sasha continued with the tale. "Jamison allowed Katherine to become his student and when he was satisfied she could match his talents, he brought her over. They've been together off and on ever since that time. There is no love between them. She would break him in a heartbeat if she could, but she is afraid of what he would do to her if she failed."

"Why does he let her stay with him?" Gabriel didn't understand Jamison's reasoning

"He sees her as nothing more than a beautiful, poisonous pet. Katherine keeps him on his toes. Our sire likes the chase and she keeps him guessing." There was nothing else she was willing to share on the subject.

"And they have Montgomery?" Michael's face paled at the thought.

"Katherine might not be with Jamison now. From time to time they do split up." Sasha thought to comfort them with the idea.

"Not this time, Sasha darling." The lilting voice, accompanied by the faint scent of sandalwood, served better than a loudspeaker announcement.

"Katherine." A rough sound slip past Rafe's clenched teeth. Silver eyes focused with astounding accuracy on the slight form of his sire.

"Very good." She kept herself far from his murderous clutches. "You were always so quick, Rafe. That's the only thing I ever liked about you," she taunted as her eyes drifted around the room. "Hmm, Michael and Gabriel as well. What a nice little reunion, too bad your lover couldn't be with us." She evaded the dark immortal with little effort, exhilarated by the panic that warred with the fury in his eyes. "Temper, temper," she admonished him as the three men advanced on her. "Don't you want to know about Montgomery?" The question stopped them all in their tracks. "I thought so."

"Where is she?" Rafe demanded, his voice an icy blast in the heat of their combined rage.

"She's safe for now," Katherine answered with an indifferent shrug of her shoulders. "She's very pretty, if you like sleek, aggressive animals. I think Jamie will like her." She smiled when Rafe blanched at her implication.

"Give her to me now and I'll kill you quick," he promised.

"She really is something, you know. Begging in that pretty drawl of hers for me to help while she sat there on the floor, her life seeping through her fingers." Katherine took a deep breath, sniffing the air. "Can you smell the blood? Isn't it exquisite? All that blood. I shiver just thinking about it. How much more do you think has spilled from her body while I've sat here and visited with old friends? Can you still feel her, Rafe? The pain? The fear?" She taunted him, reckless in her victory. "This is for you, my love. This is your hell. The one I promised you that night. It's all for you. The agony. The suffering. All without me laying a finger on you."

"Don't do this, Katherine," Sasha spoke up, weaving magic through the words in a desperate attempt to end it now.

"Save the parlor tricks, princess. Nothing about this concerns you." She dismissed Sasha with a contemptuous glance.

"What do you want from me in return for her?" Rafe's question was a tormented whisper.

"Your death."

"Then do it. Kill me now and end this." He stepped closer, putting himself within striking distance.

Katherine was tempted, then and there, to rip his heart out but that would never do. Jamison had taught her to savor a victim. "Not yet. What fun would it be if the game ended now? Besides, Jamie really wants to try her out."

Michael and Gabriel grabbing Rafe from behind was the only thing that kept him from tearing her to shreds. The snarl that erupted from his throat was enough to freeze the blood in their veins.

But not Katherine. She pushed harder, searching for a crack

in that control of his. "I wonder if Jamie's gotten started on her yet. Ask Sasha what he's capable of sometime. Or better yet? Just wait and you can feel it for yourself."

"Why not just kill me? Think of how much pleasure you would get from it."

"Not enough. Your suffering would end too soon. This way it lasts past the act itself. This way, your suffering lasts forever."

"Why are you doing this?" Rafe had to know.

"Because I can." Katherine vanished with a snap of her fingers.

No one stood in Rafe's way as he made his way from Montgomery's apartment. No one stopped him as he left Heavens Gate and disappeared into the pouring rain.

ᛉ   ᛉ   ᛉ

The pain was almost bearable, as long as she didn't move. Or breathe. Or think. Montgomery crawled from the bed as fast as her weakened condition would let her and staggered to the door. Pounding on it took all of her strength, and in muted agony, she collapsed to the floor.

"You called?"

Her lashes fluttered open at that familiar voice and she was stunned to see Katherine Darien standing in front of her. "How did you get in?"

"Oh, I've been here awhile."

"I need your help," Montgomery whispered, her face pale as sweat beaded on her skin. "God, this hurts." The pain was miserable but still she struggled to her feet.

For some unknown reason, Katherine couldn't hold back the pity she felt for the injured woman. With a gentleness she'd long thought destroyed, she helped her victim to the bed. Without stopping to second-guess the wisdom of it, she used her magic to put the woman to sleep. While she watched her sleep, she gave in again. Using an old spell, she started the wounds healing. Although the action went against her plan, it couldn't be helped. Rafe would never know that the pain he though was his lover's wasn't real, but a clever simulation planted deep within Montgomery's dreams.

"I should send you away before Jamie sees you," Katherine murmured to the slumbering woman, her hand smoothing a chestnut curl from her forehead. Then she got a grip on her way-ward emotions. There was no way she would lose this golden opportunity to get at Rafe. What the hell had gotten into her? She hadn't felt compassion for a mortal since those days she had spent with David Mallory. Even that affection hadn't stopped her in the long run. The plan had to go on. Rafe had to pay.

"She is magnificent." Jamison appeared at Katherine's side, his voice full of wonder as he stood beside the bed and stared down at the slumbering brunette. "There is a strength in her I would just love to consume. A desire, I long to claim as my own." He knelt beside the woman. "Come to me, my sweet," he whispered the words against her throat, his hunger growing in unison to his body's arousal. Lust swamped him a fierce wave that rivaled the bestial craving for blood that he had never tried to curb. "Come to me."

"There's nothing special about her." Katherine tried to nudge him away from Montgomery. "I told you to eat earlier; she's not your dinner. Keep your teeth to yourself." If only she could distract him from the woman.

Jamison growled in protest, but he drew his mouth away from the honey-skinned morsel. "I think I'll keep her," he mur-mured as he tangled his fingers into her chestnut curls.

Katherine flinched away from the open lust she saw reflected in his soulless eyes. Very few times in her existence had she seen Jamie hunger after anything but blood. Now here he was, a mortal woman lying helpless before him, while he planned only God knew what. She repressed a shudder. What he had put her through before the change had been bad enough, and that had been with little sexual interest on his part. He had used her body, but he hadn't *wanted* her. What would he do to a woman who fired his lust? A woman who made his blood run hot?

"She is the darkness my soul has craved since the beginning of time. All she needs is my blood to set her free of her mortal cage."

The odd look in his eyes frightened Katherine and she stumbled back from the obsession that filled his soulless eyes.

ᛏ   ᛏ   ᛏ

"Did you find her?" Michael asked as the dark one appeared before him. "What's wrong?" No longer could he ignore the pallor that bleached the color from Rafe's bronzed features. Their differences would just have to wait until after they had Montgomery back.

"I can feel her torment. I can feel it." Rafe sank into the chair, no longer able to stand the pain that pulsed through him.

"We'll get her back," Michael promised. "Gabriel's out looking now and Sasha is working some of that magic of hers. Now that you're back, I can go help. Stay here in case Katherine comes back. You can get more information out of her than I can. I lack your flare for interrogation."

"How is Morrigan taking this?" Rafe asked of the blonde woman.

"Dammit," Michael rasped out, his blue eyes blazing. "We forgot about her in all the chaos. I don't even know if she's back yet." He stood up quickly as he sorted out his thoughts. Clearing his mind, he called to Gabriel searching for the answer. The one he received didn't make him happy. "She left the police station an hour ago."

"Where would she go?" Rafe asked even as another spasm of pain racked his body.

Michael reached out a hand to steady him. "Here. She'd come back here," he replied.

"She'd go to the apartment," Rafe added, his thoughts were bleak over what she'd find there.

Michael didn't express his intentions before he left the

room. The sight that greeted him when he opened the door to Montgomery's apartment wasn't one he would ever forget, no matter how hard he tried.

Rafe edged in behind him and went to where she knelt on the floor. She didn't remove her eyes from the blood that stained the palm of her hand. "Morrigan." Rafe spoke her name soft and low even as everything inside of him screamed at the sight of Montgomery's blood.

Michael sank down beside her. Taking her hand in his, he used the edge of his shirt to wipe it clean. She didn't protest when he laid her hand back in her lap. Nor did she blink as her eyes shifted to the dark streaks on the wall in front of her.

Grasping her chin with his fingers, Rafe turned her head in his direction. "Morrigan," he broke off when he saw the shock in her eyes. The little blonde was way past anything he could say to help her.

"Where's Montgomery?"

They were surprised to hear the calmness in her voice. The sound was so serene they could have been discussing the weather.

"She's not here," Michael's tone was harsher than he'd intended. Her dazed gaze swung in his direction and he knew he needed to get her out of here. He looked to his friend for a suggestion.

Before Rafe could help, another stabbing pain hit him. Pulling himself upright, he staggered to the couch, drawing a ragged breath against the agony.

"I need you to come with me." Michael softened his tone as he tried to coax her away from the violence of the room. Morrigan didn't budge.

"This is so much like before," she whispered.

"Before when?" Rafe asked from the couch. The silent lasted for so long he was sure she wasn't going to answer. She surprised him when she did.

"It's like it was in Paris." Morrigan turned anguished eyes on Michael as she confessed.

Rafe gained his feet then, walking closer until he stood over where they still knelt on the floor. What she spoke of wasn't a mystery to him. The version of that night he'd gotten from Montgomery hadn't answered many of his questions though. Morrigan's would. "What happened that night?"

"We were supposed to work together on the Paris mission, but I had a problem develop and she went over without me. By the time I got there it was too late." Morrigan shook off the dangerous lassitude that filled her. Now wasn't the time to buckle under to the pressure of old fears.

"Why weren't you there?" Rafe ignored the sharp glance Michael shot his way. If retelling the story broke her, he would leave it up to the fair one to pick up the pieces. Her state of mind wasn't his concern right now. "What did you need to settle that was more important than keeping Gomery in one piece?" His words were condemning and hit her hard, but he couldn't stop. Morrigan met his accusations head on and the self-loathing he saw on her face was dark enough to rival his own.

"The day before the mission was to start, I accepted a marriage proposal from an operative working with me." The smile on her face was bitter. "I took the ring with every intention of going with her even though he'd begged me not to. An hour before I should have left, I was hospitalized and my fiancé was sent in my place. When I was well enough to travel, I joined them in Paris. There was a big party going on that night and little for me to do. After finding out the room arrangements and the coverage schedule from the technical op, I went to Gomery's room and waited for her. When I got bored, I started to look around. You couldn't imagine my surprise when I found his class ring in the sheets."

"Whose ring?" Michael didn't see where a ring fit into the story.

"My fiancé's. His ring was in Gomery's bed. His clothes were in her closet and the smell of his cologne was all over the sheets." Morrigan smiled slightly at Michael's incredulous expression.

"What did you do?" he asked.

"Nothing. Montgomery didn't know about us. I never told her that I was seeing him, let alone thinking of marrying him. And I'm pretty sure he didn't volunteer the information while he was screwing her."

"Did you confront him?" Rafe was already ahead of this part. He remembered what Gomery had said about her lover betraying her. Now he knew that the lover had been Morrigan's as well. The man had used them, one against the other, getting inside information to aid him in his assassination. No wonder the man hadn't wanted both women in Paris.

"Before I could do anything, there was a shot fired in the garden below. At the sound, I went out to the balcony, climbed over the railing and swung down. There were four more shots fired in the minute it took me to find them. I couldn't even tell if Gomery was alive for all the blood.

"At first I couldn't understand why Nik was just standing there staring down at her or why she hadn't drawn her gun. Her client was dead and she hadn't even drawn her weapon." She shuddered as her gaze locked on the bloodstains.

"Gomery told me that one of her team shot him. Did he ever know you were there that night?" Rafe asked. Had it been difficult for her to watch him die? Or had there been vindication for her in the death of the man that had betrayed her with her best friend? Not for a second did he believe she held Montgomery to blame for any of it. He doubted Morrigan had ever shared with her the facts that had surrounded that fateful night.

"Nik never saw me that night, not even when I killed him."

ፐ   ፐ   ፐ

Come to me.

Montgomery heard the words echo in her dreams as she struggled against the invading waves of consciousness.

Come to me.

The command came again as wakefulness nudged her with an unkind elbow, but she didn't want to wake up. If she was asleep, she could pretend the pain didn't exist.

"Come to me."

The voice was a whisper against her ear and no longer could she elude reality. However, reality didn't prepare her for large man who laid so close to her on the bed. So close in fact, that his very breath brushed her skin. Montgomery didn't even blink at the harsh, sculpted features that filled her line of vision. Nor did she express a thought as he rose from the bed. He was easily as big as Gabriel, but she didn't sense Gabriel's gentleness in this man.

"Where am I?"

Her lack of fear intrigued him. Never had he seen a mortal who didn't fear him. Even before he had become a vampire, he had invoked terror in others. Humans feared just the look of him, the soulless savagery that was his eyes. That had been his gift and he had gloried in that power to terrorize. But this woman didn't show any fear.

"You're in my home," he answered, leaning over her with a slight smile. Still no reaction. Just those brave green-gold eyes staring up at him. Jamison wanted more from her. Trailing a finger down the valley between her breasts, he waited. The wait didn't take long and the right cross that smashed into his jaw pleased him. The woman had spirit.

Rolling from the bed, Montgomery placed herself far from his reach. "Don't you dare touch me!" The threat behind the words didn't seem to faze the big man and she wasn't sure how much of a defense she could gather in her weakened condition.

"Come to me, my sweet." He beckoned her to him with a curl of his large hand.

"Go to hell!" She edged closer to the door, the palm of her right hand pressed against the pain in her stomach.

Jamison watched her for a moment, missing nothing of the fatigue in her eyes or the lines that bracketed her mouth as she fought against the muted agony that still rippled through her body with each breath. Although Katherine had helped the woman, she still suffered. Nevertheless, it pleased him that she fought against it. Pleased him that she defied him enough to reach for the door handle. Now to see if she was worthy of his pleasure.

He crossed the room in long strides, reaching for her with large, rough hands. Montgomery didn't hesitate for a second as she struck out with a kick that should have sent the big man crashing to the floor. Instead, he caught her foot in his hand, laughing even as he dropped it and pulled her against him.

"Isn't she glorious, my pet?" Jamison spoke to the immortal that had brought him such a prize.

"Yes, she is." Katherine came forward from her place in the shadows.

"Can you feel the darkness? The raw animal instincts that are even now causing her to fight me, when she has no chance of winning?" he asked. "Can you see the rage and hate that gather just beneath the surface of that beautiful skin? Do you still wonder what your dark immortal saw in her? In what I want from her?"

Jamie never turned his soulless eyes from the woman struggling in his arms. He didn't want to miss a second of that glorious drive, that fearless determination. "Where's your dagger, pet?"

"Why do you want it?" Katherine didn't trust his need for her ceremonial blade.

"Get it for me, pet." Jamison watched the alarm that filled those gold-flecked pools. Finally, a reaction he could anticipate. A reaction to feed to his hunger.

"Let go of me, you bastard!" Montgomery raged as she fought against the arms of iron that held her.

"Get it now."

Katherine continued to stand frozen in place, her eyes locked on the battle that Gomery waged against her captor. How she wished she had never brought the woman here. No one deserved what Jamie would do to her. No one.

"Why do you need it?" She glared at him with hate-filled eyes. "That blade is mine; it's sacred to my people."

"I'd have thought you had learned not to question me by now." Jamison looked at her. "Maybe I need to remind you again. I guarantee it will be the last time. Now, get me that damned blade or I'll allow you to share her pain."

Katherine flinched away from the red glow that consumed his eyes. Before he could retaliate, she fled the room, the door banging closed behind her.

Montgomery redoubled her efforts to escape when he turned back to her. The look on his face should have scared her, but it didn't. Fury consumed her instead, hot and burning, it released from within her, a reckless, treacherous, dangerous darkness that refused capture.

Jamison smiled when he saw all that was to be in those eyes. The search was over; he'd found what he had been searching for.

"Here it is, Jamie."

He didn't even look over his shoulder as Katherine slipped the dagger into his hand. The ancient dragon's claw that made up the handle of the weapon was a relic of a long forgotten people that had excelled in magic and sorcery. He had lived longer than most cultures, had seen empires rise and fall, but this dagger was older. The tortures he'd inflicted with it over the centuries were too numerous to count. Tonight he would add more.

Before either woman could move, he pressed the tip of the blade to Gomery's throat. He watched in fascination the bead of crimson that welled and then rolled down the honey colored column of her neck. Lowering the dagger, he brought his mouth to her skin.

CHAPTER 18

They couldn't find her. Two days had passed and all of Sasha's magic hadn't located even a trace of Montgomery. She had even gone to other vampires, some which had shown outright fear in the presence of the golden immortal. All had denied knowledge of Jamison and Katherine.

When Rafe had gone back alone with Gomery's pain racking his body and stealing his control, they'd still refused to give him the answers he demanded. Not even when he left them bloody and beaten had they caved in and revealed their secrets. Fear of the brutal, ancient immortal ran rampant through the underworld and not a single lost soul wanted to be the one to betray Jamison.

Rafe didn't stop his search though, no matter how great the pain or strong the fear that racked him. In the endless hours, he was never left to wonder if she was alive, only how much more she could endure. For her sake, he wished it could end but knew that wouldn't happen, not until Katherine had received her measure of revenge. Only when they laid Montgomery in the ground and his suffering was eternal, would Katherine be satisfied.

Then his revenge would begin.

The little bitch would rue the day she'd ever taken what was his. He would hunt her until the end of time. When he found her, when he had her at his mercy, he would destroy her. Piece by piece he would rip her apart and when nothing but her black heart remained, he would tear it out and offer it to the demon gods she worshipped. Only then would it be over.

Sasha's hand on his shoulder drew his attention. A quick glance confirmed his worst fears. The golden one didn't have good news. There was a deep well of worry in her eyes when she looked his way. Worry for him. Several times, she had tried to wipe away the pain he shared with his missing lover, but he had refused. He needed to feel the pain. Needed to know she was alive.

Instead, Sasha had used that magic to erase Morrigan's memories concerning Montgomery's disappearance. In the time it had taken Sasha to answer their summons, it had been all they could do to keep the little blonde at bay. Her need to find her friend had been ferocious. The strength of will she possessed had amazed him and that little bit of magic was nothing short of a blessing.

Sometimes though, he didn't think all those bleak memories were gone. More than once he had looked up to see an alarming expression on Morrigan's face or an ugly little gleam in her bright purple eyes. When he saw those brief flashes of intent, he almost wished they could sic her on Katherine. That would have served the bitch right.

"What would you have me do?" Sasha asked as she sat down beside him on the couch.

Rafe flinched away from the pity in her eyes. Out of all of them, she understood his sorrow the most. For centuries, she had shared as strong a connection with Gabriel, so she was no stranger to what he was going through.

"We have to find her," he murmured, closing his eyes as fatigue defeated him. "I need her back with me." He hadn't meant to say those words ever again, but couldn't stop now as they tumbled past the ice that had kept them at bay all these hundreds of years. "I need her."

"We can't find her, Raphael. No one will help us." Sasha pulled him into her arms and tried to absorb some of the pain that racked him. There was so much of it and if anyone knew what her sire could do, she did. She knew what he was doing to Montgomery. What he would still do to her.

In knowing that, she also knew Rafe's beautiful lover would not survive, but she had yet to tell him and never would. But there was one last offer to make now, one last attempt to ease his pain. She watched on in silence as another spasm crossed his face. Watched as his knuckles tightened in response to an agony he could not control.

"I can end her suffering if you let me," she spoke, her voice a soothing whisper. "All I need is your help."

"He wouldn't be able to hurt her anymore?"

"She would be beyond his reach," she evaded.

"How so?" His silver gaze missed nothing of the secrets she couldn't hide.

"I can use her connection with you to release her. Then her suffering would be over." Sasha saw the refusal in his mind before it emerged from his lips.

"Because she'd be dead." The pretty explanation hadn't fool Rafe.

"Dead is better than what Jamison is capable of."

"What is he doing to her?"

Sasha couldn't look at him for the torment in his whispered words. "I don't know." She wouldn't tell him of the atrocities Jamison excelled at. No matter what, he could never know.

"In the morning." Rafe stood up and moved away from her. "Come see me in the morning."

She didn't have to ask why as he left to go search one last time.

ʏ   ʏ   ʏ

Gabriel stood back from the door of the club. He didn't really want to go in and have to look Morrigan in the eyes and try to act like nothing was wrong. Something *was* wrong, so wrong that none of them would ever be able to fix it. Part of him didn't want to think that finding Gomery was a lost cause but in his heart, he knew they would never find her until Katherine wanted her found. As much as he wanted to, he couldn't hide out here forever. Just as he turned the knob, he felt a tingle up his spine, like fingernails on a chalkboard. Setting his feet and squaring his shoulders, he took a deep breath.

His night had just gotten better.

"Now that's a damn shame. A man holds a woman at gun-point and he's back on the streets in a few days. What is the jus-tice system coming too?" The question was a slow taunt as Gabriel turned to face his partner "Have something you want to say to me, Jordan?" The fool didn't have enough sense to fear the elated gleam in his eyes and took a step closer.

"Where is my wife?" No emotion colored Seth's voice as he made his demand. "I know she's with you. Where do you have her hidden?" He stood close to Gabriel now, so close their breaths mingled in the still night air.

Jordan wasn't afraid of the larger man. He didn't think the pretty boy had anything in him. The way his friend had stepped in front of him the other night proved that. The blond piece of fluff had held Arden back with ease. Now the dark-haired bas-tard was a different matter. Fahlan had brought him to his knees. Those cold gray eyes had given him a moment of fear, but that man wasn't here. He had watched Fahlan leave over an hour ago. There would be no help for Arden from that quar-ter. When he was through with his partner, it would be his wife's turn to pay.

"Sarah's in a safe place," Gabriel answered. "A place where you can't touch her with your filthy hands." A slight smile curved his lips. All he needed was for Jordan to throw the first punch, then every dark thing inside of him could break loose. Decades had passed since he had felt this way; decades since the animal inside of him had fought so hard to gain freedom. For once, he relished what he was capable of.

This time he could let the demon inside go, but first he would let Jordan sign his own execution papers. The human part needed just a minimum of justification for what he would do. Just a little nudge.

"Do you want to take this inside?" Gabriel opened the doors. Once he started, he didn't want to have to stop, not until nothing remained of this disgusting excuse for a man but bloody pulp and shattered bone. When he had told Michael his plan to exterminate Seth Jordan, he hadn't been overstating his intentions. Death was the very least this man deserved and he had so much more planned.

Gabriel turned his back on the older man and preceded him inside. There would be nothing to stop him now; no one to see and not a single person to stand in his way. Even the thought of cleaning up the mess didn't daunt his pleasure.

Jordan couldn't believe that Arden was playing it so cool, as if he didn't have a care in the world. But he would care. Before he was done, the wife stealing punk would care. The bastard would beg for mercy before this was finished.

Reaching into his pocket, he slipped out a switchblade knife he had lifted off a drug dealer years ago. That punk had learned the hard way what cheating Seth Jordan entailed. The kid's face had never been the same after he'd finished carving on it. Arden would never be the same either, but it wasn't his face he intended to cut. Not at first.

"Where's the stupid bitch at? I don't have all day to wait on you. Give her over and I won't hurt you too bad," Seth promised with an insincere smile. The other man's laughter brought his head up with a snap.

"That's so understanding of you," Gabriel taunted. "If somebody took my wife away from me and screwed her, I don't think I'd be as forgiving. But, at your age, you should be grateful. Now that I've tired her out, you might be able to handle her. Of course, it took me two or three times a night the first few nights, but I aim to please." Gabriel watched with satisfaction as Jordan flicked open the blade. "You just give me a call when she gets to be a handful again. Better yet, why don't I just keep her for awhile?" Light glinted on the knife as Jordan changed his grip on it. "I doubt she'll want you after me."

Gabriel caught the hand holding the blade as it swept toward his face. "Took you long enough." Closing the knife, he slipped it back into Seth's T-pocket with a gentle pat. Curling his fingers into the cotton of Jordan's shirt, he hauled him in close.

"It's not nice to play with knives," he chided as he tightened his grip.

The tread of footsteps on the stairs took Gabriel's gaze, but not his attention. Turning his head, he met the eyes of the one person he couldn't explain any of this away to.

Morrigan watched in fascination as Gabriel reluctantly removed his hand from Jordan's shirt front. She lingered as Jordan made his escape.

"I'll get back to you, Arden," Seth promised with a foul expression on his flushed face.

"Not if I get to you first."

The smile on Gabriel's face didn't confuse Morrigan at all. Nor did she turn her gaze from the viciousness of it even when their uninvited guest slammed the door on his way out.

"I know a good place to hide the body," she broke the silence. "No one would ever know."

Gabriel relaxed under the steady purple of her gaze and studied her, seeing the lines of exhaustion that framed those Liz Taylor eyes. "Maybe next time," he returned with a rueful twist of his lips. There would be a next time.

Looking over Morrigan's head, he stiffened as Sasha glided into his range of vision.

Sasha met his guarded gaze and then ignored him. "Still going out, Morrigan?" she asked of the blonde when she came abreast of her.

"I was on my way out, but Seth Jordan slowed me down a little." Morrigan turned to Gabriel. "I'll be back later. Let me know if Gomery calls. It's not like her to leave and not call me."

He looked away from the confusion he saw on Morrigan's face. Sasha's little mojo didn't seem to be working very well. "I'll let you know."

"Jordan was here?" Sasha took her time reading the intent in his eyes. What she saw there caused her to sit down on the steps. She had made him into this. All those ugly thoughts and plans in his head were her fault. When she'd given him her blood, she'd done this. If she allowed him to go after Jordan, he would become the monster he accused her of making him.

"You will leave him alone," she ordered as she rose to her feet.

"Not hardly." Seth Jordan wasn't something he planned to discuss with her. In the few days she'd been in residence, they had avoided each other. Or rather, she had avoided him. He had tried to talk to her several times, but she had refused. What surprised him was that she bothered to expend herself enough to interfere with his business now. "Jordan is mine to deal with, angel."

"I won't let you become the monster you accused me of making you." Her voice was harsh, the honey tones washed away by the sorrow in her heart.

"What has he to do with any of that?" He viewed her through narrowed eyes.

"There is no way I'll let you kill him. You still carry the guilt from the part you played in your cousin's unfortunate death. How much more would you suffer if you took a life on purpose?" She grabbed his arm, not trusting him to stay and hear her out. "I can't let you do this. It's not your true self that wants to hurt this man, but the demon I planted in your soul that night when I gave you back your life. That you carry such murderous thoughts at all is my fault." She couldn't ignore the laughter that bubbled up from her amused highlander. "What is so funny?" she demanded when he settled down.

"This is priceless." His shoulders shook with mirth. "You didn't give me any murderous inclinations, angel. I had those long before I ever looked up into your amber eyes. Ever since I was a wee lad training in the wild Highlands with my father's kin, I've had a vicious temper and a need for vengeance. That's how I was raised, the way of my clan. I'm not a product of your blood; I'm a product of mine." He stopped when she shook her head at him again.

"You were noble and proud and perfect." Sasha wanted to cry her heartache to the world. She had changed this man into a demon. "You challenged your cousin to defend that poor girl."

Gabriel placed a finger against her lips to still her words and felt her shudder at the contact, but he refused to give into the fire that shot up his arm at the feel of her skin against his. He had a point to make and no matter what, he would see it through.

"Leave the poor girl out of this, Sasha. She was never any of your concern." The tears in her eyes almost made him hold back his next words but he couldn't allow her to think she had created within him the demon he had lived with since his life began. "I killed him on purpose, angel. I didn't want to wound him; I didn't want to teach him a lesson. I wanted him dead. If that bullet hadn't killed him, then I would have beaten him to death with my bare hands. There was no way in hell he was surviving that day." Sasha sat down on the step, her eyes huge in her face as if seeing him for the first time. "When he touched Emily, he signed his own death warrant. I was just the executioner."

She didn't call out when he turned from her and walked away. Gabriel wasn't as circumspect. When he reached the door and looked back, there was a warning in his eyes. "Jordan is mine, Sasha. He ended his life the day he laid his hands on Sarah. The bastard's a walking dead man; he just doesn't know it yet. Very soon, he will. Very soon. Don't cross me on this. You might think you're responsible for what I am, you might think you can help me but you can't. Nothing will stop me until he's dead. Nothing will stand in my way." He wondered at the determination that crossed her face when she stood and approached him.

Sasha knew what she had to do. Regardless of what she would suffer for it, she would see it through. But first she needed something he had. Standing on tiptoes, she pulled his head down to hers, chanting a little spell in her head as she moved her lips against his.

She needed his cooperation for just a few seconds and he

gave it. Then she felt something move and what she had needed from Gabriel slid from his body and slammed into hers. It didn't happen gradually as it had when he had taken it from Sarah, but all at once, with no reprieve. Sasha pulled away from him and dropped to her knees panting against the agony that invaded her.

When she looked up at him with all that pain in her eyes, he knew. Gabriel knew what she had taken from him. The suffering that had kept him focused on his revenge was gone. She had stolen all the torment away from him that he had gathered from Sarah. The legacy he had intended to return to its rightful owner was nothing more than a memory.

"How could you?" he rasped the accusation, coming down on his knees beside her. "You had no right. This doesn't concern you." Digging his fingers into her loose auburn curls, he jerked her against him, his mouth slanting across hers. "Give it back." He demanded. "Give it back, damn you!"

"No. It's mine now." She refused him through pale lips, panting helplessly as she worked her way through the pain.

"This changes nothing. I'll give him some new pain and misery to remember his abuse by. He'll beg for death before I'm through." His smile was cold as he let her go. "This isn't over between us, angel," he challenged from the doorway. "I won't forget your interference. I won't forgive."

"So be it," she whispered as he walked out on her.

᛭   ᛭   ᛭

Michael couldn't believe his luck at having caught this trail. He climbed the ten-foot high fence that surrounded the old four-story house. Not bothering to knock on the door, he kicked it in. There was no place for subtlety in his life right now. Gomery was here. They held her in this house. Somewhere upstairs in one of those rooms they had her; he climbed the stairs without hesitation. Nothing would keep him from her. Nothing. She needed him.

He kicked in doors as he stalked down the hallway. Gomery was so near that he could smell her. Reaching the next landing, he stopped. Someone else was here. The faint odor of sandalwood confirmed who.

"Hello, Katherine." No part of him was surprised when the petite beauty emerged from the inky shadows. She seemed to float across the distance as she approached him, as stunning now in tight blue-jeans as she'd been in jeweled-satin two centuries ago. In his confusion the other night, he had failed to appreciate that fact. Stunning but lethal; he'd learned that lesson well. Time had given him an edge though and he owed her one.

"Hello, lover." Her sultry expression would have done a harem girl proud. "Come for the woman? Or did you miss me?" Katherine watched his fists clench. "My, my, has the party boy developed a temper?" Not threatened by the display, she took a reckless step forward. After all, this wasn't Rafe. She didn't have anything to fear. Michael was just a purring pussycat. "Are you mad at me, Michael?" She pouted up at him, feeling a little thrill at the fire that blazed from those pale eyes. He had such pretty eyes. "For what I did to you all those years ago?"

"No, Katherine, you made me the man I am today. How could I be anything but grateful?"

Feeling a warm glow of lust fill her body, she leaned in closer. Just being near him made her tingle. Knowing what he could do to her body fired her blood. If he had taken her control when he was a mere human, what could he do as an immortal?

"I gave you a gift," she fairly purred as she ran a delicate hand down his arm. "Rafe didn't appreciate his." She smiled as he pulled her closer to his powerful frame. "I'm glad one of you realizes the benefit of living forever."

"Eternity," he whispered the one word as he wrapped her into his embrace. With her head resting against his chest, she missed the hatred in his eyes. "I have eternity to watch people

I might come to care about grow old and die."

Katherine flinched as he tightened his hold but was unable to decipher anything from the serene expression that graced his angel face.

"I have eternity to live with the ghosts I created. To live with my guilt. I have eternity to stare at the blood that stains my hands. To dream of the hell I should have died and gone to years ago. I have eternity to suffer through alone. Yes, I have so much to thank you for."

The calm façade dropped and she wanted to flee from the emotions that played over that perfect face. She struggled against the iron strength of his embrace.

Michael let her go. This wasn't what he had come for. He needed Gomery. When she was safe, he would deal with Katherine if Rafe didn't get to her first. With the dark one, anything was possible. He smiled at the thought. "Tell me where she is."

"She's not here," Katherine denied with a careless shrug. Jamie had taken the woman at dusk and she had no idea where he had gone. After what he had done the last two days, she was glad he was no longer here. What he had inflicted on Montgomery Sinclair had been enough to cause her to protest and had gotten her special punishments she shuddered just to remember. If she never saw Jamison again, it wouldn't be too soon. Maybe Rafe would find him. She brightened at the thought. It would almost be worth telling the dark immortal what Jamie had done to the woman just to see who would survive the battle.

In light of what had transpired, the woman would no doubt be dead by now. How she wished she could be able to watch Rafe rip her sire apart, but she had other plans. She was clearing out. This town was not a safe place to be anymore. It was only a matter of time before one or both of the other *Angels* found her. Michael she could handle, Rafe was a different story and she didn't even want to think about Gabriel.

Michael lifted her face to his. She was lying to him. He

doubted the little demon had ever told the truth in her whole life, but he would get the truth from her this time, no matter what it took. No matter what he had to do. With her, he felt no need to be the man he pretended. With Katherine, he could be himself.

"Not going to tell me, are you?" he asked her with a great deal of amusement. "Afraid of Jamie that much? I would like to meet the man that has you so scared. Hell, you took me out that night without breaking a sweat. Well, maybe you did sweat a little." She flushed at his reminder. "You caught Gabriel off guard, too. That was quite a feat. I don't think anyone has ever caught him unaware." Michael leaned down until his mouth was only a breath from hers.

"He's really a savage when he's provoked. You did that in spades. Rafe was the only one who didn't fall for your little act. He saw right through you, didn't he? Knew what you were about from the second he saw you with David. You remember David, don't you? Or have you killed so many that their faces all blur together? He was a great man. A true noble." He drew her to him until the heat from his body mingled with hers.

Katherine shivered at his touch, fighting back a moan when his lips nuzzled the corner of her mouth. Then she did moan when her nipples hardened against his chest.

"Did you kill him yourself or did you hire someone?" he coaxed as he slid his mouth down the curve of her throat.

"I did it myself," she answered, lost in a daze as he slid his hands around her waist to stroke the arch of her back.

"Did it give you pleasure to cut his throat? Did you get off on killing a man whose only sin was loving you? How do you walk the shadows without fear? Retribution is an ugly thing, Katie my darling. You close your eyes at night and every life you've ruined, every soul you've destroyed, comes out to play in your worst nightmares. You can't escape them and no matter what you may think, they never go away. I bet you have a lot of playmates locked up in your dreams, don't you? Can you even close your eyes for what you will see?" He tilted her chin up until he could see the passion that filled her black eyes.

Katherine didn't try to look away. What she saw on his face held her spellbound. He knew what he spoke of; he lived with his own shadows. David had told her he had a darker side, but she had ignored his words. She had been so sure that Michael was a man simple in his needs and easy to control. She'd assumed wrong.

"Where is Montgomery?" he demanded, all playfulness forgotten as he gripped her arms.

Katherine knew he wouldn't believe her. Knew there was nothing she could offer to make him see reason. "Jamie took her. He left with her but didn't tell me what he had planned."

A gasp slipped from her as Michael walked her back against the wall. He hadn't hurt her but he would, she could see that as clear as she could feel the strength of his body pressed against hers. "I can't help you," she whispered as she placed her hands on his broad shoulders. Wriggling her body against his, she looked for any sign of emotion.

That night in London she had given him pleasure, maybe she could use her body to her advantage again. Leaning into him, Katherine pressed her full breasts to his chest and caught the faint hiss that escaped him. Moving her arms higher, she curled them around his neck. "Forget about her, Michael. She's probably dead by now. For her sake I pray she is." She turned her face up to his and pressed her lips to the underside of his jaw.

"Katie."

He whispered to her as she moved her lips across his. No one had ever called her that. She would have been offended if they had, but on Michael the shortened version of her name was like a caress.

"It's not that easy." He pushed her away with a steady hand.

"Forget about her, lover, and everything could be like it was before. We were so good together. We could have that for eternity." She saw the indecision on his face. Saw something flicker, then shift, in those blue eyes and gloried in the heat of it.

"You want to play with me, Katie?" His words were a sensual whisper over her senses. Then he reached for her, his fingers tangling into her raven hair. His hold was far from gentle as he pinned her to the wall. "Then let's play," he gritted out through bared teeth. "Where is she?"

The savagery of his expression stole her thoughts. "I don't know, Michael." The press of his body on hers was a blatant warning of what could be.

"Still want to play, Katie?" he taunted as he wedged a knee between her legs.

For the first time in a long time, she felt the very real fear of a mortal woman. Jamie had taken her like this before, but she knew what to expect from him. Michael was a different story. She had no clue as to the hurt he could inflict with those deceptive eyes and skilled hands. "I don't know where she is. Please, I'm telling the truth." She flinched from the smile on his face.

"It's different, isn't it? When you're not the one calling the shots? When you're not the one playing with peoples' lives? Don't you like being the victim, Katie?"

Had Jamie not stolen all her tears long ago she might have cried. She had no doubt that Michael would use her, that he would hurt her.

Michael had never used force in his life and had she only used her head, she would have been able to tell that having her at his mercy wasn't turning him on. However, he wasn't going to enlighten her to that fact, not until he had what he needed. Pulling on her hair, he tilted her head back until she could see the threat in his eyes. She couldn't escape as he brought his mouth crashing down on hers.

The brutality of it ended abruptly and she could only guess what had caused him to pull away from her. Then she didn't care as she slid down the wall and slumped on the floor. Katherine listened as he stalked down the stairs and slammed out of the house. Dragging her hand across her face, she couldn't quite believe the tears she found there. She hadn't cried in six hundred years, not since that night she had buried her hopes, her heart, and her soul all with the battered body of one man.

Michael stood out on the street and cursed himself for a fool. He had let the witch get the better of him. Maybe she didn't know where Gomery was, but if he found out later that she had lied to him again, he would be back. Nothing would stop him then, not her magic, not her pleas, and sure as hell not her tears.

CHAPTER 19

Rafe was alone again and there was only one thing on his mind; the pain had stopped. He could no longer feel her. His head knew what that meant but something within him refused to believe it. They had ended her life. Sasha had warned him that Gomery would die, but he had thought to beat the odds. In his arrogance, he had thought to keep her safe. He hadn't even gotten a chance to tell her he cared. She had died thinking he felt nothing. Died in an agony unlike anything on earth. Died while those monsters had her.

Now it would be their turn. Katherine and her bastard sire would never have a moment of peace if it took him until the end of time.

Opening the door, he didn't bother with the light as he crossed the living room. Out of the corner of his eye, he saw the outline of a large figure. Only one man took up that much space and he needed the understanding that the big man was capable of.

"It's over, Gabriel." His voiced sounded hollow in the twilight.

"I wouldn't say that, Fahlan," a deep voice answered back. "I would say things are just beginning."

With a simple thought, Rafe flooded the room with light. The dark intruder didn't even blink at the brightness that encompassed every corner. He was a big son of a bitch, bigger even than Gabriel, but Rafe wasn't intimidated by the cruelty reflected in those deep ebony eyes. He and Sasha had seen some scary characters in the last few days and not one of them would ever forget him now. A minimum of thinking and a healthy dose of physical violence had seen to that.

The paleness of the man's skin was Rafe's first hint that his intruder was a true vampire and not one of the half breeds that Katherine and Sasha were able to create. Alabaster skin coupled with his black hair and eyes made the fact even harder to miss. Maybe his message had gotten to the right ears after all and this demon was here to furnish him with some useful information.

"What can I do for you?" Rafe challenged, his misery not forgotten but put on hold. He watched with avid curiosity as the black-haired vampire moved closer. Although the man was very broad across the shoulders, he didn't step back, not even when he could feel his breath on his skin. He had much bigger inner demons to wrestle with than what this huge immortal could represent.

"It's more of what I can do for you," his visitor replied with a cruel twist of his lips. "You've been searching for a woman. I know where she is." Jamison watched the coldness that encompassed the silver of Fahlan's eyes. He could actually see as the dark one closed down each and every emotion and was impressed. Very few people had that much control, and none who had ever shared even a drop of his blood. Even if he didn't know it yet, Fahlan did share his blood. The same blood he had given Katherine long ago was even now rushing through the dark immortal's veins as he prepared himself for battle.

"Where is she?" Rafe asked as if it mattered not in the least. "If your information is useful, I'll let you leave in one piece. If not … " He trailed off with a cold smile that would have frightened a lesser revenant.

"I heard that you were making your way through the ranks," Jamison chided him. "You've made quite a name for yourself. Not that you didn't already have a formidable reputation. You have been the talk of our kind since the day of your creation. The three of you are very unique."

"Why is that?" Rafe had a slight curiosity.

"You're the first of Katherine's creations to turn on her. Most appreciate her charms. Granted, the fair one isn't as immune as you would think, but you have them all puzzled. All of that control you value is very unusual among us. They keep waiting for the leash to snap. So am I. That's why I'm here." He looked into Fahlan's eyes and waited.

"Why don't you tell me what you know about the woman. All of this other information is interesting, but I don't see what the opinion of the underworld has to do with me. I don't care what they, or you, think of me and my control." He flashed that cold smile again and gestured the big man to continue. Something about him put Rafe on guard. There was something about the man that had been lacking in the rest. A rather amused knowledge that hinted at dark secrets. This vampire wasn't like the others.

"Katherine had quite a little plan in mind for you and the woman."

Rafe froze. Not once had he mentioned that Katherine had Gomery. In his search he had been looking for Jamison. He took a step closer to the vampire.

"Beware the fury of a woman scorned and all that." Jamison didn't move back from the dawning awareness that flitted through those unusual silver eyes. He watched, knowing that the threads in the leash were snapping one by one. Before he was through, chaos would rein supreme.

"Where is she?" Rafe gritted out through bared teeth, no longer pretending indifference.

Another thread snapped.

"Where is she, you son of a bitch?"

Jamison ignored the fist that Fahlan used to pull him nose to nose. Almost there. "I haven't seen Katherine since this afternoon. I assume she's long gone by now. We didn't part on good terms. She was a little miffed with me over the methods I use to obtain obedience. Women." He watched in growing fascination the fury on Fahlan's face. All that rage and still he managed to hold it in. Unbelievable.

"Where is my woman?" The words were brutal hiss in the silent room.

Jamison shrugged off the clenched fists with a little less ease than he would have liked. The boy was strong. Stepping away, he prowled around the room. He wanted to watch the explosion from a distance. The fireworks would be better than he'd expected. "She's close," he assured him. Then he started to set the scene. "She's a real beauty. All that fire inside. The woman doesn't like to give in, even when she has no choice. Not many could survive what she has." He stopped at the low growl that sounded from Fahlan. Just a matter of time now.

"What did you do to her, Jamison?" Rafe knew without a doubt who stood before him. He also knew that he wouldn't let him out of this room. The vampire had seen his last sunset.

"I was going to keep her all to myself, then figured I'd give you one last chance to possess her. I don't mind sharing. After all, I can have her back with just a snap of my fingers. I have her tamed to my touch now, but it took so much more than I thought it would." His smile broadened at the cold fury that emanated from his target. "Where did she get all those scars?" he asked with marked innocence. "Guns are such ugly weapons. I much prefer blades. They have so many more possibilities."

Rafe gathered himself, then launched his body across the room. He hit Jamison with brutal force. Straddling him to the ground, he brought his fury into play with a barrage of fists to the vampire's endless smirk.

Jamison let him have his way for a long moment, feeding off the rage that flowed unchecked through his body. It had been a long time since he had encountered such strong emotion. As much as Montgomery had pleased him with her defiance; this man pinning him to the ground had exceeded even her massive emotions.

He would have liked to keep Fahlan around for a while; a man such as this would make a fine addition to the chaos he had planned, but it could never be. To keep such a ravening beast so close was a sure way to lose a head. The man's blood would have to suffice. When the time was right, he would drain the dark one and claim all that power for his own. Maybe he would make a gift of it to his new pet. Maybe he would even let her drain him herself.

"Do you really want to waste your time with me?" Jamison asked as he caught Rafe's fist in his hand. "Wouldn't you rather spend it with her while you still can? While I still let you?" He watched the iron control that again took over the dark one. Amazing.

Rafe stood up, allowing the vampire to gain his feet. He would deal with this demon later, right now his concern was Gomery. "Where is she?" he asked for the last time, his voice so frigid the room should have dropped by at least ten degrees.

"I left her all ready for you." Jamison waved a leather-clad arm in the direction of Rafe's bedroom. "She is a woman fit for a man's darkest and deepest appetites." He let his words sink in, pleased with the thrilling fury that again filled Fahlan's expression.

"This isn't over," Rafe vowed as he pushed his way past him.

"You're right," Jamison assured him. "It's just beginning." Pleased with the situation he had wrought with his clever words and plans, he willed himself away. He would give it a few days. Then he would reap the rewards of his efforts. While it bothered him to leave the woman, he knew that also would be to his advantage in the end. She would need to see his way of thinking. Montgomery would have to come to him to find release from the magic he had wrought.

Rafe paid no attention to his new nemesis. Not after those last words were spoken. Instead he directed his gaze to the bedroom door, his feet followed. He didn't know what he would find on the other side, didn't know if he was ready for it. Hell, he didn't even know if she was still alive. Pushing open the door, he walked into the night shadows.

Then he found her. She lay on his bed, her body clad in nothing but moonlight. Sitting on the edge, he allowed his eyes to gaze upon her. He saw the honey glow of her skin, the blush color of her nipples, the dark curls that shielded her deepest heat.

There were the faint scars from that night in Paris, the new scar that had already healed to a shiny circle on the flatness of her stomach. Every breath that raised her chest while she slept drew his eyes.

Rafe saw all of that, but saw nothing. Not a cut, not a scratch, not a bruise, nothing of what Jamie had done to her. He knew nothing of what the vampire had put her through, or what methods he had used to create the pain he had felt the last few days. Pain that spilled over from her unto him.

If only he could see what physical and mental anguish that fiend had visited upon her. If only he could take away the last few days. If he could wipe the nightmare from her mind. But he couldn't. What he had suffered second hand from her trials was still enough to send a cold shiver down his spine.

He couldn't even begin to imagine how it would have seemed to her, a mere mortal. Nor could he make it better. All he could do was keep her with him always. Not even death would part them, for when she died he would go with her. Never again would his heart know this agony.

Rafe caught his breath as she stirred, her body arching as she moaned in her sleep. He wanted so much to hold her against him, to feel the beat of her heart, the warmth of her breath on his skin. To know she was alive and in his arms. Stripping off his clothes, he climbed onto the bed beside her. With the gentlest of care, he cradled her close until not a single heartbeat separated them. The warmth of their entwined bodies soon soothed him and within minutes, he drifted off into a dreamless sleep from which nothing would ever be the same.

ᛏ   ᛏ   ᛏ

Seth Jordan arrived home several hours after his run in with Gabriel Arden. He had walked for a long time trying to burn through some of the restlessness that had plagued him. That blonde bitch had ruined all of his plans. Maybe he would take care of her after he dealt with Arden. She was such a pretty little thing, smaller even than Sarah. He liked that. Morrigan St. John wore that little girl look well. He liked that too.

After he eliminated Arden, he would deal with her. Pausing in front of his house, he fit the key in the lock and pushed the door open. When he stepped into the hall, his eyes flew to the lamp that cast a dim glow in the living room.

"I don't remember leaving that on," he broke the silence in the house.

"You didn't."

The lilting voice came from the depths of the armchair and Seth tightened his fist in anticipation. The pitch was different but the voice was the same. Wanting to lull his victim, he plastered on a smile. "So you finally came home," he chided her as he walked farther into the room. "Where have you been?" He stopped behind the chair looking at the long copper curls that gleamed in the dim light. Waist length curls that looked nothing like the straight silk of his wife's.

"Hello, Seth," Sasha murmured as she stood up and faced him.

The woman was not his wife. This one was taller and made his Sarah look plain in comparison. His eyes followed the curves and valleys of a body displayed by a stretchy black jumpsuit that clung to every hollow.

"I've been waiting for you." She took a graceful step in his direction.

"Who are you?" he demanded as his eyes roved over her body. "You look like Sarah, but I know she doesn't have any family other than her sister."

Sasha saw the lust reflected in his eyes and it was all she could do not to shudder with disgust. "I'm a friend of a close friend of hers." She smiled as she took another step toward him. Only a few feet separated them now and she could feel every sin this man had ever committed. If it had a smell, she would have gagged it was so strong. The evil of the man was overwhelming. "A very close friend," she drawled slowly, then wanted to laugh as understanding dawned, but he still didn't know what to make of her.

"Arden have a weakness for redheaded whores?" Jordan snarled the words at her.

She stood so close now she could have touched him without raising her hand. The thought gave her such pleasure that she let a little of her magic out. It reflected in a golden glow that brightened the amber of her eyes.

Seth staggered back a step. "Who the hell are you?" he whispered, fear stealing much of his bravado. The woman closed the distance between them until he could see the wicked delight in her glowing eyes. "What the hell *are* you?" He changed his question as the glow shifted and intensified.

"I'm all your nasty little secrets come back to play with you."

The smile alone would have sent him running from the room, if fear hadn't glued his feet to the hardwood floor. Seth couldn't even flinch back as she touched him with the tip of one finger. The jolt of pain that followed that touch brought him to his knees. He scrambled back on all fours as she took a step forward.

Sasha laughed at the astonishment on his face. He hadn't liked the little zap she had given him, but it would only get worse. What she had let out had been just a weak taste of the agony that Sarah had suffered. A mere fraction. She struggled to hold the unholy thrill that tickled through her at bay, but it had been so long, and it felt so *good*.

For far too long, she had let men rule her life. Her father, Jamison, Gabriel, even Rafe had used her to find his own way. In this little interlude with Jordan, she was the hunter. The one with all the power. It was a heady rush. Her eyes feasted on the pathetic picture he made, cowering at her feet. Then a frown flitted across her face; this was too easy. Easy had never been her way. "Get up, Jordan. Get on your feet." She gave him a less than gentle nudge with her booted foot.

Seth stood up, his expression ugly as he convinced himself he had been wrong. She was just a woman. That was all. He had imagined the glow behind those witchy eyes, imagined the brief flash of pain that had drove him to his knees.

Sasha could see him gathering his male pride, his abusive repertoire again in place. She'd let him have his say, and then she'd squash him. With pleasure. First, she had to give him enough rope to hang himself. She *let* him tangle a brutal hand into the bright copper curls that cascaded down her shoulders. *Let* him jerk her against his aroused body. *Let* him think he had it in the bag.

"Think you're smart, don't you? What did Arden think he would accomplish by sending you here? He want to trade or something? His bitch for mine? I might take him up on that. Let's see what you got to offer." He held her head still with both hands while he crushed her mouth under his.

She didn't fight him not even when the kiss turned ugly, but let him have his way.

Ruthlessly he worked his fingers through her hair, not content to take her docile cooperation. What he wanted was a fight and she would provide him his outlet. If he couldn't get at Arden tonight, he would expend some of his anger on this witch who looked so much like his wife. The small gasp that escaped her when his hand moved from her hair to squeeze her breast wasn't enough so he dug in his finger-nails wanting to hear her cry out. He loved it when he could make a woman beg.

Sasha could feel the excitement that raced his blood through his veins. He relished the thought of hurting her but he would be disappointed. A master of brutality had used her, and very few creatures on earth had the talent for torture that Jamie did. This pathetic mortal was laughable with his overblown arrogance. He thought he could bring her to her knees, but she'd see him in hell first. Placing a hand against his chest, she pushed and he hit the wall with a resounding thud.

Coming off the wall full of disbelief and fury, Seth drew back his arm and swung. His hand connected with a force that turned her head. The blow should have sent her to the floor.

He knew his own strength, knew what power he possessed in his large hands. The look she threw his way stopped him when he would have struck her again.

The livid handprint on her cheek took nothing away from her pleased smile. Took nothing away from the golden glow that lit up those strange amber eyes. He raised his fist again.

"Oh, no, it's my turn now," Sasha murmured as she lifted her hand and lowered his arm.

He didn't understand what she meant until she sent him sprawling with the merest flick of her delicate wrist. This time he wasn't as quick to gain his feet or so eager to prove his male dominance.

"What's wrong, big boy?" She came down on her haunches beside him. "Don't you want to play anymore?" Sasha couldn't help but see the fear in his hazel eyes. It was the fear that caught her attention. Helpless, mind numbing fear was what she had felt when Jamison had held her down on the ground and tore her clothes away.

Fear like that was what had frozen her magic while he had forced his body into hers. Her fear had all but choked her when he had explained the nature of monster he was. It had stolen her life as she'd struggled against him that last time. When he had slowly taken her blood, making sure that she felt every nuance of his possession, every second of his greatest victory. She saw Jordan's fear and she reveled in it.

"Are you afraid of little old me?" she quipped as she ran a fingernail down his cheek. "A big, strong man like you?"

Color flooded his fair features. Masculine pride rose over fear. Making a last stand, he pushed back and she hit the floor with a little laugh. Seth gritted his teeth at her amusement and contented himself with the picture of her on her butt on the floor while he towered over her. She would not get the better of him again. No matter what he might have thought she was, she was just a woman. That she was stronger than most could just be a drug she was shooting up. Maybe Arden had her strung out on crack or something. He had seen men put their fists through windshields while they were under the influence of that crap.

Coming down on his knees beside her, he grabbed her head in both hands. Just a glance was enough for him to see the amusement in her eyes before he slammed her head back against the wall. Without giving her a second to recover, he back-handed her across her face. It was his turn to smile as he watched the thin trickle of blood seep from the cut on her lip.

"Not very original, are you?"

Seth couldn't believe his ears as he heard her taunt him. Couldn't believe his eyes as she trailed her finger through her own blood and looked at it through bright amber eyes that had lost all of that golden amusement.

"Isn't this the same thing you did to Sarah? It gives you a thrill to beat her, doesn't it?" She reached out and caught the collar of his shirt in a clenched fist. "It gives you a thrill to have her at your mercy."

This time there was no question of strength as she hauled him to his feet by no greater show of effort than that one hand. "You're nothing but a coward who gets off on hurting things smaller than you. You're an animal, Jordan. I'm amazed some-one didn't put you down the first time you turned rabid. Nobody saw you for the threat you were and those who did, you made sure they ended up dead or at your dubious mercy." She shook him until he hung limp from her hand.

"You betrayed trust and friendship for no other reason than greed and lust. You used the love of one sister for another to serve your own pleasures."

Seth couldn't escape the death grip she had on him. He couldn't even find the breath to deny her accusations.

"You're now at my mercy and it's less than a sympathetic one. I have a gift for you, Seth," she promised as she slammed him against the wall with enough force that several framed pic-tures fell from their supportive hooks. "Gabriel wanted to be the one to share it with you, but I didn't want him to dirty his hands with scum like you, so I took it."

He stopped struggling, drawn like a moth to a flame as the amber of her eyes lit from within and began to glow.

"I really have to make this worth my effort because in taking away Gabriel's victory, I gave up any claim I might have had to his heart."

The woman smiled again as she released him, a sad little smile that raised the hairs on the back of his neck. "You're crazy," he breathed out as he tried to skirt his way around her. His hand slid inside his jacket, fingers coming to rest on the familiar comfort of cold steel. Using all of his concentration to steady that hand, he pulled out the revolver and leveled it point-blank to her forehead. "Who's the boss now, bitch?" he demanded as he pulled back the hammer.

"That would still be me." She relieved him of his weapon with the all the effort of a bird soaring on the breeze.

Seth blinked twice as she grasped the gun in both hands and bent the barrel until it resembled nothing but a hunk of metal, then he turned and ran as fast as he could. He needed to reach the bedroom. There was another gun in the dresser. That was the only coherent game plan he could formulate as he lunged up the stairs and flung the door closed behind him. Locking the door with trembling hands, he leaned his head against it and took a second to draw air into his oxygen-starved lungs.

"Okay," he rasped out. "She can't get in here."

"Who can't get in where?" drawled that same lilting voice from behind him.

He swung around so fast he fell against the door. She sat on his bed, her expression all innocence as she stared up at his perspiring face. "What do you want from me?" Seth demanded in a near shout as he came away from the door. "*What do you want from me?*" He was furious now, the blood thrumming through his veins. "I don't even know who you are. I don't know *what* you are. I don't want you here."

Sasha needed him like this; it gave the forgiving side of her a reason. A reason the rest of her didn't need. Watching his every reaction, she stood up. "Gabriel is the best part of me. He is my soul. If I let him touch you, that would change him. He would no longer be the same man I love. The same man that Sarah loves." She ignored the hate-filled expletive that emerged from him. "It would make him no better than you."

He took a step toward her but he never got a chance to decide what he would do. The absolute fury of her expression stopped him cold.

"You cost me so much with the vileness of your actions. Now it's my turn." There was finally an outlet for her hurt and anger. Seth Jordan was to blame for the treatment of his wife and the loss that she had sustained in the defection of Gabriel's fickle emotions. She couldn't bring herself to hurt Sarah or to punish Gabriel, but this man was fair game. The weapon was ready and she'd already paid the price for being the one to wield it. The price was her soul and her soul was Gabriel.

CHAPTER 20

Opening her eyes with a start, Montgomery took a second to look around. She was in bed. Rafe's bed. Her heartbeat slowed by degrees as she made herself believe the past few days had been nothing but a nightmare. A terrible, dark dream that just thinking about caused her to panic. No pain followed her movements as she rolled her shoulders; no healing wounds or welts greeted seeking fingers. No dark bastards with sharp blades and glowing eyes hid in the shadows. There was nothing lurking out there to hurt her. Nothing. She was safe. No dark devils could touch her again except the one who held her in his arms.

Her eyes fed upon the beauty of his sculpted features and she wanted to cry for the strength of emotion that crushed her. Life started and ended for her with this man. Giving into an urge she couldn't seem to stop, she pressed her mouth to his. Sliding her tongue along the seam of his lips, she tasted him. Her lover came awake with a swiftness that never failed to amaze her.

Rafe pushed her away, his hands gentle as he searched every nuance of her face. "Gomery?" he asked.

Montgomery didn't understand the question that lurked in his silvery gaze. "Who were you expecting, sugar?" she teased, rolling over him until she could look down into his stunning face. Settling herself against him, she held his hips between the strength of her silky thighs. The feel of his arousal, hot, hard, and straining to explore the depths of her heat coaxed a low moan from her throat. They were only a tilt and thrust of her hips away from heaven, but first he needed to answer her question. "Who were you expecting?"

"Only you." His moan of pleasure was an echo of hers when

she took him into her body. Grasping her tiny waist in his hands, Rafe held her against him, his movements uncontrolled as he slammed against her. He increased his pace at the wild cries that fell from her lips. The lust that filled her gold-flecked eyes was almost his undoing. God, she had never looked so beautiful as she did now, with the faint morning light flowing over her tumbled mink curls as she slid her body against his. Never had he seen her so desperate in her passion, so wild for release.

"Rafe!" Her back bowed with the force of her need. "Please, Rafe," she begged, moaning his name in a chant to urge him further. His body arched under hers as she raked her fingernails down his chest in a fit of passion.

Leaning over him, Montgomery clenched her fingers in the sheets on either side of his head. She wanted to reach the bliss on the other side of this sweet agony so bad, she had to bite her lip to hold back her scream. She moaned instead when he released her waist and dug his fingers into her hair. Then her lips fused to his in a kiss that seared her to the tips of her toes.

Pushed that much closer to the edge, she rocked her body against his, desperate for completion. It slammed into her all at once and unable to stop herself, she buried her face in the crock of his neck. The salty taste of him teased her tongue; the scent of the blood on his chest filled her nostrils. She forgot to breathe as the waves of pleasure hit her full force.

"Wow," Montgomery whispered when she had the strength to lift her head. The first think she noticed was the tautness of Rafe's body under hers. The intense pleasure had so captured her attention that she'd failed to notice if he had followed with her. "Your turn..." The teasing words died away when she saw the guarded awareness in those silver eyes. "What's wrong?" Her gaze drifted down to the side of his neck where she had leaned into him.

Nothing of the open wound that marred his throat or the blood that stained the tawny skin did she miss. With a trembling hand, she touched her own lips. The wetness there confirmed her worst fears. Jamie hadn't been a nightmare. He was real.

Every vile and terrible thing he had said and done was true.

Rafe watched the terror building in her eyes, but was help-less to combat it. His whole focus remained locked on the second she had pierced his throat and taken his blood. In that moment everything Jamie had said to him had flooded back. The pleasure of having Montgomery hadn't been physical for the evil immortal but something spiritual. The bastard had turned her and she hadn't even known.

There was only a second to overcome his shock before the woman astride him freaked. Grabbing the sheet, she flew from the bed with a speed he didn't think she noticed. Her panicked words stopped him when he would have left the bed to go to her.

"Oh, my God. Oh, my God," she chanted over and over as she stared down at the sticky wetness staining her fingers.

Rafe raised a shaking hand to wipe the bloody evidence from his skin before she could notice the extent of the damage she had done. Her eyes followed the motion.

"What have I done?" Montgomery whispered through chat-tering teeth as she knelt on the bed. "What have I done to you?" She reached out to touch him, needing to feel the heat of his skin under her hands.

A tingle up her spine, a shadow glimpsed out of the corner of her eye was all the warning she was given. Before logical thought could intrude she threw herself at the large, dark fig-ure emerging from the night shrouded corner. Protecting Rafe was her only priority as she found herself nose to nose with her worst nightmare. A nightmare with deep green eyes.

"Problem, Rafe?" Gabriel asked as he looked into her wild gaze.

Montgomery stumbled back from him, her eyes shifting from one to the other. A frantic heartbeat was all the time it took before her new immortal sight allowed her to see what her human heart had long failed to notice.

Neither man seemed shocked at what she had done. They didn't cower or run for cover at the appearance of a bloodthirsty fiend in their midst. Even as she took a reluctant step in Rafe's direction, she sought out the brutal wound she'd inflicted.

The wound was no longer there. Nothing remained in testimony of her attack but the blood that shined wet upon his skin. She blinked against the bright dots that danced a merry gig across her vision. This couldn't be real. This couldn't be happening. Then she no longer cared as the floor rose to meet her and blackness claimed her weary mind and shattered soul within its comforting embrace.

Rafe fell to his knees beside her, his eyes tortured as he lifted her into his arms.

"What happened?" Gabriel asked as his friend smoothed the tumble of chestnut curls back from her pale face.

He laid her down on the bed without answering and watched until her breathing evened out and she slid into a more natural slumber. Only after he'd pulled on his jeans did he utter the first words he had spoken since her teeth had pierced his throat.

"Katherine took her from me, Gabriel. That bitch took her from me and gave her to that monster. He did this to her, then left her in my bed. They did this to her. They did this," his voice rose with each word until the windows rattled with it.

The words, filled with so much pain and torment, were impossible to ignore and only seconds passed before the others descended.

Sasha felt the presence of another from the second she stepped to Rafe's side, but it took a single look into his defeated silver eyes to realize that new immortal was the woman sleeping on the rumpled bed.

"Gomery's back?" Michael asked, his eyes following Sasha as she approached the bed. The undercurrents in the room were strong, but his tired mind didn't notice it right away. He watched Sasha reach out and touch Gomery, saw the color leave her face as she jerked her hand back after a brief second. He heard the brief whimper that passed the fairy's lips, but didn't understand what could have caused it. "What's wrong?" he asked when the color returned to her cheeks.

"Nothing." She wasn't able to meet their eyes. There was no need for Rafe to know what Jamison had done to his lover. Knowing wouldn't change what had come to pass. It couldn't take back anything that had occurred. Nothing could do that anymore, not even time or death. Jamison had seen to that.

Gabriel wasn't as trusting of her answer and before she could protest, he was beside them, his long fingers curving around Montgomery's bare shoulder. He didn't pull back from what he was *seeing* like Sasha had. He *saw* each act and felt each deed as if he had been in the room with them. The emotions were muted and second hand, but the impact was enough to steal the breath from his lungs.

"Is this what he did to you?" the highlander asked Sasha, his eyes searching for any clue of what she herself had suffered all those centuries ago. Her refusal to look at him was answer enough.

Rafe remained silent for several minutes, his fists clenching and unclenching in a telling motion as he struggled against what howled inside of him. "What do you see?" He asked Gabriel, his voice an empty echo. "What do you see?" he asked again, this time his eyes showing all the emotion his first question had lacked. He met Gabriel's steady regard and knew the highlander could tell him in simple words or he could *share* what he had seen. For all that he was, he needed to know. "Show me."

Sasha's soft protest went unheeded as Gabriel stepped toward the silent man that was his best friend. What he had seen from Montgomery's slumbering mind had disturbed him. What she had experienced was of the nature of nightmares. He couldn't begin to guess how Rafe would react. Never had he seen the dark one without some shred of his famed control and this would no doubt blow that out of the water.

When the storm finished its destructive havoc, he could only hope to pick up the pieces. He held back nothing, made no effort to soften what she had gone through. Every sensation was released to slam into Rafe with the subtly of a sledgehammer.

Not by word, sound, expression or deed did Rafe betray himself. He took in all that Gabriel released and accepted it as punishment for his arrogance. He ignored the others as he turned to the bed, his eyes seeing nothing but the woman who slumbered there.

The gentleness Rafe employed as he lifted Montgomery into his arms and disappeared from their sight awed Michael. "Somebody want to fill me in?" he asked.

Gabriel just shrugged his wide shoulders as he wished himself away. He had too many things to work through right now to explain to Michael the craziness that had descended upon them.

Sasha remained behind, her eyes bright with unshed tears as she looked at Michael. This had hit too close to home for her. The brief contact with Montgomery's pain had brought the past crashing back with a vengeance. Eight hundred years had dimmed her memories but it hadn't erased them. Nothing ever would. Just thinking about what had happened in that moon bright clearing all those centuries ago sent a wave of revulsion rolling through her.

Michael took a step toward her, he had never seen that look on her face before and it worried him. They had always looked on Sasha as their balance. Now she stood there looking for all the world like a lost little girl with no hopes of rescue. He didn't know what to do, or say. For the first time in memory, he didn't have a way to put a smile on her face. Sasha took the decision out of his hands in the next moment.

"You were asking about Gomery?" she asked with all of her usual serenity.

ϯ   ϯ   ϯ

Katherine gathered her things as fast as she could. She wanted out of this house before Jamie got back. He hadn't come home last night and she had no idea where he was or what he was doing. That she wanted out while she still had a head on her shoulders was all she knew.

If he had done to the woman what she thought he had, things were going to turn ugly. It was one thing to steal an insignificant girl, but another to torture and kill the woman of a man like Raphael Fahlan. That man would never stop until he had gained revenge.

All those years ago, she had wanted to destroy all his icy control. She'd wanted to see him suffer in a way she would never be able to inflict on her sire. Her grand plans had failed. He'd been even more dangerous than she had imagined. If not for Sasha's timely arrival, she would have fallen prey to the very beast she had created. Katherine shuddered as she remembered his hands wrapped around her throat that night long ago and the cold, killing rage that had lit those eyes.

The plain and simple truth? She had messed up, both then and now. If she'd had an ounce of sense, she'd have left the man in peace. But no, she'd wanted her pound of flesh from him for something that hadn't even been of his doing and now she had it.

Jamie had convinced her that the woman was the key. Montgomery had been, but to the wrong door. The woman meaning so much to the dark one was something she hadn't counted on. She hadn't seen it until that first night Jamie had her here. It wasn't until Jamie had gone out to hunt and she had taken it upon herself to help the woman that she had realized her mistake. While she had healed most of Montgomery's wounds, she had explored her thoughts and memories. What she had seen had made up her mind.

She had tried to protect her from Jamie when he came back, but it had been useless. He had done what he wanted, and when he had pushed Montgomery as far as he dared he had turned his skills on her for her interference. She had tried twice more to get her away from Jamie, but again she had underestimated Montgomery's appeal to the sadist who was her sire.

His attraction for the woman should have been a passing thing. When the thrill of bloodletting had dwindled, he should have grown bored. That hadn't happened. With every cut and slice he'd grown even more determined to keep her. Montgomery fighting him until she could no longer remain conscious, had brought a glow to his soulless eyes she had never seen before. It was so much worse than that first night when he had stood over Montgomery's bed that Katherine shivered just thinking about it. Now that the woman was gone, there was no telling what was going to happen.

Katherine packed up her spell books a little faster. There was no sense in tempting fate and she wanted out before Michael gave Rafe the address, or Jamie gave in to his need for mayhem and invited the silver-eyed demon to the front parlor for tea. Tossing the last book in her bag, she snatched up the handles. With a last look around, she raised her hands over her head and started an ancient chant that would take her far away from the mischief she had caused.

"Going somewhere, pet?"

His voice sent a chill slithering over her skin. Katherine dropped the books, cursing the damned things as they fell to the floor. Why hadn't she just left them behind? Now she needed a plan; one that would get her out of here with the skin still on her back.

"Jamie!" she cried out with feigned delight. "When did you get back?" The old one wasn't the least bit fooled, she could tell from the cruel smile that flitted across his pale lips. His next words confirmed it.

"You don't really think I'm going to let you leave, do you? This is your great chance for revenge, my pet. Don't tell me I've gone to all this trouble and now you're going to leave me. The fun is just starting."

His idea of fun was even more warped than she had thought. Somehow she didn't think death, especially her own, was going to be *fun*.

"I'll pass." Picking up her books, she started past him. He didn't let her take two steps before he had her pinned to the wall.

With a convulsive shiver, Katherine met the blackness of his gaze.

"You're not going anywhere until I tell you to. Do you understand me?" he asked, his face only inches from hers.

There was no amusement in his eyes, none of the tolerance she had come to depend on after all these years. Jamie in this mood was something she had rarely seen. Even when he had hunted in the past or tortured, there had been a kind of glee in his actions. Not now. All there was in that gaze was the certainty of her own death if she betrayed him.

"Yes, Jamie." Before she could stop herself, she asked the one question she had sworn not to. "Where is she?" She hadn't wanted to know. As Michael had pointed out before, she had enough ghosts playing in her dreams without adding this particular one. There was no doubt in her mind that the woman was dead and for the first time in a long time, she felt a keen sense of regret.

The woman had done nothing to deserve what had happened to her. She had just had the misfortune to love the wrong man. If anyone knew what it felt like to love someone so much you were willing to die for him or to let yourself become what you most feared just to be at his side, it was her. That same emotion had led her first to Sasha, then to Jamie. The same emotion had turned her into what she was.

"When I finished with her, I left her in Fahlan's bed. You couldn't imagine his surprise when he came back from looking for her and there I was, waiting," Jamison explained with a satisfied smile.

Katherine couldn't breathe for the shock that sat like a rock on her chest. Jamie had killed Montgomery Sinclair and left her body in her lover's bed. She couldn't believe it. Now they were *so* dead and it was this great big idiot's fault! He had brought this all down on her head. Working her way through the collection of spells buzzing in her head, she tried to remember all the words for a terrible burning, blinding death. That was no more than what the bastard deserved.

"You killed her and left her in his bed?" She could no longer contain her disbelief. "You left her in Raphael Fahlan's bed? Are you crazy?" she demanded, almost hysterical at the thought of what that would bring about. Not only would Rafe come down on them, but Gabriel and Michael wouldn't be far behind. And she didn't even want to contemplate what would happen if Sasha joined the fray.

"She's not dead," he answered, not trying to dispel her sense of impending doom so much as to gain her undivided attention. It worked like nothing else could have.

"She's alive? You mean you didn't kill her? Fahlan has her and she's still breathing? You just took her there and left her?" She fired off those questions in quick succession as she stared at him, bug-eyed in disbelief.

"Yes. Yes. Yes. No."

The no was accompanied by such a smirk of blatant satisfaction that she had to sit down. Katherine looked at him then, searching for any clue that would give her advanced warning of the cause for the glow in his eyes. She didn't like the conclusion she reached.

"For love of the Gods, Jamie, please tell me you didn't." The very thought filled her with dread. Then she came to her senses; he wouldn't have turned Montgomery. That would have been the very worst thing he could do. With the darkness of her soul and the blackness of Jamie's blood, Montgomery as an immortal had the potential to be a living nightmare. Couple that with the woman's affection for Rafe and not a soul could stand against them. "Please tell me you didn't change her?" There was no shame in begging, not if it got her the answer she craved. Jamie's smile warned her that begging would be of no use.

"Of course I did, my pet, so settle back and enjoy the ride. You're not going anywhere until it's over."

T   T   T

Gabriel dreaded work, his day not having improved much in the last five hours. As if finding out that your best friend's lover, someone he had come to like very much, had been tortured and turned into the same monster he was wouldn't have ruined anyone's day was beside the point. Had he taken care of Jordan when he first wanted to, he would have never had the chance to come into the club that night and caused the problems he did.

If they had not been so distracted, Katherine and Jamison would have never gotten their hands on Gomery. That they did was something they would die regretting. If Rafe didn't take care of them, then he would. He still owed the little witch for that sword and Jamison for the torment he had put Sasha through.

It had taken two centuries, but now he knew a part of what that bastard had done to her. A small part of what Sasha had had to live with. Of what she still lived with. Memories like those didn't go away, no matter how long you lived. He didn't believe for even a minute though, that that was all he had done to her when he had her under his control. Jamison had been pure vampire when he first came upon the fairy clan. Pure vampire when he had stalked her through the forest and thrown her to the ground. Pure demon when he had raped her.

Sasha's blood had mellowed him and Gabriel couldn't begin to contemplate how terrible the bastard had been before, but Sasha knew. She had protected all of them from her dark sire since they had come into existence. That interesting fact had come to light on one of his shadow inquires the other night. The vamp he had stomped into the ground to get that information would never be the same again, but at least he had gotten to the bottom of what all the fuss was about.

Gabriel was just sitting down at his desk when one of the other detectives walked over and further spoiled what was becoming one of the worst days he'd had in decades.

"That prowler struck again last night. Hit one of the big houses on Prytania." The younger man warmed to his tale. "Guy bypassed the security somehow."

He would have gone on if Gabriel hadn't interrupted. "I'm not on the case, but I'll bear with you. What do you mean, he bypassed the system? It was shut off?"

"Nope. According to the main computer, it never went down. There was no halt to the system. No one entered any codes and the power never went down. But somehow he got in and lifted two hundred thousand dollars in rubies. The owner is throwing a fit and blaming the security system, and the firm is denying all knowledge." He was waiting to see what theory Gabriel had. The man had an uncanny ability to see even the smallest little clue. He handed the papers he had been holding to him and waited while Gabriel looked through them.

"St. John Securities again. That's the third time in the last two weeks. Some coincidence," he drawled out, his eyes focusing on the young detective even as he neglected to mention that he had two former heads of St. John's living with him. He didn't think that was a point he would be bringing up, not until after this thing with Gomery and Jamison was over. Maybe he could talk it out with Morrigan and see if she had any idea how their systems kept getting breached.

"That's what I said, but the big boss over there wasn't open to suggestions," the detective confided. "Speaking of big bosses, the captain wants to have a word with you. Let me know if you think of anything on this."

Gabriel stood up with a heavy sigh and wondered what else could go wrong today. He knocked, then entered the captain's office.

"Have a seat, Arden," his captain ordered.

A sideways glance took in the suit sitting in one of the chairs in front of Captain Davidson's desk. The man had the decided look of Internal Affairs and Gabriel couldn't help but wonder what crap Jordan had dumped on him now.

"There is a delicate matter I need to discuss with you. As Seth's partner I thought you should be among the first to know," Davidson paused for a second and looked him square in the eyes.

The captain was one of the few men who did that and it never failed to amaze him that the man couldn't see the demon that lurked there.

"Have a seat, Gabriel."

Uh oh, first name. That could only mean bad things and Gabriel tensed against what could be a wide range of problems.

"We found Seth's body this morning. He'd shot himself with his own weapon during the night. We will provide you with any counseling you need but right now, we have a bigger problem. His wife isn't home and we were wondering if Seth had mentioned to you where she might have gone. We need to contact her and let her know what has happened."

Gabriel showed no reaction to the news of his partner's death. He did give a momentary thank you to the foresight that had prompted him to deleted all memories of what had happened with Seth at the club the other night. Had that little confrontation still been on record or the food for station gossip, this little meeting could have taken a very ugly turn.

"She went to her sister's to help her plan for her wedding. I was very close to Seth and of course to Sarah. So, if you would allow me, I would like to call her first and let her know what has happened." He lied without a flick of an eyelash and spent a few more minutes making sure everything would go as he wanted. Back at his desk, his thoughts were in a tangle.

He had to call Sarah and he wasn't sure how that was going to go. The one thing he did know was that he was going to strangle Sasha as soon as he saw her. Hadn't he told her not to interfere? She had done so much than that. The woman had taken away his prey, denied him his hunt. He had warned her and now she would pay the price for her betrayal.

ᛟ   ᛟ   ᛟ

A leisurely afternoon at Café du Monde was just what Morrigan had needed to take her mind off her problems. Of course, the beignets didn't hurt either. Lounging back in her chair, she smiled in response to Sasha's observations of the passing crowd. The colorful atmosphere was due in part to the Mardi Gras tourists that flocked to New Orleans every year. Such mild weather had only served to increase the numbers to near staggering proportions.

"Have you talked to Michael?" Sasha asked, brushing powdered sugar from her apricot sweater. The fair one had been the logical choice to inform Morrigan of Montgomery's return and sudden departure.

"Haven't seen him today," Morrigan replied with a negligent shrug of her shoulders.

"I guess Montgomery came back while we were gone last night," Sasha dropped the news and waited to see how the blonde reacted. Morrigan did nothing but turn her cool purple eyes in her direction. "She wasn't here long before she left with Rafe. I guess they wanted to spend some time alone."

Sasha thought she caught a brief flash of awareness pass through the girl's eyes but that wasn't possible. No memory of Gomery's shooting and kidnapping could still remain. She shook off the strange sensation that tickled her mind. There was no way that Morrigan could have seen through her magic. "Montgomery's going to call before they start back." The lie came with ease. She had been spinning tales for years. Anything to keep her true self hidden from the mortals she walked among.

"I bet she will," Morrigan drawled out, not buying the whole story everyone kept shoving her way. There was more going on than they wanted to tell and she was going to find out. One way or another. "Did she mention how long?" She struggled to ignore the ache that throbbed in her left temple.

"No, she didn't but I'm willing to bet that it'll be soon." Sasha broke off eye contact with Morrigan as she sensed the presence of another. Before she even saw him, she knew it was Gabriel.

From fifty feet, she could feel the rage that seethed in the air around him. In that instance she knew what he knew. She hadn't tried to hide the suicide of his partner. If she had wanted to, she could have. No, this was something that needed to be out in the open. She'd only hoped for a little more time to armor herself against the fierce emotions that roiled around in him.

Morrigan followed the line of Sasha's vision and couldn't help the little jump she gave when Gabriel brought his fist down on the table. The force of the blow toppled the small table as if it was nothing but match sticks. She had never seen him like this and it was interesting to see the anger burning in those gorgeous eyes.

"Hello, Gabriel, did you want to join us?" Morrigan invited with a sweet smile.

Gabriel spared her nothing but a hard look before his eyes returned to the target of his displeasure.

Sasha refused to bend under the force of that gaze "Gabriel." The one word she uttered spoke volumes.

In a second, he took in all the avid interest his outburst had garnered. Meeting Sasha's eyes, he tried to communicate his displeasure with his thoughts alone but she wouldn't allow his trespass. Gabriel gritted his teeth in frustration. "Might I have a word with you?" he asked with exaggerated politeness.

Sasha shrugged her shoulders and turned her attention to Morrigan. "Would you mind if I go? Gabriel will pay for lunch and the table before he leaves," she added with a sideways glance at the enraged immortal, ignoring the tightening of his fists as she waited for the little blonde to decide.

"That's just fine. You two have a blast." Morrigan didn't bother to sugar-coat the sarcasm. She watched as Gabriel stalked to the counter and paid the quaking manager. Sasha followed at a more leisurely pace. In fact, Gabriel had to stop on the sidewalk and wait for her to catch up. The action did little to erase the anger from his rugged face.

Morrigan watched it all but the antics of those two were low on her list of concerns. What she needed was Gomery and she needed her now. She rubbed the back of her neck, the throbbing in her skull growing worse. With or without

Gomery this had to be finished soon. She'd delayed her stay in New Orleans as long as possible and now she had a choice to make.

Chapter 21

Sasha followed a step or two behind all the way back to the club. She wasn't in a big hurry to hear what Gabriel had to say, but to refuse outright would have brought down the full force of his displeasure then and there. And, she didn't think the crowd of onlookers would have stopped him. She had never seen him so mad before and she was more than a little nervous. So, into the club she followed, then his apartment.

For a second she looked over his current domain. He had kept many of the things from the past and it gave her a strange feeling to realize that several of the things he had were items she herself had given him. She wondered why he bothered but couldn't bring herself to ask; not when he turned the full force of those heated emerald eyes on her.

"What do you think you have accomplished?" he asked, his voice intense as he struggled to reel in his temper. "What right did you have to seek revenge? He was mine to deal with. Mine!"

Sasha flinched from the seething force of those whispered words. That he stayed across the room from her gave a good indication of his restraint. He didn't trust himself to get close. Didn't trust what he might do to her.

"I gave him back what he so loved to give. Coming from you, it would have held little meaning. He would have reacted badly and you would have killed him too soon." She met the condemnation in his eyes. "Coming from me it was poetic justice. While he tried so hard to show me the error of my ways, I got closer and closer, until I knew every evil thing in his heart. When I had enough, I gave him back the dagger of his cruelty, blade first."

The expression that crossed her face was unlike anything

he had ever seen before. "What…"

Gabriel never finished the question as she turned glowing amber eyes on him and explained in dark detail what had transpired last night. "I let him hurt me and gain confidence until he felt he had everything mastered. When he decided I would make a good stand in for Sarah, I gave a little back."

He gritted his teeth against the thought of Jordan laying his filthy hands on his golden angel.

Sasha saw his reaction, read his outrage and ignored it. She had closed that door behind her when she had gone to Seth's house last night. There was nothing that could come of this now. "He ran to the bedroom and locked the door. It was funny when he realized I was behind him. In that moment he realized I wasn't what he had thought." She smiled then, a dark smile. "His punishment lasted for hours. He writhed on the floor, his agony so great he couldn't even beg. Couldn't even breathe. The promise that I would be back was all it took for the worm to put the gun in his mouth and pull the trigger. What a shame, I was having so much fun with him." Again that smile pulled at the corners of her full lips.

"What did you do to him?" he asked, soft and low into the quiet.

"Just this." She touched him with one fingertip and let loose a little of what she had retained from last night. The jolt sent him to his knees. Sasha showed him no pity. Instead, she knelt down beside him and met his stunned eyes. "I gave him that. Not just once or ten times, not even a hundred times covered what I did. I didn't stop until the sun came up and he could no longer hide what he was." She stood back up and walked away from him.

"That was Sarah's pain?" He didn't remember it being quite like that.

"I didn't need Sarah's agony after the first few times. It was gone quickly. When I used up the memories of all the others suffering, I found a deeper source of pain and anguish to share with your partner. Something deeper and darker that had taken centuries to create. Something shown to me by a master. What I just gave you, and what I gave him until he preferred death to another round, was mine to give. It was all that I am, all that I had locked up inside. You talk much of the demons under your skin, Gabriel. You just caught a glimpse of mine."

ፐ   ፐ   ፐ

Montgomery came awake in a flash of awareness. The faint sunlight streaming through the windows gave testimony to the lateness of the hour. She didn't have to work through a flood of harsh and horrible memories from the last days and nights. Like negatives on a strip of film, they played through her head. Everything that had happened to her was there. Any magic Jamie had used to block her memory had faded away with the onset of understanding. She knew what she was.

Jamie had kept no secrets from her from the first time he held that cursed blade to her throat. From the second he had slid his mouth along her neck to taste her blood, she had known what matter of creature he was. He was a walking nightmare. The evilest of night creatures. Jamie was an vampire without a soul, without a heart.

If not for Katherine's help, she would not have made it past the first night, but Katherine had helped and she had healed and she had given her the strength to survive. But, Jamie had taken her from the house where Katherine could no longer help her. Then, he had he showed her what he was capable of.

Montgomery slid from the bed, her mind taking in things she would have never noticed before, not even with the heightened sense of observation she had cultivated from her work. She knew she was in Rafe's house; she could feel him in every room. Could smell him on the gentle breeze that fluttered the curtains on the floor to ceiling windows.

Not only did she know where Rafe was; she knew what he was. Her lover was like Gabriel and Katherine and Jamie. Now all she needed to figure out was the nature of the beast inside of him.

It hadn't taken much to peg Jamie and even Katherine had been simple to size up, but Rafe had defied any category since the first time she had seen him.

Never by any slight of hand had Rafe given away the truth of what he was. She knew she should be shocked to realize the man she'd held against her body, the man she had given her heart to was an immortal nightwalker. A vampire.

She should have been, but she wasn't. Nothing could surprise her after the last few days. Something inside her refused to let her rant and rave for all she had been through and what she had now become. The same something that relished the power that flowed through her veins. There was no need to weep and whimper now.

Only one goal filled her mind. A single concern that overrode every thought in her head, every ache in her heart.

Jamie.

He would die with her name on his lips. She would be the last thing he ever saw.

"Hello, sweet thing."

His voice was like music to her senses. In the drawn out hours when Jamie had tested her resolve, she'd imagined that voice, low and smoky in her ears. Turning her eyes on him, she had to blink against the rush of emotions that threatened to overwhelm her. He was so beautiful she wanted to weep with the pain of it. If he hadn't loved her before when she was *normal,* how could he ever love her now?

Rafe might be as she was, but she would always remember the look on his face when she had taken his blood last night. How could she make him understand that last night would never happen again when just the thought of touching him, of having his body under hers, of her teeth at his throat, sent heat burning through her.

Gomery's lack of response was as telling as the slender back she turned on him in rejection. She knew what he was, *what* she was and wanted no part of him. Rafe tried to ignore the hurt that cut into his heart. "Sleep well?" His control allowed him to stand tall under the pain. There was no reason to mention that he had held her in his arms until just an hour ago. Until the memory of her taking his blood had aroused him to a point that he had feared for her safety in his embrace. Only thoughts of hurting her had forced him from her side.

"How did you…" Montgomery couldn't finish the question. She didn't know what she wanted to ask, only that his eyes burning into her back was stealing all her thoughts. Wanting so much to see the silver of his unearthly gaze, she turned to face him. "How did you meet the others?" she decided that was as good a place to start as any. Snuggling deeper into the silk shirt he had dressed her in last night, she settled into a large armchair and waited for him to explain.

He stared at her for a long moment before he spoke of the past. "Gabriel, Michael and I were still mortal when we meet in London two centuries ago. For personal reasons, we had left our homes and the city was the place to lose yourself. We were social outcasts for the most part, our families had disowned us for various reasons and we had become friends." He wouldn't go into the reasons behind his leaving. Some things he couldn't discuss while her eyes burned with such loathing.

"At night we roamed the streets searching for something to ease our frustrations. On one of those nights, we met the man who changed our lives. David Mallory helped others to see past our flaws to the men we should have been. Along the way, we attracted the wrong kind of attention from a woman well known for her appetites. Katherine became a lover of David's to get close to us. She had him killed in order to win our sympathies. On the night of his wake, we left Michael to comfort her while we went looking for the killer. Little did we know."

He smiled at that point and Montgomery struggled not to cringe from the chill of it. She had never seen him this bitter, not even the morning he had left her.

"When Gabriel and I got back, we found Michael bloody and unconscious while Katherine fed us some pathetic story about an intruder. Gabriel was the next to fall to her treachery. The scar he carries is a gift from Katherine and the broadsword she used to bring him down." He stopped at the question he could see on her face.

"Katherine didn't turn Gabriel?" She would have thought they were all of one creator. That it was blood that held them together.

"Gabriel is of Sasha's making. In two hundred years, he has yet to forgive her for giving him back the life that Katherine had tried to steal from him." Rafe could see her thinking it through.

"The woman you're talking about helped me, Rafe. Katherine tried to keep that bastard away from me. She let him hurt her so he would leave me alone. She helped me," Montgomery said it again, needing him to understand.

"Katherine had David's throat cut. Then she turned Michael into a demon before she skewered Gabriel for no other reason that his refusal to believe her lies. When I found her, she was leaving him to die, his blood spilling onto the carpet at her feet," his voice picked up volume as he spoke. "I won't bother you with all the details of her offer to me because that wasn't an option I was willing to take. All of that wasn't enough for her; she had to take you from me, not to help you but to turn you over to Jamie. She wanted to hurt you to get at me, Gomery, and now she has. Katherine has gained my undivided attention. Now let's see if she can handle it." He took a deep breath, his control back in place.

"Jamie was the one that hurt me. He was the one that did this. It's him that should be punished," Montgomery tried to reason with him. She had never dreamed the cruelty on her lover's face. Not even in her nightmares could she have placed so much hatred in those silver eyes. "What is he to Katherine anyway? I only know what I was told and he wasn't in to answers so much as idle chit chat." She wanted to stall him. Needed time to cool the fire in his eyes.

"Jamison is the oldest known vampire. Eight hundred years ago he found a clan of people he hoped to exploit. They were

people of magic called the *Sidhe*. The harbingers of light. He'd
gone there for a girl of pure blood. When he was refused, he
went on a killing spree. In desperation the elders gave him the
clan's princess. When Jamie came that night he let her go. Sasha
thought he was giving her her freedom. Before he was through
with her, she realized he just liked the thrill of the chase. Before
he took her blood he was a true vampire. Blood drinking,
killing, fear of the sun, all those old myths. After he had acquired
the gifts of her people, all that changed. Daylight was no longer
a burden, the blood hunger was no longer absolute, but he
was still a destructive, vicious, inhuman monster.

"To use Sasha's words it took the best of both worlds and
combined them. Jamison didn't change his ways, though. He
still went about his usual business. I guess after all that time it
was just too hard not to rape and kill and torture." Rafe waited
while all he had revealed sank in. "Katherine went to Sasha six
centuries ago and when she refused to change her, she sought
out our sire and begged him to do the honors. Unlike the rest
of us, she begged to be what she is.

"What's so funny is that she kept such close tabs on us over
the years when we could find no trace of her. You would have
thought she'd have learned from past mistakes and stayed away.
This time she will. She should have left you alone, honey." He
approached her, unsure how she would react to a lover who'd
hidden his true nature every time he'd laid with her like a man.

"Do you love me?"

That was the one question he hadn't counted on from her
but should have.

"In all of this mess, with all that I now am, do you love
me?" She held his gaze as if bands of steel linked them together.

"I loved my mother until she left me. I loved my wife until
I found her in bed with my father. I loved my son, even after
the illusion that he was mine shattered. I held him in my arms
while he died. Love doesn't exist for me now, Gomery. To me,
it's a reflection of the scars on my back and the loss of my soul.
I have no heart with which to love you, but I know I want

you." Rafe refused to lie. He would never love. The past had cut that emotion from him.

Montgomery wanted to rage against the sincerity she glimpsed in those fathomless eyes. Wanted to strike out against what she could never have. Now she had eternity to tolerate his lack of emotions for her and she couldn't even blame it on Katherine or that demon bastard. This was a mess of her own making and she had no one to blame but herself.

"You want me? Even knowing that I could drink of you while I bed you down, you still want me?" She wanted to hear him admit that it didn't matter, that she didn't matter. She needed to hear it so she could walk away. When she accomplished that, she'd find Jamison.

"I want you to stay with me." Rafe needed to touch her so much it hurt but he knew that if he did it wouldn't end there. He tried to reach her thoughts as he had done before, but found himself locked out. Jamie had seen to that, of this he was sure. "I will give you what I can, baby."

There was rejection in her eyes. "What more do you want from me?" he whispered at last, desperate to break past the hurt on her face.

"Maybe after I take care of Jamie, I won't bother to come back," she taunted as her temper emerged from behind the locks that had held it for years. "By then you'll have found some other toy to play with, I'm sure. Some other stupid fool to *want*. Then you won't have to worry about what *I* want."

"You'll stay away from him."

That going after Jamie was the only thing that caught his attention in her whole outburst had her swinging for the fence. "Don't you tell me what to do!" She was shouting now, but she didn't care. It hadn't even bothered him what she'd said about not coming back. She shuddered with her rage as she remembered the gentle way he had held her last night. It had all been a lie. "If I leave and never come back, then that's my business. What do you care anyway? Go find some other demon to amuse yourself with! Go find Katherine! She wants you so bad she's willing to deal with devils and kill people!" She ignored the look of complete amazement that crossed his dark features.

Come to me.

Montgomery heard the voice in her head and knew with a flash of deep fear who was calling to her. It was the same voice she had heard over and over again while she'd been in his clutches. She rose from her seat, so agitated that she forgot all about Rafe in that instance.

"I'll take care of him, Gomery. I don't want you hurt. He's not going to let you take him down. Hell, I don't want you even that close to him. Let me handle him." Rafe wondered at the expression on her face, but at least she wasn't yelling anymore. "Let me take care of you. We can be together. I want you with me. Don't you know that I care?" She didn't struggle as he pulled her into his arms.

Montgomery clung to him in desperation. The voice in her head caused so much confusion she would have given anything for the comfort of Rafe's embrace, regardless of their contrary views on love. Maybe she should let him deal with the brutal vampire. Just the thought of what he had done had the power to make her shake.

Then again, what did she really have to lose? What could he do to her now? He couldn't touch her, she was what he was now. She was an equal to Jamie. All she needed was a weakness and she could beat him down. A soft spot she could drive the knife into.

Katherine would know what to do.

Rafe took a deep breath; the feel of her in his arms was more than he could have hoped for. After last night, he wasn't sure it would happen again. The look in her eyes when she had drank from him still felt like a fist in his stomach. He had feared what she would do to herself. What she could do to him. Tilting her head up, he brushed his lips over hers. When she kissed him back, it was all he could do not to carry her to the rumpled bed across the room. Montgomery didn't make it easy, moving her body against him, sliding to meet the hardened contours. With the very tips of his fingernails, he held onto his control.

There was no need to rush her. Last night had been a shock for both of them and he didn't want to scare her again. Maybe after some time she would let him show her what it could be like between them. The feel of her taking of him had been so erotic he could barely restrain his desires at the memory. Now he understood the pleasure Katherine had received as she had held him down and drank from him, why she had wanted him to do the same.

The glory in the possession had been unbelievable, beyond anything he had ever experienced. Even the heated rush he had felt when he had taken from her the night before he had fled to Sasha couldn't compare to the feel of her mouth on his skin. Of her body sheathing his while she sipped of his essence.

Sweeping her up in his arms, he moved to the bed. To hell with control. He wanted to lose himself in her. Needed to touch the every edges of her soul and give her his in return. She would never leave his side again. He wouldn't let her. No one would ever be able to hurt her again. Even if he had to give his life for hers, he would. She would be safe. Lying her on the bed, he followed her down, not breaking contact for a second.

Montgomery was drowning in the sensations that bombarded her. Rafe touching her had always stolen her reason but now everything was so much *more*. She fought against herself, not wanting to give into the pleasures his hands and mouth were giving her. He didn't love her, he only *wanted* her. That little mantra did nothing to block out the heat that invaded every part of her body. There was no fighting her need. It was stronger than pride, stronger than reason. The hunger to be one with him, to sink her teeth in and fill herself with his taste and strength was overpowering. She wanted to...

That's right, pet. Bite down and drink until there is nothing left. Take him. Take his strength and power. Taste the darkness. Feel the rush. It could all be yours. He could be yours.

Jamie's commands filled her head and brought her to her

senses just as teeth broke skin. Pulling away from Rafe with a determination borne of fear and disgust, she made for the other side of the room. She could only stare at the marks on his skin, at the tiny trickles of blood that escaped. The smell of it reached her from across the room, stirring to life a hunger that had her taking a step in his direction.

That's good, pet. Go to him. Drink of him.

Putting her hands over her ears did nothing to block out the words. They were inside of her, testing her love, her sanity. She sank to her knees as the voice continued.

You can have him now while he still wants you, my pet. Before he knows what you want. Before he sees the hunger in your eyes.

"No. No." She held on tighter, not wanting to hear any more. But it was too late; she'd heard enough. Tasted enough. Jamie had done this to her. Jamie had put those thoughts in her head. He had better run for cover. Before she was done with him, he would be nothing but a pile of bones. Montgomery jumped at the feel of a hand on her shoulder. Unable to stop herself, she looked up into cautious silver eyes and her heart sank.

"It's okay, sweet thing. I feel the same hunger that you do. If doing this gives you pleasure, then don't run from it. Don't run from me." Rafe slid his arms around her and pulled her up into his warm embrace. The shame and fear in her eyes tore at him.

Maybe his heart could love again. Never had he felt so helpless before as in that moment when he held her so close but she was so far away from him.

Rafe could feel her rejection of his words, could read the doubt in her eyes. "I've felt the same hunger." She needed to understand. "We are joined. To want to share of me and me of you is a pleasure we can't deny. It won't harm us now. We are equal." He drew her fingers through blood on his throat. Then he brought those same fingers to his mouth and with his eyes locked on hers, he licked the dark wetness away.

Her insides turned to molten lava at the sight. Leaning into him, her mouth closed around the wound her teeth had made.

Rafe tensed at the feel of her tongue against his skin but tried his best not to react. The desire to throw her down and take until they couldn't move again pounded through him but she needed time. Time to learn of her hunger. Of her new desires. He wanted so much to give her that time.

Very good. Do it again. Drink until your dark lover is dead in your arms. Drink until there is nothing left. Drink until you can no longer feel the beat of his heart, the warmth of his body. Then you will come to me and we will share the bounty of your dark desires.

Montgomery tore herself away from his throat, from the heady exotic taste of him. God, she needed help, needed to get away before she hurt Rafe. Before she killed him. Katherine would help her. Together they would get rid of Jamie. When his voice no longer filled her head, she would be able to control this. Then she would be able to come back.

Rafe watched in anguish as Gomery pulled away from him and vanished. He sat down on the bed, his head in his hands as he wondered where she had gone. If she found Jamie, she wouldn't live to see the new sunrise. The vampire would have no tolerance for her defiance. Reaching out to her with his mind, he tried to find her but it did no good. Jamie had taken her from him again. This time he could only hope she found her way back.

T   T   T

Gabriel didn't wonder long about Montgomery. Almost as soon as he sent a questing thought in the dark one's direction, Rafe showed up before his eyes. What he did wonder about was the shattered expression on his face and the fury behind those clenched fists. He didn't have to ask.

"That bastard's inside her head. I couldn't pick up on the wavelength but he scared her enough to make her run. I think she's gone after him. No, I'm damn sure she's gone after him.

We need to find him first. We need to find him and smash him into the dirt before he can touch her again. We need..." He didn't finish as Gabriel laid a hand on his shoulder.

"We need to calm down and think," he countered, calm and smooth. "We need help from the others. Sasha can be of assistance. She's been hunting him for years and will have an idea where to look. Call for her and we can start."

Rafe didn't stop to wonder why the highlander didn't call her himself, he just closed his mind to his turmoil and beckoned the golden one to his side. That Michael would follow was never in doubt.

He had calmed down some in the few short minutes it took them to *pop* in, but they would have been blind to miss the silent rage that boiled so close to the surface. It seethed and writhed with a life of its own and Sasha feared what would come of so much emotion.

She didn't have to guess who it was directed at. "What do you need, Raphael?" Her eyes skimmed over Gabriel before she ignored him. She didn't want to deal with that yet. Rafe was her main concern. That gleam in his eyes had her worried. It spoke of a violence she wasn't ready for.

"I want to find Jamison."

There wasn't another word added and Sasha knew she would have to wait until hell froze over to get one. Instead, she reluctantly turned her questioning gaze on the highlander.

"He's inside of Gomery's head, confusing her, giving her commands. She took off and all we can assume is that she's gone after him. We need to find him first, before she goes and gets her immortal life cut short. She thinks Katherine helped her, she might go to there." Gabriel didn't go any farther. There was no need to bring up Gomery's new habit of nibbling on her lover. If Rafe wanted that fact known, he'd have to mention it himself.

"We should split up. I'll go back to the house where I found Katherine. You three can go look elsewhere," Michael suggested even as he took a step back. He wanted to get out before they exploded.

"You found Katherine and you let her go?" Rafe's voice shook the windows.

Gabriel's fists wrapped into his shirt shook him. Michael had known this would be ugly. That was why he had kept that little visit with her to himself. If it hadn't been for Katherine's tears, he *would* have turned her over to the rest but she *had* cried. She had shown a side of herself he hadn't thought she possessed. A side that showed she wasn't what he had thought. Either that or he was a fool. He didn't want to be a fool about her now. That was a role he'd played too often. Shrugging off Gabriel's hands, he turned his attention back to Rafe.

"Katherine hadn't known at that point where Jamie had taken her. It seemed wisest to let her go in case we needed information later. Now it's later and I'll go find out what she knows." He defended his choice.

"What else have you done, Michael, that you haven't seen fit to share with us?" The cold accusation in Rafe's voice sent a shiver through the room. Never before had he turned that icy control on one of his own.

"I don't answer to you," Michael's temper flared against the hostility Rafe didn't bother to hide. "I didn't drag her back here for reasons that are none of your business. Think what you want, I don't give a damn." He wouldn't answer to them. His secrets were his own.

"Jamison said you're not immune to Katherine's charms. What the hell does that mean, Michael? What the hell did he mean?" Rafe advanced as he threw out those questions.

"Leave it alone." The fair one threatened through clenched teeth.

"I don't think I will." Rafe drew back a clenched fist and let it fly with a force that leveled Michael to the ground. "I don't think I will." He followed the blond to the floor, his silver eyes glowing with fury as he pinned him to the ground. "What the hell did he mean?"

Michael didn't let the hand clenching his throat intimidate

him, nor did he back down from the rampaging fury that held the others in the room at bay. "Go to hell," he gritted out. "I don't answer to you, Rafe."

"You fucked her, didn't you?" Rafe saw the small flicker of guilt that flashed through those pale blue eyes. "Son of a bitch. You and your talk of trust." He swung again, making contact with the side of Michael's face. "I send you to find Gomery and you take a tumble with that black-eyed witch." His fist flew again before anyone could think to stop him. "Back off." Rafe snarled at Gabriel without taking his eyes off Michael. "Get the hell away, highlander. This doesn't concern you."

"I didn't." Michael had no defense against the hatred that burned within that silvery gaze.

Rafe looked at him for a long minute, allowing himself that small time to hear what the fair one wasn't saying. "That night in London." He watched the emotions that chased each other across Michael's angel face. "It was that night in London. While we searched for David's murderer, you were screwing her. That's how she got the drop on you, isn't it, Michael? You rotten bastard." His fist smashed down again, this time drawing forth a stream of bright red blood.

"Dammit, Rafe," Gabriel muttered as he pulled the furious immortal up by the back of his shirt. If Michael had made an effort to defend himself against the powerful blows Rafe had rained down on him, he might have let it go on. But the fair one made no move to strike back, just took the punishment. "Tell him he's wrong, Michael. Tell him you didn't betray David, that you didn't betray us." He demanded as he watched Michael rise to his feet.

"I can't."

Both Gabriel and Rafe stared at him in disbelief. Neither had wanted to think him capable of such betrayal. Sasha's presence kept them from reacting to the guilty truth they could read in Michael's pale eyes.

"We need to split up," she ordered, trying to dispel the brutal tension in the air. "We'll go back to the same places we hit before. Someone might have heard about her. One made by Jamie would draw much attention. There should be talk of her at the very least. If you find anything out, call for one of us. We don't want to confront him on a one on one basis. He is one of the most powerful vampires in our history and not above all things vile to get his way," she continued, her eyes locked on the defiance that flared in Gabriel's expression. "He'll be searching for you, angel. He's wanted a piece of you for years.

"Stay here, Michael, in case Gomery comes back or Morrigan needs you. Don't let her go out tonight. I would hate for something to grab her." Sasha looked at him then. She knew he would see her order as a sign of contempt, but there was nothing she could say now to dissuade those thoughts. Michael needed to stay here. Vampires were way too interested in his pretty face for her to want him roaming the dark.

"So I get to baby sit?" he murmured, his face blank of expression. "You want me to stay here and play watchdog over little miss sunshine while you three go out and search for Gomery? You don't want my help?"

There was so much self-contempt in those words that Sasha almost rescinded her decision.

"Think you can do it right this time?" Rafe snapped at him. "Think you can keep your pants on, you rotten bastard?"

Michael didn't answer, but the expression on his face spoke volumes. He took a step in Rafe's direction, his fists clenched in blatant threat.

Rafe didn't back down. He wanted a fight. Needed something to gain control again, something to give him an edge. Michael had betrayed them with Katherine. Michael would do.

"When this is over, I want you gone." Rafe ignored the harsh grip of Gabriel's hand on his shoulder, the shocked gasp that escaped Sasha's lips. "I want you gone, Michael. Don't make the mistake of ever crossing my path again. You betrayed us, you betrayed David and you betrayed Gomery, all for a piece of ass."

"This is not going to do us any good." Sasha shot him a

quelling glance. Then she looked at Michael and was surprised at the fury that burned in those blue eyes. He had never shown so much emotion as he did in those tense moments, with his rage and hurt coming off of him in waves. Rafe had hurt him with his words and now Michael was ready to strike back. She couldn't let him. "We need to focus on Gomery now."

Rafe eased off, his mind again focused on the search at hand. Michael relaxed by slower degrees, but Sasha saw that the rage never eased. That things would never be the same between the two men was a given. What could make it right again was a mystery.

"Can she kill him?" Rafe asked, his question an echo of what they all wanted to know. "If she finds him before we do, can she kill him?" he asked again.

"No."

Chapter 22

Morrigan watched him from the doorway, her eyes glued to the blond head bent over the inventory printouts. She'd made her decision and now she was running out of time. So little time. How she wished Gomery was here so she could confide her fears. Forcing back a bitter sigh, she realized she was on her own. Nobody was going to shake her awake and tell her it was all just a bad dream.

Nobody was going to say, *Oops! Sorry, we made a mistake!*

There wasn't even any comfort in the belief that everybody died sometime. She was going to die. Soon. And there was nothing anyone could do about it. The doctors had prepared her for this. They had told her the best scenario; now she was living out the worst. If the last few days were any indication, she had reached a critical stage. A month, a few weeks were all she had left. Hell, maybe all she had was a few days. No one knew. Not the doctors. Not her. She was going to die and she was afraid.

There was still so much she had to do. So many things she'd left undone. But she wasn't going to die alone, tied to a hospital bed. That was why she had come to New Orleans, to finish her goal and to take care of that *other* problem while she still could. The one she wasn't sure she'd accomplish now that Gomery was gone, but she'd sure as hell take care of that other one. She wasn't going to die with it hanging over her head.

Do what you have to do, Morrigan, she chided as she continued to hesitate in the doorway. This had nothing to do with emotions. Nothing to do with hopes and dreams. Absolutely nothing. She pulled herself away from her thoughts, cleared away her doubts and fears. There was a job to do and for better or worse, she always finished what she started.

"Michael."

He looked up, his pale blue eyes locking on her. "Morrigan," he returned, cautious of the fey looking female. That little girl look went a long way in cloaking the will of steel she kept hidden from others. Glancing at his watch, he wondered what she could want from him at this late hour.

"Did you want something, *cher*?" Michael asked at her continued silence. She blinked at his question and seemed to shake herself. He watched the look of determination that flew across her face. Then she straightened from the doorframe and strolled to where he sat on the couch. Resigned, he set his papers on the table.

"Will you come out with me?" she asked, her whispery voice softer than usual.

They had warned him not to let her go out and for the first time he noticed her clothing. Or lack of clothing. Her plum silk mini-dress went a long way in proving there was not a single tan line on her golden-brown body. Who would have thought that someone so tiny could have such long legs? His body stirred at the sight. Going out was a very bad idea, but her being with him wasn't any safer.

"I can't tonight, *cher*. I need to finish this so I can fax it in the morning. Some other time?" His smile was cool and she returned it without answering him. Michael forced his eyes to focus on her face. There was no need to tempt fate by admiring that tiny waist or those full breasts. He wondered what she was wearing under that scrap of silk. Caught up in his silent investigation he missed her reply. "What?" he asked, shaking his head to clear his thoughts.

"Can I stay here for awhile?" she repeated as she perched on the edge of the table.

"I do need to finish this." His eyes never left the smooth thigh that beckoned inches from his clenched fingers.

"Please?" she whispered as her soft pink lips trembled.

"Sure," he gave in with a sigh. "Can I get you something

to drink?" A distraction from those big lavender eyes staring at him with such loneliness was just what he needed.

"That would be wonderful." Getting him smashed would make this so much easier. It would still work if she got him intoxicated. The practice was one she'd employed in the past to get information. She was not above trickery to get what she wanted, and Michael had something she wanted.

When he handed her a glass of wine, she noticed his other hand was empty. "Aren't you going to have anything?" she asked, her voice sharper than she'd intended.

"I don't drink." There was a harshness to his smile as he sat down, pinning her to the spot. "What do you want, Morrigan?" His mind probed the edges of hers, looking for something, but she had a tight grip on her emotions and thoughts. He could read nothing of her desires or intentions and it bothered him more than he cared to admit.

One look at the wary expression on his face and she realized that pretty words would get her nowhere. Michael had been prey for women who batted their eyelashes and swayed their hips to get what they wanted for way too long. If she wanted something from him, she would have to take it, not sit around and ask pretty please. She rose to her feet, setting the full wineglass aside as she slid off her stiletto heels.

"You're right, Michael." Morrigan looked at his surprised face from under platinum lashes. He leaned back against the couch as she bridged the few steps that separated them. "I do want something from you." She didn't stop to watch his reaction as she placed her knee on the sofa by his thigh. Didn't second-guess the tightening of his fists as she braced her hands on the back of the couch behind his shoulders. Nor did she take mind of the harsh in drawn breath that escaped his clenched teeth as she slid her other leg on to the seat and straddled his hips. "The question is, will you give it to me?" She felt an unexpected thrill at the fire that blazed in those pale eyes.

Michael banked the flames that licked at his libido. He didn't buy this whole seduction scene for a minute. A few days ago, she was using his ego for target practice and now she was sitting on his lap with her butt wiggling against his groin. What was she up to and how far would she go to get it?

"What do you want from me, *cher*?" Urges he had never been able to deny softened the suspicion on his face, but he didn't bother to hide the distrust that hardened his eyes.

Why was nothing ever easy? At what point in all her planning did she actually think a womanizer of Michael's caliber would stoop to playing hard to get? It just boggled the mind. "I want *you*, Michael," Morrigan murmured, struggling to maintain eye contact. "I want you to carry me into that bedroom, take off my dress, lay me on the bed and make love to me." He shifted his hips under her and she felt the hard press of his arousal. Then she saw the hesitation in his eyes. Damn! When had this man developed restraint? "Please, Michael," she enticed with a husky whisper as she rocked against him.

Michael felt a surge of anger at the lust that flowed through his veins. He had learned nothing! All those years, all that pain, all of Rafe and Gabriel's hatred and disappointment, and he still couldn't control his animal urges. Anger gathered, built and redirected. If he couldn't deny himself her offer, then he would get her to withdrawal it.

"I don't *make love* to women, *cher*. Love has nothing to do with what I do for them. What I offer is recreational fucking, pure and simple." He watched her draw back from him. If only he could get her off his thighs, then he could think. "Women come to me and I provide them with a service. When it's over, we go our separate ways. Nothing promised and nobody gets hurt. I don't think you could handle that, little girl." Michael smiled at the outrage that tensed every muscle in her body.

"You think you're that good?" she challenged with a raised brow, forcing herself to relax against him.

"You wouldn't believe what I'm good at," he returned, his voice husky, silky.

Morrigan wanted to smack that look off his pretty face. She

didn't though, she needed him. "Then show me."

Michael settled for scare tactics. Shifting his fingers into her loose curls, he held her still. Never breaking contact with those pansy eyes, he stated simple facts. "If you want hearts and roses, you're looking in the wrong place. If you're looking for a soul mate, you're not even close. If you need a replacement for the lover who walked away, I'm not your man. I don't want love or commitment, *cher*. I don't need a tease who's just trying to get her kicks by playing turn-on games." He didn't let her pull away, instead he tightened his hold and brought his mouth closer to her ear so she'd miss nothing of the words he spoke.

"When I play, I play for keeps, little girl. If you want to stay, the rules are very simple. We leave our clothes and pretenses on the floor. I'll lay you on that bed in there and I'll fill your body with mine. No regrets. No promises. Nothing but sex and pleasure. If that's not what you want, then by all means don't let the door hit you on the ass."

There was no hint of a smile to soften the harshness of his words. All in all, that suited Morrigan just fine. She knew she surprised him when she leaned forward and bit his earlobe, her tongue snaking out to soothe the sting. Just as she knew he was unprepared for the bold and arousing words she purred into his ear. "If it's really that simple, then just fuck me, Michael."

†   †   †

Katherine arrived back at the house under the cover of night. Jamie wasn't around, she had made sure of that before she'd ventured up the long flights of stairs. She wasn't in a real big hurry to see him again. Ever. Caught up in her private thoughts, she entered her darkened room. Any other time she would have sensed the presence of another immortal a mile away. This wasn't one of those times.

"Hello, Katherine."

That the new immortal would come back to this place had Katherine baffled. She hadn't thought of Montgomery Sinclair as a stupid person.

"What can I do for you?" Katherine inquired as she turned to face the tall brunette. She had to get her out of here before Jamie returned from his hunt. If he caught her with his new prize, things would go badly for her and she wasn't up to another tangle with Jamie. There'd been enough of those to last her a life time. Maybe two. She just hoped Montgomery hadn't come for a pound of her flesh. Right now, she didn't feel up to a fight. Not tonight.

"I need some help." Montgomery sensed the hesitation in the sorceress. "I need to know how to hunt, how to block my thoughts. I need to know how to evade others like us," she explained, choosing her words with careful precision.

"It's not safe here for you. Jamie will be back soon." Katherine cast a worried glance out the window.

"We can go somewhere else then," Montgomery countered. Katherine wasn't getting off that easy. She needed her help and she was going to get it. There was so much this tiny woman could teach her, so much she needed to learn. There was no way she could trust herself around Rafe anymore and she couldn't go to the others, they would only lead Rafe to her and she feared too much for his safety if he got close to her.

"If Jamie finds me gone, he'll hunt me down and when he finds me, he'll kill me. This is the last chance I have to keep my head attached," Katherine explained with a cynical little smile. "I got on his bad side this time. He's a little miffed with me."

"Why have you stayed with him all this time? Why haven't you destroyed him? Brought him down like the rabid dog he is?" Montgomery was curious about the hold he had on her.

"Keep your loved ones close and your enemies closer," Katherine paraphrased. "I can't kill him, I don't have the power. If I tried and failed, he would kill me with so much glee it would take an eternity." She shuddered at the thought. "I had hoped that Gabriel would take care of him for me but I haven't been able to get close enough to ask. He's still pissed over that whole sword thing."

"Trust *me,* Katherine, Jamie won't hurt you again. He won't hurt anyone ever again."

ㅜ   ㅜ   ㅜ

Morrigan stared up at the ceiling with glazed eyes, struggling to focus on anything except the pleasure that pulsed through her body with enough force that even her toes tingled. She was beyond caring about her nakedness in light of Michael's clothed state and the fact that she'd only succeeded in removing his shirt before he had laced his fingers through hers, pulling her hands above her head. Then she saw the smile that softened his mouth as he watched the last waves of her orgasm pulse through her.

That same mouth had fused with hers and smothered her objection when he had refused to let her touch him. Those same lips had left a trail of fire down her body, never stopping until they reached the hidden parts deep inside of her.

Then there was those hands that stroked her flaxen tresses from the damp skin at her temples. Those same hands had followed the fire of his mouth and had wrung from her body a response she hadn't believed she was possible of giving.

But her mind wouldn't allow her to savor the experience of Michael's expertise. For all of the ecstasy that had racked her body, she was still alone. No sharing. No joy of togetherness at the moment of release. Nothing. There was nothing but a blinding flash of rapture and a dark well of fear and loneliness. It was that fear that had her begging for more. "Please, Michael, I need you with me." Her eyes glinted with unshed tears he didn't see as he slid down her body.

"Don't you like this, *cher?*" His warm breath brushed the platinum curls that shielded her heat from his pale gaze. He didn't wait for an answer as his fingers began to slide along the slick folds of her femininity.

"Michael…" Her words ended on a gasp as his tongue again found the small bud of nerve endings that started her body to shaking anew. "No more." She moaned as her body crashed on the first wave of sensations.

"More," he whispered against her as he sent her over the edge and into the abyss of gratification.

As her heart slowed and her breathing smoothed out, Morrigan pushed a hank of damp hair off her forehead with a limp hand. Ignoring the small tremors that continued to pulse inside of her, she watched Michael remove his belt and unbutton his jeans. She blinked back the longing and reverence in her eyes as she watched the ripple of muscles that danced across the washboard of his stomach.

Michael didn't miss the small gasp that reached him from the center of the bed. The reaction wasn't new to him. "Don't worry, *cher*, I promise I won't hurt you."

Morrigan blinked again at the sight of that magnificent body washed golden in the half-light from the living room. Then she raised her chin and met the concern in his eyes. "You can't hurt me." She hid her flinch at the slow smile of satisfaction that spread across his face.

When he came down on the bed beside her, that smile disappeared and the lust that flooded his eyes brought a hard edge to his face that would have scared her spitless if she'd had a choice. Then she was too busy as her eyes feasted on the hard male body that rose above her. On the long legs that eased her thighs apart. On the hand that held her body open for his possession. Morrigan pulled back as her gaze again fell on his impressive arousal, the hardness of which was already pressing into her.

"Michael," she gasped before she could stop herself.

He looked at her for a long moment before he brought his mouth down on hers. There was no need to rush this. For the first time in his life, he wanted to savor the needs of a woman. Wanted to experience every nuance of her desire as he slid in to the hilt. In two hundred years, there had never been a woman who could make him feel past the dark lust that fired his blood to the gentle passions that lie within him. There was something about the uncertainty on that stunning face that touched at his heart, that stirred something he'd thought never existed.

"Don't you worry, *cher*," he whispered in a low purr against her ear. "We'll take this as slow as you want. We have all night to do this. I have all night to give you pleasure."

Morrigan felt the crushing weight of fear as he eased into her body a little more. The stretching was almost more than she could endure. She knew that slow was only going to lead to panic, that she needed to take control again. Somewhere down the line she let Michael take charge and this was no longer her decision.

"Hey, *cher*," she drawled in her patented little whisper, refusing to flinch from the sudden heat in that crystal gaze. "Don't slow down on my account, baby. Unless you're afraid you can't deliver?" She watched as the tenderness left his eyes, and wished that God had struck her mute. Or, at the very least, she could take back those foolish words. Anything that would erase the look of ruthless, savage eroticism that now filled the face so close above hers.

Her eyes never left his as he grasped her slender hips with his large hands. She refused to look away from the dark promise on his face, no matter how much she wished she could. As he brought his lips down to hers for a kiss that spoke more of conquering than passion, Morrigan wrapped her slim legs around his waist, preparing herself for the worst.

Nothing could have prepared her for the pain that tore though her when Michael slammed through the fragile barrier of her virginity with a single powerful thrust that lodged him inside of her body as far as possible. Morrigan trembled with the pain of his entry and no matter how hard she bit her lip, she couldn't hold back the sobs that echoed in the darkened room.

Michael froze above her, his fingers gripping her hips hard enough to bruise the silky skin. For several moments he couldn't do more than watch the slow slide of tears down her flushed cheeks. It wasn't until her internal muscles began to flex and stretch around him, that he lifted his eyes to hers.

Then he brought his hand to her face and with shaking fingers, he wiped away the tears. With a gentleness she wouldn't have thought possible, he started to ease away from her.

Morrigan panicked. She couldn't let him leave her now, no matter how bad it had hurt to get this far. She needed him to finish what they had started. There was no way she'd leave this earth without knowing the closeness of a man's body holding her tight. She refused to give up the feel of a lover taking her into his arms, into his bed in the darkness of the night. If she had one night left or a hundred, she would make sure that she spent every one of them with her body tangled with his. The right or wrong of it could be worried over when she was dead.

"Don't leave me," Morrigan whispered. "Please," she added, tightening her legs around his waist. For everything she was worth, she couldn't fathom the expression on his face. There were more tragic things in this world than finding yourself in bed with a virgin. Some men even found that a turn on.

Morrigan could only guess that the pain he had caused her was the root of his upset. If only she could explain that in the long run the pain he had unwittingly inflicted would seem like a pleasant memory compared to some that she would experience. To some she had *already* experienced. But she couldn't tell him. She couldn't tell anybody.

When he didn't respond to her request, she flexed her hips against him, lifting away before she eased down again taking him back into her body. She ignored the discomfort that followed the movement. When he didn't take up the pace she did it again, and again, gasping as her body eased the way with a rush of moist heat. Without saying a word, Michael grasped her waist and held her still. She looked up in question at those expressive eyes and it was so easy to read the wanting in the pale blue depths.

"Like this, *cher.* "

There was no laughter on his face, no smug smiles, just a heavy remorse as he began to move into her body with long, slow strokes. After several moments, she felt a pressure build deep down inside of her. She couldn't control the wildness that consumed her as she arched up to meet his quickening thrusts, wanting nothing more than to ease the urgency. When the pressure tightened and intensified, she moaned with it. As her awareness tunneled in, she felt nothing but the tension in her muscles, saw nothing but the stars that flashed before her eyes. Unable to stop herself, she reached for his shoulders, her nails digging deep as she moved under his body, mindless to anything but what lay on the other side of the wanting.

"Michael," she gasped his name, searching for release, but not certain how to ask for it.

"I won't hurt you again, baby." He gentled his pace, misinterpreting the plea in her voice.

Morrigan found that the slower he moved, the more the pleasure slipped from her grasp. "Faster," she demanded.

He took in the enraptured expression on her face before he obeyed her. When no pain crossed her features he moved even faster, their bodies rocking in a rhythm that sent the canopy swaying above them. Michael's moans mingled with hers as she twisted and turned with him.

"More." She was so close to the edge that she wanted to scream.

He hesitated a brief second, ignoring his own needs for the care of hers. With a little more power, he thrust into her.

She gave a little moan at the sensations that brought her. "Again."

He gave up the fight. Her need for completion was just as desperate as his and he thrust again and again. Within seconds, her body went as taut as a bowstring under his as she soared over the edge, straight into the fires of release. Michael gave one last thrust and followed with a climax so violent that not even Katherine's exchange of blood could compare to it.

ᵀ   ᵀ   ᵀ

Michael lay very still in his big, tousled bed, Morrigan's warm body curved to his side as painful memories, centuries old, galloped through his troubled mind.

The worst of those memories centered around one girl. A tiny little slip of a thing so sweet, so innocent that he hurt just to remember her. His parents had taken Amanda as their ward and he had bedded her for no greater reason than to prove he could. But that hadn't been his biggest crime against her.

Weeks later, she had come to him, desperate to find her lover and share her news. Which of his *friends* had escorted her to his room, he would never know. All had thought it a grand joke to leave her standing there in the doorway. It had been a drunken joke for him as well. A cruel jest that had left him on that rumpled bed with the whores that had come to the lodge with him. He could see it as if it was yesterday. Could see the way her eyes had flooded with tears at the sight of him humiliating her. By heart, he could recite the words she had spoken to him that night. About the baby and their need to elope to Greta Green.

Amanda had cried and begged on her knees for him to leave with her. Too drunk to care and too much of a bastard to listen, he had sent her away with his harsh words of rejection.

The next morning, hung over and reeking of cheap perfume and debauchery, he'd gone home. What had greeted him upon his arrival had changed his self-indulgent life forever. Amanda had slit her wrists with a knife she had taken from the kitchen. She hadn't been able to live with what he had done to her. With what they had done in his bed. All of her reasons were spelled out in a bloodstained letter that his mother had pulled from her cold fingers. He had left that very day, his family's horror-filled accusations still ringing in his ears.

For a time, he'd done his best to thwart the ravenous sexual hunger programmed into him by his father's creative mistress. Inevitably, the erotic lessons taught to a boy of thirteen had exerted a depraved pull all their own and his efforts had gone for naught. He served one purpose and he couldn't escape his calling.

Lilith had pounded that into his head over and over in her need to create the perfect toy. So brutal honesty and a jaded reputation had become his weapons of choice from there on, to keep the innocent from his bed.

Women had flocked to him in droves, regardless of the blood staining his hands. Married, single, lady or serving wench, they'd seen that same something in him that had drawn Lilith. And he'd given them their fill without hesitation. Anything went in his bed. No desire was denied. No urge was too dark. Just one thing remained the same in the ever-changing parade of willing women; no promises were ever given in the heat of pleasure and no emotions ever touched him while he attempted to relieve his insatiable need.

That vow had held true for endless years until last night. Morrigan had changed all that with her bold eyes and lush body. In taking her, he'd taken an innocence he wasn't entitled to.

Rafe was right about him after all. They couldn't trust him to take care of a woman as he should. He hadn't kept Morrigan safe from harm, instead, he'd hurt her, bringing tears to those beautiful purple eyes while she urged him on.

"Good morning."

The greeting was whisper soft and matched the satisfied gleam in her eyes. She stretched against him, her body a warm reminder of what had transpired between them. "Morrigan," he began in a husky whisper, as he searched for some sign of hurt, some lingering pain he could soothe. Reaching out a tentative hand, he smoothed back the tumble of white curls that framed the sleepy sensuality of her face.

There was something on his face that surprised her. Uh oh, that wasn't part of his guidelines. Guilt had no place in this, or love, or ever after. He had promised sex without complication, but *that* look spoke of big complications. Complications she didn't need. Not now. "Last night was perfect. You're as good as the rumors said you'd be." Morrigan waited for a reaction.

Embarrassment wasn't an emotion she'd thought Michael Wyhndym capable of feeling but it was there in the faint blush on his face. Didn't his bed partners believe in compliments? Or were they just incapable of forming coherent thoughts after he reduced them to puddles of mindless hormones? She couldn't fault them their inability to speak. The man was a walking sin. But that was all he was. What woman could trust a man like this? Faithfulness wasn't even in his vocabulary and no matter how good he was at scrambling her brain, she wasn't going to waste her limited time trying to reform him.

"About last night, *cher.* I didn't mean to hurt you."

"Don't sweat it, baby. You more than made up for it. In fact, I would love going another round."

Michael swallowed down the moan that snaked up his throat at her invitation. He wanted nothing more than to bury himself inside her, but that wasn't an option now. Things needed to be said between them. Those promises he'd always ran from needed to be made. He owed Morrigan for what she'd given him last night. After all those decades of inescapable guilt, he had a chance. "Come out with me, *cher.* We'll go to Jackson Square and have breakfast."

"Don't waste your time, baby." Morrigan gave a little chuckle she was far from feeling. How did she tell him that his body and the distraction it offered from the dull ache pounding in her temples was the draw here and not his company? "I'm a sure thing, *cher.* Why should we waste time with social niceties when all I want from you I can get right here?"

"All you want from me is a tussle?"

She failed to notice the irony that crept into his silky-smooth voice. Missed the bitterness that invaded the paleness of his eyes. Michael felt his temper rise at her careless shrug. The little tease thought she was going to screw him out of his chance to make amends but she was wrong. It was his turn to set things right and if he had to keep her on her back until she wanted more from him than that, he'd just have to accommodate her.

"That was how you explained the rules to me. Remember?" Morrigan could tell something was wrong, but she didn't for the life of her know what. Shouldn't he thank her for her cooperation? Didn't he want entanglement-free, mind-blowing sex on tap? Men were so damned complicated.

"What about the game that precedes the victory, *cher*? What if I need the challenge to arouse my interest?" Michael wanted to see if she would back down.

"Do you like to play games, Michael?" She didn't trust his wounded expression. Men, no matter how innocent they looked, could never be trusted. That was a lesson she had learned in spades and she never made the same mistakes twice.

"Every man likes to play games, *cher*. It's the nature of the beast."

Morrigan rolled over him until she had his body pinned under hers. He could talk all he wanted of games and challenges but he was so ready for her that she couldn't resist taking him. "The game doesn't have to end yet, Michael. Not when you want to play as bad as I do." The breath shuddered from her lungs as his hips thrust up against hers, fully seating her on his straining body.

Chapter 23

"If Jamie had wanted her dead, I think he would have done that by now," Gabriel expressed his opinion as he sat with Rafe and waited for news of Montgomery to reach them. "He wouldn't have turned her if he didn't have a specific reason. Whatever that might be."

He didn't look at his friend sitting across from him, he couldn't stand to see the deep emotions that burned there. Part of him was sure that this whole mess would come to a cataclysmic finish. Jamie had a lot to answer for and before this was over, one of them would die. If it was him, or Rafe or Jamie, they had yet to know. But, if he had any say, it wouldn't be a fallen angel that ceased breathing.

"How did Sarah take the news about Seth?" Rafe changed the subject. He no longer wanted to talk about Jamie's reasons for taking Gomery from him. The bastard would have all of five seconds to explain himself before he drove a stake through his black heart. Five seconds to realize he had made the biggest mistake of his life.

"She didn't really ask many questions. It's as if she's afraid of what the answers could be. But she's not coming back. She's going to take care of all the arrangements from there. I don't blame her. There's nothing for her here but bad memories. Someone's going to close up the house and take care of putting it on the market for her. It's about time she realizes that she doesn't have to do everything on her own." Gabriel leaned back in his chair, stretching out his denim-clad legs.

"Does she think you did it?" Rafe asked, his curiosity getting the better of him.

"She must but she doesn't *want* to know. From what I've

told her and from the reports, she knows it was ruled a suicide, but I don't think she believes it," he continued with a rueful shake of his head. "Even if she asked me, I couldn't tell her the truth. She would never believe it."

"What *is* the true story?" Rafe hadn't yet heard what had happened the other night. He hadn't been able to get an answer out of the elusive Sasha, and if anyone knew what went on between Gabriel and his partner it would have been her. "What went on in that house? What pushed Jordan so far? What did you do?"

"I wasn't afforded the privilege of dealing with him. Someone beat me to it. Someone with a lot more at stake than me."

Rafe took in that statement with nothing more verbal than an arched eyebrow.

"Sasha took care of it."

"So the golden one released her claws and went for blood. Did she kill him then?" Rafe wasn't at all surprised to know that their savior was involved.

Gabriel couldn't help but wonder at his easy acceptance. "She didn't pull the trigger, but she gave him enough incentive not to be there when she came back. I guess death was the best the coward could come up with." He clenched his fists as he relived the jolt she had given him as a lesson. If she had done that to Seth for any length of time, he could see where a mere human wouldn't have been able to withstand it. That she had that much pain inside of her and was still the caring, giving person she was gave him much to consider.

All that she had revealed to him of herself in the last weeks kept his mind in a whirl. She was different than he had thought. Strong and serene. Deep and fragile. That she had loved him despite all he had put her through, amazed him. That he hadn't seen it until that night she found him with Sarah burned through him like a flame. He hadn't realized he'd let his own pain blind him. There was so much about her he didn't know. So much he had never allowed himself to see.

"Did you find anything?"

Gabriel knew what the dark one was asking. He knew the fears that ran through Rafe's head and shared many of them. Everyday it became a little clearer that Rafe was lost without Gomery. Clear to everyone but Rafe and that was past strange because the man saw everything. His cool analytical mind missed nothing. No emotions ever colored his thinking or judgment. Until her. This one woman had turned his whole world upside down and he was blind to it. Completely unaware. Gabriel might have found the whole situation amusing if he wasn't sinking in the same boat.

"Nothing new. Not about Jamie, or Gomery and sure as hell not about Katherine. On a different note, there were two murders down in the French Quarter last night. The bodies were mutilated and drained of blood. If I didn't know that vampires didn't exist, I would have had cause to worry." His sarcastic smile brought an answering one to Rafe's troubled face.

"There was just enough made to make it look *normal.* Judging by what Sasha has shared of his past, I would say that Jamie got hungry last night and ate out." That comment brought Rafe to his feet. "I think he's sending a message. Both victims were females, tall with reddish-brown hair. It was too hard to tell what the eye color was after he had finished with them, but it doesn't take a genius to see he's sending out a challenge to you. He wants you to come out and play, but the question is, if he wants to play so bad, why doesn't he just knock on the front door and ask?"

"That's what I am going to find out." Rafe paced the floor, his face set as he sought out the elusive answers to his burning questions. "Where would Katherine go? If she had Gomery with her, where would that little witch go?"

Gabriel couldn't answer that one. That was another woman he'd never figured out. Other than the fact that every time he looked at his chest was a reminder of her perfidy, he tried not to dwell on the antics of that certain immortal. He found that the mere thought of Katherine fired his anger to a dangerous level and that was a rush of emotion he chose to deny whenever possible.

"We always hear about mental ties. Sasha hears me, I hear her. Why shouldn't that work with you and Katherine?" Gabriel threw out the possibility. He needed to give the dark one some hope, even if only for a little while. Every hour that Gomery was gone, he sunk that much deeper into a fury that colored the icy coldness of his gaze and fisted those strong hands at his sides.

"When should Sasha be back?" Rafe gritted out, already searching the darkening sky for signs. "I would call to her, but she seems to have blocked all of us from her mind. Any ideas why she would do that?" He challenged with a hostile glance in the highlander's direction, needing a distraction from the pain in his soul. Sparring with Gabriel would accomplish that.

"She should be back soon and it's none of your damn business," Gabriel answered, a smile softening the words. He wasn't in the mood to cross swords, so he picked a different subject, one that had the whole precinct in an uproar of unanswered questions and speculation.

"Our prowler lifted two hundred thousand in jewels the other night. That brings the grand total to about three million dollars. The guy's clever. He never leaves a trace and always seems to know how to get past the security systems. No one thinks it's a coincidence that all the hits have been on St. John Securities client list."

"Since when is that an area you cover?" Rafe asked, half-listening to his friend as he sent a mental call to Sasha.

"It's not, but that whole locked room scenario has me intrigued." Gabriel shook his head as he gave some of the particulars. "What do you think?" He listed the last of the details that had the local police and now members of the FBI, all in a tizzy.

"Sounds like an inside job at St. John's. Did they question the owner? What would he have to gain if this all came through?" Rafe asked, distracted as he searched the darkness encroaching on the city beyond his window.

"Nothing to gain and everything to lose. If this happens a few more times, he's as good as done. Not that we got that from him. We have a source that was more than willing to come across with that and another little piece information that I found very interesting. It seems that Malcolm St. John had the same idea about this being an insider, so he set out a reward that would tempt a saint to turn in his own mother. Funny thing is, nobody's snitching. From what I gather, there is no way a person can break through one of these systems. A person would have to know every little component and every little wire to begin to break through one of the coded systems and no one has that knowledge. Not even the Feds can figure it out." Gabriel shrugged off his unease with the whole thing.

"Did you ask Morrigan what her thoughts on the subject are? I thought she was a wizard when it came to that stuff." Rafe reminded him.

"That's what I have in mind to do, but she's been pretty elusive the last few days. Michael's been keeping her occupied." He hated to bring up the fair one's name in front of Rafe. The silver eyes that turned on him with such coldness increased his discomfort.

"Screwing her too, is he?" Rafe didn't want to discuss Michael right now. Maybe never. The bastard had betrayed them for the sake of lust. Had desecrated the memory of David Mallory for a moment's pleasure. Worse than that, he allowed the one who held the key to Gomery's whereabouts to get away without so much as a protest.

"You need to let it go." Gabriel wasn't happy with what had transpired between Michael and Katherine either, but he wasn't going to throw away centuries of brotherhood over what they couldn't change. He knew what it was like to live with mistakes you couldn't right. To live with sins committed in a single night.

Rafe didn't respond, his attention focused instead on the woman stepping from the inky shadows into the light. "What did you found out?" he asked Sasha with as much patience as he could muster.

"Nothing as yet, but I hear he was busy last night." News of the murders had assaulted her ears from the minute she had hit the underworld. The bloody atrocities were all the true vampires could speak of. They weren't happy that Jamie chose to play his little games so close to their backyard. Most tried to be discreet when it came to feeding.

Rumors that Jamie hadn't even fed on the women he had taken, but had slaughtered them had several up in arms, while others hid in the shadows, avoiding his wrath. After all this time, stories of his vast cruelties still evoked fear in immortals. Talk ran rampant of stopping him, but only one mysterious warrior had accepted the challenge centuries ago. All hoped Hunter accomplished his goal.

"So Gabriel told me." Rafe saw the bitter look that passed between the two but didn't comment. Their little tragedy didn't concern him right now.

"I do know he doesn't have Katherine with him," Sasha revealed. "Seems he's been looking for her as hard as we've been looking for him. Word is he's wanting her head this time."

"Doesn't she pull this little stunt all the time?" Rafe had heard much of the witch and her antics in the last few days. He had learned as well that Katherine's true name was unknown in the darkness, whereas tales of the sorceress and her escapades abounded. Real names had no place in the shadows; strange little nicknames were the norm and every creature of the night had one.

"To hide from Jamie is one thing, it's another to run from him. Our sire doesn't take defiance in stride and I'm going to guess that when he finds her, Katherine will no longer be our problem." A small frown crossed her face, part of her would miss the little one.

"He won't get the chance, not if I get to her first." Rafe spat out the threat.

"She's what Jamie has made her, Rafe. Katherine was very different before he took her under his *care*. Maybe had I not been so full of rage when she came to me, things would have been different. *She* would have been different." Sasha knew it was time to break her silence about Katherine's past. About Christian.

"What's this all about?" Gabriel asked, joining the conversation.

"Katherine was very young when she came to me, younger even than I had been when my father abandoned me in that field, but she had great magic for one so young. Greed didn't bring about her downfall, or lust for power, but love for a man. A man destined to die in her arms." She ignored the disbelieving snort that erupted from Rafe.

"It had been prophesied that a great warrior would come to save her people, not through any great feat of arms but through death. For anyone to save him or give warning of his coming doom was forbidden. None of that mattered to her. Katherine fell in love with this warrior and in begging him to leave with her, revealed all. For reasons never shared, he refused. Fear of his death forced Katherine to seek me. She begged for immortality so she could save her lover and I refused." Sasha closed her eyes, memories of Katherine's desperation still fresh after six centuries.

"Jamie kept her mortal for months. That so tiny a creature would seek him out amused him beyond all reason. What he did to me must have been nothing compared to the tortures he inflicted on her. She stayed and let him do as he wanted, until such a time as he deemed her worthy. The deed done, she returned home to find her warrior lying on the ground, his life seeping into the dirt. In the end all she could do was hold him in her arms and watch him die." She wiped a single tear from her cheek.

"How did she end up with Jamie again?" Gabriel couldn't believe that Katherine could go back to him.

"Jamie wasn't ready to give up his new toy so he hunted her down. It took him time, but he broke her to his hand. I tried once to get her away, but he had done his work well. He produced in the child she was, a reckless bitter woman who could no longer love anyone, least of all herself. The only time I think she's at any kind of peace is when she thinks of Christian. Whenever she can get away from Jamie, she goes back to the valley we buried him in." Sasha released a sad sigh. Things would have been so different had she just listened with her heart then, instead of her misery.

"I don't see Katherine languishing at a lost lover's grave." Rafe refused to believe her capable of softer emotions.

"Don't let what she did to you blind you. Nothing is ever black and white, but many shades of all encompassing gray. To think that she has no heart is to make a lie of all she did to try to save him. In her grief, she took his dagger and slashed her wrist, trying to force her blood into him. He was too weak to take it and when the wound healed over, she did it again and again. Over and over, she cut into her flesh and when it finally healed for the last time, it left a deep and ragged scar behind. Who lost more blood that day, she or Christian, is hard to guess. If I hadn't found her, she would have died from the wounds she had inflicted. After I healed her, we buried her warrior."

"She hated you, but she let you help her?" Gabriel spoke again.

"Katherine's love for him was stronger than her hatred of me."

"Can I find her?" Rafe reached for her, taking her hands in his. "Can I find her how you always find Gabriel?" He was no longer asking but demanding. "Can I find her, Sasha?"

ᛏ   ᛏ   ᛏ

Morrigan stood away from the glowing streetlights on St. Charles Avenue, her dark clothing blending into the shadows of the trees growing next to the fence surrounding the four-story antebellum plantation. The house being deserted for the night was a pleasant treat in her favor, but not a necessity.

With unhurried movements of such fluid grace, it appeared that she glided over the damp grass, she approached the fence. Dropping her backpack on the ground, she studied the tall wrought iron fence.

Reaching into the black bag, she drew out a sturdy length of dark rope. Forming a loop, she tossed her makeshift lasso and caught one of the tall spikes that adorned the uppermost part of the fence. Ignoring the dull ache in the back of her head, she hooked the bag over her shoulder and climbed the fence. Reaching the top, she swung her legs over and slid down the rope until her feet touched the ground.

She didn't need to consult the notes in her bag. The layout was so implanted in her mind, she could have made the trip from the fence past the security triggers blindfolded. After all, she had designed every system that her uncle had ever sold.

Malcolm St. John had yet to guess that she sent system designs through his office under a dummy corporation. Just as he'd yet to figure out that she was the one who'd bought up all the outstanding St. John stock. The rotten murderer didn't know that she had enough evidence to prove that not only had he had her father killed, but that he had disposed of the two men he had hired to do the deed. He didn't know of all the nights she bypassed his security system and stood at the foot of his bed, her gun clenched in her hand, but he would.

Before this was all over, when his stolen company lay in tatters around his feet and the police came knocking on his door, he would know. In vivid detail, he would know everything she had done to bring him to his knees. And when the end came, there'd be nothing he could do about it. No law that could stop her from gaining justice. No one who could stand in her way.

And when she went to sleep and never woke up, then she would answer for her sins. If God deemed hell a suitable punishment for the act of vengeance, then so be it. She was prepared to burn so long as she had dear uncle Malcolm to keep her company.

Stopping next to the building, Morrigan glanced up at the small rectangular window that allowed fresh air to circulate into the full-length attic. There was no sensor on that window, no trigger to the alarm. All she had to do was get there. Putting her rope over her free shoulder, she grasped a rung on the rose trellis. Ignoring all the fancy equipment in her bag, she settled instead on an old fashioned method. With steady hand over hand climbing, she made it as far as the second story balcony. Grasping the railing, she walked the outside edge, careful not to put her toes past the invisible light sensor that kept the floor of the balcony secure.

Moving with as much speed as a three-inch wide ledge would allow, she reached the other side. Grabbing the gutter that they'd over looked in the final layout, she climbed up to the next floor without hesitation. Now all she had to do was get up the next ten feet to the window.

Ignoring the sharp pain that pulsed through her head, she reached behind her and pulled the grappling hook from the side pouch of the bag. With steady movements, she attached her rope and with a quick eye and sure aim, she tossed it out and up. With a sturdy tug, she tested the security of the hold. Confident in the placement of the line, she swung out and climbed the line until she came level to the attic window. Wrapping the rope around her right arm, she tugged on the frame that opened as if by magic.

Morrigan levered herself through the small opening. Leaning back out, she freed her hook with a flick of her wrist. Bundling her rope up she tucked it and the hook back into her bag. She wouldn't need them again tonight. There was no way in hell she planned on going back out the way she'd come in. There were a lot of things she was, but crazy wasn't one of them.

She crossed the floor with unhurried strides. There were hours available if she needed them and only one item on her mind. A rather special item that would be impossible to replace. The disappearance of it would be something her dear uncle couldn't buy his way out of this time.

Taking it would be a cakewalk. It wasn't even in the room-sized safe on the second floor, but in a special glass case in the library. No triggers guarded this particular item; no alarms would announce its removal from the house. Nothing so complex guarded this little treasure.

Sliding open the door, Morrigan crossed to the back stairs that would lead her to the third floor landing. Opening her bag, she took out her pen light, the small beam lighting her way down the dark hall. Her black tennis shoes moved over the carpet without sound as her eyes searched the shadows.

On the third floor, she pulled the floor plans from her bag and scanned the sensor layout on the main staircase. Not every step had a trigger and if all was as it appeared on paper, it would save her the time of climbing down her rope off the high side rail. With her luck holding true, she stepped down the first riser. In the barest of seconds, she had maneuvered the stairs and was walking with sure steps down the hall.

The locked door that barred her from her coveted prize was of little consequence. Snapping open the small black case she'd removed from her bag, Morrigan slid out a slim metal tool. In the time it took to draw a deep breath, the door was swinging open. The dim room beckoned and with it, the reason she'd added it to the list.

This house had been one of the first that Malcolm had done after her father's death. The case against the back wall drew her feet across the floor. What was in the case squeezed her heart with the same strength it had when she'd seen it a few years ago. There was no surprise this time though, just a deep-seated sense of wonder. She had never thought to see it again. If a faulty wire hadn't necessitated a service call, she wouldn't have.

The treasure that had her so enthralled was nothing more than a simple painting. A painting the size her backpack, framed in nothing more than delicate, carved cherry wood and worth no more than the canvas it was painted on. A simple, beautiful painting of a pair of lovers wrapped in each others' arms as they stood in the middle of a sun-dappled field of wildflowers. A man and a woman sharing an embrace full of gentle passion and earth shattering emotion.

Morrigan gasped against the pain that lanced through her head with a fierceness that almost sent her to her knees. Closing her eyes, she fought against the darkness that seeped into the edges of her vision, fought against the weakness that caused her legs to shake. Steadying herself against the glass case, she took a deep breath, forcing the air in and out of paralyzed lungs.

Concentrate. Focus. Finish. The mantra did nothing to block out the agony that pierced through her brain. This was what her revenge was all about and revenge was all she lived for now, all she had left. A gasp rippled up her throat as another pain lanced through her and this time she couldn't keep her knees from buckling. Morrigan slid to the floor, her head in her hands as she struggled against the demons that sliced into her skull with razor sharp claws.

On and on the pain continued until it was all she could do not to slam her head against the wall. Nausea churned her stomach and sweat beaded her body until the dampness of it sent shivers dancing over her skin. The passing of time held little meaning as every breath whispered past her lips in an exhalation of desperate misery. Curling into a ball, she weathered the storm until the intensity lessened.

When she could move again, Morrigan wiped the cold sweat and tears from her pale face, her blurry eyes focusing on the painting that had drive her to take such a chance. Slowly she staggered to her feet and with unsteady hands, pulled open the case, easing out the frame. There was no time to look at it as she slid it into her bag. Too much time had passed while she'd huddled on the ground and her cakewalk was now a dangerous situation.

She hadn't expected this to happen now, hadn't planned for the eventuality of an attack so close on the heels of the lesser one that had occurred just that morning. No amount of planning would have prepared her for the intensity of what she'd just experienced though. Even now, the dull pain that throbbed through her had no impact compared to what had preceded it.

There was no need to close the case, or the door behind her as she left. At this point, she no longer cared about maintaining the mystery surrounding her night work. Right now, all she wanted was out of here.

Circumstances conspired against her as she struggled under the added weight of the black bag on her shoulder. Her body demanded sleep to replenish the energy the episode had taken and as much as she wanted to curl up and sleep, she couldn't. Stopping now meant getting caught and that meant putting herself within her uncle's grasp. Either way, her end was near, but there was no way she'd go to hell at his mercy.

ϯ   ϯ   ϯ

Michael rested his shoulders against the large tree that dominated the section of yard under the second floor balcony. Breathing deep of the humid night air, he waited. There was not a clue in his head as to what had possessed him to follow Morrigan tonight but something had. Maybe it had been that little smile or maybe the guarded look in those bright purple eyes.

The reason no longer mattered. Nothing mattered after watching the cat like grace and amazing skills that had gained her entry into the house of New Orleans' police commissioner. With a patience that was as foreign to his nature as savagery, he waited for hours until the pale head peaked out a third story window.

Morrigan shimmied down the dark rope with monkey like agility until she touched the ground, black bag looped over her shoulder. She still hadn't seen him where he lounged in the shadows, but only because he didn't want her to. The advantage of surprise was still his and he observed the graceful sway of her body as she made good her getaway.

"Well, well. Just what have you been up to tonight, *cher?*" He drawled out as he stepped into the dim light cast from the streetlamp. To give her credit, she didn't even flinch at the sound of his voice. There was no hurry to her movements as she turned and took in his unexpected appearance.

"Miss me?" The taunt was unmistakable as she drew away from the security of the stone pillar.

"What's not to miss, *cher?*"

His easy smile didn't fool her for a second. She didn't need this right now, not when all she wanted to do was get back to the club and crash. Then the smile evaporated and he lunged for her, grabbing at the bag on her shoulder. Morrigan refused to let go and tightened her grip on the black nylon. "You're so right, honey. I'm hell on wheels and twice as fun."

"All that and a lousy thief to boot."

"Oh no, Michael." She denied his accusation with a shake of her head. "You've got it all wrong."

Part of him was relieved to hear she wasn't the elusive prowler that Gabriel had been searching out the last few weeks. He didn't think he could turn her over to the police and he didn't want to test his loyalty to the highlander, not now when he and Rafe were so much at odds.

"I'm not a *lousy* thief at all; I'm a very good one." She didn't wait for his reply but jerked free of his hold and turned away.

"Where do you think you're going?" he demanded.

His words as much as the hand at her elbow stopped her escape. She turned to face him, her arched eyebrow and sardonic expression worth a thousand words. "To the club. Let me go or call the police." The ultimatum was delivered without a flicker of platinum eyelashes. "I don't care which, but I'm not going to stand here and debate the issue with you."

This time when she shrugged off his hand, he followed.

CHAPTER 24

Katherine paced the living room of the little house she'd confiscated, her nerves on edge. Something was going to happen soon, she could feel it in the air and she was scared beyond reason. Jamie had been looking for her and Montgomery last night. He'd almost found them. If not for his devious desire to send a message to Rafe, he would have had them. Instead, he'd allowed a woman exiting one of the many bars on Bourbon Street to distract him. A woman with the same looks as Montgomery Sinclair.

She'd had to physically restrain Gomery to keep the young revenant from confronting their vile sire then and there. The struggle had been fierce but her magic had served her well in the end. Maybe not so this time. Montgomery had left hours ago and she had yet to return. While she had taught the tall brunette much, Katherine didn't think it was going to be enough to ensure her survival in a direct clash with Jamie.

Maybe she was just overreacting. There was no evidence that the woman had gone after Jamie. There was every possibility she'd slipped out in her desire to see her dark lover, to recruit him to her cause. Now *that* would be a deadly combination not even their ancient sire would stand a chance against. No one could stand against one such as Rafe. He was a force to reckon with. A dark warrior. He reminded her so much of…

"Thinking of me, sweetheart?"

She heard the voice drawl from behind her. "Yes, I am," she replied as she placed the width of the gold brocade couch between them. Katherine didn't turn around; she didn't need to. She would have known that voice anywhere. It was that voice that had first caught her attention. That voice had sparked her interest all those years ago. Every silken vowel, every smoky consonant reminded her so much of *him*.

"I'm flattered, but you don't have to look to find me anymore. I've come to you."

Again, that voice purred down her spine just as it had two centuries before. Its caress was softer than the black velvet covering her skin. If she closed her eyes, she could almost pretend. Rafe didn't let her as his hand caught her elbow and turned her around.

"Miss me?" he taunted with an amused smile.

Katherine opened her eyes and met the cold certainty of his. His lips might hold a sardonic smile, but there was none of that in his eyes. Only by sheer self-mastery did he hold onto the pain and anger she saw reflected in those pure silver eyes. It was only by his great strength of will that she wasn't even at this very moment dead at his feet.

She didn't try to get away.

There was no need to run. Now she could leave this hell and go on. She wanted to close her eyes and rest. Rafe could give her that.

Michael had been right about the many ghosts that haunted her dreams. They kept her from sleep. From peace. But none so much as the one ghost she'd done so little to create. The one she'd been unable to save. Until it was too late. The one she saw every time she closed her eyes. The one she had embraced to her heart.

She needed to be with Christian again. She needed the comfort of death and Rafe could do that for her. As much as he hated her it would be quick, and even if it was not painless, it would be a far cry better that the demise that Jamie no doubt had in mind for her.

Rafe watched the emotions that flitted across her face and wondered at the momentary torment, then the deep resignation that came to rest there. He didn't wonder long. Nothing in him cared about the misery he could see in her eyes. All he wanted from Katherine was what he had craved for the last two hundred years. Revenge. It was that simple emotion that had kept him grounded all these years. That emotion had kept him in control.

"Where's Montgomery Sinclair?" His face was so close to hers that every breath feathered the hair across her forehead. "What have you done with her?"

"She left this morning." Katherine remained steady under his icy gaze. There was no reason to say more. She just wanted it over with.

"You let her leave," Rafe drawled the words out nice and slow as if they were a rare treat to be savored. "You took something that was not yours to take. For nothing more than blood lust you decided my fate."

Katherine repressed the shiver that the ice in his gaze evoked. She wouldn't show fear. Not ever again. "I would change nothing of what I did that night in London, except that maybe I would have started with you," she goaded him. Then she pushed just a little bit more. "Gabriel and Michael weren't the ones I sought out that night. It was you I wanted. You I wanted to see suffer and die."

"Why?" he asked the one question that had been denied him.

"You're so like Jamie, those cold soulless eyes, that cruel, hard face. You were my chance to get even with that bastard for all he'd ever done to me." There was no reason to lie about her motive.

"You came after the three of us for nothing more than a chance to kill me in Jamie's place?" Rafe moved his hand up her arm until it settled on the curve of her shoulder. "For nothing more than petty revenge, you took David's life?" His expression hardened at the memory of his mentor. "Was that few minutes you had me at your mercy worth all that you've done? Was it worth what I'm going to do to you?"

"Not really. Not as much as it was when I took the woman to get your attention." She waited for his anger to take him over. Waited for him to snap, but she should have known better.

"You wanted it, now you've got it." His mouth softened and that smile emerged again. This time true amusement curved his full lips. "Be careful what you wish for," he whispered close to her ear.

"I was really quite surprised by your girl. She wasn't at all what I expected her to be." Katherine threw out that bomb and waited for the fall out. She knew she had hit the mark when his hand moved from her shoulder to her throat, but she refused to flinch from the fury she saw in his eyes. If death was what she craved this night, then she had found her man. "Jamie is very taken with her. I have never seen him so enthralled by a woman. "

Not even the tightening of his fingers around her neck or the unholy glow in his silver eyes slowed her words. "He wants your woman, Rafe. He wanted her when she was mortal but now that she's not, he burns for her even more. He said he would wait until she came to him. That their coming together would be beyond measure if she came to him willingly. But, you already know that feeling, don't you? You've felt the power of her body as she accepted yours. You felt the rush as she drank from your veins while her body fed of your passions. It's a feeling beyond mere pleasure, isn't it?" She needed his angry enough to drain her. Nothing else would work. As painful as his hold on her was, breaking her neck wouldn't bring the sweet oblivion of death. Katherine knew that and so did he.

Rafe took a deep breath and a few seconds to clear the rage-induced haze from his mind. Then he saw the satisfaction on her face and the determination in her black gaze. In that second he knew what she wanted from him. Her desires for his services had changed since that night in London but *he* hadn't. He wouldn't do her bidding then and he sure as hell wasn't going to now. No matter how far she pushed, he wouldn't give her the satisfaction. Meeting the question in her eyes, he released her.

"Nice try, Katherine, you almost had me, but it's not that

easy. I'm not that easy. Feeling mortal, sweetheart? Finally seeing all that you've done? You screw with others people's lives all this time and now you want me to end it for you? Do you think I'll make it quick?" His expression was a thing of cruel beauty.

"Do you really think I won't make you suffer, Katherine? You should take your chances with Jamie. He'll show you more mercy than I will. You would be amazed at what I'm capable of. Of what I've dreamed of doing to you."

The last words came out in a dark purr that brought goose bumps to her skin.

"I've killed you a thousand different ways in my mind and not one of them was quick or merciful. Not one of them didn't end without you begging for mercy."

She took a step back, the hatred in his eyes even more than her jaded sensibilities could handle.

"When you took her from me, you decided your fate. It won't be pretty and it won't be now. Every time you lay your head down to sleep, you can wonder. Every time you open your eyes, you can know fear. I'll even take care of Jamie for you, just to make sure that nothing comes between us. Nothing is ever going to be simple for you again." He would have walked away if not for the small hand that came out to grab his.

"Please, believe me." She didn't want to beg, but she would if that was what he demanded. "I tried to help her, to keep him away from her as much as I could. I let him hurt me to protect her, but I couldn't save her. I tried," she whispered, silent tears falling.

Rafe took her hand in his. Turning it over, he ran a finger across the nasty scar that marred her wrist. Sasha had not exaggerated. "Did you love him?" he asked. "Did a part of you die when he was taken from you? Did you ever wonder what your precious Christian would've done if he could've seen what you'd become? Would he have welcomed you into his arms, his heart? Would he have thanked you for letting Jamie use you any way he wanted? Would he have forgiven you? Or would your virtuous warrior have done as honor demanded and destroy the abomination that you had become?" He traced his finger over the faded scar, his expression gentle.

Katherine couldn't pull away from the understanding in his eyes.

"Think about it. Every time you close your eyes, dream of what he would have done." He lifted her wrist to his lips and the kiss he placed there brought fresh tears to the wounded pools of her eyes. "See the same disgust in his eyes that I see when I take Gomery into my arms. See the terror that *I* see on her face every time she looks at me. Look at this mark of your *devotion* and wonder if he would have thanked you had you succeeded in changing him. Think about it and wonder."

"I wanted to save him. I loved him," she murmured, her face a pale mask of grief. "There was no other way. Sasha wouldn't help me. I had to go to Jamie. I had to let him." Rafe's amused laughter stilled her desperate words.

"And Jamie kept you mortal until it was too late. He changed you just in time, so you could hold Christian in your arms while he bled the ground red. Didn't you ever wonder why? Why did he wait so long, Katherine?" He wanted her to feel the same as he had when Gomery disappeared. The same cutting uncertainty. The same deep down anguish. She needed to know what it felt like to have everything you thought you knew about yourself ripped out from under you.

"Maybe after he finished with you and you lie there deep in sleep, he willed himself to Christian's side. Maybe he told your hero what he'd done to you. Or maybe, he just thrust a blade into him without giving him a reason. Maybe he planned it from the very moment you sought him out," he said that last part with such cold amusement she wanted to scream. "Doesn't that seem like something he would do? Isn't it similar to his perverse delight in leaving Gomery in my bed the way he did?" He read the flare of rage that flashed across her face.

"Makes you think, doesn't it?" Rafe chided her. "If you hadn't gone to Jamie to save your lover, maybe he would have never been in danger. You killed him, Katherine, as surely as if you had thrust home the blade that took his life. What wonderful irony that is."

She didn't see the humor in any of what he had described and the brilliant glow in her ebony eyes said as much.

There was so much fun in it that Rafe couldn't let it go. "Jamie took your life and your lover. He made you into what you now are," he explained carefully, his eyes as cold and dangerous as frost. "Then you came to me, you took my life, then you took something even more precious. You took her from me. You stole her from my very arms like you had the right."

Rafe stepped away from her, no longer trusting himself so close. "You wanted my undivided attention, Katherine. Now you have it. Bask in its glow while you can because it will be the death of you."

т   т   т

"Any news of my little pets?" Jamison asked one of his many minions.

"None, sir," the youngest answered. Being this close to the ancient vampire always made him nervous. A person never knew what Jamison had planned until it was too late and more than one unlucky immortal had lost his life to one of his temper tantrums. That was why he had lost the coin toss and had thereby won the unfortunate job of giving the old one the bad news.

"No news," Jamie mused as he settled into a large wing-backed chair that dominated the corner of his study. He liked this chair. It reminded him of a throne he had ruled from many centuries ago. Back in a time when a man could have all he wanted. A time when a strong arm and fear were the greatest allies a ruler could have. The good old days, when blood flowed and death was an animal that man couldn't cage. How he missed those days.

"None, sir," the young vampire said again as he eased back

a step. When it went unnoticed he eased back another. Then another. He wanted out of striking range, not believing even a second that unconcerned look upon his sire's face.

His mistake was in believing that distance would keep him safe. In a flash too quick to be seen, Jamie was out of his chair and upon him. Before anyone could blink, the young revenant was on the floor, his spine crushed and his immortal life draining from his body through the large wound that used to be his throat.

"Anyone else have bad news for me?" Jamison asked of the other nightwalkers within the room. The rest shuffled back, their fear of him so strong he could smell it. Glory in it. "Good. You have until sunset to find them. If you don't, there will be no place you can hide." He turned his back to them and settled in his chair, flicking specks of blood from his silk shirt. The remaining three were too afraid to move. "Time is wasting, children," Jamie chided as they continued to stand there frozen with fright.

As if freed from a spell, they scurried as one to the door. "Not so fast." Jamison wanted to laugh as they stopped cold, their expressions filled with unspeakable dread. "Don't forget the trash." He waved a careless hand at the body on the floor, waiting until they had gathered up the remains of their fallen comrade before he spoke again. "Don't fail me, children. I will not be so merciful come sunset."

Jamison leaned his head back and closed his eyes. If he tried, he could almost hear her cries of pain echo in his head. He let his imagination wander and could almost feel her silky skin under his hands. Could almost believe he had her body under his, almost hear her moans of pleasure as he moved within her. He could almost...

With a single thought in his mind, he crashed back to reality; someone was here. His eyes searched the shadows as he wondered which of his little immortals had wandered back into his domain.

"All alone, Jamie?" Katherine taunted as she stepped into

the light.

He couldn't hold back the smile that crossed his lips. This one would do for now until he found the one he really wanted. She would do until he finished with her and had drained the life from her exquisite body again. As much as he hated to loose the amusement she brought him, he no longer had a choice. Katherine had run from him for the last time.

"I'm never alone, pet. I have my memories to keep me company," he answered as he came to his feet.

"Why don't you search those memories, Jamie, and share some of them with me." She kept the distance of the room between them. There was a purpose for this visit and she wouldn't let him get the better of her.

"There are many, any ones in particular, pet?" He walked the perimeter of the chair; his black eyes missed nothing of her position in the room. Jamison could have closed the distance in a heartbeat. Could have had her under him on the floor before she had time to draw breath enough to scream. However, he bided his time, wanting to see what his little Katherine had to say. He wanted to know what had put that fiery glow in her ebony eyes.

"Think back, to when I came to you for your blood," she demanded of him with a tight smile. He returned it with one of his own. A smile so dark and malicious she had to force herself not to flee.

Jamie angled to the left, his steps measured and concise. Katherine didn't seem to notice his stealthy advance. "Some of my favorites," he confided with a purr, pleased at the shudder that racked her body. "You want what, Katherine? What of that time do you want to know about? Have you forgotten so soon how you begged me to change you? Have you forgotten the sweet agony? The overwhelming pain? Have you?" He advanced another step.

"No," she whispered, shaking her head against the waking nightmares that passed through her mind. Jamie had been exacting in his punishments, imaginative in his tortures. "I have forgotten nothing of what you did to me. Nothing." Katherine watched his stealthy advance. Her sire was close but she needed him closer.

"Do you remember the night I held your sister down on the ground and drained the blood from her very heart?" Jamison taunted, ruthless in his pleasure. "Do you remember how she begged me for mercy? Do you remember how you begged and pleaded for her life?" He took another step.

"Yes, I do." Her voice was a small sound in the room. "I remember what you did when you finished with her. I remember what you made me do." She trembled with revulsion at the scene her mind refused to let her forget. "I remember."

"How about the little village we visited in the mountains?" he asked, his eyes bright with glee. "Do you still hear the cries for salvation? How they begged you for help? They knew what you were. They knew of your magic. You could have saved them but you didn't, did you?" He took another step. "You wanted my gift more than you wanted to save them. The children were especially sweet."

Katherine closed her eyes against the visions his words evoked. She recalled all to easily the delight he had taken in draining the children. It was a struggle to hold her nausea at bay as he spoke on and on, his words firing her rage to a whole new level and with each sentence, he moved a little closer.

Jamison watched her open her eyes and his excitement grow. He hadn't ever seen such a glow there before, had never felt such rage in her fragile body. She would taste like heaven.

He had her within arms reach now. She was right where he wanted her. Lifting an arm, he wound her long black hair around his fist and she let him. Katherine let him pull her against him. Let him walk her back against the wall until not an inch separated her body from his.

"You forgot something," she whispered, her eyes locking with his. "You've forgotten your most favorite memory of my time with you," she continued at his puzzled expression. "The night you changed me, you went somewhere. Where did you go, Jamie?" The smile her words evoked was chilling in the extreme.

"I went to see a certain brown-eyed warrior, my pet. A warrior strong of body and pure of heart." Jamison fed off the pain in her gaze. Relished it and with the utmost of care, he nurtured it. "He was standing out in the valley watching the sunset. When I asked him what he was looking for, he said he was waiting for his heart to return." He delighted in her apparent agony, and when he was sure he had her undivided attention, he continued. "Then he spoke of a girl, so beautiful and innocent he didn't know how he lived without her. What was his name?"

"Christian." The name escaped her in a whimper of misery.

"I'm surprised you remember that after all this time." He arched a black eyebrow at her. "Christian spoke of his lady love in such glowing terms I almost didn't realize it was you. I told him that and then I told him what you were *really* liked. What made your body burn, what stirred your blood. He almost got the better of me, Katherine. Your warrior was fierce. You would have been proud. It took quite a bit of work on my part before I was able to thrust my blade home." Jamison watched the lone tear that slid down her face. "You can't imagine what it felt like when I thrust that blade into his body, how smooth it slid in and how deep it sank. You can't even begin to know the feeling of pleasure I got when I pulled it out and did it again."

"Did it feel like this?" Katherine asked as she buried the blade of the dagger she had kept hidden behind her back deep into his belly. "Did it feel like this?" She asked as she grasped the dragon claw handle in both hands and jerked up with all her might. "Did it feel like this?" She asked again as his blood spilled over her hands.

CHAPTER 25

"Given that information, is there anyone you can think of that would be able to pull off the robberies?" Gabriel asked of Morrigan as they sat in his living room and discussed possibilities. After trying for days, he'd finally cornered her this morning leaving Michael's apartment.

"Very few people could accomplish them. He would need layout plans, access codes, and the knowledge to loop the system input." Morrigan continued in detail, looking him straight in the eyes as she gave away every aspect of how she'd done the jobs. She did everything but confess, and he knew it. Damn his gorgeous green eyes, Gabriel knew she was behind it all and still he said nothing. He just sat there listening, a half-amused, half-respectful expression on his rugged face.

"Why would somebody want to do it?" he asked when she finished with her explanation. Just as easy, he could have reached out and with a single touch of her hand, have an in-depth answer to that simple question. Instead, he waited to hear it from her own lips why a woman would destroy her own company.

"Revenge."

Long after Morrigan left him, he brooded over her answer. The reason didn't get any simpler then that and it was enough. Now one question remained; what had Malcolm St. John done to bring about such a strong need for vengeance in his niece?

The answer was something he wanted to know and it wasn't something she'd share with a cop. Maybe Michael could find out for him. Morrigan and the fair one had been sharing a bed for a few nights now and if anyone could get information from a woman when she was on her back, Michael could.

"Why bother, Gabriel?"

There was no warning before Sasha was standing in front of him. The part of herself she'd always kept open to him was closed now and no hint of her emotions or proximity reached him before hand.

"You of all people know about revenge."

He didn't trust the look she slanted his way or the cool irony that laced her little accusation, but he waited for her to continue. When she did nothing more than settle on the arm of a chair, Gabriel decided to take the bait.

"Meaning what?" His eyes narrowed at the burst of amused laughter that failed to reach her eyes. Had she come at long last to discuss Seth Jordan with him? For days, she had avoided the subject and he was more than ready to have it out with her.

"You're so good at seeking revenge whether it's warranted or not. You decide someone's fate and then deliver the punishment."

"Are you saying that Seth Jordan didn't deserve to die?" He didn't like what she was implying, and clenched his fists as he waited for her answer.

"Oh no, he deserved what he got. He deserved every terrible thing I did to him and so much more but that, unfortunately, is no longer an option."

The coldness of her smile made him take notice. Gabriel had never seen her like this before and it troubled him. "Then what's your point?" What the hell was she getting at?

"Other women are beaten. Other wives go through what she did, some even worse. What made her so special? Who made you judge, jury, and executioner? What gave you the right?" Sasha watched the play of emotions on his face and didn't like what she saw.

There was a reason for her visit today. They had to end this little standoff between them. Two centuries of her begging forgiveness had taken a toll and this time Gabriel had proven beyond a shadow of a doubt that there was no future for her with him. She needed to go on with her existence; one without him in it. The look on his face made it that much easier.

"Any man that does that to a woman deserves what he gets," he spat out the words through clenched teeth. "He had no right to touch her, no right to force her, no right to treat her as he did." Gabriel drew a deep breath. "He had no right."

Part of her wanted to leave things alone. Part of her wanted to keep that last thread of hope intact that someday he would come to her with love in his eyes. Until she saw the look of contempt he sent her way. The same one he'd been shooting at her since that night in London when he realized she wasn't what he'd envisioned. She tried to hide it, but that look never failed to cut to the quick.

"Would you have cared so much if you hadn't been fucking her? Was your outraged anger the act of a concerned cop or a vindictive lover?" Sasha refused to step back when he shot to his feet and closed the distance between them.

Gabriel stared at her for a long minute, struggling to contain his rage. He brought it under control, every muscle tensed until he felt able to continue what she had started without causing her physical injury. Unclenching his huge fists, he smiled. Trailing a finger across her lips, he felt her tremble.

"Jealous, angel?"

The soft, rolling brogue glided over her skin like a caress even as the meaning behind the words drew blood. But she didn't cry out with the pain of it, or let him see how deep the barb had cut. Instead, she returned his smile. A cruel, amused smile that had him blinking in confusion.

Only then did she return fire. "Jealous?" She forced herself to laugh and the sound grated against her nerves. "Jealous of a man who stands by my bed while he thinks I'm asleep? Jealous of a man who lays beside me and touches my skin while he feels safe that I don't know he's there?" Leaning into him, she whispered her next words against his ear. "Jealous of a man that takes my picture while I lay there pretending I don't see him? While I lay there sometimes dressed in nothing but moonlight and sheer silk? Jealous,

Gabriel?" She moved away, needing space between the violence in his eyes and what she had to say next.

"Why should I be jealous of a man that has made love to me a thousand times in his dreams? A man, who every time he takes a woman in his arms, closes his eyes and pretends it's me?"

She laughed again and the mockery of it was more than he could take. "I didn't pretend with Sarah, did I?"

"Isn't it lucky you found a girl that looked like me to slack your lusts on? It must have been a thrill not having to use my image in your mind to find release." She saw the vicious intent on his beloved face, but she pushed anyway. She wanted him to suffer as much as she had all these decades. Wanted to hurt him as much as his words wounded her. "You should have told me a long time ago how bad you wanted it, Gabriel. I might have taken pity and given you a tumble. But not now that I know how pathetic you are."

He erupted across the room in a fury, grabbing her by the shoulders. Sasha didn't bother to struggle against his excruciating hold, nor did she flinch away from the green fire in his eyes. She'd expected retaliation. His temper was infamous and she had done all in her power to court it.

"What's wrong, angel? Can't take the truth?"

Before the last word fell from her lips, he had again reined in the beast that existed within him. As he stared into amber eyes he had dreamed of for two centuries, he saw what she was so desperate to hide from him. He saw her heart and the love she couldn't fight. He saw the pain he had caused for centuries and he saw her determination to leave him behind.

He could do no less than finish what she had started. For her sake, if not his, he would see this break through to the bitter end. As much as he needed her, she needed to be free of what he was. Free of what he had always been, of what she had always refused to see.

"Let's just test that theory." Gabriel swung her up into his arms and carried her into his bedroom.

Sasha hit the mattress with a bounce and a gasp. She hadn't planned on this. If he touched her, she had no idea how she would finish this. "I don't want you," she whispered the denial.

Gabriel ignored the words and her attempts to scramble away from his descending body. He tried to ignore her soft moans; the way she melted under him as his mouth found hers. It was a struggle to remain in control when he deepened the kiss further and her tongue met his and slid into the heat of his mouth.

"Liar," he whispered in her ear with an amusement he was far from feeling. "You want me so bad you'd give up breathing for just a taste." Words didn't matter then as she reached for him, fitting her mouth and body to his with surprising strength.

The past melted away as he shifted over her until her body cradled his with an intimacy unique to lovers. He drowned in the softness of her lips, of her arms and legs pulling him closer. Unable to deny the desire she kindled to life inside of him, he pulled at their clothes with desperate hands until nothing separated the thrusting of their bodies but the faded denim of his jeans and the thin lace of her panties.

Sasha sank into the emotions that flooded her. Lost to everything but the overwhelming love she felt for the man touching her with such exquisite passion, she opened herself to him, holding nothing back as she arched against the arousal he couldn't hide. What mattered now of the past but the wonder of this moment? His kiss had the power to fill her thoughts for decades, but to have him? Belonging to him, even if only for a moment would make her existence bearable. To know that she had held her highland warrior close to her heart. To know that she had given him pleasure.

"Love me." A moan vibrated in her throat as his hand moved down between them and he stroked the heat of her through the lace the protected her vulnerability.

Love her. The words clawed at Gabriel with vicious accuracy. He couldn't love her. Wouldn't. Ever. His eyes raked her flushed face and what he saw there almost destroyed his resolve. What man didn't crave absolute possession? She was his, heart and soul. Only sheer determination kept him from taking her body as well. "You don't want me, angel?" he forced the words out with a mocking smile as he locked onto misty amber eyes.

This had to end. Now. There could be nothing left for her when he walked away. No hope. No pride. Not even the love that burned so bright in her eyes. "Say you want me." Gabriel touched her then, his fingers tracing the lush flesh between her thighs. Finding the small nub through the damp lace, he stroked it once, twice.

"Please," she whimpered as shivers danced through her body.

"That's not enough; I need more. Say you want me, angel. Say you need me. Tell me how much you want me inside of you," he demanded. "Tell me!"

Grasping at his broad shoulders, she pulled him close and in a voice that shook with her desire, she gave him what he wanted. "I need you so much I ache. I want you inside of me until there is room for nothing else. Not a wish, not a breath, not a prayer." She moaned, arching up against him, her nipples brushing the roughness of his chest. "I want you inside of my body until there is nothing between us but sweat and skin and heat and pleasure."

He crushed her mouth under his before she could say more. Before she could destroy his vow, his honor.

"Now, Gabriel. I need you now," Sasha whispered against his lips. Drawing in a shaky breath, she almost shattered with pleasure when he wrapped her legs around his waist.

Gabriel danced on the edge of honor as he held her body locked to his. Everything inside of him screamed for her. For what she made him feel, but it wasn't enough. She deserved more than just a single night in his bed and a lifetime of hatred for his weakness. Wasn't two hundred years enough for her to suffer for his sins? If a kiss could wrought centuries of loathing, what horrible emotion could complete surrender deliver unto him?

Taking her hands in his, he stopped their urgent exploration, holding them above her head where they could no longer touch his overheated skin. Pressing down against her hips, he stilled the restless writhing that was almost killing him.

Sasha looked up at Gabriel as he loomed over her. His glacial expression should have clued her in to what lay ahead, but it didn't, not even a sledgehammer could have broken through the ecstatic, rosy glow that colored her world.

"On second thought, angel, I don't want *you*. I guess Sarah was better than you gave her credit for." He rolled off the bed. Turning away so he wouldn't have to look at her face, he studied the wall, his body ridged with tension. Had she touched him now, he would have splintered into a million pieces.

Gabriel didn't know what he had expected from her after that, but not the dead silence that followed. It was all he could do not to look at the bed. He wondered why she waited, why she didn't lash out in wounded fury. She had to be furious beyond reason and he was amazed she wasn't sharpening her claws on his flesh even now.

There was nothing; not even a breath of sound and he knew in his heart that she had left him without so much as a damning word or scathing retort. He should have left himself but he needed one last look at the bed they could have shared together for eternity had the past been different, had his vows allowed it. Holding in a pain he hadn't felt in years, he turned around.

Sasha hadn't left him, but knelt there in the middle of his bed, her amber eyes huge in a face streaked with tears of anguish and misery. His green eyes missed nothing of the trembling hand that clutched her disheveled clothes to her breasts. Missed nothing of the quivering fingers she held over her mouth to hold in her heart wrenching sobs. He didn't know what power held him in place, what inner strength he called on to remain impassive.

When she was able to breathe again, Sasha lowered the hand from her mouth and stared at him, her gaze never wavering. Her very life depended on keeping contact with his deep green eyes. On controlling the splintering pain that pulsed in her chest. Once, twice, she tried to speak. On the third try, she was able to whisper a single word that expressed all her pain and bewilderment. "*Why?*"

Why had he said those things? Why had he given her such a gift just to stomp it into the dirt under careless, hateful feet? Had he taken a blade to her, he couldn't have done as much damage as he had with those few words. Words he'd spoken as if she meant nothing. As if she mattered less than an animal.

He had destroyed her, Gabriel could see it in her eyes but she remained, willing to give him a second chance. He knew all he'd have to do was reach for her, take her in his arms and soothe away the hurt and all would be forgiven. She loved him that much.

Because of that love, he forced himself to smirk and point to the door. He forced the words passed a throat that felt as if a fist was lodged in it. "The door's that way, angel."

᛭   ᛭   ᛭

Montgomery returned to the house that had been her prison just days ago and felt none of the fear she had expected. She felt nothing in fact but a deep sense of excitement. Jamie was here. A vampire that had been following her had strayed a little too close and she had gotten her information the hard way. It was nice to know her job training would still come in handy given her new lease on life.

The last few days had been a revelation for her. All she had learned from Katherine had shown her the wonder of the gift Jamie had forced on her. She had never felt such strength! Never had she experienced so many sensations, the very air seemed to talk to her. It was as if she had walked in shadows her whole life and the sun had just decided to shine. Everything was so clear now, so intense.

Katherine had taught her much, but there were things

that had come to her on their own. Things that had come natural. Dark things, ugly things. Those were what she wanted to share with her sire. Those were the terrible things she wanted to inflict on him. He should have never touched her. She would make it so he was never able to again. Once he was gone, she would be able to bury the nasty impulses that plagued her. Once he was out of her head, she wouldn't have that impolite desire to snack on Rafe.

Montgomery stopped in front of the closed study door, every muscle in her body tensing. She could smell him. Jamie was in there. Just the demon she wanted to see.

A glance told her Jamie wasn't in the room. Montgomery walked in and took a deep breath. The smell of his blood was so strong it filled every corner. She could get used to that smell. Searching the room, her hazel eyes settled on where Katherine sat in a big black chair.

The desolation in her dark gaze was impossible to miss. "What happened, Katherine?" Montgomery asked as she knelt by her side. "Where is he?" She pried the dagger from the older immortal's clenched fist. The blade was covered in as much blood as the sorceress that had wielded it. "Did you kill him?" Gomery asked softly as she tipped Katherine's head up. She could decipher no emotions other than anguish in those ebony eyes.

"He killed him," were the first words to emerge from her pale lips. "He killed him," Katherine repeated with a shaky sigh.

Montgomery was confused. "Rafe killed Jamie?" That was all she could come up with. Katherine seemed to gather herself before Montgomery's concerned eyes. She watched as the strength flowed back into her and hatred flooded her exotic features.

"Jamie killed Christian." The glow in her black eyes was almost blinding.

"Who's Christian?" Montgomery had not a clue as to what was going on now and tried again with what she did know. "Who killed Jamie?" That was what concerned her now; she needed to know who had beaten her to the finish line.

"Jamie's not dead," Katherine replied, her smile radiant. "But he'll wish he was." She looked at the dagger in Gomery's hand. "You might want to give that to me. It has a nasty little poison on it. If the blade even pricks your skin, the poison is released and the agony it causes is quite unbearable."

She relinquished the knife without protest.

"Jamie killed Christian?" Montgomery repeated what her teacher had said earlier. She didn't know who Christian was but the news seemed to have upset Katherine. For the first time in six hundred years the little witch had taken revenge on her sire. "Will Jamie still be able to get in my head?" That above all was her greatest concern now. The subject of Christian could wait for another time.

"He'll be in no condition to enter your thoughts. All of his concentration will go to keeping the agony under control. In his weakened condition, he'll be no threat to us. As immortals, we will be safe from his fury at this sudden turn of events."

The satisfaction in Katherine's eyes would have been frightening had she not shared it. "Where will he go? What will he do?" Montgomery was curious as to the fate of the monster that had inflicted so many unpleasant *tests* upon her.

"Jamie will try to find a cure for the poison slithering through his veins. Will try and fail. There's no one in existence that knows the cure to *hell fire*. No one that can help him but me."

"Will he come after you? Us?" Montgomery looked forward to the chance to face off with her sire.

"No. He will go after those weaker than us, those who can't defeat him. He will do what he can to hurt those I hold dearest in order to force my hand," Katherine theorized.

"Will he succeed?"

"There is nothing he can offer that would make me help

him. Nothing he can do to force my hand. He has already taken from me what I held most dear."

T   T   T

Morrigan ignored the shaking of her hands and again tried to set the code numbers into the palm-sized computer she held. She had been working on this for the last twenty minutes and didn't know if she wanted to scream in frustration or sob from the pain in her head. Giving up altogether, she tossed the little machine into her backpack.

Maybe she would wait until tomorrow night to do the last house. Blurry eyes focused on the pill bottle setting on the coffee table. She had never touched them before, no matter how bad the pain had gotten. She had never given in to the promise of relief the strong narcotics would provide. This time she was more than tempted. In the hours since she had left Michael, she had done everything she could think of to take her mind out of the pain. Nothing had worked and she'd spent the majority of her day in the bathroom, her head hanging over the sink as she heaved her guts out.

No longer could she ignore the excruciating hurt in her head or the burning sensation behind her eyes. Using all of her concentration, she worked at getting the lid off, sighing when her hands refused to obey. Frustration had her tossing the bottle aside and with a gut-wrenching sob of defeat, she dropped back on the couch cushions. When her body could no longer take the agony, her eyes drifted closed and sleep claimed her within its ebony embrace.

Hours could have passed or mere minutes, Morrigan didn't know. Opening her eyes, she had to bite her lower lip to hold back the moans of agony that clawed their way up her throat. If the pain was bad before, now it was unbearable. Rolling off the couch, she landed on the floor with a thud. The slight sting in her palms and knees from the impact was a welcomed diversion as she searched for the little plastic bottle.

Not even trying to loosen the lid this time, she set it on the table. Reaching into her backpack, pulled out a metal bar and focused on the white cap. The lid shot off with a loud pop at impact and trembling hands scooped up a few of the small white pills. Concentrating on putting one foot in front of the other, she made it to the bathroom and water.

Slumping to the floor, Morrigan drew her knees under her chin and waited for it to stop. The pain eased. Seconds turned into minutes until almost an hour later she felt in control of the steady throb in her abused skull. Bracing her hands against the wall, she lurched to her feet, stopping just before she could tumble back to the floor. The sound of laughter echoed in her ears.

"Wow." She staggered into the bedroom, holding her head with both hands as she tried to stop the room from spinning. Falling onto the bed with none of her usual grace, she made a desperate grab for the mattress to keep the world from tilting. What was worse she didn't know, the blinding pain or the feeling of complete helplessness. Instead of deciding, she focused on a shadow creeping across the ceiling.

"This is so weird." The words sounded strange to her ears.

"What's weird, *cher*?" Michael sat on the edge of the bed.

Tearing her eyes away from the ceiling, she forced them to focus on her best chance of getting through what was going to be a very bad night. "How I can't stop wanting your body," she improvised as he leaned toward her.

Michael flinched at her answer. If she had said she wanted *him*, he would have done anything for her. He would have given her anything, had she only said that one word. She didn't want him, only the pleasure he could give her. Hell, if someone else had been handy, she would have moved on when he'd proven so difficult with his questions. But there wasn't anyone else and she had to settle for him if she wanted sex.

And she did want it, he could tell from the way she turned into him as she sprawled on the bed, from the way her breathing altered. Body language was as loud sometimes as the spoken word and her body was screaming for what he could provide. He could have given into the lust that burned in her pansy eyes, but he wouldn't. Giving in would accomplish little, when the sweat had cooled from their skin; they would have gained nothing.

He was tired of feeling nothing, of giving nothing. He wanted peace and acceptance, and contrary to what Morrigan seemed to think, she could give it to him. But first, she had to see that it was *him* she wanted and not the physical pleasures he had introduced her to.

This was the woman he needed in order to make peace with himself. She was the one he needed to put the ghosts in his past to rest. Why she had chosen him didn't matter; she had and he wasn't giving her a chance to duck out now. He didn't want her to make the same dreaded mistake he had in assuming pleasure was enough.

Reaching up, Morrigan wrapped a hand around the back of his neck and tried to pull him to her. He wouldn't budge. She tried again and failed. Stretching up, she moved her parted lips against his. Michael remained as still as a statue. Drawing back, she blinked in bewilderment. Maybe the pills had her confused. This time when she kissed him, her tongue slid along the seam of his lips, seeking access. He denied her.

"What's wrong, lover?" she whispered against his mouth as he continued to refuse her advances.

"I'm not your lover," Michael contradicted as he set her away from him.

"Then what are you?" Tilting her head to the side, she waited to see what the pretty boy had to say. It would prove interesting, she was sure. Already, he had distracted her from the foggy feeling that plagued her.

"I'm just the stud you mount whenever you want that itch inside of you scratched." His eyes missed nothing of the smile that faded from her face or the bewildered look that entered her eyes. "Lovers share more than just their bodies with each other, Morrigan. They share feelings, thoughts, dreams and enjoy what they have together," he tried to explain something he'd never experienced, but wanted to. "There is caring and respect and desire. I'm not your lover, sweetheart. I'm the body you use when you can't stand to be alone anymore." He watched as understanding filled her beautiful face.

"You're right." She ignored the surprise that crossed his face. Rolling from him, she stood up on legs that refused to support her. Unable to stop, she sank back down on the bed.

Michael hadn't expected her calm acceptance of his explanation. He had contemplated fire and anger, not this docile acceptance agreement.

"Please leave." She refused to meet his eyes as she pressed trembling hands together.

"Don't shut me out, *cher*. We could be so good together. If you let us." Kneeling on the floor beside the bed, he eased her against his chest.

The kiss he pressed to her lips was as stirring and as exquisite as anything Morrigan had ever experienced in her life. It made all the lust and desire that had passed between them seem cheap and easy. That simple kiss showed her all she had lost in her rush to gain so little.

Morrigan watched him go, her eyes opened wide against the tears that threatened to steal away her resolve not to beg him to come back. Already, the pain was seeping back through her body. She staggered back to the couch. One by one, with her concentration so focused a herd of alligators could have snapped their way through and she wouldn't have noticed, she gathered up the pills.

ᛏ   ᛏ   ᛏ

Sasha needed to talk to the dark one. Something wasn't right. The feeling tiptoed up and down her spine and she had to tell Rafe. Once she did that, she was leaving. For good. If Rafe or Michael needed her, they would have to seek her out. No longer would she keep contact with the three. No longer would she leave herself open to Gabriel.

"What's wrong?" Rafe asked, feeling the emotions that writhed in her like snakes in a pit. Hurt flowed through her soul and he wondered at the cause of such heartache. "Sasha, tell me what's wrong." He stopped her from turning away, unwilling to let her out of his sight. Not until he knew what had put that broken misery in her amber eyes.

"Gabriel."

The one word was answer enough. That he hadn't guessed from the start was due to a lack of concentration on his part. Gabriel had been putting her through hell for years. Why she tolerated it, he would never be able to figure out, but he had offered his opinion on it long ago and he wouldn't voice it again.

"That's all?" he asked as he stepped away.

Sasha couldn't stop the little laugh that escaped her, the bitterness of it leaving a terrible taste in her mouth. She had asked for that casual reply from the one man who had always held out his strong arms when she needed a shoulder to cry on. That Gabriel causing her pain was such a cliché was something she had allowed to happen, but not again. Never again would she let him near her. If he were drowning, she wouldn't hold out a hand to save him. If he were on fire, she wouldn't spit on him. If he...

"Is that all?" Rafe asked again. He could feel something moving in her he hadn't felt before. Defeat. That did worry him. With all that they had seen and been through, she had never given up. Not on him, not Michael, and sure as hell, not that damned fool highlander. What had the golden fairy all lost?

"Something is wrong. I saw something that I can't figure out, Rafe. Something we need to beware of. Jamie..."

She never finished as a third immortal descended upon them.

"Jamie is not going to bother us for a long time," Montgomery declared as she leaned against the door and allowed her eyes to feast upon her lover.

Rafe forced himself to stay still when every instinct inside of him demanded he reach for her. He didn't want to frighten her again. Didn't think he could stand to see the fear in her eye. To see the disgust on her face that had been there the last time he had touched her. He would wait until she came to him. Until she wanted him. Until she loved him again.

"Why do you think that?" Sasha asked. "He's not dead. I can still sense him, and I find it hard to believe that he's turned over a new leaf. What has happened?"

"Katherine took care of him."

"Katherine?" Rafe and Sasha blurted together in disbelief. Neither believing that she had the guts to move against their evil sire.

"Yeah. She used that vicious little dagger of hers on him and sliced him up pretty bad. There was blood everywhere," she explained with relish.

"That won't hold him down for long. He'll heal and when he does, he won't rest until she's begging for death. Then he'll come after you." Sasha didn't want to scare Gomery, but she couldn't leave her with the idea that Jamison was no longer a threat.

"I'd agree if she hadn't put a little something on the blade. She said the *hell fire* was real nasty and that he won't be able to find the cure to remove it from his system. As long as the poison flows through his veins, he will do nothing but suffer all the agonies of hell and beyond." She laid out the facts as Katherine had explained them.

"*Hell Fire,*" Sasha repeated with a small whistle. The poison was an ancient and vile creation. If given to a mortal, his torturous death would be inevitable. An immortal wouldn't have that luxury. He would suffer, writhing in agony, his very insides smoldering as his blood burned like liquid flame. The torment would last an eternity with only an occasional reprieve to keep the victim from going insane.

"I wonder what he did to push her that far," Sasha

mused. Jamison had done so many horrible things to the sorceress in the past, but nothing had ever driven Katherine to such measures.

"He killed someone she called Christian. She wouldn't say more and I didn't want to pry," Montgomery offered.

"So I *was* right," Rafe murmured, his eyes never leaving Gomery.

Neither woman paid him any mind as they continued their discussion.

"Jamie killed Christian." Sasha hadn't ever made that connection, but she should have. She should have realized he wouldn't be able to resist such a treat as the young lovers. "We still have to be on guard. Did you tell him anything that he could used to his advantage?"

"We didn't have very many soul searching conversations." Montgomery's smile was so cold the very air shivered with it.

Rafe reminded them then of someone who would make an ideal target if Jamison decided to use her. "What about Morrigan?"

Chapter 26

Everything inside of Morrigan screamed for the relief the little pills would bring but she wouldn't take any more. She couldn't allow the pain to win. Instead, she would just have to deal with the agony that was already screaming through her head and the nausea that rolled through her stomach.

Gripping the pills in her hand, she reached for the painting she'd set next to the coffee table just this morning. Her gaze never left the entwined couple as she caressed the curve of his face, the soft purple of his eyes, the length of her hair pale blond hair, the wicked smile that looked so much like her own. This painting was all she had left of the two people she had loved most in her life. It was a portrait of her parents. One her mother had painted herself as a gift. A gift that had comforted her father long after her death.

Morrigan knew the painting better than her own face in a mirror. For hours she had stared at it, loving the memories it stirred in her. Her father had felt the same, had in fact never traveled without it.

The night he was killed in Boston had been no exception. The painting was one of the things they had taken from him after killing him. When it had turned up in New Orleans, she had seen it as a blessing. Hard found information had reveled that her uncle had sold it to the man she had stolen it from last night.

"I see you got the painting," Montgomery murmured from behind her.

Morrigan was so numb to everything but her inner turmoil that she didn't even jump at the sudden presence of her best friend behind her. She did nothing but nod her head. Leaning forward, she placed the painting on the table, then she turned and looked at her best friend.

Montgomery could see the pain in her eyes. "What's wrong?" she asked, sitting down beside her. "What happened?" Sudden fear that somehow Jamie had gotten past them all and had injured the tiny blonde filled her. She looked her over but could see no physical signs of Jamie's handy work.

"I'm tired," Morrigan spoke the truth. Never had she been so tired in her whole life. Never had she wanted to lie down and sleep as much as she did now. She couldn't though, not until she told Gomery why she'd come to New Orleans. "I'm not going back to Chicago. I'm staying here. I'm staying because…"

"You need to go home," Montgomery told her urgently.

"I'm not finished with Malcolm," Morrigan didn't understand the hard look that entered Montgomery's eyes.

"You're going home and I'm going to deal with Malcolm." Morrigan had to leave before Jamie gathered himself enough to hurt her. Montgomery needed her gone tonight and she didn't care at this point, what she had to do to accomplish it. There was always later to make it up to her, when things settled down and she figured out a way to explain it all.

"But *I* need to finish this."

Morrigan breathed the words with a desperation that cut at her heart, but Montgomery wouldn't back down. "I'm not going to let you. I'll take care of it myself. I don't need you getting in my way." The shock in those deep purple eyes almost destroyed her resolve. "I don't have time to baby sit you anymore." How she forced those words out, she'd never know. She wanted to beg forgiveness at the anguish those words brought to Morrigan's face. Instead, she got on the phone and booked her on the next flight to Chicago.

Long after she left, Morrigan continued to sit there in silence. That rejection on top of the other should have had her on the verge of hysterics but she was so past that she almost laughed at how pathetic her grand plans had been. She'd failed at everything she'd wanted so much to accomplish, and now she couldn't land on her feet long enough to try again. She didn't even know if she wanted to try again.

Now she just wanted to sleep, to forget about the hurt and the pain. To sleep and not dream about the cold arms of death that waited just on the other side of the agony. The very arms that would wrap around her until she could no longer escape them.

Unclenching her fist, she stared at the damp, ragged looking pills. There was no hesitation now as she swallowed them two at a time. She didn't worry about the future, or the past. She had done that for too long, all she wanted now was to lie down and sleep.

ᛏ   ᛏ   ᛏ

Rafe took a deep breath and wondered how he would be able to let Gomery walk away from him again. From the minute she had appeared in his living room, it had been all he could do not to grab her close to his heart and never let go. Then she had looked him over, her eyes touching him in an almost physical caress that had sent the blood burning through his veins with brutal intensity.

God, he wanted her so much! But she had turned and left without saying a word to him. She had left him standing there clenching his fists against the hunger in his heart.

The only thing that kept him calm was the knowledge that she was still in the building. He knew where she was. She had gone to send Morrigan home. Above all else, she wanted to keep the small blonde safe. When this was finished, he would track his lover down and when nothing else clouded her mind, he would make her understand.

His head turned to the door as it creaked opened. He waited while Montgomery stuck her head around the door. Her eyes locked on him and he felt his heart clench at the look she sent his way.

"Can I come in?" she questioned even as she shut the door

behind her.

"Since when do you ask my permission, sweet thing? By all means, come into my parlor," he invited when she hesitated. Rafe couldn't figure out the need for caution she was exercising around him. How could she not know that he would end his own life before he ever hurt her?

Montgomery was scared. She didn't want to hurt him like she had before; didn't want him to be afraid of her because of what she had done when they had come together. Now that Jamie was no longer in her head, everything would be better. The reminder helped and she stepped closer.

She didn't have to be afraid to hold him in her arms now. Didn't need to be afraid that she would lose control and drink from him while they made love. Montgomery fought down the thrill just thinking about the taste of him sent through her. Her confidence faltered, but she refused to give up.

"How is Morrigan?" he asked, when she remained silent.

"Are you going to be able to deal with the change of plans concerning Katherine and Jamie?" she asked her own question instead, not feeling up to discussing her meeting with Morrigan. It was only when his smile faded and his gaze hardened that she regretted her choice.

"All that will come to an end soon enough," he said as he closed the distance between them. He stopped just inches from her; so close he could feel the heat from her body. Reaching out with a hesitation he had never shown before, he stroked the silkiness of her chestnut hair through his fingers. She leaned into his caress and he breathed a sigh of relief at her acceptance of his touch. The feel of her body against his went through his system like a bolt of lightening. Only days had passed since he had touched her but the uncertainty made it seem like years.

Montgomery gloried in the strength of his body against hers. It had the power to make her forget what Jamie had done to her. To forget the fear that had filled her. She would give up her foolish hope for his love if it meant being in his arms forever.

"Rafe," she whispered, pulling his head down to hers.

He gave himself up to the seduction of her lips, the sirens call of her desires. Then, when the wanting became too much, he swept her into his arms and carried her to his bed.

Nothing came between them as they sank down on the cover. Clothes came off without words, longings were expressed without sound. It was if they were of the same mind. The same heart.

Only as their bodies joined as one, the climax of their cravings realized, did Montgomery find the one thing that could take it all away. She jerked away from his sated, sweat-slicked body in stunned disbelief, the taste of his blood still on her tongue.

This shouldn't have happened! She couldn't have just taken from him while he had no chance to defend himself.

The hunger inside wasn't appeased by the small taste that had passed her lips; it wanted more. Panic assaulted her as trust in herself vanished. What if she drained him completely next time? What if she killed him? She tried to leave the bed, but strong hands gripping her waist held her locked to his body.

"Not this again," he chided, his eyes searching hers. "Haven't we been through this before? Is this little flood of guilt going to happen every time you lose control? Is this going to happen when I do?" Rafe wouldn't let secrets or fear come between them again.

"When you do? What do you mean?"

"You are so much a part of me that I can't control it either. I need all of you. Your body, and mind, and spirit. Your heart, your blood. Your love. I need everything that you are, Gomery. I need you so much I can't breathe without you," he told her as he rolled over, pinning her to the mattress.

"You need me?" she whispered in awe, hardly able to believe what he was saying.

"I love you. I would give up everything for you. My life, my heart, my soul. They are yours. Everything I was, everything I am, everything I will be, is in your hands," Rafe vowed. "I live for you and would die for you. Nothing touched me before, Gomery. Without you, I would no longer exist."

† † †

Michael waited at Morrigan's door and knocked again. Still no answer. He had come back to explain, to make things right, to take away the hurt he'd inflicted. What right did he have to set rules? To preach of right and wrong? That she had let him was a surprise but he would make it up to her. He would show her that he cared, that he could take care of her. When everything was over and he left, he wanted her to go with him.

Stepping across the threshold, he looked around the room, his gaze finding nothing of who he sought. Closing his eyes, he concentrated. She was here; he could smell the sweetness of her shampoo, the subtle scent of her skin.

Morrigan was lying on the couch, an arm flung over her head while the other curved around her bare midriff. He stood there for the longest time, his eyes just admiring the curves and valleys of her exquisite body. She was the most magnificent thing he had ever seen.

Kneeling beside the couch, he put his hand over her heart. The faintness of the rhythm had him calling her name. When she failed to respond, he gave into his growing panic. What seemed like forever to him was only seconds before the room was crowded with immortals.

Montgomery reached them first and with a strong shove, she pushed him out of the way. Gathering Morrigan's limp body into her arms, she turned stricken hazel eyes on him. "What happened? She was fine when I saw her. Fine." Guilt for what she had said to her friend flooded her. "Oh, God." A whimper slipped out as she cradled her fair head against her shoulder.

Rafe had to get Montgomery under control before he could sort this out. He eased Morrigan out of her arms, ignoring her protests as he led her away from the couch. "Come on, baby," he soothed. "Move away so Sasha can help her." He held her close as she cried against his shoulder.

"I tried to get her to leave so Jamie couldn't get to her. I told her I didn't need her." Her voice broke under the strain of her explanation.

"Dammit." The soft-spoken expletive turned every head in Michael's direction. He met accusing silver eyes head on and waited to see who would make the first accusation. Rafe didn't let him down.

"What the hell did you do?" he demanded, his voice holding the same cold threat it had held the other night when the subject of Katherine had been tossed out for open scrutiny.

"I did nothing to harm her. I just turned down an invitation," Michael replied, his eyes glowing with pale blue flames.

"Well that would be a first. The great whore, Michael Wyhndym, turning down a quick tumble between the sheets. Why do I have a problem believing that?" Rafe challenged him. "It's not like you've ever done it before. I find it hard to believe that you've finally learned to keep your pants on."

"You son of a bitch!" Michael gathered himself to lunge at the dark one.

"That's enough," Sasha interrupted their male posturing, but remained kneeling at Morrigan's side, her eyes closed, her brow furrowed in concentration. She placed her hands on Morrigan, her healing powers searching for the cause of this unnatural sleep. "I find a deep illness inside her. There is a natural force causing great pain."

"You can fix it?" Montgomery asked from within Rafe's embrace.

Sasha wanted to help but this was something she couldn't fix. Morrigan St. John's death was meant to be.

"Will she wake up?" Michael asked from his corner of the room.

"There is something at work here I don't understand. This sleep is unnatural; it's not due to the illness," Sasha explained, her hands still on Morrigan as she searched for a cause within her body.

"Does this explain it?" Gabriel handed her the small brown bottle he had found on the floor.

Sasha refused to look at him as she retrieved the bottle from his grasp. She didn't bother to read it, just the presence of the empty container gave an explanation that was all to clear to the people present.

"We can fix this," Gomery filled the silence that had invaded the room. "We can turn her, like Jamie and Katherine did. She'll be all right then. Rafe can do it."

As much as Rafe wanted to take the pain from her gold flecked eyes, he couldn't do it. Just the thought of someone else's blood flowing through him was enough to fill him with loathing. To acknowledge that dark side of his nature was something he wasn't prepared to do. He had come too close to that darkness to ever want to go back. "I can't, baby." The look in his eyes explained what he couldn't put into words.

She accepted his answer with a small nod, her eyes settling on Gabriel where he stood at Sasha's side. The backlash of his tormented thoughts kept her from voicing the question in her mind. She had seen too much of his and Sasha's strife over the very concept to ever ask him to do what she so desperately wanted.

"I can do it." Montgomery decided, although the thought made her feel ill. She would do anything to save Morrigan. She owed her so much.

The amber-eyed immortal moved closer until she could place a comforting hand on her shoulder. The bad news she had was something she couldn't hide. "You're too young to change her. To do so would kill her and you," Sasha explained. Not looking at anyone, she promised to do the one thing she'd sworn to never do again. "I'll do it."

"No, I'll do it." Michael stepped forward. "She's my responsibility. I'll do what needs to be done."

The cold determination in his eyes was something they had never seen before. Moving past the others, he lifted Morrigan into his arms. Without another word, he left the apartment. None of the others followed but remained in the living room, all the questions they wanted to ask locked in their throats until Gabriel broke the silence.

"Did you accomplish what you set out to do?" he asked Montgomery, his eyes taking in the protective embrace Rafe still held her in. The instance he'd seen them together in the weight-room all those months ago he'd known she would be the one to melt the ice that surrounded Rafe. He had even warned the dark one of the potential she had to take his heart. Would this be an appropriate time to say he told him so?

"Katherine had an agenda of her own and she got to Jamison before me." Montgomery raised her eyes to meet Gabriel's.

Mixed in with her grief over Morrigan was a deep devilment that had him asking despite himself. "What did the little witch do?" While Katherine would never be far from his darker thoughts, he could take a minute to appreciate any plan that brought Jamie low.

Gabriel listened as she explained what had transpired in the library this morning, not bothering to hold back a ferocious smile. Things would be very interesting now. "Where is our little sorceress by the way?" He had a thing or two he needed to *discuss* with the sword wielder. A scar or two he wanted to *reminisce* over.

"She said she needed to go home, that she had been away too long," Montgomery repeated the words that Katherine had spoken just hours before. "Will Michael be able to do what he said he would?"

"He'll see it done. We can only hope she doesn't hate him when it's all over," Sasha answered.

"I can't bring myself to feel pity for him," Rafe was still furious over Michael's betrayal.

"There is much about the fair one that you don't know, Rafe. There is so much even you couldn't understand. He's suffered so in his life and his past haunts him in ways beyond nightmares. Even as we speak, he could be throwing away his only chance for peace and redemption. He's willing to take that risk. Willing to give up his dreams of life to preserve hers."

Sasha spared Rafe nothing of the sadness in her eyes. "To decide what is worth more, the life and future of someone you care about or your own heart and soul is a choice I hope you never have to make." She refused to look at the brooding stranger whose deep green eyes she had given up so much for.

T   T   T

Michael laid her limp body on his bed. He knew what he had to do, and he knew it was something that would forever lock him in the nightmares of his past. Every part of him rebelled at the thought of doing this. Morrigan had made the decision to end her life on this plane of existence. What right did he have to gain say her sacrifice?

The look in her eyes when he had left her sitting on that bed tonight was one. The wonder in her lavender gaze when he had kissed her that last time was another. That was what had made him step forward when he could have left it to Sasha to damn her to eternal life.

He had lied to Morrigan today when he had denied being her lover. She meant more to him than any woman ever could. Never had someone touched him the way this purple-eyed siren had. Holding her had made him believe in himself. It had made him believe that he was more than just a body living without a soul.

Maybe she would have come to love him; maybe he could have loved her. That was something he had never done before. He had never been in love. After all these years of being alone, he needed that closeness of spirit. He needed what he had seen in Rafe's eyes when he had held Gomery close to his heart.

Stretching out on the bed, he pulled Morrigan into the curve of his body. Reaching out with a hand that trembled, he smoothed her blond curls out on the darkness of the blanket. She was so beautiful he could have spent hours just looking at

her, but time was running out. He could see it in the paleness
of her golden skin, could feel it in the slowness of her pulse.

Michael was so scared he would hurt her, so scared that
she would hate him. The fact that he'd never done this
before didn't help. The only blood to ever pass his lips had
been Katherine's and truth be told, he remembered very
little of that exchange.

Katherine had claimed that physical lust had brought on
her blood hunger. He had no such advantage as Morrigan lay
in his arms so deep in her death-like sleep that the only emotion she stirred in him was grief. But he had no choice. Pressing
his lips to hers, he allowed himself the comfort of a kiss.

Leaning over her, he arched her up against the hardness of
his chest. Bringing his mouth down to the curve of her throat,
he ran his tongue over the faint throb that was one of the few
signs she still lived. Knowing what he had to do, he suckled
the damp patch of skin into the heat of his mouth. Before he
could let himself reconsider, he bit down.

ᛏ   ᛏ   ᛏ

Sasha and the others were waiting where he had left them.
They looked up as one when he walked in, but Michael would-
n't meet their eyes. He couldn't let them see what changing
Morrigan had done to him. Couldn't let them know what the
taste of her had made him feel. What the thought of her blood
inside of his body did to him. In the minutes that her life had
flowed into him, they had become one. One heartbeat, one
breath, one mind. He had seen everything that had ever touched
her life, felt every emotion.

When that happened he'd seen a part of himself that had
shocked all notions of his own humanity from him. From the
second he could taste her, he'd changed. The strength, the
hunger, the lust, had flooded him until he had taken all he
could from her. Only then did he rip open his own wrist. He
hadn't pondered the rightness of it as he'd held his wrist to her

mouth, commanding her to drink. All he had felt was the deep, all consuming pleasure that had bombarded him while she'd taken her fill of him.

Long after she'd fallen asleep, he'd held her in his arms. He'd held her close until he could no longer stand the pain of what he'd lost. Only then had he covered her lips with his, the mingled taste of their blood bringing back the hunger he had never felt before. Then he'd left her, needing the distance to keep him sane.

"How is she?" Montgomery asked as she came to her feet. She saw in a glance the defeated set of his shoulders, the blood that stained the once pristine white silk of his shirt. Coming forward, she took his fisted hand in hers. Turning it over, she looked at the healing wound that still seeped his blood.

Michael pulled his arm away from her gentle hold. "Please, tell her why I had to do it," he said no more as he turned his back on the two men he had loved as brothers and walked away.

Ϯ   Ϯ   Ϯ

Sasha left as well, her eyes never focusing on the large man that followed her out. Gabriel stopped her desperate retreat with nothing more than the sound of his voice.

"Running from me?"

She clenched her teeth against the frustration that demanded release. "I'm going to check on Morrigan. She's going to wake up soon and I need to tell her what has happened. I need to explain why Michael did what he did," Sasha answered without looking at him.

"Then what?" He took a step closer.

"Then I'm leaving you." She finally looked at him then and let him see her determination. "You won't have to look at this honor stealing fiend ever again." The smile that curved her lips had little to do with humor. "You won't have to wonder if I'm lurking in the shadows. You won't have to wonder if I'm plotting your downfall. You're free of me, of my pathetic love, and my foolish hopes."

"Sasha," he began, but all the things he had held in for so long refused to come out.

When a minute past and he said no more, she stood on tip-toes and pressed a kiss against his lips. "Goodbye, Gabriel."

🜊   🜊   🜊

As the sun came up on a new day, Montgomery snuggled closer to her dark lover and gloried in the warmth of his stunning silver eyes.

Rafe pulled her closer until she lay over the heat of his body. Part of him still refused to believe that she was his. He had never thought he would feel such emotion, that his heart could feel such devotion and love for another. "I love you."

"I know you do, baby."

"That's not nice." He scolded even as a hand moved in threat toward the firm curve of her backside.

"After she stopped giggling hysterically, she took the news in stride. I don't think she even sees it as a curse so much as an avenue to fulfill her goals. It's Sasha that has me worried. I think Gabriel burned that bridge," Rafe spoke with concern at the sudden departure of the golden one.

"I don't think so. I think she's just giving him enough space to realize he needs her. Denial is the way to a man's heart, you know," she chided him. "Michael has me concerned though. He needs you and Gabriel. The three of you are part of something special, sugar. All that you are you owe to each other. Whatever he did that was so wrong is in the past. Leave it there."

"What's between Michael and I needn't concern you, sweet thing." Rafe wasn't in the mood to discuss his feelings about Michael. Not now.

Montgomery let him have his way. She had a long time to make him see reason, and with Gabriel and Morrigan's help, they would have her dark lover seeing things her way in no time. "What about us? Do you concern me?" she taunted even as she straddled his hard body. "Does this concern me?"

Her throaty purr fired his blood. "Everything about me concerns you." His voice was husky with need. "From now until the end of time there is nothing you won't know about me. Every thought, every hope, every prayer. We are one, joined together by blood, by desire, by love."

"I love you, Rafe." She couldn't say more for the tears that choked her.

"Nothing will keep us apart, Gomery. You're mine until the world stops turning, until angels fall from the sky."

She gasped in surprise when he flipped her on her back and under the demanding heat of his body. "And you're mine, " Montgomery vowed as he slid into her, filling the deepest recesses of her heart, her soul.

Cindy Gengler

Cindy credits her love of strong heroes and independent heroines to the relationship between her parents. Their out in the open, thirty-plus year romance gives her the ability to look for the happy ending at the end of the fairy tale and the capability to slay her own dragons along the way if need be.

A native of Joliet, Illinois, Cindy married her high school sweetheart and now resides in a lovely four-bedroom farmhouse with her husband of twelve years and their two children. When not working full time as a dental assistant in a prominent Naperville dental office, she is writing about and researching new ideas for her immortal star-crossed lovers and the battles they must wage against the evil plotting of their ancient foes. In her spare time, Cindy enjoys watching old movies and reading the various works of her ever-growing selection of favorite authors. Other hobbies also include photography, walking in the great outdoors and collecting various styles of art dedicated to depicting myths, legends and fantasy weaponry.